THE COMPLETE CASES OF THE MONGOOSE

THE COMPLETE CASES OF THE MONGOOSE

JOHNSTON McCULLEY

INTRODUCTION BY

PETER POPLASKI

ILLUSTRATED BY

JOSEPH A. FARREN

STEEGER BOOKS • 2019

PUBLISHING HISTORY

"Introduction" appears here for the first time. Copyright © 2019 Peter Poplaski. All rights
reserved.

"Alias the Mongoose" originally appeared in the March 26, 1932 issue of *Detective Fiction
Weekly* magazine (Vol. 66, No. 3). Copyright © 1932 by The Frank A. Munsey Company.
Copyright renewed © 1959 and assigned to Steeger Properties, LLC. All rights reserved.

"The Voice from Nowhere" originally appeared in the April 23, 1932 issue of *Detective Fiction
Weekly* magazine (Vol. 67, No. 1). Copyright © 1932 by The Frank A. Munsey Company.
Copyright renewed © 1959 and assigned to Steeger Properties, LLC. All rights reserved.

"The Mongoose Strikes Again" originally appeared in the May 7, 1932 issue of *Detective Fiction
Weekly* magazine (Vol. 67, No. 3). Copyright © 1932 by The Frank A. Munsey Company.
Copyright renewed © 1959 and assigned to Steeger Properties, LLC. All rights reserved.

"Smoke of Revenge" originally appeared in the September 3, 1932 issue of *Detective Fiction
Weekly* magazine (Vol. 70, No. 2). Copyright © 1932 by The Frank A. Munsey Company.
Copyright renewed © 1959 and assigned to Steeger Properties, LLC. All rights reserved.

"Jewels of the Rajah" originally appeared in the September 17, 1932 issue of *Detective Fiction
Weekly* magazine (Vol. 70, No. 4). Copyright © 1932 by The Frank A. Munsey Company.
Copyright renewed © 1959 and assigned to Steeger Properties, LLC. All rights reserved.

"Ransom for Vengeance" originally appeared in the November 26, 1932 issue of *Detective
Fiction Weekly* magazine (Vol. 72, No. 2). Copyright © 1932 by The Frank A. Munsey
Company. Copyright renewed © 1960 and assigned to Steeger Properties, LLC. All rights
reserved.

"Six Sacks of Gold" originally appeared in the February 4, 1933 issue of *Detective Fiction Weekly*
magazine (Vol. 73, No. 6). Copyright © 1933 by The Frank A. Munsey Company.
Copyright renewed © 1960 and assigned to Steeger Properties, LLC. All rights reserved.

"Profit for the Mongoose" originally appeared in the February 25, 1933 issue of *Detective
Fiction Weekly* magazine (Vol. 74, No. 3). Copyright © 1933 by The Frank A. Munsey
Company. Copyright renewed © 1960 and assigned to Steeger Properties, LLC. All rights
reserved.

"Trap of the Mongoose" originally appeared in the May 27, 1933 issue of *Detective Fiction
Weekly* magazine (Vol. 76, No. 4). Copyright © 1933 by The Frank A. Munsey Company.
Copyright renewed © 1960 and assigned to Steeger Properties, LLC. All rights reserved.

"About the Author" originally appeared in the January 23, 1932 issue of *Detective Fiction Weekly*
magazine (Vol. 64, No. 6). Copyright © 1932 by The Frank A. Munsey Company.
Copyright renewed © 1959 and assigned to Steeger Properties, LLC. All rights reserved.

ASSOCIATE EDITOR
Ray Riethmeier

Visit steegerbooks.com for more books like this.

TABLE OF CONTENTS

PETER POPLASKI

THE MONGOOSE STORIES BY JOHNSTON McCULLEY

ADVENTURE TALES. DETECTIVE mysteries. Western yarns. Spanish California historical romances. Sport narratives. Christmas and New Year short stories. This list of magazine literary genres embodies the focus of the imaginative range of Johnston McCulley and his large output of stories as a successful American pulp magazine writer over the first half of the twentieth century.

Beginning in Peoria, Illinois, and traveling widely as a tramp newspaperman, he learned his craft and married young. His earliest known writing, "In the Arms of the Octopus," appeared in 1903 in *The Daily Journal,* a newspaper in Quincy, Illinois. In 1905, while working on staff on the *Portland Oregonian,* he managed to write a play titled "The Heir Apparent," which debuted at the Empire theatre. It was popular enough on a local level to be revived in 1907. However, a short story that appeared in *Pacific Monthly* in May of 1906, "The Rotting Log," actually began Johnston McCulley's magazine career. Inspired, the young writer sold two other stories: "The Song of the Sand" to *Red Book* and "The Escape" to *Blue Book* by the end of the year. Then he made a second sale to *Red Book* and his first sales to *Argosy, All-Story Magazine,* and *Railroad Man's Magazine* in 1907. And so, like a Horatio Alger dime novel character, Johnston McCulley had "pluck" and he needed "luck" and through diligence built a magazine writing career that in his lifetime eventually overlapped into over fifty hardcover book collections of his many pulp short stories and serials, and then Hollywood movie adaptations and film studio commissions, until his death in Los Angeles in 1958.

This particular book brings together for the first time a series of nine stories featuring a character Johnston McCulley created called "The Mongoose," which began appearing on an irregular basis with the March 26th, 1932, issue of *Detective Fiction Weekly*. He originally worked up the idea in October of 1931 for Street and Smith's *Detective Story Magazine*, but the project was suddenly cancelled. McCulley quickly cut and redeveloped his manuscript, selling the first two episodes of this project to the other magazine before the year was up.

"The Crook Who Hunts Human Snakes!" is how The Mongoose is labeled on his first and only magazine cover appearance. The visual metaphor image depicts the snake-killing animal from India staring up eye to eye with a King Cobra. Actually, the mysterious Mongoose in these short stories is two shape shifting masters of disguise, a Mr. Sidney Carleigh and his sister Eleanor, who for ten years have planned vendetta operations against a good number of prominent financiers, bankers, and guilty wheeler-dealers for the frame-up of an innocent bookkeeper, William Cratch, their father, who died in prison because of perjured testimony and false evidence. Having used siblings in his pulp stories earlier—identical twin brothers in "The Green Glove" (1910) and The Avenging Twins series (1923–1926), and identical twin sisters in "Held As Hostage" (1910) and "Alias Madame Madcap," a 1919 serial republished in hardcover as *The Masked Woman* (1920)—this *Detective Fiction Weekly* feature seems to be the first time that Johnston McCulley uses a brother and sister team as protagonists in a detective adventure series. One doesn't know for sure because of McCulley's large story output during his career, with many stories and characters yet to be rediscovered.

Consistently, the plots recall the old saying, "behind every great fortune lies a great crime." It is all for the love of "swag" that greedy men sin. Johnston McCulley the writer uses this dime novel formula to manifest the vengeance his many righteous "bent" heroes initiate to balance the scales of justice in their own manner. Thus, bold dedicated daredevils like John Warwick in McCulley's Spider series of 1918–1919, John Flatchley, masked in The Thunderbolt stories of 1920–1921, Richard Staegal, masked three times as The Man In Purple in 1921, Peter and Paul Selbon, both masked in The Avenging Twins episodes of 1923–1926, all appear in the pages of *Detective Story Magazine,* while James Peters, masked as The Rollicking Rogue, turns up twice in 1930 in *All Star Detective Stories.* These ethical heroic characters handing out retribution betray, no doubt, the preferred reading material of McCulley's youth— plus his love of theatre—as sources, and since pulps are totally about action, this makes these nine clever tales of revenge seem to read today like enjoyable early radio or television scenarios. However, it is because of the success of Señor Zorro, the Curse of Capistrano—in print and on the silent screen—that they all incorporate the use of a mask. The mask, of course, is the device that erases the hero's social identity to protect close friends and family members, and to make his opponents fearful of the unknown. It also puts him above the law where the view of the truth and retribution can be seen as justice, allowing the hero to then act with violence to square things right. This is every skinny kid's fantasy of how to deal with the big bully of the neighborhood. Interestingly, as the Depression decade wore on, the more picaresque and gritty hardboiled detective characters became; this elevated their pulp stories to a new literary style level that led to Film Noir, while McCulley's direction led his masked mystery characters to inspire the comic book super-heroes of the near future via the movies, making this kind of intellectual property now part of a billion dollar industry.

The mask of Zorro was Johnston McCulley's good luck charm. He may have begun with an earlier Fantomas-type super-criminal, The Black Star (1916), who was in demand in the pages of *Detective Story* until 1930, but then he followed him with the masked "Yellowjacket," the cowboy good guy of *Range Land Justice* (1919). The important thing is that the mask trail leads to Zorro and then to Douglas Fairbanks and great success. Fairbanks commissioned a sequel to *The Mark of Zorro* in 1921. Naturally, McCulley rethought the basic concept. If he didn't, other writers would, and did. So, as he continued with Zorro, he came up with as many variations on the theme as he could, to an eventual total of twenty-two known masked adventure characters. The most recent masked character (#14) to be rediscovered is "The Lone Vigilante," who tamed a town by riding into the pages of a *Western Story Magazine* in 1928. Anyway, at this moment, The Mongoose places fourteenth in a list of nineteen series of continuing characters, and number sixteen in the list of twenty-two masked characters because of the use of the mask in his final published appearance on March 21, 1933.

The super-villains of these McCulley adventure stories are, naturally, predatory Wall Street bankers, a breed of ambitious and aggressive individuals with questionable ethics, who, in building their vast wealth to become high stake players in the shark pool of business, easily accepting the collateral damage of crushed little guys they've stepped on as they climb up the money ladder. Is self-interested indifference reflective of a sociopathological state of mind, one might ask? In the tradition of the Dime Novel formula, isn't blind injustice just a social Darwinism principle caused by the privileged class aristocrat's ability to pay off and manipulate the law and authority? After all, there was a stock market crash around 1908 and a bigger one in 1929. Wasn't there a Wall Street bailout within the last decade and an Occupy Wall Street protest? McCulley's Depression moral to his working class readership seems to be that you just can't trust bankers. Somebody has to do something! And he says it over and over in every piece of a puzzle that is never complete because McCulley never came to an "official" ending with the characters he created in the 1930s. Like El Torbellino the Whirlwind, and the Green Ghost adventures to come, The Mongoose stories, as a series, just abruptly stops. Perhaps it is because McCulley simply got distracted, first in keeping Zorro alive for a future film version deal, and then by selling his backlog of western stories to

Hollywood studios for their B-movie line-ups.

So, even in their simplicity, these action tales contain the voice of social protest of this "little guy against the world" period. There were still human beings in those days, instead of the little information processors we have become. Johnston McCulley and his fellow pulp writers, Clarence E. Mulford and Edgar Rice Burroughs, are, after all, voices from the American Midwest, initially country boys from the state of Illinois, not New York or Los Angeles. Mulford, who originally hailed from Streator, Illinois, created the Hopalong Cassidy and the Bar 20 stories of the old west, beginning in 1906. Burroughs was a Chicago boy and started with John Carter of Mars in 1911 and Tarzan of the Apes in 1912. McCulley created Zorro in 1919, and this masked avenger appeared in *All-Story Weekly* just as Tarzan did. Robert E. Howard was from Cross Plains, Texas, and he was creating Conan the Barbarian for *Weird Tales* in 1932. Surprisingly, the combined characters of these three popular Illinois pulp authors plus one from Texas, inspired 183 films (66 Hopalong Cassidy, around 54 Tarzan, 1 John Carter, 1 Lad And The Lion, 43 Zorro, and 14 California romances and westerns, and 4 Conan). There is a message in them. It is a legacy that continues to be viable even after a century. Perhaps it was "pluck" and "luck," but it was also something more embodied by these simple good versus evil heroes, a moral sympathy that means something hopeful to humanity. Put simply, it is a feeling that, through my own actions, "I control my own destiny." Picked up from the original text of these adventures, this escapist attitude is adapted by new forms of media. They still entertain because they still speak to the great working class audience about freedom and the indifference of the wealthy. So how did these voices of the Midwest, these storyteller dreamers, do it?

Return to the middle of a balmy autumn season at the end of October 1931, as a pulp story commences. Words are being typed out on a sheet of white paper. With the success of *The Shadow* magazine published by Street and Smith, the age of the hero pulps is beginning. In the wings are *Doc Savage* and *The Spider* magazines, and with more adventure characters following as darkening skies lead this world into the third cold winter of the Great Depression of the 20th Century.

From the window of an eleventh floor apartment in the landmark Hotel Ansonia at Broadway and 73rd Street in New York City, a certain pulp magazine writer, recently described as "an alert, middle aged man of ordinary stature" in the pages of *Argosy*, paces across the carpet of his study room, and pauses to look out. He is holding a dessert plate and eating a slice of lemon pie. Between bites he takes small sips from a cup of hot coffee.

Twilight is diminishing as the streetlights and the electric signs of the Great White Way blink on, illuminating the congested traffic and "the hurrying throngs of people" on the sidewalks below. For a man who writes by night, this panoramic view always ignites a story idea. Nearby, there is the physical evidence of his work, of a narrative in progress, as slowly, hour by hour, something comes into a tighter focus, paragraph by paragraph, accumulating casually as a pile of neatly typed double-spaced manuscript pages of text with corrections, on the table next to an Underwood typewriter. Three pencils and a gold fountain pen aid this performance. A small rack of well-used pipes and a can of tobacco perfume the air. At hand is a small stack of current pulp magazines, *Ace-High, Best Detective, Clues,* and *Argosy* issues running the "Zorro Rides Again" four-part serial.

Syncopated dance band music plays low, emanating from a radio cabinet against the wall opened for use and tuned into WOR.

Typing is resumed. Underscoring the present moment is the melody and lyrics of the newest tune hanging on the invisible airwaves:

> *Life is just a bowl of cherries / Do not make it serious / Life's too mysterious / You work, you save, you worry so / But you can not take your dough when you go, go, go / So keep repeating it's the berries / The strongest oak must fall / The sweet things in life / To you are just loaned / So how can you lose what you've never owned? / Life is just a bowl of cherries / So live and laugh at it all.*

Finally, several hours later, Johnston McCulley types "The End" to his latest tale and rips the last page from his typewriter. It had been another long night. Yawning at the dark silent city before him, he studies the orange morning sun from his Upper West Side perch as it slowly climbs through the silhouettes of skyscrapers that now stand embossed against the vivid blue dome that announces another Depression day. He can hear his third wife, Louris, in the kitchen making fresh coffee. Clearing his throat and taking a sip of the cold coffee left in the bottom of his cup, McCulley begins to make a word count of his first draft text to estimate how much money he will be making. "What was this deal with *Detective Fiction Weekly*," he asks himself again as he searches around the room for a note he wrote to himself, "five cents a word, or three cents a word?"

Times were getting tougher and they were going to get worse, but the little guy on the street in 1932 will have to take whatever the world dishes out. This message can be found in all of Johnston McCulley stories, somewhere amidst their momentary distraction!

Peter Poplaski
Sauve, France
August 8th, 2017

(This introduction was written from material compiled by Peter Poplaski from his 20 year project: Zorro—The Myth, The Mask and The Image*).*

ALIAS THE MONGOOSE

"The Mongoose" This New and Mysterious Criminal Called Himself, Because His Prey Was Snakes—Human Snakes!

THE MESSAGE OF MENACE

LIKE A MAN on the verge of a physical and mental break-down, Stephen Wazer was pacing back and forth from corner to corner of his rather ornate private office, on the twentieth floor of a prominent building in the commercial center of the city. It was Saturday afternoon, about two.

That office possessed the atmosphere of the home more than it did that of a place of business. There were expensive rugs, some rare tapestries, a few valuable paintings. The furniture was of heavy carved mahogany, including a huge desk which sat in the center of the room. It was all a bit garish, a trifle overdone, as though there had been a vulgar attempt at display.

Stephen Wazer had superintended the furnishing of that private office personally, but he did not seem to be enjoying it now. He was in a highly nervous state. His entire body trembled at times. He wiped the cold beads of perspiration from his face with a handkerchief held in a hand that shook. The emotion which was slowly wrecking him was a combination of anger and fright.

He was trying to tell himself that the whole affair might be only a hoax. He had certain friends who were thoroughly capable of indulging in such a practical joke, expert at playing such pranks. However, there remained the disturbing possibility that it was not a hoax, that there really was some grave danger impending for him.

He stopped beside the desk, and for about the twentieth time he read the penciled scrawl on a yellow slip of paper, which had got into his personal correspondence in some strange manner as yet unexplained:

> STEPHEN WAZER:
> The time has come for you to pay! Prepare to suffer for your sins! The transgressor must be punished!

WAZER CRUMPLED the sheet of paper in his hand. Rage more than fear dominated him now. With sudden decision in his manner, he reached forward and pressed a button. Almost immediately a door opened softly, and just as softly Stephen Wazer's confidential secretary slipped into the room.

An efficient secretary in every particular, this Guthrie Jayne. He knew his way around. Always attended strictly to business, never watched the clock, acted like a man afraid of losing his

"Look!" he called excitedly. "Look!"

job. Possessed tact and diplomacy, and knew how to use them. Also knew how to keep his mouth shut about certain things, which was a valuable asset for anybody working in the offices of Stephen Wazer.

Guthrie Jayne was rather a queer specimen, though. He was an inconspicuous person, always dressed in quiet clothes, was stoop-shouldered and pasty-faced, and wore huge, thick spectacles which almost hid his eyes. He had a mop of curly blond hair which always looked dusty and lifeless. Efficient rather than impressive—that was Guthrie Jayne.

"Sir?" he questioned.

Wazer looked at him sternly. "I've been thinking about this note that got into my mail, Jayne," he said. "The note in itself amounts to nothing. But the fact that it got into my personal correspondence amounts to a lot."

"I do not blame you for being angry, sir," Jayne said.

"It reveals a flaw in the office system. There's a weak cog in the machine somewhere, Jayne. That means the machine must be repaired. You've learned nothing?"

Sprawled on the floor were the two policemen who had been guarding the office

"Not a thing, sir. I questioned the clerks, stenographers and file girls, and the two office boys. They all impressed me as being innocent."

"Jayne, I am determined to learn who inserted that note in my mail. The person who did it must be dismissed from my organization immediately. It may have been only a childish prank, but this office is no place for childish pranks. Or—it may be something more important, even criminal. The thing is a sort of—well, a sort of threat."

"Sir?" Jayne gasped.

"A threat, I said. It's an intimation that I have—er—transgressed in some manner and am to be punished for it. Preposterous!"

"Certainly, sir," Jayne agreed.

"You get right at it again the first thing Monday morning. Try to discover the culprit. Understand, Jayne, I do not suspect you of such a childish thing. That would be preposterous, too. But, whether it is a joke or a serious threat, I want to know who put that note in my mail!"

"I'll do my best, sir."

"Anybody in the outer office now?" Wazer asked.

"Nobody is out there, sir. They've all gone for the week-end," Jayne replied.

"Is everything in readiness for the meeting?"

"Quite ready, sir."

"This is a sort of secret meeting, Jayne, of the board of directors for one of my companies. Don't let anybody into the suite except the directors you know are to be present. When they arrive, usher them into the directors' room. Let me know when they're all here."

"Yes, sir."

"You've got a box of those special cigars ready—and ash trays, and all that?"

"I have attended to it, sir."

"And the cocktails—?"

"They are ready, sir," Jayne replied. "I gave my special attention to the cocktails, sir."

"Good! I want you to remain in the outer office, Jayne, and make sure that we're not disturbed. May want you to get something out of the file cases for me. Sorry to cause you to lose your half holiday, but I'll make up for that in a financial way."

"Thank you, sir. You're always generous, sir."

"That's all, Jayne."

JAYNE SLIPPED quietly out of the office and closed the door behind him. Stephen Wazer began pacing the floor again. He tried to tell himself that the note was only a joke, and that it was utterly absurd for him to be frightened.

He was a prominent man, and well protected. An important man. The commercial agencies rated him at a million. He held a certain position in the social world, though more by virtue of his parentage than by his own qualities. But in the business world it was whispered that Stephen Wazer would combine with other commercial rogues at any time to put through a shady deal, and that, lacking other victims, he was not above turning against those with whom he was associated. He was generally regarded as a business buccaneer.

A telephone buzzer sounded, Wazer stepped swiftly to his desk and picked up the receiver. The signal had come from his private wire.

"Hello!" he called.

A deep voice addressed him: "Retribution is at hand! The scales must be balanced! I am ready to strike!"

"What's that? Who are you?" Wazer almost screeched the words into the transmitter.

A soft laugh answered him, and then the connection was broken. Stephen Wazer returned the receiver to its hook. That voice had sounded determined, and the laugh had been one of self-confidence. He could not put up an adequate defense against a thing like that. He had no chance to question, demand the meaning of it. And he could not merely shrug his shoulders and try to laugh it off—a guilty conscience precluded that.

Once more he jabbed at the button on his desk, and again Jayne hurried into the room.

"Did you handle that telephone call at the switchboard?" Wazer demanded.

"Yes, sir. Everybody else is gone. Is there something wrong, sir?"

"Tell me about it."

"Why, the gentleman who called gave the private code signal, sir, so I connected him with you immediately. I believed that he was one of your business associates, sir."

"He wasn't!" Wazer snapped. "It was another threat. This time over my private telephone line! It's too late now to have the call traced. Jayne, I'm going to get to the bottom of this affair! Joke or real threat, I'm going to find out who's doing it!"

"I'm sorry if I made a mistake, sir."

"You didn't, if the caller gave you the private code signal. But how did he get the signal? That's the question. Have to change it, I suppose. That's all, Jayne!"

Stephen Wazer wanted to be alone. Jayne hurried out of the office and closed the door again. Wazer strolled across the room and came to a stop in front of a window to look out across a sea of roofs. His hands were clasped behind his back, his brow was wrinkled, his eyes contracted until they seemed to be only mere slits. He was trying to shake off all disturbing and alien thoughts and concentrate on a business problem with which he found himself confronted.

The section of the city was almost deserted. The huge office buildings were almost empty of tenants and their employees on Saturday afternoons. So there would be few to spy, and possibly talk afterward, if a group of prominent financiers met for a conference.

Wazer had called a special meeting of the board of directors for one of the corporations he headed. They would be arriving at almost any minute now, and he did not want them to find him disturbed. He wanted to be calm and inscrutable.

He glanced up at the sky to see whether there was a threat of inclement weather, for he expected to spend the following day in the country. Not a cloud marred the perfect blue. But his attention was caught by two large kites, flying high in the air, with an advertising streamer between them.

He had noticed those kites often before while standing at the window. They were being flown from the roof of another building not far away. The sign was changed frequently, as different products were advertised. Some poor devil made his living with those kites and signs, Wazer supposed.

He glanced up again, wondering who was paying for the advertising today. There were only two words on the sign. The letters were enormous, easy to read:

REMEMBER CRATCH

Stephen Wazer wondered vaguely what that might mean. There did not seem to be any sense to it. Cratch! The word had a sort of familiar ring to it. He felt certain that he had heard it before somewhere. But he told himself that it certainly was nothing for him to bother about now. He had more important things to consider.

He took his eyes off the kites and banner, and glanced down at the broad roofs of some other buildings across the street and below him. He gasped his surprise at what he saw. There was a sign spread out on one of the roofs, too:

REMEMBER CRATCH!
IT IS TIME TO PAY

There was that word again—Cratch! It seemed to have some special significance for Stephen Wazer, some direct association with the past. He began searching his memory.

And suddenly the solution came to him like a blinding flash, and he crossed the room to sit down quickly before his desk, as though a weakness had seized him.

Cratch!… That affair about ten years ago!… So that was it!… Those signs were meant for him!

CHAPTER II

THE VANISHING CYLINDER

SUDDEN FEAR CLUTCHED at Stephen Wazer again, and he could not shake it off. He tried to tell himself that such fear was ridiculous. Here he was, safe in his own private office. Friends and business associates would be there shortly. His secretary was in the adjoining room. And, if he wished, Stephen Wazer had only to telephone and call to his aid a detective he retained, a man capable of handling almost any emergency.

The thing had happened about ten years before, too, and the public forgets a lot in that length of time. Who would dig it up now, and why? Who would be making threats? For there was no doubt in the mind of Stephen Wazer that those signs were meant to be subtle threats. And the note he had received, and the telephone call over the private wire! All this looked like a preliminary to blackmail.

Stephen Wazer's mind traveled swiftly back a decade, to a time when he and some of his associates had skated on ice too thin, had put through a swindle which almost had been their undoing. They had escaped prison only by fastening the guilt on an innocent man, a bookkeeper named Cratch. It had seemed safe enough at the time. Cratch had been a nobody, a man without influential friends. He had died in prison, and Wazer and his associates had believed the affair closed forever.

And now—those signs!

If somebody knew the truth, and was in a position to convince others of it, the possibilities for blackmail were stupendous.

Stephen Wazer and the others implicated would have either to pay or fight—and they dared not fight. If they found themselves in the clutches of professional extortionists, there was disaster ahead.

Jayne suddenly returned to the private office. He stopped just inside the door and coughed apologetically to attract attention to his presence.

"Well, Jayne?" Wazer asked.

"Pardon me for disturbing you at this time, sir, but a messenger just left a package for you," the secretary said.

"He was told that it's important for you to receive it at once, and personally."

"A package?" Wazer asked. "Bring it over here to the desk, Jayne. It may be something that calls for immediate attention."

"Shall I open it for you, sir?" Jayne asked.

"It isn't even addressed, is it?" Wazer said, after a quick glance at it. "I'm a bit afraid of mysterious packages, Jayne. I have enemies, and I've received some threats recently."

"I don't blame you for your caution, sir. I'll open the package for you, sir—take it to the outer office."

"Nonsense! Open it here on my desk. I'll walk over by the window while you do it. I hope it isn't an infernal machine of some sort, Jayne. You're a valuable man, and I'd hate to have you go up in smoke."

STEPHEN WAZER smiled as he got out of his chair, but it was a nervous, twitching sort of smile. He went over by the window, and turned to watch Jayne. The secretary quickly severed the string with which the package was bound. He unwrapped several layers of coarse paper, and exposed a small pasteboard box. Removing the lid from the box, he took out an object which had been packed carefully in layers of cotton.

"What is that thing, Jayne?" Wazer demanded.

"It appears to be a cylinder record for a dictating machine, sir," Jayne replied.

"So it does! Now, who would be sending me a thing like that—and why?"

"I'm quite sure that I haven't the slightest idea, sir," Jayne replied.

"Isn't there a letter with it—a note of explanation, or something of that nature?"

Jayne searched swiftly and carefully. "There's nothing of the sort, sir," he answered. "Not a mark of any kind on the box or wrapping paper, either. Possibly it is only some new sort of advertising scheme. Do you care to put the cylinder on the machine and listen to the record, sir?"

Wazer walked back to the desk, hesitating a moment. "Might as well," he finally decided. "Haven't anything else to do at the moment. Fix it up for me, Jayne. It's a fine way to send a billet-doux, what?"

Jayne gave a sickly smile in acknowledgment of his employer's pleasantry, put the cylinder on the machine, and stepped back. Wazer sat down, adjusted the ear tubes, and started the machine.

Stephen Wazer scarcely knew what to expect. He feared that it would be something more about the Cratch affair, another threat, possibly a demand for hush money. He braced himself mentally, and tried to act in a natural manner before his secretary.

He smiled. But, in a moment, the smile fled from his countenance. In its place came an expression of bewilderment as he listened. This changed to astonishment—and then to something like fear. Stephen Wazer's rather florid face turned to a sickly white.

Jayne took a swift step forward, and there was alarm in both his face and voice as he spoke.

"What is it, sir?" he cried. "Are you ill, Mr. Wazer? Is there something I can do to be of service?"

"I—it's quite all right, Jayne," Wazer stammered. He had stopped listening to the record, and was slumped down in his chair looking at the machine.

"If you'll pardon me for saying so, sir, you look rather—rather ill." Jayne was very careful to avoid the use of the word frightened.

"Silly of me," Wazer muttered. "I felt a bit faint for a moment. Need more exercise.'

"Shall I call your physician, sir?"

"Nonsense! I'm all right now, Jayne. That thing on the dictating machine—it was a sort of threat, and startled me. New way of sending a threat to a man, what? Where did it come from, did you say?"

"If was left by a messenger, sir, from the usual messenger service office."

"Would you know him if you saw him again?"

"I believe so, sir."

"Try to remember him, Jayne. I may want to get in touch with him later. I'm getting sick of this sort of thing. Telephone to Detective Mark Graddon, and tell him to come here immediately. Keep at it till you locate him. That's all."

GUTHRIE JAYNE hurried out of the office. Stephen Wazer looked at the dictating machine again, and at the little cylinder which bore the message that had disturbed him. He seemed to be making a great effort to pull himself together, to become master of his emotions.

Once more he adjusted the ear tubes, and compelled himself to listen a second time:

> Hello, Stephen Wazer! About ten years ago you and your crooked associates got caught in a shady deal. You made a scapegoat of one of your bookkeepers, a man named William Cratch, and saved yourselves by giving perjured testimony and having him sent to prison.
>
> He died in prison. His wife also died, of a broken heart. His son afterward unexpectedly inherited a large estate. This fortune enables him to devote his time to his main object in life— having vengeance for the wrong done his parents.
>
> That son is here now. He has spent considerable time and

money investigating you and the others. His plans are complete; he is ready to strike! He has taken precautions against discovery. The name he uses is not that by which his father was known to you.

I am that son! You must pay the debt, all of you, in humiliation and anguish, in worldly goods, perhaps with your lives.

You probably have heard of the mongoose, an animal that kills reptiles, even the most deadly snake of all. It seems appropriate, under the circumstances, for me to call myself

THE MONGOOSE.

Stephen Wazer stopped the dictating machine once more, and slumped down in his chair. He shivered with apprehension. The cold perspiration popped out on his face again, and he wiped it away with a trembling hand.

The Cratch case—he recalled it well now. The others would remember it, too, especially Clark Donnibell and Harvey Blandale, who had been vitally interested. They had passed through some dark moments together before they had been able to escape the clutches of the law by fastening the crime on an innocent man.

And so the man they had made a scapegoat had a son who was vowing vengeance! Stephen Wazer had anticipated blackmail after seeing those signs, but this was worse. The victim's son probably could not be bought off, especially if he really had inherited a large estate and was rich already.

But it would not be the first time that Stephen Wazer had been made the object of an attack. He decided that he would have Detective Mark Graddon take charge of the affair. Graddon was concerned in this, too. Mark Graddon had helped arrange the bogus evidence that had sent William Cratch to prison.

He wondered how Graddon would go about it. Probably he would want to question Jayne. He would run down the messenger who had delivered the package. He would make an examination of that cylinder, look for fingerprints on it.

That thought reminded Stephen Wazer that he should wrap

up the cylinder carefully and keep it safe for the detective. He reached toward the machine to remove the cylinder—and recoiled with a cry of amazement.

The cylinder seemed to be dissolving, melting into the air. The surface of the portion which still remained seemed to be alive with little bubbles, as though some vicious acid was at work there. Astounded, Wazer bent closer to watch. A pungent odor struck into his nostrils, and he jerked back his head. The bubbles grew larger, seemed to be working faster. The cylinder was swiftly disintegrating before Wazer's eyes.

An instant later it was gone.

CHAPTER III

BUSINESS ROGUES

FOR A MOMENT, Stephen Wazer was rigid, stricken with surprise and awe, staring at the place where the cylinder had been. The last few bubbles disappeared. There was not even a damp spot remaining. The pungent odor he had noticed was dispelled by the soft breeze that came through the window.

Stephen Wazer aroused himself to action. He jabbed a finger against the desk button again, and an instant later Jayne came hurrying into the office.

"Look!" Wazer cried, huskily. "That cylinder! It's gone! It melted away before my very eyes!"

Jayne did not betray that he was aware of his employer's highly nervous state, his evident fright. He bent over the dictating machine and made a close inspection of it through his ugly thick spectacles.

"Astounding, sir!" Jayne declared. "Just how did it happen?"

"It happened right before my eyes, Jayne. I was watching the thing at the moment, and I saw it disappear. There's something terrible behind all this. It may be something utterly new—a different sort of danger. There was a threat on that cylinder, Jayne. I wanted to give it to Detective Graddon, so he could attend to it professionally—and now it's gone! Did you locate Graddon? Is he on his way to the office?"

"I haven't located him yet, sir."

"You keep right after him, Jayne. Telephone his home. Try to get in touch with one of his assistants, and learn where Graddon is. I want him here as soon as possible."

"I'll do my best, sir."

"When Mr. Donnibell and Mr. Blandale arrive, show them into this office immediately. None of the others, understand—only Donnibell and Blandale."

"Is it really something serious, sir?" Jayne wanted to know. "Are you in actual danger, Mr. Wazer? May I suggest telephoning to the police?"

"The police? Certainly not!" Wazer exploded. "This is not a thing for the police—nor for the newspaper reporters!… That confounded cylinder! How do you account for it disappearing that way, Jayne? It seemed to melt into nothing."

"I'd say, sir, that it'd been treated with some chemical, which worked when subjected to contact with the open air for a certain period of time," Jayne replied. "That would not be a difficult thing, sir, for a person skilled in chemistry."

"That's it, probably. Clever! Evidence all gone—fingerprints, if any. Look alive, Jayne!"

"Is there really some sort of danger for you, sir?" Jayne persisted.

"I'm not quite sure. It may be a hoax, and it may not be. We'll be careful, Jayne, until we know. Keep a sharp lookout for any strangers loitering around. You'd better lock the outside corridor door as soon as everybody has arrived for the meeting. And don't forget to bring Donnibell and Blandale in here the moment they arrive."

Jayne hurried out of the private office again. Alone, Stephen Wazer got up and paced around the room. He tried to convince himself that there was no cause for alarm, but could not quite do it. His nerves commenced jumping again, prodded by a guilty conscience. He was remembering that day in court, visualizing it again—remembering the white-faced, bewildered bookkeeper who had seemed stunned when branded a felon.

Presently, the door was opened. Wazer whirled toward it, half frightened, and gave a sigh of relief when he saw Jayne ushering two men into the office.

CLARK DONNIBELL came first—a jovial sort of business bandit much given to raucous and bombastic talk. He was followed by Harvey Blandale—a small, nervous man whose eyes continually shifted in a furtive manner.

"What's all this, Steve?" Clark Donnibell bellowed at Wazer. "Why the secret session? The other directors will get suspicious of us if we meet alone like this—think that we're trying to put over something on them."

"Sit down!" Wazer snapped. "I've got something to tell you two…. That'll be all now, Jayne. Let me know when the other gentlemen arrive."

Jayne bowed in Acknowledgment of his dismissal, and went into the front office. Donnibell and Blandale had dropped into chairs at either end of the desk. Wazer resumed his own chair, seemed to collapse into it. He wiped a trembling palm across his forehead.

"What's it all about?" Clark Donnibell demanded again. "Anything gone wrong with any of our schemes? What's the matter with you, anyway, Wazer? You look like you'd seen a ghost."

"It's something like a ghost," Wazer admitted. "Do you remember that Cratch affair, that bookkeeper, about ten years ago?" His voice dwindled and died, as though he did not possess the strength to continue speaking.

"Sure, I remember it!" Donnibell replied. "It certainly cost me enough."

"Heavens!" Blandale exclaimed. "Has something come up about that, at this late day?"

"Step over to this window," Wazer requested. "I want to show you something."

He got out of his chair and went across to the window, and they got up and followed him, wondering. Wazer pointed through the glass.

"Look at that sign in the air between those two kites," Wazer said. "And then look at that other sign, down there on the roof."

Donnibell gave a grunt of surprise as he looked, and Blandale an exclamation of fear.

"Probably a practical joke," Donnibell declared, "or else a case of blackmail coming up. Might be either. A couple of signs don't mean much."

"But that isn't all," Wazer told them. "Let's sit down again. You'll probably feel a bit weak when I tell you the rest. It seems that this man Cratch left a son behind him. Now, the son is out for revenge—out to get us. Understand? He calls himself The Mongoose."

"What's that?" Donnibell exclaimed. "The Mongoose? You'd better consult a specialist, Steve. I've heard of pink elephants and purple crocodiles, and even green snakes. But when a man begins seeing mongooses—"

"Listen to me!" Wazer begged, as they resumed their chairs. "This is nothing to laugh about. When I tell you the rest of it, maybe you'll not think it's a joke."

He told of receiving the cylinder and listening to the message it carried. He repeated as much of the message as he could remember, and described the peculiar destruction of the cylinder.

WHEN HE concluded, Harvey Blandale was showing symptoms of acute fright. But Clark Donnibell got up and moved around the room, a man fully in control of himself and reasoning systematically, and finally stopped beside the desk again.

"It's probably true," Donnibell declared. "Sounds like the real thing. Our sins have found us out, as the saying is. But, what if it is true?"

"We're in danger?" Blandale cried.

"Rot! Suppose this man Cratch did leave a son behind him, and the said son is now out to get us? What of it? Let me recall to your memories, fellow conspirators, the fact that others have started out to get us, and we have never been got, so to speak."

"That cylinder—" Wazer began.

"Don't let that cylinder thing worry you too much," Donnibell said. "Mr. Cratch's son has some unique ideas, let's say. He probably wants to frighten us badly. Do you mean to sit there, Wazer, and admit that you're scared of a chemical reaction? What's a chemical reaction? The world's full of 'em. Your man Jayne probably was right—the cylinder had been treated chemically, so it would be destroyed at a certain time by contact with the open air. It's nothing more than a schoolboy trick!"

"But what about this fellow, this Mongoose?" Wazer asked. "What are we going to do about him? We've got to do something at once. We must have protection. He may be a half-idiotic youth brooding over what he thinks are his wrongs—the type to assassinate."

"Judging from what you've told us of that cylinder message, he won't be in any hurry to shoot," Clark Donnibell declared. "He isn't the type to do that. But he may try all sorts of fancy tricks on us. He spoke of humiliating us, didn't he? And he'll probably try to rob us, too—try to collect."

"Buy him off," Blandale suggested.

"According to that message, he's rich." Wazer reminded him. "He probably can't be bought off."

"None of us is safe until the fellow has been apprehended and put out of the way," Blandale declared.

"And how is he to be apprehended?" Wazer asked. "Nobody knows his identity. He said on that cylinder that he was using a name which wasn't his father's."

"Suppose we leave all that to Mark Graddon," Donnibell

suggested. "That's Graddon's line of business, and he'll have a personal interest in this case, too. Try to pull yourself together, Wazer! You, too, Blandale! Are we to be scared by a few cheap tricks and threats? Let's go after this fellow as soon as he shows his hand, and clean him up!"

"We must!" Blandale said.

"That's the stuff! Never say die!… We're here to hold a directors' meeting, I believe. Then let's go into the directors' room and hold it. When Graddon gets here, the three of us will have a conference with him. Meanwhile, don't lose your nerve. We're safe enough in this suite of offices, at least."

He flayed them to their feet with his scorn, made them recover a measure of their composure. Wazer picked up a bundle of papers from his desk, and led the other two out into the front office.

Four rather suspicious men were awaiting them there—the other directors. They looked askance at the three who emerged from the private office. Donnibell laughed at the expressions in their faces.

"Gentlemen, your unjust suspicions are written in your countenances for all the world to read," he told them. "We haven't been plotting against you. Word of dishonor! You should be ashamed of yourselves for thinking such a thing! How we all trust one another!"

"Private matter—" Wazer began.

"The truthful explanation is that the three of us have received certain threats—a consequence of a little deal that happened years ago, and in which none of you gentlemen was concerned," Donnibell continued. "Now, let's go into the directors' room and hold that special meeting. I want to get done—intend to catch a late train for the country."

THEY WENT into the directors' room and found their places around the long table. At Stephen Wazer's signal, Jayne carried forward a big silver tray bearing cocktail shaker and glasses.

"Steve Wazer certainly knows the proper method of calling a

meeting to order," Donnibell observed. "Let's drink to our own success and the confusion of all our enemies, whether they be of the past or present. A dash of grog for all hands, skipper! A pannikin of rum! There's a prize in the offing!"

They took their drinks, talked and laughed. The suspicions of the four were allayed. Guthrie Jayne silently passed the special cigars, and each man at the table took one and lighted it.

"That'll be all for the present, Jayne—thank you," Wazer said. "Please remain in the outer office within call. Lock the outside corridor door. And keep trying to locate Mark Graddon for me, and tell him to get here as quickly as possible."

Jayne bowed and left the room, and closed the door behind him. Then Stephen Wazer got up from his chair and went to a corner of the room, where there was a vault to which only Wazer had the combination.

He worked at the knob, finally pulled open the heavy door. He disappeared into the vault, and returned almost at once with a ledger and a bundle of documents. These he put on the end of the table, and beside them he placed a thick sheaf of banknotes of large denomination.

"It begins to look good," Donnibell commented. "So we're going to cut a melon!"

"A fat, juicy melon, stolen at midnight from the farmer's patch," Harvey Blandale managed to say, as he made a further effort to shake off the feeling of fear which assailed him.

Wazer tapped on the table with the end of a pencil. "The meeting will please be in order," he announced. "Kindly give your attention to this report."

Wazer began reading from typewritten pages. But his voice sounded tired, a bit thick. He droned on, mumbling statistics about stock sales and bond issues.

Clark Donnibell interrupted him suddenly. "Pardon me, Wazer, but it seems a bit close in here," he complained. "Mind if I open one of the windows?"

"Go ahead," Wazer replied.

He removed his spectacles to wipe them with a handkerchief as Donnibell got up to cross the room to open the window. But Donnibell seemed to have some trouble with that window. He could not quite decide whether it was stuck or he was wanting in strength to open it. He looked back toward the table, and one of the others gave a cry of alarm.

"Donnibell!" he exclaimed. "Your face, man—it's white! Are you ill?"

Clark Donnibell gave a sickly smile. His lips moved, but no sound came from them. He lurched suddenly toward the table, and the others started to get to their feet, for they saw that he was falling, pitching headlong to the floor.

But, when they sprang up, they found that a sudden weakness had come upon them. They reeled, their knees sagged. They looked at one another with expressions of bewilderment in their faces. They tried to talk, to call out, ask what this meant, and could not. Some of them collapsed on the floor. Others dropped back into their chairs.

"Wh—what—?" Blandale mouthed. He tried to say more, but sprawled across the table unconscious.

Stephen Wazer found himself in the clutch of a sudden terrible fear. He remembered the signs he had seen, the cylinder he had received, the threats of The Mongoose.

"That warning—" Wazer gasped.

He struggled to get out of his chair, made a great effort to get upon his feet, tried, ineffectually to brace himself against the end of the long table.

His senses were reeling. The interior of the room was dancing before his eyes. His vision became confused. He realized dimly that his thoughts were getting confused also. He tried again to brace himself and gather his faculties, made a last effort to pull himself together and summon assistance.

"Jayne!… Jayne!" he tried to call, his voice coming as a thick murmur.

And then he sagged back into his chair again, his lips still moving voicelessly, and his head fell forward upon his arms as they were spread upon the table.

CHAPTER IV

THE MONGOOSE

BACK IN THE outer office, Guthrie Jayne had traveled the length of the big room and locked the front door as he had been instructed, so nobody could enter the suite from the corridor. Then he went to the telephone switchboard and sat down before it. There was no haste in his movements, no trace of excitement in his manner.

He did not make an immediate effort to telephone to Detective Mark Graddon, nor to anybody else. He lighted a cigarette, and puffed at it lazily and with evident enjoyment, as he sank back comfortably in his chair. He glanced at his wrist watch and made a mental note of the time. As though coming from a far distance, he could hear the drone of voices in the directors' room.

Guthrie Jayne's demeanor now seemed to be undergoing a strange metamorphosis. His usual servile attitude disappeared. His shoulders straightened, his head went up, and his eyes flashed behind his thick spectacles. His thoughts seemed to be making a different man of him.

Presently, he left the switchboard and went leisurely across the office to an old filing cabinet. From the lower drawer of this, he took an old, worn, black traveling bag. He tossed the bag out of sight beneath a nearby desk, where he could get it easily when he wished to do so.

At the door of the directors' room, he stopped and bent forward as though listening to what was happening inside. A confused murmur came to his ears. Jayne smiled, and glanced at his watch again.

Now he walked the length of the office to a front window,

and leaned out, letting his eyes search the windows of the building just across the street. At one of those windows, a short distance below him, he could see the soft blur of a face. Something flashed for an instant, as though a handkerchief had been waved at him in signal.

Jayne smiled slightly, but he did not reply to the salutation, if indeed it had been one and directed at him. He drifted away from the window and returned to the switchboard. Having finished his cigarette, he carefully extinguished the butt of it in an ash tray.

Once more, he glanced at his watch. His manner was that of a man timing something, waiting for a certain moment to arrive. And presently he got up and hurried over to the door of the directors' room again, and listened there once more. There was no babble of voices now, only an ominous silence.

Guthrie Jayne opened the door slowly and cautiously for the space of about a foot, and peered into the room. An exclamation of satisfaction escaped him, and his eyes gleamed. He darted inside and closed the door behind him, and locked it with the spring lock, so he would be secure from interruption and discovery.

Seven unconscious men were in the directors' room. Three were sprawled across the big table. The four others were on the floor, where they had fallen. They were all breathing heavily, as though drugged. Jayne's lips curled into the suggestion of a sneer as he looked them over.

"Cocktails and cigars!" he muttered.

THE DOOR of the private vault was standing open as Stephen Wazer had left it. Jayne took a pair of thin gloves from his coat pocket, and drew them on. Then he hurried across the room and disappeared into the vault. He remained there for about ten minutes. When he emerged, his arms were full of documents and account books. On the end of the long table, he piled what he had collected.

There were two thick packages of banknotes, and to these

Jayne added the package which Stephen Wazer had taken from the vault to distribute to the directors. There were also several documents that Jayne selected, and an old ledger with its leaves yellow with age. Jayne handled this old ledger lovingly, as though it had some special value for him.

Carrying the loot he had selected, he hurried across to the door, listened there, and heard no sound in the front office. He opened the door and left it standing partway open, and went out. Into the old traveling bag he had taken from the filing cabinet, he stuffed his loot.

Then he sped noiselessly to the front of the office and leaned from the window again. Once more he saw a little flash of white in another window across the street. This time, Jayne answered the signal by waving his own handkerchief. He disappeared from the window immediately afterward.

Into the directors' room he hurried again, and closed and locked the door. And now he did a surprising thing. Commencing with Stephen Wazer, he began divesting Wazer, Donnibell and Blandale of their outer garments. He piled their coats, waistcoats and trousers on the floor near one of the windows. Then he stretched the three victims side by side on the floor, like a row of dead men in a morgue.

Guthrie Jayne did not seem to have the slightest fear that any of those in the room would return to consciousness and catch him at his work, and identify him. None knew better than he the duration of the effects of the drug they had received from the cocktails and cigars.

After his work was finished, he rushed back into the front office. He hurried to the corridor door and waited there a short time. When a soft knock came, he unlocked and opened the door immediately.

An elderly woman slipped into the office, a woman stoop-shouldered and dressed in rusty black. She carried an old traveling bag, a duplicate of the one into which Jayne had stuffed his loot. Jayne took it from her.

"Is everything all right?" she whispered.

"Everything's fine, Eleanor," he whispered in reply, "No slips so far—and we sure don't want any. There hasn't been a single hitch in the plans. Everything on schedule. Wazer saw the signs and got the phone message, and the cylinder scared him half to death. The drugged drinks and cigars made everything easy."

THE BAG she had brought was tossed beneath his own desk. Jayne got the one into which he had put the currency, documents and old ledger, and handed it to her.

"So you were able to get into the vault?" she asked.

"Yes. Wazer left the door open after he got out the things for the meeting, as I'd expected him to do. Scads of money! We'll take out our expenses and pass the rest on to charity. And something even better than the money, Eleanor—absolute proof!"

"You got it?" she gasped. Her voice sounded eager, enthusiastic—young.

"Documents—and an old ledger that tells the story," Jayne told her. "After we've punished them, we'll clear our father's name, put them where they put him! But we must be careful now. No slips! You're not afraid, Eleanor?"

"Certainly not! Why should I be afraid? Haven't we rehearsed this enough times?" she asked.

"Yes. But doing the actual thing is different," he explained. "Be cautious—don't make any mistakes. So much depends on our success in this first venture."

"Trust me, my brother," she said. "Do you think I can forget our father and mother, and how their lives were ruined by these men? Haven't we spent years planning for this moment? I'll make no mistakes!"

"We'll make them pay, over and over," Guthrie Jayne said. "We'll wreck them, break them! Three of them are in that other room now, drugged and helpless. I—I scarcely can keep my hands from their throats!"

"Hush!" she warned, grasping his arm. "This isn't the time

to let yourself get worked up about it. It's a time to be cautious and carry out plans."

"I know. I—I'll control myself," he said.

"I came as soon as I saw your signal at the window. I got off the elevator at the seventeenth floor and walked up the rest of the way. I'll use a different elevator when I leave. If anybody questions, I'm only a poor woman taking orders for soap." She laughed a bit.

"And nobody would dream that there's a fortune in currency and negotiable bonds in that old bag," Jayne replied. "How about your disguise?"

"I'll get rid of it as we planned," she said. "An old lady will go into a telephone booth at that busy drug store on the corner—but a young woman will come out of it. This old-fashioned bonnet I'm wearing not only hides my face but also covers a chic hat. This baggy black dress hides a gown of the sort you'd expect a fashionable young woman to wear. The same with the shoes. Don't my feet look enormous in these? I'll make the change in less than two minutes."

"And how about the clothes you must leave behind?" Jayne asked her.

"That telephone booth is almost dark. One jerk on a string and this black dress will fall off me. I'll drop the clothes on the floor and kick them into a corner. The gray wig, too, and even these spectacles I'm wearing. I'll be away before the stuff is found."

"Good girl!" Jayne exclaimed. "We've got to remember every little detail, Eleanor. A little mistake might wreck us. And we must leave a trail that can be followed easily—to the wrong destination."

"I'll be so glad when this first affair is over," she said. "Then you can stop being Guthrie Jayne, and be yourself."

"It'll be a welcome change," he confessed. "Being stoop-shouldered and humble for about ten hours a day is a strain."

"My part is easy," she said, "but you—"

"Don't you worry about me, Eleanor. Our plans are fool proof. Just be ready to help me, as we've arranged." He opened the door and peered out into the corridor. "Everything's clear now," he reported. "Better be going."

She slipped out of the office immediately, and shuffled along the corridor toward the nearest elevator. Guthrie Jayne locked the door after her exit, and hurried back into the directors' room.

Now he made a swift search of the garments he had taken from the three drugged and helpless men, removed everything from the pockets, and made a heap of the articles on the floor in a corner. Jayne did not want them, nor did he wish to send them where the clothes were going. The owners could search through the pile and find their belongings.

He raised a window its full extent, leaned out, and looked at the street far below—a side street which was almost deserted now. That window could not be seen from any of the other buildings near. Jayne picked up some of the garments, and prepared to toss them out of the window. There would be some startled persons below, when clothing began raining upon them.

Working as rapidly as possible, Jayne threw out the garments, sent a shower of coats, waistcoats and trousers sailing through the air. The window was closed again before the falling articles were halfway down to the street. Jayne glanced around the room swiftly, to make certain that everything was as he wished it, and then fixed the spring lock on the inside of the door, stepped out, and jerked the door shut. His unconscious victims were locked in the directors' room, and that lock could be worked only from the inside.

Out in the front office, he went to another file case and opened a drawer. From beneath a heap of old papers, he took a card. On that card were some words which had been printed with pen and ink:

WITH THE COMPLIMENTS
OF THE MONGOOSE

JAYNE FASTENED the card to the door of the directors' room with a pin, and hurried back to the file case. This time he took out a small package similar to the one which had contained the cylinder for the dictating machine—and which contained another. He put the package on a desk almost in front of the door of the directors' room, where it was sure to be found.

Then he hurried across to the telephone switchboard. He tore off his gloves and tossed them into a waste-basket. He made himself comfortable in front of the switchboard, plugged in, and called a number.

"Hello!" a man's voice answered, presently.

"Mr. Graddon?" Jayne asked.

"Yes, this is Graddon."

"This is Jayne, Mr. Wazer's secretary. Oh, Mr. Graddon, please hurry right over to the office! Something terrible is happening! If you don't hurry, you may be too late!… Oh!"

Jayne ended the conversation with a sort of choked scream, as though he had been the victim of a sudden violent attack. He smiled grimly when he heard Detective Mark Graddon's frantic yelps at the other end of the wire, his shouted demands for further enlightenment. Those yelps ceased suddenly. Detective Graddon, Jayne knew, was on the way.

Now Jayne plugged in again, and this time he called Police Headquarters. A grouchy desk sergeant answered the call.

"Police—help!" Jayne cried into the transmitter. Come quick—Stephen Wazer's office—National Building! Oh, hurry—hurry!" Jayne's voice was that of a man in agony.

"Hey! What's the trouble there?" the sergeant bellowed.

"Be quick, please! Something terrible… robbery… murder… help!"

Again, Jayne ended the conversation with a choking cry, as though being throttled. He severed the telephone connection. And now he called two leading newspapers, spoke in the quiet tone of a man giving a confidential tip, and informed two city editors that there had been a sensational robbery at the offices of Stephen Wazer, and that an attempt was being made to keep it a secret. That would bring out the star reporters, he knew, men who would overlook no sensational detail when they wrote their stories of the affair for the press.

Leaving the switchboard, Jayne went to a water cooler in a corner of the office, and filled a paper drinking cup with water. Into the water he put three drops of a liquid taken from a tiny vial which he had been carrying in a vest pocket. He drank the mixture.

Then he removed the lid of the water cooler, emptied the contents of the vial into the water, and replaced the lid. He hurled the vial against the wall and shattered the glass into a hundred fragments.

"I'll be awake about the same time as the others," Guthrie Jayne estimated. "Now to make everything look natural."

Returning to the telephone switchboard, he plugged in as though to make a call. He sprawled across the table, one hand clutching the cord, his position that of a man who had passed out while trying to telephone. He shifted a little in the chair, and rested his head comfortably on his left arm.

And he smiled faintly as he felt unconsciousness stealing upon him.

CHAPTER V

RIVAL SLEUTHS

DETECTIVE MARK GRADDON drove his own car, a battered old roadster that looked like a wreck but could show remarkable speed with Mark Graddon at the wheel. Regardless of traffic rules and corner policemen, Mark Graddon made the distance to the National Building in record time. He stopped at the curb with screaming brakes, yanked the emergency and twisted off the ignition, and sprang out.

At the same instant, a police car came tearing around the corner with its siren screeching, and drove to the curb behind Mark Graddon's roadster. Graddon was already on the sidewalk when the police car stopped. He turned to look. A squad was getting out of the police car. In the squad was Doc Pimms, medical examiner, and it was in charge of Detective Sergeant Tim Ladman.

Mark Graddon's face burned and his black mustache bristled. Between himself and Tim Ladman there was professional enmity of long standing. Before he could get into the lobby of the building Tim Ladman was beside him.

"Probably the same case," Ladman suggested.

"What case?" Graddon wanted to know.

"Got a call from Stephen Wazer's office—sort of frantic call—man said something about robbery and murder."

Graddon showed increased interest. "I got one, too," he admitted. "Wazer is a client of mine. The call came from his secretary."

"Must be something up, then," Ladman said. "Won't take any chances." He issued swift orders, stationed men in the entrance with orders to detain everybody wanting to leave, and sent men around to the side entrance and to an alley door.

Mark Graddon hurried on to the elevator. Tim Ladman was right behind him, and Doc Pimms and a couple of officers. They shot up to the twentieth floor.

"Funny they called the police," Graddon said. "It's probably something I can handle alone."

"Yeah?" Ladman asked. "They always call the police when a thing is serious. You private dicks are all right when it comes to shadowing some poor cuss or gathering business information—"

"I graduated out of the Department before you got into the rooky school," Graddon interrupted.

"They didn't have a rooky school when you got into the Department," Ladman retorted. "Anybody with a pull could get in those days. Now they're more particular."

"Well, you're all right physically, Ladman, but how did you manage to dodge the brain test?" Graddon wanted to know. "Must have had a set of the answers."

Doc Pimms put in a word. "You lads do your fightin' now," he suggested. "Get it over with, so you can both concentrate on the case."

Doc Pimms had gray in his hair and was known for a caustic wit, so the pair subsided. The elevator stopped, the door clanged open, and they stepped into the corridor. Mark Graddon led the way to the Wazer suite of offices.

There was nobody in the corridor except an assistant janitor who was fussing with a window at the end of the hall. There were no sounds of trouble. The building seemed deserted. The assistant janitor, evidently surprised at this invasion, shuffled toward them along the corridor.

Mark Graddon found the front door of the Wazer suite locked. He listened with the others, but they could hear no sound from the inside. Ladman beckoned for the janitor to hurry.

"Unlock this door, and be snappy about it!" Ladman demanded.

"See or hear anything funny around here?" Graddon asked, as the janitor fumbled for his keys.

"Ain't seen anybody or heard anything," the janitor replied. "Not many folks here Saturday afternoon. What's wrong?"

"We'll tell you that later," Tim Ladman said. "Get this door open!"

THE JANITOR opened the door. Mark Graddon was the first through it, but Ladman was at his heels. The interior of the front office of the Wazer suite seemed calm and peaceful. Everything was in order. There was no wrecked furniture, no signs of a life-and-death struggle.

"Fake call!" Tim Ladman decided.

But Mark Graddon, knowing the office better, had been

glancing around it swiftly. And now he gave a little cry and started rapidly across the room. He had caught sight of Guthrie Jayne huddled in front of the telephone switchboard.

"Who's this bird?" Ladman asked.

"Jayne—Wazer's secretary," Graddon replied. "He telephoned me—probably called you cops, too. Look at that—plugged in to make another call, and passed out before he could do it. How about it, Doc?"

Pimms already was making an examination.

"Drugged, I'd say," the medical examiner reported. "Every indication of it."

"Maybe some gang caught this fellow alone, and looted the office," Ladman suggested.

Mark Graddon rushed to the door of Wazer's private office, and pulled it open. Ladman was at his heels again. A swift glance assured them that everything was all right there. They hurried back to the switchboard.

"Bring him out of it, Doc," Graddon begged. "Looks like he'd have to talk before we learn anything."

"What's that on that door?" Ladman cried.

He pointed to the door of the directors' room. Graddon ran to it with him. They read the card: "With the compliments of The Mongoose."

"Nut stuff!" said Tim Ladman. "What's it mean, Graddon? What's a mongoose?"

"I think it's a kind of monkey," Graddon told him.

"It's a marmoset you're thinking of," Ladman declared. "A mongoose is not a monkey. I remember of reading of one once. I think it's a snake. Anyhow, what's that sign mean?"

"Hey, you bulls! This gent is comin' out of it!" Doc Pimms called.

Graddon and Ladman dashed back to the telephone switch-board, Guthrie Jayne was moving his head, and moaning. His eyelids flickered, closed again.

"Snap out of it, Jayne!" Graddon said. "What's happened? This is Graddon asking you! Come alive, man!"

Jayne groaned again, and they braced him up in the chair. Doc Pimms held a bottle beneath his nose. Jayne tried to turn his head away from it as a pungent odor burned his nostrils. He gave a sneeze, opened his eyes again.

"That's the boy," Graddon encouraged. "Wake up and talk, man! What did they do to you—and who did it?"

One of the other officers had been moving around the room.

"Ladman!" he called, suddenly. "Listen here! Something goin' on in this room."

He was pointing to the door of the directors' room. Graddon and Ladman left Jayne and rushed to the spot They bent their heads to listen. They could hear a chorus of groans and moans.

Graddon tried the door, to find it locked. He pounded upon it with his fists.

"Help!… Help!" came a cry from inside. It was a weak cry, little more than a murmur, but it urged Graddon and Ladman to action.

"Smash the door down!" Ladman suggested.

Graddon sprang back, prepared to hurl himself against the door. But he was spared a bruised shoulder. The door was opened suddenly, opened by a man who was on his knees and reaching up to the spring lock, a man who tumbled over weakly as soon as his work was done.

GRADDON AND Ladman sprang over his body and into the directors' room. They stopped abruptly, astounded. Men were sprawled on the floor. Men were lurching to their feet, holding hands to blurred eyes. Men were moaning as they tried to get into chairs. Seven men—and three of them in underclothing!

"Doc! Doc!" Ladman screeched. "Come here, quick!"

Doc Pimms turned Jayne over to one of the officers, and hurried to them. Doc was a practical man. He wasted no time in horrified exclamations or in speculation. He was a medical examiner, and he examined, rapidly and superficially.

"Doped!" he pronounced. "The whole gang's been doped! What's the idea of those half-dressed birds? That the way big business men run around now?"

"Let's get some of 'em out of it," Graddon begged. "Open the window, Ladman, and let in fresh air! Can you do anything, Doc?"

"The dope, whatever it is, seems to be wearin' off," the doctor replied.

"Something big's been pulled off here," Ladman declared, as he opened the window. "Look there, Graddon! Door of the vault standing wide open! Papers scattered all over the floor."

"That doesn't mean anything. They probably were holding a business meeting," Graddon said.

He was trying to get Stephen Wazer to talk, after managing to prop him up in a chair. And he was doing some rapid thinking, too. Mark Graddon knew the dark and devious ways of some financiers. It occurred to him that Stephen Wazer might want to keep secret what had happened here—or at least tell his own version of it.

CHAPTER VI

JAYNE IS SUSPECTED

INTO THE OFFICE rushed a group of newspapermen. Though they were hardened reporters, they got a shock now. Through the open door of the directors' room they could see seven of the most prominent financiers of the city reeling and staggering around, making meaningless gestures—and three of them less than half clad.

"What happened, Mr. Wazer?" Graddon was asking. "Jayne

telephoned me to come." In a whisper he added: "Careful! Reporters!"

"Get... everybody... away," Wazer muttered.

Graddon whirled toward Ladman. "Help me handle this, Tim," he begged. "Get Jayne in here, shut everybody else out, and let's find out what's happened."

Ladman got Jayne inside and the door closed. The seven financiers were in chairs now, rapidly recovering their strength and brain power.

"I—I wish to talk to my associates—in private, please," Wazer said.

"If there's been a crime here, I want to know it," Ladman said.

Graddon thrust his way forward. "Ladman, let me handle this," he begged. "Mr. Wazer retains me. If I need help, I'll call you."

"I'll be waiting outside," Ladman promised.

Graddon shut the door and set the spring lock, and walked back to the table. "What is it, Mr. Wazer?" he asked.

I've been robbed. I had a bundle of currency on this table— seventy thousand dollars. And two packages of banknotes have been taken from the vault, each of fifty thousand."

"But who—"

"Donnibell, Blandale and I are the only ones concerned. The three of us have been threatened. Keep it as quiet as possible. Say it was a small robbery, and that I don't want any fuss made about it," Wazer said.

"Maybe I can get Ladman to agree to that."

"Donnibell and Blandale will remain, and these other gentlemen will go as soon as it is possible. If you can get rid of the police—"

"Can't shake Tim Ladman now, I'm afraid, sir. But he'll be sensible."

Graddon did his work well. Ladman chased the newspapermen into the corridor after giving them the yarn about a small robbery. The four financiers departed, having sworn to reveal nothing. Then Ladman left men on guard in the outer office, and entered the directors' room with Doc Pimms.

"Careful!" Wazer whispered to Graddon. "It's that old Cratch case—somebody out to get all of us."

Graddon's eyes grew wide, then narrowed swiftly. He understood Wazer's position now, and why he did not want this affair investigated closely. And now that he was warned, Graddon was in a position to help his employer—and himself. He did not forget that he was concerned in the Cratch case.

Jayne told his story at length, prodded continually by Ladman, while Graddon tried to interfere at times, and Wazer and his two associates writhed in their chairs. Then Ladman disappeared into the front office, and was gone for some little time. When he returned to the room, he stood in front of Jayne and looked down at him in a manner slightly accusing.

"The messenger service people say that none of their boys delivered a package here this afternoon," he said.

"Possibly he was an impostor, sir, in the uniform of a messenger," Jayne replied.

One of the elevator men remembers the old woman you mentioned. And did you ever see these before?" Ladman thrust a pair of gloves at Guthrie Jayne.

Jayne blinked at them. "G-gloves!" he said.

"Get busy and try 'em on."

Jayne suddenly seemed seized with a fit of nervousness. He took the right glove and pulled it on his hand. It was just a little loose.

"**GOOD ENOUGH** fit at that," Ladman said. "Good enough to prevent leaving fingerprints. Those gloves were found in a waste-basket in the front office."

"Are you daring to intimate, sir, that I may have had something to do with this?"

"I'd say it's an inside job. You may have been in on the deal."

"But—the stolen stuff—?" Jayne asked.

A pal could have carried it out—possibly that old woman with the black bag."

"But I was drugged, sir."

"One of your pals could have drugged you to make it look good."

"Preposterous!" Jayne cried. "Mr. Wazer, I have tried to be faithful and loyal. Why should I do such a thing?"

"For coin!" Ladman retorted. "Some smooth crook coaxes you in on a deal, shows how easy it would be."

"But why would Jayne, or anybody else, take our clothes?" Wazer asked.

"That's something to be found out. Let's get out of this room," Ladman said. "I don't want anything here disturbed. You may shut the door of your vault, Mr. Wazer, but I'll probably want to let the fingerprint man in there later."

"We can go into my private office," Wazer said. "We must telephone for clothes."

They went into the front room, and Ladman closed the door.

"See that nobody gets into that room," he ordered one of his men. "Keep that hall door locked, and the reporters out."

They started toward the door of the private office, but Jayne suddenly stopped and pointed. "That package on the desk!" he said. "It looks like the one Mr. Wazer received, containing that cylinder. Perhaps it is another cylinder, sir."

Ladman picked it up. "We'll take it along. Lead the way, Mr. Wazer."

Wazer began doing some rapid thinking, trying to devise a means of getting hold of the cylinder, of hearing its message before anybody else, of destroying the cylinder before any of the others could listen to it.

He passed through the door and into the private office, and the others followed. Jayne shuffled along in their midst. He lurched to one side as he came to the door, acted as though seized with a sudden spell of dizziness. His hand clutched at the edge of the casement for a moment—and his forefinger touched a button hidden there....

WAZER SAT down in his desk chair, and the others found seats around the room. As Wazer started to speak, his telephone buzzer sounded. His private wire! And there was nobody at the switchboard in the outer office!

He reached for the telephone instrument, trying to act in a nonchalant manner. "Hello!" he called.

"Mr. Wazer?" It was a woman's voice. "The Mongoose told me to thank you for your little donation. He may visit you again soon. And he'll visit the others, too."

Wazer heard nothing more except a feminine laugh. A little click came along the wire to tell him that the woman at the other end had hung up.

"Quick!" Wazer said. "Into the outer office!"

He dashed to the door with the others crowding behind him. He opened the door to see one policeman standing near the door of the directors' room and another at the other side of the office. Neither was near the switchboard.

"That telephone call, on my private line—it had to come through the switchboard," Wazer said. "And there's nobody at the board to plug in the call. It can't be done!"

"What can't be done?" Ladman asked.

"Can't get a call through on my private wire unless it comes through the switchboard. The caller gets my general office number. If he gives a signal code, the switchboard operator plugs in on my private line. But there wasn't anybody here to plug in."

"Answer probably easy when we find it," Ladman remarked, as he examined the board. "Ah! Here we are! The trunk line has been hooked up with your private wire. "See here! Beneath the board, so the plugs don't have to be used. Little switch here. Somebody went to a lot of trouble to arrange that."

"But who—?" Wazer began.

"Jayne was at that board last, and nobody has touched it since. He probably hooked up that connection, so a call from outside would ring the buzzer in your private office. The call traveled around the board—understand?"

They went back across the front room and into the private office. Ladman closed the door, and they sought chairs again. The detective glared at Guthrie Jayne, and the latter seemed to be a bit frightened. Mark Graddon had been remaining in the background, observing everything, trying to catch signals from Wazer.

"Mr. Ladman," Wazer said, "I feel that we are on the wrong track in this investigation. I told you that I've received threats from somebody, calling himself The Mongoose. I believe that name is given to represent one of these so-called master criminals, perhaps the leader of a lawless band. This affair may usher in a series of attacks on wealthy men."

"It's possible," Ladman admitted.

"I dislike publicity of this sort. The newspapers will make enough of it as it is. I—I'd appreciate it if the whole thing could be dropped now."

"Going to let 'em get away with it?" Ladman roared. "That's a wrong attitude. It's my job to catch crooks. Let 'em go, and one of your friends may be a victim tomorrow. Don't worry about some crook stealing your pants. It'll cause a short laugh—but what of it?"

"A man in my position—"Wazer began.

"Rot! A few of your friends will roast you at the club, and some of the common mob will giggle to think of a rich man having his pants stolen. But you can offset that prettily by giving the reporters an interview, in which you say that you'll use every means to discover the crooks. That stealing-your-pants thing may be some new boss crook's way of attracting attention. Like leaving an ace of spades at the scene of every crime, or something like that."

"I—I'd rather have Graddon handle the case," Wazer declared. "I retain him—pay him—"

"The citizens of this man's town retain and pay me, too—to run down crooks," Tim Ladman said. "That's my job. Mr. Wazer, why are you so eager to have this case dropped? They took a wad of money from you, didn't they? Don't you want revenge? It's very human to want revenge."

Revenge! Human to want revenge! That was what The Mongoose wanted, Stephen Wazer thought.

"Get into that little package, and let's see if it is another of those cylinders," Ladman said. "Might get a clue there."

Wazer gave Graddon a glance of helplessness. Donnibell and Blandale glanced at each other swiftly. They, too, were eager for Ladman to leave, transfer his activities elsewhere. They wanted to talk to Graddon alone.

But Wazer was compelled to unwrap the package. He did it slowly, and finally exposed a cylinder for the dictating machine. If only he could delay things until that cylinder melted into nothing! Yet he wanted to hear the message, too.

He put the cylinder on the machine, but he took plenty of time about it. Finally, he adjusted the ear phones, and gave all his attention to the message:

> Hello, Stephen Wazer! I have struck my first blow! Others will follow rapidly. Donnibell must be punished, and Blandale. And Graddon, the crooked detective. Then I have more of your associates to punish, including a crooked judge.
>
> You cannot escape—any of you! The scales must be balanced. Retribution is at hand. You, who sent William Cratch, an innocent man, to a living death in prison, must know fear, anguish, humiliation, and finally disgrace and ruin! If you get this cylinder, it will mean that I have got, out of your vault, proof of William Cratch's innocence and your own guilt.
>
> THE MONGOOSE.

CHAPTER VII

THE DOPED GUARDS

"**ANYTHING INTERESTING THERE**, Wazer?" Tim Ladman asked after the machine had stopped.

Stephen Wazer played for time now, hoped that this cylinder would be destroyed as the other had been. He fussed with the machine, adjusted the ear tubes again.

"Something I didn't quite catch," he said. "Just a moment, please."

So he started the record again, bent forward as though listening intently, while the others watched him and waited. Wazer kept his face free of incriminating expression. He was looking intently at the surface of the cylinder, praying for the little bubbles to appear and herald the destruction of the record. He certainly did not want Detective Sergeant Tim Ladman to listen to that revelation of the meaning of this affair.

Donnibell and Blandale guessed what he was doing. Donnibell tried to strike up a conversation with Ladman, attract his attention.

"Haven't you any idea, officer, what crook might do a thing like this?" he asked.

"Any crook who's big enough might," Ladman replied.

"How about you, Graddon? You got any ideas about it?"

"The cops seem to be handling this case," Mark Graddon said. "When they get through messing around I'll get busy and probably solve it."

"When we get through messing around it'll be solved!" Tim Ladman assured him. "I'm going to cultivate Mr. Jayne more. I think he's going to be interesting."

"Preposterous!" Jayne cried. "You'll do better service to search for the real culprit. I'll not endure this, sir! I'll retain an attorney! I'll sue the city!"

"It's being done every day," Ladman told him. "Another little suit won't bother much."

"You cannot connect me with this crime," Jayne said. "If I did it, where is the—er—loot?"

"That's easy! Your pals carried it away, and you'll get your split, later—if your pals are honest with you. I never said you did it, Jayne. That'd call for heavy mentality. I said it's possible that you're in on the deal—that you doped those drinks and cigars and let the others into the office. Maybe I'm wrong. Time will tell."

Donnibell glanced at Wazer and saw the ghost of a smile on the latter's face. It disappeared instantly, but it had been there long enough to warn Donnibell. He looked swiftly at the cylinder. Little bubbles were appearing on the surface.

Jayne had been glancing at that cylinder also. He did not want Ladman to hear the message it bore. He wanted to handle his victims in his own way, did not want the reason for his attack to become public yet. That might interfere with his vengeance.

"Look!" Wazer cried suddenly.

Ladman whirled toward him. Wazer had removed the ear tubes and was pointing at the cylinder. Ladman gave a cry of chagrin.

"Just like the other," Wazer said. "Watch it disappear! The thing is uncanny!"

"Let me have those tubes!" Ladman said. "I want to hear that thing."

WAZER DROPPED the tubes, stooped to recover them. And then, when Ladman put the tips into his ears, Wazer fumbled about starting the machine. It would not operate. The needle stuck in the soft composition of the cylinder. And it was a cylinder no longer—was rapidly becoming a soft mass that was seemingly evaporating.

"What did the thing say?" Ladman demanded.

"I—I really don't remember," Wazer replied.

"You mean you won't tell!"

Stephen Wazer became indignant. "I do not intend to tolerate any more of your impudence, sir!" he cried. "I have endured enough this afternoon, and can stand no more! Mr. Graddon, you take charge of this case."

"Oh, I'll keep on the job!" Ladman said.

Mark Graddon did not like the situation. He did not want Tim Ladman to grow angry and suspicious. Ladman was an officer of worth, and far from being a fool.

"You're nervous, Mr. Wazer, and I don't blame you," Graddon said. "You just let Ladman and me handle it together. We'll manage to get along."

He tried to flash a message to Wazer. The latter started to turn away from his desk. Again, the telephone buzzer sounded.

I'll answer that!" Ladman snapped. "This private wire is still hooked up with the outside." He jerked up the receiver.

"Hello!" he called. "What's that? Yes, he's here! Who wants to talk to him? None of my business, huh?"

Ladman glanced up, smiling cynically. The others looked at him with keen interest.

"It's a call for Mr. Jayne," Ladman said. "A lady at the other end of the line."

Guthrie Jayne betrayed sudden nervousness. His hand seemingly shook as he accepted the receiver. He gulped, and licked at his lips as though they suddenly were dry.

"Hello!" he said. "Yes… yes, I'm all right!… I can't talk just now!… I'll telephone later!"

Nervously, Jayne replaced the receiver on its hook.

"So you can't talk just now?" Ladman mocked. "One of the gang, wasn't it?"

"Just a—a lady friend of mine," Jayne replied.

"I wouldn't take you for the sort to have many lady friends,"

Ladman said. "Sit down there, Jayne! We're going to have a little talk with you!"

Guthrie Jayne sat down. He fumbled with his cravat. His eyes traveled around the office. He was a consummate actor at the moment. That telephone message had come as arranged, with his sister Eleanor at the other end of the wire—had come with the intention of arousing suspicion against Guthrie Jayne!

"Now, Jayne, you'd better come across!" Tim Ladman told him. "You may get off easy if you tell us all about it and turn up the others. They coaxed you into it, didn't they?"

"I will not endure your suspicions!" Jayne cried.

"Talk quick, so we can get the swag back, and maybe I can fix it so you'll only get a short jail sentence," Ladman said. "That is, if Mr. Wazer agrees."

"Do you really think Jayne had a hand in it?" Wazer asked.

"I do!"

Jayne sprang to his feet. I'm not going to remain here and listen to any more of this!" he cried. "I'm going home! Don't you dare try to stop me!"

He made a dash for the door, reached it, jerked it open and sprang into the main office. Ladman was only a step behind him, clutching at him.

But Jayne came to an abrupt stop, so that the others crashed against him. "Look!... Look!" he cried.

They looked. Sprawled on the floor, unconscious, were the two policemen who had been guarding the office.

CHAPTER VIII

JAYNE'S GETAWAY

THERE WAS SOMETHING else that they did not notice just then—a brackish odor in the air. Not for nothing, had Jayne pressed a button in the door casement as he had gone into the private office. Pressure on that button had opened a dozen tiny vents in the moulding of the room. Gas had seeped into the office, a heavy gas that spread as it slowly dropped toward the floor.

That gas had got into the nostrils of the two men, into their throats. It was a harmless gas in itself. And it had taken Jayne months, working at odd moments at nights, when he had sneaked into the suite, to store that gas at different points along the moulding, and to arrange the electrical control which released it. Stephen Wazer did not know that his secretary knew more chemistry than many men who taught it.

Harmless in itself, that gas. But it parched men's throats— and made them want to drink water. And into the water cooler in the corner of the front office, Guthrie Jayne had dumped the contents of that little vial!

Now Ladman and the others rushed forward, crying in alarm. Doc Pimms knelt beside the nearest victim and made a swift examination.

"Doped!" he judged.

"But how did they get it?" Ladman cried.

"You don't suppose they were toying with those cigars, or emptying the cocktail shaker?" Graddon asked. "Didn't warn 'em about it, did you?"

"The fools!" Ladman exploded. "They'll hear from me, if that's the way of it! You watch 'em, Doc. Now, Jayne— Where is Jayne?"

Jayne had crossed the room to the water cooler, and was pretending to drink. As they approached him, he crushed one of the paper cups in his hand and dropped it into the waste-basket, then brushed the back of his hand across his lips.

"Thirsty—" he muttered.

Suddenly, the others realized that they were thirsty. Like sheep following one another, they followed the suggestion given them by Jayne. One by one, they drank of the water—all except Doc Pimms, who was working over the unconscious men.

"Back into the office!" Tim Ladman said. "Let's get at this thing, now!"

Detective Sergeant Tim Ladman had the fond belief that he was striking while the iron was hot. He drove them before him into the private office and closed the door, ordered them to chairs.

"We've got to have clothes," Wazer complained again. "We've got to telephone—"

"I've got a couple of men below looking for your panties," Ladman said. "If they don't find 'em pretty quick, you can telephone. Don't take time to do it now. I want to settle this thing. Now, Jayne—"

"I won't say anything!" Jayne declared, suddenly.

"Oh, you won't? Want to see your lawyer first, huh? Is that it? Maybe the mob you're working with has a dandy mouthpiece. You'll need one, Jayne."

"See here!" Jayne cried. "What gives you the idea I have something to do with this—this robbery?"

"Everything points to it. I think we'll go into your history. How'd you get hold of him, Mr. Wazer?"

"He applied for a position just as my old secretary left me to go into business for himself," Wazer replied.

"A man like you doesn't pick up anybody and make him a confidential secretary."

"He had splendid references, from Boston and Philadelphia—as to his professional ability, integrity, and all that."

"Ever investigate to see whether they were forged?"

"Matter of fact, I didn't," Wazer replied. "But I watched him, and he seemed honest and hard-working. He's been with me over a year, and never before—"

"Even a percentage of today's haul would pay him for that year, wouldn't it?" Ladman asked. "It's my idea he was tempted and drawn into this by some clever professional crooks. That's why I say that, if he'll come clean right now and help us, I'll do what I can to make his sentence light."

JAYNE GLANCED around at the five men. Donnibell and Blandale were sitting at either end of the desk, and Wazer was in his own chair. Mark Graddon was walking around the room. Ladman stood against the wall like a man trying to dominate the scene.

"Well, Jayne, what've you got to say?" Ladman demanded. "Want me to take you to the station and sweat it out of you?"

"Putting me in jail wouldn't get Mr. Wazer his money back," Jayne said.

"So, that's it! That's the game, huh? Trying a hold-up on us, are you? We'll see about that, my lad! I think I'll just take you to the station!"

Guthrie Jayne threw up his head and laughed. It was a laugh utterly unlike him. It did not seem to fit in with his character.

"Take me to the station?" he asked. "You'd better look around! What's the matter with Mr. Wazer? Look at Donnibell and Blandale, the financial crooks! And Mark Graddon—what's the matter, Graddon?"

Graddon was slowly collapsing to the floor. Wazer had toppled forward across his desk. Donnibell and Blandale were slumped down in their chairs unconscious.

"Why, you—what—?" Ladman mouthed.

He started to lurch toward Guthrie Jayne. His knees seemed to give way suddenly. His head swam. He tried to shout a warning, and only gurgled. The last thing he heard was Jayne's soft laugh.

Jayne darted to the door and listened a moment, made sure that Doc Pimms was not at the point of entering. Then he got Tim Ladman's service revolver, and Graddon's, slipped the former into his coat pocket and tossed the latter into a corner of the room after extracting the cartridges. Chuckling, he got Ladman's handcuffs out, and fastened Ladman's right wrist to Graddon's left.

He gave a swift glance around the room, made the gesture of kissing it good-by. Then he opened the door.

"Doctor!" he cried, alarm in the tone of his voice. "Doctor—come quick!"

"What is it?" Pimms shouted; as he came running across the room.

"Hurry! I'll get some water!" Jayne cried at him. "Look at them! Terrible!"

Doc Pimms rushed into the private office—and Jayne jerked the door shut after his entrance. He turned the catch, and Doc Pimms was prisoner for the time being.

Now Jayne sped across the room, past the unconscious officers, and to a locker. He grasped his hat, ran to the corridor door and opened it. There were newspaper reporters in the corridor, as Jayne had expected. They beheld an excited man, hat in hand, rushing from the scene of the latest sensation and howled a volley of questions at him.

"Go in—go in!" Jayne cried at them. "I'm going for a doctor! Go to the private office!"

He brushed past them, sped on. As he neared the elevators, he glanced back and saw that nobody was in the hall. All had gone into the suite. So Jayne darted on past the elevators, went to the stairs, and hurried down them.

He suspected that police officers were stationed in the front lobby of the building and would let nobody out unless he had permission from Ladman to leave. But Guthrie Jayne did not intend to leave in that manner. He had planned a different route of escape.

On down the stairs he sped, betraying the athlete. He did not appear to be the stoop-shouldered, near-sighted Jayne those in the building were used to seeing. He had to get down to the fifteenth floor. And he wanted to do so without being seen.

But on the sixteenth floor he crashed into a janitor who was just starting about his work. Jayne acted swiftly. The revolver came from his pocket, and the janitor was menaced. He found himself thrust into a supply closet, locked in. Jayne sped on as the janitor began howling.

On the fifteenth floor he raced to the end of a corridor, threw up a window, leaned out. Directly opposite, only a few feet away, was an open window in another building. A narrow ledge of fancy masonry connected the two buildings.

Without hesitation, Jayne crawled out on the ledge. He did not look down, looked only at the other window. He shuffled along the ledge slowly, an inch at a time. The draft in the court seemed to be trying to pull him down. He fought against the draw of it.

He reached the edge of the ledge, grasped the sill, managed to get through and into the other building. And now he walked briskly to the elevator, putting on his hat and pulling it down almost to his eyes. He rang, and when the elevator ascended for him, he was calmly puffing a cigarette.

"Some men never keep appointments when they make 'em," he growled at the elevator man.

Jayne left the elevator at the ground floor and walked through the lobby. Out in the street, he went leisurely to the corner. Quite a crowd had collected there.

"What's the row?" he asked a bystander.

"Cops after somebody. Robbery, I think."

"They probably won't catch the guy," Jayne observed.

His eyes were twinkling behind his thick spectacles as he crossed the street. He got a taxicab, gave the chauffeur the address of the apartment house where he had a suite of two rooms, and leaned back against the cushions and puffed at his cigarette as the cab rolled swiftly along the avenue.

CHAPTER IX

THE VOICE FROM
THE EMPTY ROOM

DOC PIMMS, FINDING himself locked in the private office, spent a moment howling maledictions. Then somebody pounded on the door, opened it, and the newspapermen tumbled into the room.

"What's goin' on?" one of them demanded.

Doc Pimms could only wave a hand helplessly. "Drugged!" he said. "Doped! That's all I know. They all got it except me."

The air seemed to pulsate with the heavy breathing of the drugged men. Doc Pimms did not know what restoratives it would be safe to use, and did not have them with him had he known. He could only wait. Donnibell regained consciousness first.

"What was it this time?" he asked, weakly.

"More dope," Doc Pimms replied.

"But where—how—?"

"Some sort of gas in that outer office—I got a whiff of it," Doc replied. "But that didn't make you go under, or I'd have gone under also. I was out there working on those two coppers."

Blandale recovered consciousness at that moment, and had a spasm of fright. Donnibell shamed him to silence, warned him with a glance to be careful what he said.

"You're having a lot of experience," Donnibell told him. "You might even get your name in the papers, Blandale—if you talk too much."

"This is terrible—terrible!" Blandale cried. "I'll go to Europe! I'll—" He realized that Doc Pimms and the reporters were present, and that they knew nothing of The Mongoose, and allowed his voice to dwindle away.

Stephen Wazer began muttering, and in a moment was awake. Then Ladman and Graddon regained consciousness almost at the same moment, to find themselves handcuffed together. They liberated themselves and reeled to their feet.

"What happened?" Graddon cried. "And where's Jayne?"

"He trapped me in this room, and beat it," Doc Pimms said.

"That funny secretary?" one of the newspapermen asked. "He took it on the run down the hall. Told us to get in here. Said he was going for a doctor."

"Did he dope us, Doc?" Ladman demanded.

"You ought to know more about that than I do," Doc said. "I was in the other office. He called me, and when I rushed in here you were all asleep. Don't you know what happened?"

"It—something just struck us," Ladman admitted. "Let's do something. We've got to get him! I knew he was guilty. When I get my hands on him—"

"I've got it!" Doc Pimms cried. "Gas loose in the outer office. Made you thirsty. You all took a drink of water—all except me. The dope was in the water. That's why it got the rest of you, and never touched me."

"But Jayne took a drink," Graddon protested.

"He probably only faked it," Doc Pimms guessed. "I'm commencing to admire that man's tricks."

One of the newspapermen stepped forward. "What's it all about?" he demanded of Ladman. Are you going to come across, or do we have to dig it up?"

Ladman took a deep breath, brushed aside Mark Graddon's restraining hand, and faced the reporters.

"There was a robbery," he explained. "I accused Jayne, Mr. Wazer's private secretary, of being in on the deal. He managed to trick us and escape. We've got to get him! Don't know who his pals were, yet."

"What was taken?" one of the reporters demanded of Wazer.

"No statements now!" Wazer cried. "No statements by anybody! The first thing is to catch the fellow. I trusted him. He'd worked for me a year or more."

"But why take your clothes?" another asked.

Wazer became conscious of his appearance again. "Don't know," he replied. "Gentlemen, please go into the other office. We can tell you nothing. I'm sure Detective Ladman will give you what information he thinks can be made public. If you'll respect our—er—unconventional attire, and spare us further shame—"

The reporters laughed and trooped out into the main office. Doc Pimms hurried after them, to inspect the two officers there, who had returned to consciousness.

"Detective Ladman!" Wazer said. "In the top drawer of my chief clerk's desk, just inside the railing, is a little blue book. It has the addresses of all my employees. If you'll kindly get it for me, we can—"

Ladman waited to hear no more. He darted away to get the address book—and left Graddon alone with the three.

"GRADDON, YOU'VE got to get Jayne ahead of the cops," Wazer said swiftly. "If they catch him, he may talk. That Mongoose—he says that he's old Cratch's son—rich—spending time and money to punish us. Understand? He'll be after you the same as the others."

"I get it!" Graddon said.

"I don't know what part Jayne had in all this. Possibly The Mongoose has a band, and Jayne is one of it."

"I'll have to play along with the cops, and try to throw them off at the last moment," Graddon said. "Leave it to me! You gentlemen get clothes and get home—and don't talk."

The telephone buzzer sounded. Stephen Wazer flinched. In obedience to Graddon's gesture, he answered the call.

"Mark Graddon there?" a man asked.

"Just a minute!" Wazer handed the receiver to Graddon.

"Well?" Graddon snapped.

"Hello, Old Sleuth! This is Guthrie Jayne speaking. Did you all have a nice nap? Has Wazer told you more about The Mongoose, or are the cops still hanging around? I've got some news for you, Graddon. I'm The Mongoose. But you'll never see Guthrie Jayne again!"

"I'll get you, Jayne!"

"You're on my list yourself, Graddon. I know the part you played in the Cratch case. You'll hear from me about it later— but you'll never see Guthrie Jayne again."

Ladman appeared in the doorway with the book in his hand. Mark Graddon made frantic signals which Ladman understood. He rushed out to the switchboard, plugged in on one of the lines, demanded a tracing of the other call.

"I'll see you in jail—that's where I'll see you!" Mark Graddon told Jayne, striving to hold him in conversation until the call could be traced. "You and your gang!"

"I've got a pretty small gang, Graddon. Don't need a gang to fight a nest of snakes like you and the others. Before I'm done with you, I'm going to put you in the pen!"

"You expect to get away with this, you poor sap?" Graddon cried.

"Certainly! Brains always win," Guthrie Jayne said, laughing a bit. "You're too obvious, my dear Graddon. For instance, I know quite well that you're having this call traced. You'd have saved some work if you'd merely asked me where I am. I'm at home, Graddon, talking to you over the telephone in my parlor. Go ahead and check up on it!"

Jayne laughed, and broke the connection. Tim Ladman came charging back into the office.

"Got it!" he said. "The poor sap is talking from his own apartment. Number checks with the address in the book. Let's get going!"

LADMAN SHOUTED orders for some men to remain behind, brushed aside eager reporters, rushed out into the corridor and along it toward the elevator. Graddon was at his heels. Wazer, Donnibell and Blandale were left alone in the office, to make arrangements about getting some clothes.

When the street was reached, Graddon sprang into his roadster and dashed up the avenue. The police car, with its siren screeching, was only a short distance behind. That siren cleared the way for Graddon's car.

Graddon knew a shortcut to the destination. He was eager to get there first, to catch Jayne if possible, and handle him before Tim Ladman could reach him and begin questioning. He used the shortcut, but the police chauffeur simply followed his car, and gained on it rapidly.

There was not a hundred feet between them when they pulled up with smoking brakes in front of a second-rate apartment house on a side street. They rushed into the lobby, howling questions at the clerk. The newspapermen had been left behind, but they would be there soon. It would not take them long to pick up the trail.

Up in the elevator they went, to rush along a hall and come to a stop at the door of Guthrie Jayne's suite. An excited manager demanded to know what it was all about. There must be some mistake, he said—Mr. Jayne was such a quiet man.

Graddon tried the door, and found that it was locked. There was a key inside. Tim Ladman pounded on the panels.

"Who's there?" a voice demanded. "Why smash the door?"

"Open up!" Ladman ordered.

"Why should I? What do you want?"

"Open the door and come out, Jayne!" Mark Graddon called. "We've got you in a trap!"

"That you, Graddon? I told you, didn't I, that you'd never see me again? I don't want to make myself out a liar."

"Open the door, or we'll smash it in and come after you!" Ladman cried.

"Go ahead and smash it—I don't care!"

Then there was silence inside the room. The apartment house manager protested against destruction of property. One of the detectives took him by the arm and led him gently aside. Graddon drew back and hurled himself against the door.

It withstood the shock, and Graddon attacked again. There was an ominous crack.

"Give her another one!" Ladman called.

For the third time, Graddon hurled his bulk against the door. And this time it crashed in, and he sprawled over it and into the room. Ladman sprang in also, with the others behind him. They half expected to find a suicide, but they found nothing. There were but the two rooms. There was only the one door. The windows were closed, and locked on the inside, and none of them was on a fire escape anyhow. There was no way for Guthrie Jayne to have escaped.

Yet he was not there. They searched beneath articles of furniture, searched closets, looked into every nook. There was no place to hide—yet Jayne was not there.

"Where the deuce—?" Ladman cried.

"We heard him talking in here, didn't we?" Graddon said. "The door was locked on the inside, and all the windows are now."

"But where?" Ladman seemed to choke. Rage suffused his face. He brandished his fists in impotent ire.

"He's got to be here!" Graddon exclaimed. "He can't be anywhere else. Examine the walls!"

They worked for a quarter of an hour, examining the walls, but found nothing unusual. Exhausted, they dropped into chairs. There the newspaper reporters found them.

"You make the statement, Ladman," Graddon said, with a suspicion of gloating in his manner. "Take care of the newspaper boys, Ladman! Tell 'em how great and infallible you cops are. Tell 'em first where Guthrie Jayne went. Go ahead and tell 'em, for I want to know myself!"

CHAPTER X

EXIT MR. JAYNE

IT TOOK GUTHRIE Jayne about fifteen minutes to reach the apartment house. He got out of the cab, entered the lobby, greeted the clerk, and ascended in the elevator to the seventh floor, where he walked briskly along the hall and let himself into his suite.

His movements had been leisurely, those of a tired man returning to his home after the day's work. But the moment he was inside and the door locked, his manner changed. He became snappy, alert, a different sort of man. He hurried to the telephone and called Wazer's number, hoping that his arrangement at the switchboard had not been disturbed, and that the buzzer of Wazer's private line would sound.

He had his talk with Detective Mark Graddon, and ended the conversation by snapping the receiver back on its hook. He yawned and stretched. When he stretched the stoop disappeared from his shoulders.

And now Guthrie Jayne underwent a strange metamorphosis indeed. He rushed to the closet in the corner of the room, where a modest wardrobe was hanging. He shoved suits and coats to either side, and then hurried back across the bedroom. In a corner near the baseboard was a tiny button. Jayne pressed it.

He ran to the closet again. A portion of the back wall of the closet had slipped aside. No ordinary job of a sliding panel, this! The thing was a work of art, even insulated so that there would be no hollow sound if a man pounded on it.

A false closet was disclosed behind the other. Guthrie Jayne darted into it. He stripped off his clothes to the skin, and dropped them to the floor. Then he began dressing in other garments, the laundry marks on which were not the same as those upon the ones owned by Guthrie Jayne.

He stood erect at intervals, bracing his shoulders, breathing deeply. Finally, he pounded on the back wall of the false closet. A faint tapping came from the other side.

"Good girl, Eleanor!" Jayne breathed.

He tapped again, and before him the second wall slipped back. Guthrie Jayne stepped into a shower bath with tile walls. He peered through the curtains. A fashionable, gowned, attractive young woman smiled at him.

"Oh, work fast!" she whispered.

"Trust me! They're on their way! Here's where I kill Guthrie Jayne, as far as appearances are concerned."

He left both panels open behind him, so he could hear what was happening in the hall beyond that other room. He was dressed only from the waist down. There was a basin of hot water ready, and certain bottles filled with liquids.

"Got my clothes ready?" Jayne asked.

"Everything is ready," she replied.

"Get the loot put away safely?"

"Yes. Ridiculously easy."

"Clear out, now!" he ordered.

She left the bathroom and closed the door. Guthrie Jayne locked it. He immersed his head in the hot water, poured a solution into it. He scrubbed with a coarse bath rag, applied a cosmetic, scrubbed again.

Guthrie Jayne's pallor began to disappear. It was a false pallor, a thing of cosmetics which had set into the skin and could be removed only by the application of certain lotions. Guthrie Jayne used a towel, and had a healthy face. He tugged at his hair—and a wig came away. His dusty blond eyebrows disappeared, and under them were black, thin eyebrows, almost pencil marks.

From his nostrils, Jayne removed tiny plugs which had

distended them. From behind his ears, he took bits of plaster that had held those ears braced outward. There had been a tiny speck of plaster at the corner of each eye, and with them removed the slant of the eyes were changed entirely. Jayne did not worry about those eyes—they were ordinary brown in color, the same as thousands of other pairs of eyes.

Now he affixed a wig of thin brown hair, a marvel of a wig which had cost him a lot of money in Europe. He had no hair of his own—the result of an attack of fever when he was a boy. It was a fortunate thing now.

He looked at himself in the mirror, and smiled. Opening the door, he dashed into a bedroom, slipped into undershirt and shirt, opened another door and called in his sister as he put on collar and cravat.

"HOW DOES it look?" he asked. The voice was changed, too. It was deep, vibrant.

"Great!" she said.

"Think I'll do?"

"I know it!"

"Guthrie Jayne is dead," he said. "Eleanor, there were times when I got mighty tired of it—shuffling along stoop-shouldered, using that thin voice, acting humble and servile to a man I hated! And now Guthrie Jayne has told them that he is The Mongoose. And The Mongoose will continue his work. And they will be looking everywhere for Guthrie Jayne—who no longer exists. They'll probably have his photographs and descriptions—but not his fingerprints. Those false fingertips left marks all over Wazer's office, but those fingertips are gone, too—dissolved off my hands."

"The first blow!" she said.

"It's been tough changing back and forth and playing two parts, showing myself as Guthrie Jayne, and as myself," he said.

"They'll never find the way through those double walls."

"I hope not! They may get through the first one, but not into the shower. I'll fix that right now!"

From a drawer he took a little prepared cement and a tiny trowel. But he heard a tumult from the hall in the other building.

"They're here!" he said. "Stand by!"

He hurried back into the modest two-room suite and spoke to the men on the other side of the door. When he finally retreated, he closed the panel in the closet, got into the shower bath and closed that panel. And then he carefully calked the cracks around the door in the false back of the shower.

"That's that, Eleanor!" he said. "That's the last of Guthrie Jayne! Let's check up, quickly. Facial appearance—changed completely. Voice changed. Manner of walking, swinging my arms—changed because I'll revert to the natural. As Jayne, I was acting. I'm almost two inches shorter because I'm wearing normal shoes, and I was using shoes that had been built up before. Fingertips changed. Nobody in the world can say that I am Guthrie Jayne."

She laughed a bit as she went with him through a bedchamber and into a huge living room. The second-rate apartment house on the side street stood back to back with the more pretentious one on the avenue. And the man who had called himself Guthrie Jayne owned them both. With plenty of time and money at his command, it had not been difficult for him to arrange that getaway from one house to the other—especially since he was an expert in chemistry and a man to whom the effects of electricity had few secrets.

"Perfect!" he said. "Good old Guthrie Jayne! Gone forever, as far as seeing him is concerned. What a search they'll make for him! And the work of The Mongoose will go on! One by one, we'll punish them, Eleanor. Even Mark Graddon, who arranged the false evidence. And then the climax—when I use that old ledger and prove our father was innocent!"

"Yes, we'll make them pay!" she said, her face stern for a moment.

"I had hard work to keep from laughing," he said. "Ladman thought he was so wise, getting me to convict myself. He didn't know that I was leaving a trail purposely, that I wanted him to follow it here—and see Guthrie Jayne disappear. And we made fools of them, too. A prominent financier cannot be dignified in his underwear. Wait till the newspapers come out!"

"What now?" she asked.

"Now? I believe that Mr. Sidney Carleigh and Miss Eleanor Carleigh, his sister, will take a little stroll. Mr. Carleigh wishes to inspect some of his property."

"You—you think—?" she whispered.

"Get on your hat—and don't be afraid."

MR. SIDNEY CARLEIGH and his attractive sister, Eleanor, went down in the elevator and smilingly crossed the lobby. They paused for a moment at the desk to exchange pleasantries with the clerk and manager. Out upon the avenue they went, strolling leisurely, Mr. Sidney Carleigh swinging his stick in a jaunty manner.

They went to the corner, turned it into the side street, and continued their stroll to the entrance of the other apartment house. Here there seemed to be a small amount of excitement. A crowd had gathered. Mr. Carleigh frowned as he made a path through it for his sister and himself.

They turned into the apartment house, and a middle-aged man rushed up to them.

"What is all this confusion, Gregory?" Mr. Carleigh demanded.

"It is the police, sir. They say that one of the tenants is a robber. He was in his suite—but he's gone. They can't find where he's gone."

"A robber? A thief?" Mr. Carleigh said, elevating his brows a trifle. "Really, Gregory, you must be more careful about tenants. Such things give a property a bad name. I trust you to operate this place in a proper manner."

"He has been here a year, sir," the manager defended himself. "A quiet, mild man, always friendly with everybody. Kept to his rooms a great deal, and read a lot, I believe. Never had the slightest complaint about him."

"Ah, well! We never know," Mr. Sidney Carleigh observed. "A sort of wolf in sheep's clothing—eh, what? Possibly you are not to be blamed, Gregory. You've made me a good manager. But use caution, Gregory—use caution!"

"Yes, sir. You may trust me, Mr. Carleigh! Here come some of the detectives now, sir."

Mr. Carleigh braced himself mentally and physically. He saw Mark Graddon and Tim Ladman hurrying toward him. There was a hint of aloofness in his manner as he looked them over.

"This is Mr. Carleigh, the owner, gentlemen," Gregory introduced. "He did not know the man Jayne, however. He does not live here."

"So there has been a thief in the building?" Carleigh asked. "I regret that very much.

"My manager says that he always seemed to be a quiet, nice man. One never knows, does one?"

Mark Graddon gave him a rapid glance—and there was nothing of recognition in it. Ladman glanced at him also, and away again—looking for Guthrie Jayne, possibly.

Then they went out to the street, scattered the crowd of curious, and sent a few men to look around the neighborhood. The reporters trailed them, at which Mr. Carleigh smiled. He guessed that the reporters would play up the cleverness of The Mongoose, which was a thing to be desired.

Presently Mr. Carleigh and his sister went out upon the street again and strolled down the avenue.

"What are we going to do next?" she asked.

"We're going to have an excellent dinner, and then take in a good show," he replied, smiling at her. "We're going to forget about The Mongoose over the week-end. But, say about Monday, we'll start considering him and his activities again!"

THE VOICE FROM NOWHERE

*Out of Thin Air Came the Message from
The Mongoose—and to Clark Donnibell It
Was a Message Fraught with Terror*

OUT OF THIN AIR

ENSCONCED IN THE sacred precincts of his innermost private office, Clark Donnibell was bending over his carved mahogany desk, deeply engrossed in a certain corporation report. The prominent financier was gathering important data, preparatory to making another raid on the stock market.

It was about three o'clock in the afternoon. An atmosphere of quiet efficiency and smoothly-operating routine permeated the Donnibell suite. There was nothing to indicate that trouble was just around the corner, or that a season of panic was impending—panic which had nothing to do with the market, stocks or bonds.

So interesting to him was the document he was reading that Donnibell did not even glance up when the door was opened quietly and his confidential secretary slipped into the office. The secretary coughed slightly to call attention to his presence. Without looking up at him, Donnibell gave a characteristic grunt, which was translated by the experienced secretary as permission for him to speak.

"Pardon me for disturbing you, sir—" he began.

"What is it?" Donnibell snapped.

"There is a package for you—"

"What's that—a package? Why bother me about it? Haven't we a method of handling packages in this office?"

"I wouldn't have bothered you with it, sir, at this time, except

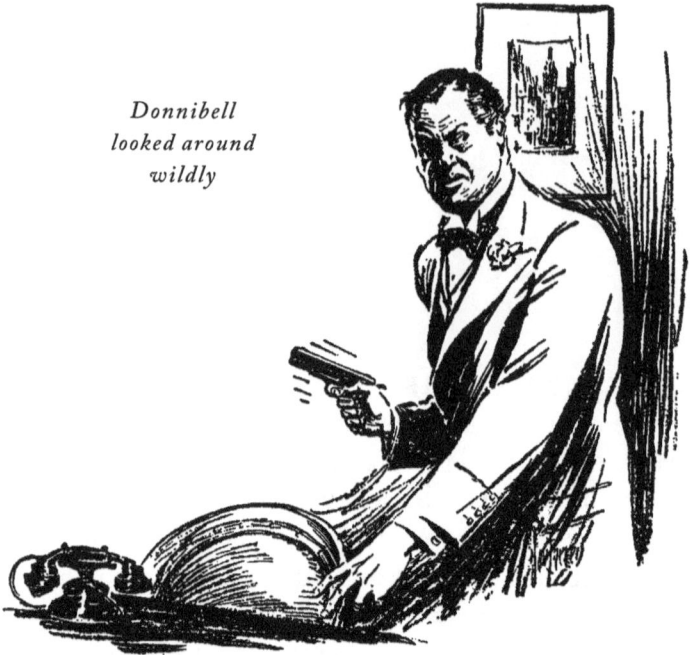

*Donnibell
looked around
wildly*

that there's a sort of irregularity connected with it," the secretary said.

"Something irregular, you say? What do you mean?" Donnibell demanded.

As he spoke, he glanced up from the document he had been reading. He looked at the small package the secretary held. He seemed to flinch when he caught sight of it. Quickly, he made an effort to control himself, to refrain from making an exhibition of his emotions, and succeeded admirably.

"I feel it my duty to make a report of something that has been brought to my attention, sir, though it may result in unpleasantness for somebody," the secretary was saying. "It concerns the discipline of the office, sir. It is possible that one of our clerks or messengers has been derelict in conduct."

"Explain!" Donnibell snapped.

"Very good, sir! The elderly Mr. Osgerd, our client, found this package, sir, as he was coming into the office to see about some bonds. Evidently, it had been dropped on the floor out in the public corridor, just outside our own door. Noticing that the package was addressed to you, Mr. Osgerd was kind enough to bring it in. It's possible, sir, that one of our employees dropped the package carelessly."

During this recital, Clark Donnibell had been fighting to retain control of himself and not betray his unusual agitation. He gripped the arms of his desk chair until his knuckles showed white, and set his jaws as though against incautious speech. He endeavored to keep his face an inscrutable mask. He did not want his secretary to observe that the mere sight of that package had disconcerted him.

"Unpardonable!" he judged, when the report had been concluded. "We can't be having things like that happening around the office. Have to look into it! But—take it up with me later. I'm very busy now."

"Very good, sir! And this package—"

"Put it there on the end of the desk. I—I think I know what it is."

"Yes, sir."

"And get out—and don't bother me again until I get finished with this confounded report."

THE SECRETARY put down the package, and turned to slip from the room with scarcely any more noise than a shadow would have made. Donnibell bent over the corporation report again. But that move was only a pose.

He was not reading the document. He merely was making a pretense at being occupied, until the secretary had gone from the office and closed the door.

When he was alone, the manner of the financier changed swiftly. Suddenly, he tossed the corporation report aside. He bent forward in his chair. His body seemed to grow tense. He commenced breathing heavily, like an agitated man. And, with glowing eyes, he looked intently at the package on the desk.

It was a small package, about eight inches long and five inches square at the ends. It was neatly wrapped in tough express paper, tied with heavy twine, and liberally daubed with red sealing wax. Donnibell made no effort to open it. He did not as much as touch it. A keen observer might have perceived that he was afraid to do so.

And now Donnibell seemed to undergo a strange metamorphosis. Leaning back in his chair again, he inhaled deeply, like a man gathering strength for some unusual ordeal. A surge of color rushed into his face—a banner of mounting rage.

His eyes flamed suddenly. His lower jaw shot out pugnaciously. His lips became a thin, straight line of determination as they were pressed back against his teeth. Donnibell became the picture of a fighting man who had received a challenge, and was prepared to accept it instantly.

For a moment, he remained motionless, as though trying to decide on a course of action. Then, turning slightly, he flipped the switch of the office intercommunication system, and bent forward to speak.

"Yes, Mr. Donnibell?" the alert girl at the outside switchboard asked, immediately.

"Get Detective Mark Graddon on the phone for me." Donnibell instructed. "Try his office first. Keep right at it till you get him. It's important!"

He threw off the switch without waiting to hear the girl's conventional acknowledgment of the order. Getting up from the chair, he strode across the room to a window, from which he could look out over a sea of roofs, and down into the man-made canyons at the teeming streets.

So it had come!

He had been expecting it for some time, and had nerved himself to face it, yet it was something in the nature of a shock, after all. Well, he was prepared to fight!

They wouldn't make a fool of him, he told himself, as they had made fools of two of his business associates, Stephen Wazer and Harvey Blandale! Wazer had been caught off guard, and

Blandale was only a weak-kneed brother at best. But he, Clark Donnibell, was made of different metal. He was a fighting man!...

DONNIBELL'S MIND flashed back a decade. He was remembering the time when he and some of his close business associates had perpetrated an outrageous stock swindle, and had faced conviction and imprisonment as a result.

They had escaped only by manufacturing bogus evidence and giving perjured testimony, and so pinning the guilt on an innocent bookkeeper named William Cratch. The latter had been convicted and sent to prison, and there he had died. The financial conspirators had been able to breathe normally again.

And now—after years of security—Nemesis!

Unexpectedly, a son of the victimized William Cratch had appeared. Taking the name of Guthrie Jayne, he had obtained the position of private secretary to Stephen Wazer, one of the guilty financiers.

Thus he had been able to learn the business secrets and personal habits of members of the group. He had visited their offices scores of times, their apartments and houses. He had played the game slowly, and with patience, making careful preparations.

Then he had thrown the mask aside, had announced himself as an instrument of vengeance—and had struck! Two victims in as many months! He called himself The Mongoose now, declaring that the unusual soubriquet was appropriate, since he was attacking human snakes.

The police had been unable to find any trace of The Mongoose. Guthrie Jayne seemed to have disappeared utterly. Detective Mark Graddon, a private operative who worked for the financiers, could not get a clue as to the whereabouts of the man. And Graddon was especially eager to do so, for he was a potential victim himself. It had been Graddon who had manufactured the false evidence that had sent William Cratch to prison.

Yet, The Mongoose was somewhere in the vicinity, sending

out his frequent taunts, warnings, and threats. Those he assailed knew only that he could be expected to strike again. They could not guess where or when....

The telephone buzzer sounded its demand for attention and brought Donnibell back to the present. He hurried across the room to answer the call.

"This is Detective Graddon—" a voice began.

"Graddon!" Donnibell interrupted. "Get over to my office as fast as you can make it. You'd better bring one of your best assistants with you."

"What's happened?"

"It's come!"

"You mean the little package we've been expecting?"

"That's it! Hurry, man! We must get right at this."

"Don't make a move till I get there," Graddon cautioned.

"I won't even touch the thing till you're right here beside me," Donnibell promised.

He replaced the telephone receiver and turned to pace nervously across the office from corner to corner, his head bent and his hands clasped behind his back, his attitude that of a man doing some deep thinking.

A fighting man—that's what he was! He was glad that this finally had come. The tedious, nerve-straining wait was at an end. Now, there could be a decision. If that ass who called himself The Mongoose thought that he could outwit Clark Donnibell, and possibly rob him of some worldly goods, he had another thought coming! A fighting man—that's what he was!...

"Donnibell!... Donnibell!"

The words were scarcely more than whispers. Donnibell had come to a stop beside a window, and now he whirled around swiftly, startled. But there was nobody in the office to receive his just rebuke for entering without being properly announced. Yet he would have taken honest oath that his name had been spoken. Imagination, probably, he thought. His nerves must be in a pretty state!

"Hello!… Donnibell!"

There it was again. There was no mistake about it this time. Donnibell could not tell from which direction the sound had come, but he knew beyond the shadow of a doubt that he had heard the words.

"This is a voice from nowhere… this is The Mongoose speaking to you, Donnibell!"

The voice seemed to be stronger now. Donnibell advanced a step from the wall, and stood there with cold shivers running up and down his spine. His moment of bravado already was at an end. This sort of thing was enough to wreck a man's determination to show valor. He remembered that The Mongoose was reported to be expert in chemistry, physics, electricity. He was capable of almost anything, a man who employed agencies of which other men knew but little.

"I know everything you do, Donnibell!… I can hear every word you say!… I can speak to you like this out of the nowhere whenever I desire!… and you hope to cope with me—you consummate fool!"

CHAPTER II

THE MESSAGE OF THE MONGOOSE

PANIC SUDDENLY SEIZED Donnibell. Again, he glanced wildly around the office, as though expecting to see the speaker. There was no possibility of somebody being hidden there— no place for a man to hide. Donnibell started across the room toward the door, but the voice of The Mongoose halted him.

"I heard everything you said to your secretary." The words were spoken in a clear monotone. "I had that package left in the corridor for you. I'm communicating with you in several ways, as a precaution, for I want to be sure you get my messages. I'll probably speak to you out of the nowhere again when you are at home. Give my regards to Detective Graddon when he arrives—and tell him I said he was a clown!"

Then the voice was silent. Donnibell remained motionless for an instant, then suddenly rushed across the room to the door and jerked it open. Adjoining the private office was a smaller one used by the secretary. And the secretary was there now, furiously typing some personal letters Donnibell had dictated to him.

"Anybody been in here with you?" Donnibell demanded.

"No, sir. I've been busy with these letters. Oh, are you ill, Mr. Donnibell? Pardon me, sir, but your face—"

"Did you hear anybody talking?"

"No, sir. Is there something wrong, sir?"

"It's all right—nothing! I'm expecting Mark Graddon. I want to see him as soon as he arrives. And don't let anybody else get in to me."

Donnibell closed the door again, and this time he turned the catch and locked himself in—and everybody else out. He hurried back to his desk, jerked open a drawer, and got out an automatic pistol. With his back against the wall, and the weapon held ready, he looked around the room again.

There was but the one door, opening into the secretary's office. There was no fire escape at either of the two windows. This was on the twentieth floor of the building, and an outside room. There was no place in the office where a human being could hide. And yet—that voice had come to him!

Donnibell knew that it had not come through the office inter-communication system, nor from the telephone. It was some trick, of course—possibly an attempt to wreck his nerves. But the fact that it was a trick did not lessen Donnibell's fright, did not stop the shivers running up and down his spine.

And suddenly soft, mocking laughter seemed to fill the private office. It seemed to come from every direction, and beat against Donnibell's ears like breakers on a rocky shore. Beads of cold perspiration popped out on his face. He glanced around wildly, brought the automatic up in a position to fire.

"Poor, poor fool!" the voice of The Mongoose taunted, as the laughter ceased. "Poor, helpless fool!"

THEN THERE was silence in the private office, except for Clark Donnibell's labored breathing. He leaned weakly against the wall, with the automatic still in his hand. He wished that Mark Graddon would hurry. This was something that he did not care to face alone.

Donnibell already had sensed that he had been selected by The Mongoose to be the third victim in the series. When he glanced at the little package on the end of his desk he felt sure of it. And Donnibell also felt sure that he knew the contents of that package.

When it was opened, undoubtedly a dictaphone cylinder record would be found. That was the way in which The Mongoose sent his threats, warnings, and demands—on dictaphone cylinders. And those cylinders were treated chemically, so that they disintegrated within a short time after being exposed to the open air, melted into nothingness.

A buzzer again signalled a demand for attention. Donnibell rushed across the room to the desk, and flipped the switch of the intercommunication system.

"Mr. Mark Graddon is here, sir," the girl out at the information desk announced.

"Send him right in," Donnibell ordered.

He hurried across the room, unlocked and opened the door. Mark Graddon came through the secretary's room and entered the private office immediately. The detective's countenance betrayed some surprise when he noticed the beads of perspiration on Donnibell's white face, his wild eyes, the automatic pistol held ready, the plain evidence of fright.

"What's the trouble?" Graddon asked. "You look about half scared to death. Why the gat? Have you shot somebody, or are you just going to?"

"Graddon, it's—it's terrible!" Donnibell whispered.

"What's terrible? Let me in on it."

"I heard his voice—the voice of The Mongoose. And yet he wasn't here—couldn't have been here."

"Calm down!" Mark Graddon advised. "Keep your nerve! Now, tell me—just what are you talking about?"

"It was right here in my private office, a moment ago. The Mongoose spoke to me."

"Why didn't you knock him on the head—or shoot him?"

"He wasn't here. He only spoke to me—said it was a voice from nowhere."

"Yeah? So he's up to some of his fancy tricks again, is he?" Graddon commented, in matter-of-fact tones. "He's probably got some kind of freak apparatus planted around here somewhere. He had a chance to plan all sorts of tricks when he was Wazer's secretary. For instance, he's probably been inside this office fifty times."

"He seemed to know everything that I said and did, Graddon. It's terrible—like being watched by unseen eyes."

Mark Graddon looked at him quickly, with a degree of suspicion in his glance. "Are you disobeying the doctor's orders and drinking hard liquor again?" he asked, grinning. "Sit down and relax. This thing is commencing to get on your nerves."

"I didn't just imagine it, Graddon, if that's what you're thinking," Donnibell protested. "It's true, I tell you! A voice from nowhere—"

"Uh-huh! But everybody with sense knows that a voice has to come from somewhere," Graddon pointed out. "There's no danger, I'm sure. You're here in your private office—and I'm with you. Your secretary is in the next room, and a score of other employees are scattered around the big office out front. So, let's get down to the facts first, and look for freak tricks later. It came, did it—the little package?"

"There it is," Donnibell replied. He gestured toward the package on the end of the desk. "No way of tracing it, either. It was left in the corridor, for one of my clients to find and bring into the office."

"Looks like the packages he sent to the other victims," Graddon commented. "I've got my best man, Jim Kreig, with me—left him in the front office. We'll get right at this thing. And, this time, we're going to land The Mongoose!"

"We *must* land him, Graddon! This can't be allowed to go on. I'll reward you handsomely if the fellow is caught. That voice—coming from nowhere—"

"Forget that voice for a moment," Graddon begged. "Don't let it make you wilt. I want to get my hands on The Mongoose. He's made a fool of me twice, but he'll not do it a third time! I'll soon put a stop to his work!"

"We must be very careful about publicity, Graddon. To the general public, The Mongoose is only a high class criminal attacking and robbing wealthy men. If he's caught, and talks—if he tells the motive behind the attacks—"

"I understand all that," Graddon interrupted. He eyed Donnibell meaningly as he continued: "Don't worry so much about it. Leave it to me. If he's caught, something may happen to keep him from talking. Now, I think we'd better have a look at that mysterious package."

"You open it, Graddon."

GRADDON IMMEDIATELY unwrapped the parcel, exposed a pasteboard box, removed the lid of that, and came upon something which had been wrapped carefully in a roll of soft cotton. Out of the cotton, he took a dictaphone record.

"You guessed right—this is it," Graddon said.

"Let's get it on the machine—quick!" Donnibell suggested. "I'll listen to the message first, and then you listen to it—before it melts and disappears."

Graddon handed him the cylinder, and Donnibell put it on the dictaphone quickly and carefully. He adjusted the ear tubes, and started the machine.

Nervously, he waited. The voice of The Mongoose—what would it say to him? What threat, what demand was about to be poured into his ears? He was almost afraid to learn. He bent forward, tensed, his senses keyed, as he listened:

> Hello, Donnibell! This is The Mongoose speaking. This is the son of the innocent man you treacherously had sent to prison, to die of confinement and shame.
>
> The time has come for you to pay for your sins, Donnibell. You are to be my next victim—the third snake to be attacked by The Mongoose. Your hour of retribution is here.
>
> I have spent considerable time deciding how to strike at you, and finally have decided to strike where it will hurt you the most—through the thing you value above all others.
>
> My plans are complete, and I may strike at any moment.
>
> And here is an important suggestion for you, Donnibell—do not forget to look beneath the bonbons!

That was the extent of the message. Donnibell removed the tubes from his ears, and motioned for Graddon to take them. The dictaphone was started again, and now the detective heard the record, while Donnibell sank back in his chair as though overcome by a sudden weakness.

Graddon heard the thing through. Then, without speaking, the two bent forward and watched the cylinder. What they expected, happened. Almost immediately, little bubbles began appearing on the cylinder's surface, as though some powerful acid was at work there. The bubbles increased rapidly in size and number. The record seemed to melt, run, evaporate.

"There it goes," Donnibell whispered.

"We both heard what it had to say," Graddon reminded him. "Just a sort of general threat—nothing specific. What do you suppose he meant by saying to look beneath the bonbons?"

"I can't imagine."

"And he says that he's going to strike at you through the thing you value most. What is that? Money—jewels—bonds? If we can get a line on what he intends to do, it may help some. What thing do you value most above all others?"

Donnibell's voice was husky, and his face ashen, as he replied. "My daughter!" he said.

Graddon seemed startled at the thought, but he did not allow it to startle him long.

"Nonsense!" he exclaimed, laughing a bit. "How could he strike at you through her? Where would there be any profit in that for him? And you can bet safely that The Mongoose is after profit. Unless he tries to abduct her and hold her for ransom— But that game's pretty well played out. The Mongoose would be too wise to try it. We can depend on him to think up something new and novel. Where is your daughter now?"

"I believe she's home. She told me this morning that she intended to remain home all day, and rest," Donnibell replied.

"Then she's all right, and there's nothing to worry about along those lines," Graddon declared. "She's home, with a butler and personal maid, and a flock of other servants to keep everybody from molesting her."

"But, this Mongoose—he seems to be able to do anything he wishes," Donnibell said. "If he harms Flora—"

"We'll protect her," Graddon assured him. "I'll have men scattered all around the place. Call in the regular cops, too, if it's necessary. Now, we'd better—"

MARK GRADDON ceased speaking abruptly. Suddenly, soft laughter had swept through the office. It grew in volume, rang back from the walls in mockery.

"That—that's what I heard before," Donnibell whispered.

"It's only some trick. There's some sort of machine hidden in the room," Graddon declared.

The laughter stopped. Then they heard a voice, which came to them at first as though from a far distance, and gradually grew stronger.

"Hello, again, Donnibell!… Greetings, Graddon!… So you've

listened to the message on the dictaphone. I sent the cylinder for fear something might happen to this, my other means of communicating with you."

Donnibell and Graddon looked at each other with their eyes bulging. The detective rushed across the office to the door, and pulled it open. Donnibell's secretary was busy typing in the other room. And, even as Graddon watched him, the voice of The Mongoose could be heard again, and Graddon knew that the secretary had nothing to do with it, as he had half expected. That was not the solution, then. He closed the door quickly.

"Afraid for your daughter, are you, Donnibell?" the voice of The Mongoose was asking. "What of the daughters of the men you've ruined?... But I don't fight women, Donnibell—not even such a worthless butterfly as your daughter Flora, who thinks of nothing but night clubs, gin and wild parties.

"I only fight men through women. You guessed right, Donnibell, I meant your daughter when I said the thing you valued most.... And don't forget to look beneath the bonbons."

"Wait!" Mark Graddon cried. "I don't suppose you're able to hear what I'm saying, Mongoose, but, if you are, listen to this: I'm out to get you! And I may not be careful how I handle you when you're caught!"

"I understand, Graddon. You'd like to murder me, to seal my lips," The Mongoose replied, distinctly. "But you haven't caught me yet, my dear Graddon. Good hunting!... Good-by!"

Again they heard that soft, mocking laughter for a moment—and then it was quiet in the office again.

CHAPTER III

THE DOPED CANDY

"**DO YOU REALIZE** what that means?" Graddon whispered to Donnibell. "He answered me—heard what I said and gave a direct reply to it."

"He can hear what's being said in this office. But he can't be anywhere near."

"It's some kind of a trick, but we'll get to the bottom of it. He'll try one trick too many, make some little slip, and then we'll have him!"

"My daughter—"

"Yes, we'd better attend to that first," Graddon agreed. "I suggest that you telephone your house. Tell Miss Donnibell to be on guard continually until we get there, to keep somebody with her. And you'd better tell your butler to keep his eyes open, especially for strangers."

Donnibell put through the call. Blake, his butler, answered.

"I was at the point of telephoning you, sir," the butler said.

"Anything wrong?" Donnibell asked, in sudden alarm.

"It is Miss Flora, sir. She's been taken ill. I've called Dr. Wanberg, and he'll come immediately. Her maid found her unconscious in her boudoir, sir."

"I'll start for home at once, Blake. And let me warn you, Blake—she may be in danger. See that nobody except Dr. Wanberg and her maid gets near her. Understand?"

"Yes, sir. Very good, sir."

Donnibell replaced the receiver and sprang to his feet, his face white and his eyes bulging.

"What is it?" Graddon cried.

"There's something wrong with my daughter. The butler says

she was found unconscious. He's called the doctor. I—I must get home, Graddon."

"We'll take my car, and make fast time," Graddon said. "I'll give Jim Kreig some instructions. Send all your employees home for the day, right now, so my men can work around here."

With Graddon in the lead they hurried out into the main office.

"Kreig!" Graddon called.

"Right here, chief."

"Telephone the office to send you a couple of men. Go through this suite—take the private office first. See if you can find any sort of hidden apparatus, such as a dictograph. Look for hidden wires. If you find wires, trace them to the other end." Lowering his voice, he added: "It's The Mongoose!"

"Okay, chief!" Kreig answered.

"I'll telephone you later. Tell the office, also, to send half a dozen men to report to me at Mr. Donnibell's home immediately. Take 'em off other work, if necessary. Get busy at that switchboard."

He whirled toward Donnibell, ready to leave the office with him. The employees already were preparing to quit work, Donnibell having told them to go. They sensed that something unusual had happened, and were growing excited.

"Come along with me, Mr. Donnibell," Graddon urged.

He grasped the financier by the elbow, and piloted him swiftly toward the corridor door. Donnibell seemed to be in a daze. Graddon was eager to get him away before the office employees noticed too much.

They descended in an express elevator, hurried out to the street, and got into Graddon's car. The detective sent it rushing through the crowded thoroughfare, signaling traffic officers who knew him to clear the way.

Into a side street he drove, where the traffic was not so heavy, and he could make better speed. Presently he turned into a broad avenue, and went along it recklessly. Donnibell crouched in the seat, holding on with one hand, clutching his hat with the other.

A shrill scream from tortured brakes—and they had stopped at the curb in front of Donnibell's town house. They hurried through the bronze gates and up to the front door. The butler had been watching for them; he opened the door as they were rushing up the steps.

"She's in the bedchamber, sir," the butler reported to Donnibell. "Dr. Wanberg has arrived and is with her, sir."

"What happened, Blake?"

"I really don't know, sir. I telephoned for the doctor as soon as I had verified the maid's report that Miss Donnibell was unconscious."

GRADDON FOLLOWED the agitated father up the stairs to the second floor, and along a hall there. Donnibell opened a door and hurried into a bedchamber. Graddon hesitated a moment, then went after him.

Flora Donnibell had been put to bed. A white-faced, weeping maid was standing beside her. A physician was just turning away.

"What is it, Wanberg?" Donnibell demanded.

"Try to be calm, Donnibell," the doctor ordered. "Your daughter has lost consciousness, and I'm trying to arouse her."

"Something serious?"

"I haven't had time to determine that," Dr. Wanberg admitted. "They tell me that she was on the *chaise longue* when the maid discovered her. There's nothing to indicate a fall, or an accident of any sort."

"Then—?" Donnibell questioned.

"I must have more time, for a fuller examination," the doctor replied. "Frankly, I believe that we have something unusual here. I'd say that she isn't unconscious because of an attack of some ordinary disease. She gives every indication of having been drugged."

"Drugged!" Donnibell cried.

"And not with an ordinary drug," the doctor added.

"But what—how—?"

Graddon touched him on the arm. "Come away, Mr. Donnibell, and let Dr. Wanberg do his work," Graddon said. "Let's go into the living room of the suite. And please have that maid come along with us. I want to ask her a few questions."

The maid was middle-aged, and Donnibell said that she had been with the family for eight years. She did not look like a person who would lend herself to an intrigue. She was frightened already, and she became still more frightened when she learned that Graddon was a detective.

Graddon's manner was not calculated to make the maid feel any more comfortable. He was an officer of the old school, and he still believed that rough methods were the most effective.

"Tell me exactly how you found Miss Donnibell," Graddon ordered.

"When I went to the bedroom and spoke to her, she did not answer, sir," the maid replied. "I thought at first that she had just dozed off. But there was a telephone call, so I tried to awaken her. Then I found that she was unconscious. That frightened me, and I—"

"Are you in the habit of ruining Miss Donnibell's beauty sleep every time there is a telephone call?"

"No, sir. But this—it was rather special, sir. The call was from Mr. Dick Hannock, sir. He's engaged to marry Miss Donnibell, and she always wants to be told when he calls."

"What did you tell Mr. Hannock?"

"I kept him waiting until I'd called the butler, sir. Then I told him Miss Donnibell had been taken suddenly ill. He said he'd come right to the house. He called from some country club, I think."

"He'll probably get here soon, then, and we can check up on that," Graddon said. "What has Miss Donnibell been doing all day, since breakfast? Think well, now!"

"She hasn't been out of her own rooms, sir. She said that she was tired, and not feeling any too well, and wanted to be quiet and just rest."

"Has anybody but you been in her suite today?"

"Nobody but one of the housemaids, sir, to help me put things to rights."

"But you haven't been in the suite yourself all the time, have you?" Graddon asked.

"Almost all the time, sir. I was doing some mending for Miss Donnibell. I was gone downstairs long enough to eat luncheon."

"Didn't Miss Donnibell eat luncheon?"

"She ate in her bedroom, sir."

Graddon began to show sudden interest. "What did she eat?" he asked.

"Only a little lettuce and tomato salad, sir, and some wafers and tea."

"Young woman, Miss Donnibell has been drugged!" Graddon informed her. "I'm trying to find out how she got the drug. Do you understand?"

"Yes, sir."

"Now—did she eat or drink anything else today?"

"I got a glass of water for her at one time, sir, out of the carafe in the bedroom. But I drank some out of it, too, and it didn't make me sick."

"Anything else?" Graddon persisted.

"Nothing, sir—except the candy."

"Candy?" Graddon questioned.

"Yes, sir. That was all right, though. It was a box of her favorite kind of candy, brought by a messenger, sir—with Mr. Dick Hannock's card."

"And she ate some of it?"

"Yes, sir. She opened the box right away. She was reading, and eating the candy—resting on the *chaise longue*—when I left the bedroom. And when I went back to tell her about the telephone call she was unconscious."

"How much candy did she eat?"

"Only a few pieces, I believe, sir. The box is still on the little table beside the *chaise longue*."

Graddon suddenly sprang to his feet, his face alight. He whirled toward Donnibell.

"Candy!" he cried. *"Bonbons!* Do you remember, Donnibell? *'Look beneath the bonbons!'* That's what he said!… You, girl! Get back into the bedroom and bring us that box of candy—quick!"

The frightened maid hurried away.

"But, if Dick Hannock sent her that candy—" Donnibell began.

"You should know by this time, Donnibell, that The Mongoose is clever," Graddon interrupted. "He's certainly clever enough to learn what kind of candy Miss Donnibell prefers, and to get hold of one of Dick Hannock's personal cards. And he mentioned something about bonbons, didn't he—and about striking you through your daughter?"

"If he's poisoned my girl—" Donnibell's voice ended in a choking sound.

IT HAD been said of Clark Donnibell that about the only redeeming trait in his character was his adoration of his daughter, his only child, who had been left motherless at the age of six. Yet this adoration had led to a criminal overindulgence of her whims.

Flora Donnibell was no pattern of maidenly modesty. She went the pace with the younger set. But her love affair with Dick Hannock, a serious-minded young man, was genuine, and seemed to have brought her to her senses in a measure.

"Oh, he probably hasn't poisoned her!" Graddon made haste to reply to Donnibell's exclamation. But he half doubted his own statement. He remembered that The Mongoose was conducting a campaign of revenge.

The maid came hurrying back, bringing the box of candy. Graddon took it from her and put it on a table which happened to be near. He handled it with extreme care. It seemed quite an ordinary box of confections of a better grade, bearing the trademark of a prominent candy manufacturer.

A dozen pieces were missing from the top layer. Graddon bent over the box and inspected it closely. Then he motioned for the maid to hand him a dish from another table. One by one, Graddon lifted the pieces of candy from the box and put them into the dish, until the entire upper layer was gone.

He removed the empty cardboard tray and put it aside, removed a sheet of tissue paper, and so exposed the lower layer of candy in the box. Once more, he made a careful inspection.

"It's been unpacked—and repacked," he judged, finally. "A fair job, but not perfect."

"You think the candy was drugged?" Donnibell asked. "Think that's where she got it?"

"We'll soon find out," Graddon replied.

Working carefully, he removed the candy of the lower layer, and put it into the dish. Donnibell stood beside him and bent over the box also.

"Look!" Graddon whispered, presently. "There's an envelope beneath the candy.... Better send the maid out of the room now."

Donnibell sent the maid. Graddon took the envelope from the box.

"Here's what The Mongoose meant, I suppose," he said. "It's a letter addressed to you, Donnibell. Handle it carefully. I may want to have it examined later."

Donnibell opened the envelope with trembling fingers, took out and unfolded a sheet of paper, and spread it out. The paper was covered with fine handwriting. Donnibell read the message quickly:

DONNIBELL:
Your daughter is probably unconscious as you read this. Be assured that she is in no immediate danger. The candy was drugged. It is a drug not known by ordinary physicians and

scientists. Certain Indian tribes near the headwaters of the Amazon use it.

This drug causes unconsciousness. There is but one known antidote. If this is administered properly within a certain time limit, the patient awakes as from a sound sleep, and with no bad after-effects. If the antidote is not given, the patient wastes away and dies. A delay in administering the antidote also may induce insanity. Tell your physician not to try the usual restoratives; they may have an unpleasant effect.

I have a supply of the antidote. I'll send it to you after you have carried out my orders. Meanwhile, your daughter is getting a much-needed rest.

The voice from nowhere soon will tell you just what to do. I'll speak to you in your library when I am ready. Keep somebody there to call you when the voice from nowhere demands your presence.

THE MONGOOSE.

DONNIBELL HANDED the letter to Graddon, who read it swiftly.

"Well, that's that!" Graddon said. "Now we know where we stand. Some plotter, this Mongoose! Do as he says, and he'll send you the antidote. Refuse, and your daughter wastes away and dies without regaining consciousness."

"He's got me! My hands are tied!" Donnibell cried. "I'll have to do whatever he says. Isn't there some move we can make, Graddon? Can't we fight him some way? But we must be very careful. If we anger him, and he doesn't send the antidote—"

"Keep your nerve!" Graddon interrupted. "We'll have to wait and see what he demands. Meanwhile, I'll get busy. I've got men coming out here, to guard the house. Jim Kreig will soon be reporting whether he's found anything unusual at the office. We aren't licked yet!"

"Shall I tell Dr. Wanberg anything?"

"Yes. Take him into your confidence and show him The Mongoose's letter. We have to do it. Then he won't be trying to use the wrong restoratives. Tell your butler to let me know when my men get here. I'll be using this telephone."

Donnibell hurried back into the bedchamber to consult with the doctor, and Mark Graddon sat down before an ornate and delicate desk and looked at a mauve telephone instrument half hidden in a cloud of lacy material of some sort. Graddon grinned as he reached for the thing. Unconsciously, he rubbed his hands on the legs of his trousers as though to remove grime. Mark Graddon was not used to such delicate telephone instruments.

But, as he was about to touch the receiver, the bell rang. Somebody was calling in. Graddon glanced toward the door of the bedroom, but the maid did not appear to answer the call. So he removed the receiver and answered it himself. Blake, the butler, was speaking from downstairs.

"There is a call for Detective Graddon, sir."

"I'm Graddon. Put 'em on."

"A moment, sir."

Graddon heard a click, and spoke into the transmitter again, and the voice of Jim Kreig answered him.

"That you, chief? Good enough! Well, we've sure found something down here!"

"What have you found?"

"I don't know exactly."

"What do you mean, you don't know exactly? You had eyes and ears the last time I saw you."

"It's like thus, chief—we found something that looked like a dictograph disk, only about three times as big. It was fastened to the bottom of Donnibell's desk. The wires ran down the leg of the desk, and through that swell rug."

"Did you follow 'em?"

"Sure thing! They ran to the outside wall, and passed through it—through a little hole. Some neat job, too! So we looked outside. We found a black box about a cubic foot in size. It was fastened outside the window."

"Any other wires run from that?"

"That's the joke—there wasn't any. I'm sure of that, because we unfastened the black box and got it into the office. The front of the thing was a sort of concave bell, with a lot of little holes in it."

"We'll have it examined—" Graddon began.

"I don't reckon so," Jim Kreig interrupted. "Not that black box! The thing had a lid, and we started to open it, to find out what was inside. The cussed thing was an infernal machine of some sort."

"What?" Graddon gasped.

"Yeah! She blew up, chief. There was a puff of black smoke and a big stink, and blue flames shot out of the thing. Some heat, too! Jackson got burned a little on his right hand."

"Blow the box to bits?"

"Nope! It was like this, chief—that thing evidently was fixed so, when it was opened, some chemicals got busy workin'. What I mean is this—when it cooled off and we looked at it good, we found that everything inside had melted. Nobody'll ever know what was in that black box."

"Foxy Mongoose!" Graddon exclaimed. "So we can't tell what kind of a machine it was. Find anything else, Kreig?"

"Nothing suspicious, chief, and we went through this suite of offices from end to end."

"All right! Have Jackson take the remains of that black box to the office, then see a doctor about that burn. You bring the other man out here with you. This is going to be the busy end of this case from now on. And make it snappy!"

CHAPTER IV

THE BLACK BOX

GRADDON HUNG UP, and got out of the chair to pace around the boudoir and do some heavy thinking. So The Mongoose had some new kind of infernal machine—a thing which enabled him to overhear what was being said, and to talk from a distance. Graddon supposed that there had been other wires, hidden so cunningly that Kreig and the men had failed to find them....

Donnibell returned to the room, and now a younger man was with him. Donnibell introduced him to Graddon—Dick Hannock, who was engaged to marry Flora Donnibell.

"Did you send Miss Donnibell a box of candy?" Graddon asked him.

"Not today," Hannock replied. "I was out in the country. I telephoned to ask whether I might see her this evening—she told me yesterday that she might decide to remain home and rest."

"Is this one of your cards?" Graddon handed him the card which had come with the candy.

"It's one of a lot I used formerly," Hannock replied. "I ran out of cards and had some new ones printed—got them just the other day. The new ones are slightly different. This is one of the old lot."

"Would it be difficult for somebody to get hold of one of your cards?"

"I suppose not. I leave them at shops, to be sent with parcels, and scatter them around the clubs—the same as anybody. If somebody wanted a card of mine, he probably could get it without much trouble."

"Any idea who might have sent Miss Donnibell a box of candy and put your card in it?"

"Almost anybody could have done so."

"Is this candy sold in more than one shop, or is there an exclusive agency for it?" Graddon asked.

"It's a rather popular brand of mixed bonbons, and probably is sold in a hundred places in the city," Hannock replied. "It could be picked up almost anywhere. Miss Donnibell has a fancy for the brand, so I frequently send her a box."

Blake the butler, entered quietly.

"There are some men downstairs asking for Mr. Graddon," he reported. "I believe they are his assistants."

"My men from the office," Graddon replied. "Let them wait for a few minutes. Blake!"

"Sir?"

"Did you receive that box of candy when it was delivered at the house?"

"It happens that I did, sir. It was delivered at the service entrance, and I happened to be near there at the time, consulting with the chef about dinner."

"Who delivered the box?"

"It was delivered by a young man, sir. He was not dressed in uniform like a messenger boy. I had a fleeting idea, sir, that he was the delivery boy for some neighborhood shop."

"Did he say anything?"

"As I remember it, sir, he merely said: 'Candy for Miss Donnibell,'" Blake replied. "He hurried away immediately, did not ask me to sign a delivery book. I unwrapped the package and sent it upstairs."

"How was it wrapped? Was it addressed?"

"I remember distinctly, sir, that it was wrapped in plain white paper. There was no shop's advertisement on it. Miss Donnibell's name and the address were typewritten on a little piece of paper, which was pasted to the wrapping."

"I want to see that wrapping paper."

"I regret to say, sir, that it has been destroyed," Blake said. "Things like that are tossed into the incinerator immediately, sir."

"Would you know that delivery boy, if you saw him again?"

"I doubt it very much, sir. I had my mind on something concerned with dinner, and did not pay much attention to the boy."

"You're a great help!" Graddon said. "All right, Blake! Please tell my men that I'll be down to see them in a few minutes." Graddon turned to face Donnibell and Hannock again as the butler left the room. "There you are—mighty small chance of tracing the candy," he said. "Easy enough for The Mongoose to buy it, dope it, put in Mr. Hannock's card to quiet any suspicions Miss Donnibell might have, and send it here."

"But suppose I'd been here?" Hannock asked. "Suppose Miss Donnibell had been out with me, and knew that I hadn't sent the candy?"

"The Mongoose," Graddon declared, "never supposes—he knows! He probably took a long time to fix up this scheme, and overlooked no important details."

"**WHAT CAN** we do, Graddon?" Donnibell cried. "My daughter is in there, unconscious—"

"It's a tough situation for you, but try to be calm," Graddon advised. "The Mongoose said in his letter that she's in no immediate danger. Wait until we hear from him, and learn what he wants from you. In the meantime, I'm going to have my men go through this house, looking for a little black box. And somebody must be in the library continually, listening for the message The Mongoose said he'd send."

"Not everybody must hear that," Donnibell hinted.

"Is Mr. Hannock—" Graddon looked at the young man significantly. "Mr. Hannock knows that this fellow who calls himself The Mongoose is bothering some of us," Donnibell said, quickly. "I've explained to him that The Mongoose is a crank who says we wrecked him financially in a recent deal. An unjust accusation—but somebody is always getting caught in the market and then blaming those more fortunate."

"True enough!" Graddon admitted. So Donnibell had not told his daughter's fiancé the entire truth. "I think I'll hang around the library myself. I'll send for you, Mr. Donnibell, if you're wanted."

"The library is on this floor, Graddon, at the end of the hall," Donnibell said….

Dr. Wanberg opened the door of the bedchamber and came into the boudoir. "I've made a few simple tests with the candy," he reported. "Undoubtedly it has been drugged with something. I'll send some to the laboratory for further testing. The poison mentioned in that letter—there are several such. The native tribes in the interior of South America have many strange drugs, and not all of them are known to us."

"How is Flora?" Donnibell asked.

"She's sleeping like a drugged person. There seems to be no immediate danger. Until I'm sure of the drug, I dislike to try restoratives."

"Don't do that!" Donnibell cried. "Wait until we hear from The Mongoose."

"And save some of that candy for me, doctor, so I can have it examined also," Graddon said. "I'm going downstairs to see my men, Donnibell. Then I'll go to the library. I'll send for you if anything happens."

Graddon hurried to the lower floor, and found half a dozen of his men waiting for him in the spacious living room. Some had been taken off other work. At the same instant, Jim Kreig arrived from the Donnibell offices with another man.

"I want the house surrounded," Graddon directed. "Watch all entrances. Let nobody in unless vouched for by Blake, the butler. You come with me, Kreig."

The men were posted, and then Graddon went upstairs with Kreig, and to the library. They closed the door, and began their search for a little black box.

"The thing we want first looks like a dictograph disk, only it's about three times as big," Kreig said.

They found it after only a short search, behind a painting on one of the walls. Then they began tracing the wires, which had been cunningly hidden. They ran along the base of the wall and disappeared beneath a window. Graddon opened the window and looked out. The wires ran along the outside of the wall toward the rear of the building.

The two left the library and went down the hall to the end, and there Graddon opened another window. They discovered the black box fastened to the rear wall of the building. No wires seemed to run from it, except those which connected it with the disk in the library.

"The Mongoose sure went to a lot of trouble on this job," Graddon said. "Probably did the work during last summer's vacation season, when everybody was gone except the caretaker."

"Yeah! From what we know about him, maybe he's been planning these tricks a year or more," Kreig said.

"But, what is the cussed thing?" Graddon asked. "I can understand a powerful, supersensitive dictograph arrangement—nothing so wonderful in that! But no wires run from this box on the other side. So, how can he hear what's said? And how can he talk back?"

"Search me! You want me to take that box down off the wall, chief?" Jim Kreig asked.

"No, leave it alone. If we disconnect the thing, maybe The Mongoose won't be able to talk to us—and he's promised to talk and tell Donnibell what he wants. Let's get back to the library, and wait."

CHAPTER V

THE MONGOOSE PLANS

HALF A MILE away from the Donnibell house, in a large and lavishly furnished apartment in a residential hotel, Mr. Sidney Carleigh stopped pacing the floor long enough to smile at his sister, Eleanor.

"It's about time to give them another shock," he said.

"They've got it coming, Sid. But I—I'm just a bit afraid for you."

"Commencing to weaken?" he asked. "Are you forgetting what our father suffered at their hands?"

"Never that!"

"And how we've spent several years getting ready for this campaign of vengeance? I can't forget how I acted the rôle of Guthrie Jayne for a year."

He laughed a little as he finished speaking, and went to a window to look down at the street far below. Guthrie Jayne! His strange disappearance had annoyed Graddon and the police. But they believed that he was somewhere in the city—whereas, Guthrie Jayne had disappeared forever.

Guthrie Jayne had been stoop-shouldered, servile, inconspicuous. His hair had been a dusky blond, his eyes hidden behind thick spectacles, his face a pasty, unhealthy yellow. His voice had been a bit grating to the ear. His own ears had protruded, his nostrils had been wide, and he had possessed a thick upper lip.

And, after the first adventure of The Mongoose, Guthrie Jayne had disappeared to give place to Sidney Carleigh, a wealthy middle-aged man who owned the apartment house in which he lived. The transformation had occurred in Sidney Carleigh's bathroom.

Chemicals had removed the sallow complexion and produced a ruddy one. The blond wig cemented to the head had been removed and a black one substituted—for the head was hairless due to an attack of fever. Nose plugs had deflated the nose, other plugs had been removed to allow the ears to resume their natural position, and the thick upper lip had become normal when another plug was removed. The stooped shoulders had become erect, the voice had changed, the thick spectacles had been discarded. Guthrie Jayne was gone forever, though Graddon and the police still searched for him.

They had photographs of Guthrie Jayne, and descriptions. They had false fingerprints which Guthrie Jayne had left behind in a hundred places—but they did not match the fingerprints of Sidney Carleigh.

"Is it necessary for you to go in person, Sid?" his sister asked.

"In this case," he replied. "I want to do it, despite the risk. They must be taught that I am not afraid to confront them. It is half the battle, Eleanor, to keep fear in their hearts."

"I know," she said. "And the plans are good. I'll do my part."

"You'll have to be the voice from nowhere at the proper time," he told her, laughing again. "Well—let's let Donnibell know the worst now."

She got up and followed him into a sort of den, where there was a huge radio apparatus. Sidney Carleigh sat down and picked up the headphones.

"Innocent enough on the face of it," he said. "Mr. Sidney Carleigh is a radio fan. Short wave set even. Got one of the most delicate instruments made, and has added a few inventions of his own. Nothing queer in that, is there?"

"No," she said, smiling at him.

"Ah! But the rest! How about the hidden closet behind this wall, my dear young lady? What do I have in there? A wonderful invention—which shall not be given to the world at large for some time, I assure you."

"And what is that, kind sir?" she mimicked.

"Speaking broadly, it is a wireless dictograph," he answered. "On the other end a special disk, wired to a machine out in the open air. With these headphones I can hear what is being said in a room a distance away. A new application of radio, my dear young lady. And I also can speak here, and make myself heard there. Not for nothing did I befriend that young inventor in Germany five years ago. Of course I had a lot of work to do on the thing after he died, but it's worth it!"

"If they get hold of one of those machines—" she began.

"They got hold of one, and it melted on them," he said. "The same thing will happen to the other, unless I have a chance to destroy it myself. Even if they knew the truth, they'd have one sweet time finding the station at this end. Even an expert could look at this outfit and say it was nothing more than an elaborate receiving set…. Now—to talk to Donnibell again. The voice from nowhere is about to speak. The Mongoose gives orders!"

He adjusted the headphones, bent forward, began fumbling with plugs and dials....

IN THE library at the Donnibell house, Mark Graddon and Jim Kreig were sitting beside the table smoking. Suddenly a voice came to them, softly at first, and rapidly growing stronger.

"This is the voice from nowhere... this is The Mongoose speaking....I want Donnibell... answer me and I'll hear."

"This is Graddon!"

"I can hear you, Graddon."

"I'll be damned if I know how! I'll get Donnibell for you. It'll take a couple of minutes."

"Let him speak when he comes into the room."

Jim Kreig had jumped to his feet, a look of astonishment on his face. Graddon grinned at him.

"Scared you, huh? That's the little black box," Graddon said. "Stick here, Jim, till I fetch Donnibell."

Graddon hurried down the hall and knocked on the door of the bedchamber. Donnibell came out to meet him.

"He wants you in the library," Graddon said. "The voice from nowhere is on the job again. We found his confounded apparatus, but didn't bother it—thought he might not be able to talk if he did."

Donnibell already was hurrying along the hall at Graddon's side. His face was pale, he was trembling. He had been looking at his unconscious daughter, stricken by the mysterious drug, and he had a horrible fear that something might happen to prevent her being saved.

"I want you with me, Graddon," Donnibell said. "Keep everybody else out of the library."

Jim Kreig was waiting for them in the open door. "That thing hasn't squawked while you were gone," he reported.

"Good enough!" Graddon said. "Jim, go to the end of the hall, and keep everybody away from here. Understand? Mr. Donnibell doesn't want things overheard."

Kreig hurried to take up his station. Graddon and Donnibell entered the library, and Graddon closed the door.

"Here's Mr. Donnibell!" Graddon spoke to the wall.

"Ah! Are you really there, Donnibell? Answer me," said the voice from nowhere.

"I—I'm here," Donnibell said.

"Good! Pay close attention to everything I say. Make no mistakes, if you value your daughter's life! Is Graddon there with you now?"

"Yes. Graddon—nobody else."

"Let him listen, too. I'll not repeat what I have to say."

"We're listening, Mongoose," Graddon said.

"First, do not destroy any apparatus you find, or I cannot speak to you—and help save Miss Donnibell. You know what happened at the office. Do not touch the apparatus at all."

"That's understood," Graddon said.

"Now, Donnibell, I have orders for you," The Mongoose continued. "Obey them, and I'll talk to you again at ten o'clock tonight. If you have not obeyed by that time, your daughter will die. First, get one hundred thousand dollars in currency, no bills larger than a hundred."

"The—the banks are closed," Donnibell whimpered.

"No argument! Get busy, if you want to save your daughter. Your checks are good. Go to your friends, your clubs, hotels—everywhere you can cash a check. One hundred thousand dollars! By ten o'clock tonight, the money must be wrapped in a neat parcel, in tough paper. Understood?"

"I—I'll do my best," Donnibell said.

"You'll do it—if you love your daughter, if you want her to live. And attend me, Donnibell! I can strike from the dark, as you know. If any of those bills are marked, if any attempt is made to trace them—I'll strike the next time so no antidote will save her! Get the money, make it into the package, and at ten o'clock tonight have that package on the big table in the middle of your library. Understood?"

"I understand," Donnibell said.

"Communicate with Stephen Wazer and Harvey Blandale, your partners in crime, and have them in the library with you at ten."

"I may not be able to—"

"Do it—if you love your daughter! You three ringleaders in the plot that ruined my father—and Mark Graddon. I want the four of you in the library at ten, with the money on the table. At that hour, I'll speak to you again, and give you further instructions. Understand that?"

"Yes, I understand!"

"That's all for the present."

THE SOUND of The Mongoose's voice died away. Donnibell turned toward Graddon and started to speak, but Graddon motioned for him to remain silent and follow into the hall.

"He can hear if you talk in there," Graddon whispered, when they were some distance from the door.

"I've got to get that money," Donnibell said. "What else can I do, Graddon? And Wazer and Blandale—they'll have to know."

"It's another trick of The Mongoose," Graddon said. "Everybody will be wondering why you're running around cashing checks. You'd better get busy on the telephone. A hundred thousand is a lot—"

"It's nothing, compared to my daughter's life. I'm wondering why he didn't ask for more."

"I've got to let the police in on this."

"No—no!" Donnibell gasped. "The publicity—"

"But we can't miss this chance, Donnibell. Listen to my scheme. He wants you to have the money in the library at ten o'clock, and then he'll talk to you again. That means he'll give you further orders—perhaps tell you where to take the money and leave it. It gives us a chance to get ready for him—"

"You can't make a move! I'll not let you!" Donnibell cried. "My daughter's life is at stake. Try to catch him, and he may refuse the antidote."

"Listen to me!" Graddon begged. "Be calm, and understand what I'm saying. You'll do as he says with the money—deliver it, and get the antidote. We'll make sure of that. We'll not make a move against him till the antidote is safe. And then—"

"What can you do?"

"I'll fix it with the police. I'll have reserves ready in every part of town. I'll have you covered wherever he tells you to go. Two minutes after I know the antidote is safe in your hands, we'll take up the chase."

"If he's caught—"

"I know what you're thinking—he mustn't talk. He'll not! I'll fix it so I and my men will be on his heels while the cops are working elsewhere. And—well, say that The Mongoose tried to escape arrest, and got shot?"

"Yes... yes!" Donnibell gasped. "But there must be no mistake, about the antidote!"

"Depend on us to be careful. You get that money. It's better to have it ready. The Mongoose may be watching to see if you go out to raise it. We'll carry out his orders, all right, so he'll have no excuse for failing to give the antidote."

"Why do you suppose he wants the four of us in the library at ten o'clock?"

"Probably wants to issue some more orders. That's why I want to catch him tonight," Graddon explained. "He may want to expose us for that old thing ten years ago. Maybe this is his last trick, and he's scheming to turn us up. We've got to get him tonight!"

"We must be careful about publicity," Donnibell said. "The police will talk."

"They needn't know everything. Not about your daughter. Just let 'em think you've been ordered to deliver money to him somewhere. I'll send Jim Kreig and another man with you, to

guard you while you collect that coin. I'll keep my men guarding the house. And I'll hurry right down to Police Headquarters
and have a confidential chat. We've got until ten o'clock to get
ready for him."

"Wait, Graddon! I—I'm afraid, for Flora! Perhaps we'd better
not try to catch him—just give him the money and carry out
his orders."

"He's got to be caught! Think, man! When he robbed Wazer,
he got evidence of what we did ten years ago. He'll be using
that next, after he completes his series of robberies. Want to
be disgraced and go to prison? Want your daughter to be the
daughter of a convict?"

"No... no!"

"We'll be careful. We'll not make a move until you have
the antidote safe. And, when you have, we'll take after The
Mongoose, and not stop till we run him down!"

CHAPTER VI

THE RASCALS GATHER

CLARK DONNIBELL TOOK Dick Hannock into his confidence to the extent of saying that The Mongoose had demanded
money, and left Hannock at the house as a personal guard for
his fiancée. Dr. Wanberg had decided to remain at the bedside,
and had sent for a nurse.

Then Donnibell did some telephoning, and after half an hour
of that called for his car and left with Jim Kreig and another
man, taking along a checkbook and a brief case, the latter for
the cash he went forth to raise.

He visited the offices of Stephen Wazer and Harvey Blandale,
where he exchanged checks for packages of currency, and told
the men to be at his house that night. He left them fear-stricken,
went to his office and got what cash he had in the vault there.

Then he visited half a dozen others, to whom he had telephoned, gathering currency, letting them think that he had an emergency need of it after banking hours. He went to clubs and hotels and got what he could. And Jim Kreig and the other man went along with him, until Donnibell had gathered the needed amount and had packed it into his brief case.

Back at the Donnibell house, he locked himself in his library, counted the money carefully, and made it into a package, which he wrapped in heavy paper and tied with tough twine. He put the package into his library safe. He ascertained from Dr. Wanberg that his daughter was still unconscious, talked with Dick Hannock, paced back and forth along the hall, waited for Graddon to return.

Graddon had hurried to Police Headquarters, where he had told of the demands made by The Mongoose. Telephones buzzed as orders were issued. In every section of the city, officers were to be held ready. High-powered department motor cars would be waiting at curbs with their engines running and their chauffeurs behind the steering wheels. A telephone message would send them rushing to the scene of alarm.

For fear that the telephone at the Donnibell house might be tampered with, Graddon arranged for the use of one at the nearest corner. He planned to have Donnibell shadowed carefully by expert trailers if he left the house alone with the money. The powerful influence of the men who were victims of The Mongoose was behind all this activity. Trusted officers of the department got the imperative order:

"Get The Mongoose!"

ABOUT EIGHT o'clock that evening, Sidney Carleigh put on a cap and a dark topcoat which had hidden pockets filled with mysterious and unusual things. His sister walked beside him to the front door of the apartment.

"Be careful, Sid," she begged.

"Don't worry about me, honey. And don't forget your part."

"Trust me, Sid!"

"The little records are in order. You can hear the folks talking in the Donnibell library. Give them the records at the proper moment. When you don't answer questions, they'll think The Mongoose has broken the connection."

"I understand, Sid."

"And don't forget to destroy the records afterward, as I showed you. I'll bring home the money, if I can. We can send it to charities. If I can't, I'll destroy it, and the government will be the richer. Donnibell probably has cheated the government out of double the amount, in taxes."

"I'll be waiting for you, Sid—and I'll not forget anything," Eleanor Carleigh said.

Sidney Carleigh left the apartment and went out like a man intending to take an evening stroll. But, at a garage two blocks away, he called for a powerful roadster he owned. He got in it, drove up the boulevard, and finally stopped and parked the car on a side street near a suburban theatre where a stock company was playing.

Entering a drug store on the corner, Sidney Carleigh went into a telephone booth and made several calls. They were to the city editors of newspapers, and to press associations. He gave all a tip—The Mongoose had attacked Clark Donnibell, had poisoned Donnibell's daughter, and was demanding a great sum for an antidote which would save her.

Leaving the telephone booth, Sidney Carleigh hurried to the theatre. He had a ticket for the performance, and it called for a seat on the outside aisle about halfway down the side of the auditorium. He passed through, was seated by an usher, and stuffed the theatre check into his pocket. The performance had started. Sidney Carleigh watched it for a short time, then got up and slipped quietly and unseen through an exit door....

AT NINE o'clock that night, there was turmoil at the Donnibell residence, a sudden deluge of newspapermen. Graddon's assistants held them in check at the front door. The other guards came hurrying to assist.

But the reporters were not to be denied. The presence of the guards told them that there was something in the tip they had received. They demanded that Donnibell come to them, and tell them what had happened.

Blake, the butler, finally informed Donnibell, and there was a conference in the upper hall. The newspapermen were not admitted to the house, but Donnibell went to the front door, accompanied by Graddon and Dick Hannock.

Donnibell knew the value of having the sympathy of the public with him, and he was too wise to antagonize newspaper reporters.

"Gentlemen," he said, "I do not know what rumors you may have heard—"

"What about your daughter—and The Mongoose threatening you?" one of them interrupted.

"My daughter is very ill, gentlemen, I beg of you to be as quiet as possible. Dr. Wanberg is with her now. She suffered—er—a stroke during the afternoon. Mr. Hannock, here, is her fiancé, as perhaps some of you know. We are all very much concerned. Perhaps, in the morning, we shall be able to tell more."

"What about The Mongoose?" one of the reporters asked.

"I have received a threat from the man who calls himself The Mongoose, as have several other men. He is a criminal preying on men of wealth. I have Detective Graddon and some of his men here for protection. Since my daughter is ill—" He concluded the sentence with a wave of his hand.

"What did The Mongoose threaten?"

"He said that he would communicate with me again and make a demand for money. Until he does, I do not know exactly what he intends. Now, gentlemen, if you'll pardon me—"

Donnibell went back into the house and closed the door. The reporters started back toward the bronze gate, talking among themselves. They were in time to note the arrival of Stephen Wazer and Harvey Blandale, prior victims of The Mongoose.

Wazer and Blandale got into the house without talking. But

the wise newspapermen did not quit the neighborhood. They could smell a story. They remained near the gate—and Graddon's men remained near the front of the house, watching them.

At five minutes of ten o'clock Donnibell was in the library with Wazer, Blandale and Graddon. Jim Kreig was keeping guard at the end of the hall, to see that they were not disturbed. Donnibell had taken the package of currency from the safe and put it on the big table in the middle of the room.

"We've got to catch the scoundrel!" Wazer declared.

"We'll get him!" Graddon promised. "Just as soon as we know where he wants the money delivered, we'll start things moving."

"It's almost time for us to hear him," Donnibell said. "The voice from nowhere—"

"Talks from a distance, by some trick," Wazer interrupted. "Find out about it later. The thing tonight is to get on his trail and run him down."

THEN THEY sat in silence, smoking, glancing at one another from time to time. Graddon got up and paced nervously up and down the room. He felt of his service pistol, to make sure he had it ready.

A little clock on a bookcase chimed the hour of ten. The four were breathing heavily. A whisper seemed to brush through the room. And then they heard the voice of The Mongoose:

"Are you there, Donnibell?… Are you there? Answer, if you are."

"I'm here," Donnibell replied, his voice shaking a bit. "I've done as you ordered. The hundred thousand is in a package on the table in the middle of the room. Wazer, Blandale and Graddon are here."

There was a moment of silence, then they heard the voice again:

"You four fiends formed the plot against my father. So far, I have done nothing but rob you and make you fools before the public. I have yet to deal with Graddon. And then I must deliver the real blow. Proof of what you did will be given the proper officials. You must be convicted, sent to that prison where you sent my innocent father to die! That will come later. Tonight, we have our little deal with Donnibell."

The voice ceased. They waited a moment, but The Mongoose did not speak again.

"Mongoose!" Donnibell cried.

"What do you want me to do now? My daughter—I must save her. You promised the antidote if I got the money. Where do you want me to meet you, to deliver the money and get the antidote?"

Again a moment of silence, and then the voice of The Mongoose replied:

"Leave the money where it is. Stay where you are, you four. I'll come there and get the money, and leave the antidote. I'll be there before long."

The four looked at one another in amazement.

"Coming here for it!" Donnibell gasped. "The last place we'd expect. Police scattered all over the city—but none here."

Graddon laughed. "My men are here," he said. "They've got the place surrounded."

"If we don't get the antidote—" Donnibell began.

"He has it on him, probably," Graddon said. "We'll get the antidote!"

"He may intend to kill us all," Harvey Blandale said. "Maybe that's why he wanted all of us here at the house."

"My men are on the job," Graddon snapped. "If he tries to get into this house, we'll land him!"

But The Mongoose was in the house already.

CHAPTER VII

THE MONGOOSE
STRIKES AGAIN

LEAVING THE THEATRE, Sidney Carleigh had hurried up the boulevard and turned into a side street. He walked along it briskly. In time, he passed in front of the Donnibell residence—and smiled slightly when he beheld a bevy of newspapermen milling around the front door.

His plans were working. He knew that the reporters would loiter there, and that Graddon's men would be watching them closely. Passing on to the corner, he turned off and made his way around to the alley. He slipped into the darkness there, making scarcely a sound.

The Mongoose had spent considerable time planning his campaign of revenge. He had overlooked no detail in the plot. In the hidden pockets of his topcoat he had the things he needed.

The first was a key which unlocked the alley gate of the house next to Donnibell's. The Mongoose passed through silently and locked the gate behind him. Through the darkness he slipped to the wall.

There was a certain spot where that wall had been repaired, where the rough masonry gave handholds and footholds. The Mongoose got to the top of the wall and stretched flat upon it, watching.

It was dark on the top of the wall, dark in the small rear court of the Donnibell place. But streaks of light shot across the yard, at the side of the house. Through these streaks of light he could see one of Graddon's men pacing back and forth on guard.

The others were near the front of the house, watching the reporters. The Mongoose spotted all of them, locate the man at the rear of the house by the red tip of the cigarette he smoked, and then dropped down beside the wall, in the Donnibell yard.

Now he reached into another hidden pocket of his topcoat, and brought forth a chunk of metal. Crouching beside the wall, he watched the guard who paced at the side of the house. As he went through one of the streaks of light The Mongoose hurled his missile.

It struck the man squarely in the back, and he gave a yelp of pain and alarm. The guard at the rear rushed around the corner of the house and toward him. And The Mongoose darted swiftly to the service entrance, used a key he held ready, unlocked and opened the door and got inside.

He knew this house well. He had studied it during the summer, while the family was gone, when only an old caretaker had been there. That was when The Mongoose had installed his wireless dictograph. So, now, he darted along a hallway and turned into a store room. He got behind a pile of boxes, made himself comfortable, waited.

With a tiny flashlight he inspected the dial of his wrist watch from time to time. At exactly ten o'clock he took a mask from beneath his coat and put it on, and drew on thin black gloves. He fumbled in the hidden pockets for other articles and slipped to the door.

THE MONGOOSE knew what the men in the library upstairs were hearing. They were listening to the words of The Mongoose, sent over his wireless arrangement—but those words were coming from dictaphone records through an amplifier. The Mongoose was here in the house, and not far away, as those upstairs supposed.

He acted swiftly now. They would be leaving the library, possibly—at least Graddon would be leaving to give new orders to his guards. So The Mongoose slipped into the hall again. He went through the rear of the house rapidly, encountering no one. He reached the rear service stairs without being observed, and started up them.

Through the rear hall on the second floor, he hurried noise-lessly. He heard somebody approaching, some servant hurrying on an errand. The Mongoose stepped into a recess, and waited.

In his hand, he held a weapon. It looked like a regulation automatic pistol, but no bullets were in it. It was Blake, the butler, who came upon him, and stopped in astonishment at finding a masked man there in the hall.

Blake's mouth flew open in a gasp of surprise. He did not have time to give voice to his alarm. That gasp sucked into his lungs a cloud of vapor which The Mongoose discharged from the gun he held. Blake muttered something, tottered, started to fall. The Mongoose caught him, lowered him gently.

"A half hour's sleep for you," he whispered.

He went on, meeting nobody, and came to where he could look into the main hall. At one end was the door of the library, closed. At the other, Jim Kreig paced back and forth on guard. Beyond Jim Kreig was the room where Flora Donnibell was stretched unconscious, with her fiancé, her physician, a nurse and a maid near her.

Jim Kreig was the man he wanted out of the way. And he had no time to lose. Time was the essence of success in this under-taking. Everything had been timed. If he delayed, plans might be wrecked, failure come.

He darted along the hall toward the front as Jim Kreig walked into the cross hall for a moment. He waited until the man started to come back. He knew Kreig by sight and name, for he had made himself familiar with all Graddon's men—that had been a part of his preparations.

"Kreig! Come here!"

The Mongoose imitated Graddon's voice. Kreig whirled and glanced down the hall. He saw nobody, and the door of the library was closed. Graddon had called to him and then closed the door again, he supposed.

Kreig started briskly along the hall. A cloud of vapor came from somewhere, blinded his eyes, choked him. He clutched at his throat, tried to call out and could not. He sensed the presence of a man at his side—and then ceased to sense anything.

THE MONGOOSE darted along the hall and stopped at the closed door of the library. He was just in time to hear Graddon's declaration that The Mongoose could not get into the house. Now, if Eleanor did her part—

The distant sister did. As Graddon would have opened the door to leave, a woman's voice came out of the nowhere and stopped him, startled the others in the room.

"Mr. Donnibell!… Mr. Graddon!… Are you there? Can you hear me?"

"Who are you?" Graddon demanded.

"Listen carefully. I'll tell you something about The Mongoose. I know him. I know where he lives."

The voice seemed to dwindle away. The four in the library were silent, motionless, waiting.

"I must hurry… can't talk too loud… get near the disk—" the voice went on.

Graddon beckoned the others; the four went over by the painting behind which the disk was hidden.

"Go ahead. We're listening," Graddon said.

The voice of the woman droned on. Eleanor Carleigh was merely killing time, attracting their undivided attention. And, while she did that, The Mongoose, out in the hall, took something else from a hidden pocket in his coat. It was a long tube—a slender tube which seemed to be filled with an amber liquid. He put the end of the tube in the keyhole, jammed it through.

"Tell us where he lives," Graddon was saying, in the room. "Let us know who you are. You'll get a big reward."

The woman began laughing in mockery. "You couldn't get him if I told you," she said.

"Who are you?" Graddon demanded again. "Where are you talking from? Why don't you—"

At that instant Mark Graddon realized that he felt faint and was growing dizzy. He reeled against the wall, his hands going to his choking throat. He saw the other three gasping, gulping. His eyes began to grow dim.

"Wh-What—?" Mark Graddon muttered.

One by one the four collapsed to the floor.

The hall door opened. A masked man slipped into the library and closed the door behind him and turned the catch. With his left hand he was holding something to his nostrils beneath the mask.

He rushed across the room to a window, and raised it, letting cool air rush into the room. A swirl of vapor seemed to lift and drift along the ceiling, sweep down and go through the window. The Mongoose stood with his eyes closed, breathing lightly. The air cleared rapidly.

Presently The Mongoose opened his eyes, tried a breath of air and found it untainted. Then he began his rapid work.

He darted to the table and ripped open the package of money. He removed his topcoat, opened slits in the lining, removed padding, put packages of currency where the padding had been. When all the money was stowed away he put on the coat again.

Now he took a bottle from his pocket and put it in the center of the table, where the package of money had been. Beside it he placed a card upon which a message had been scrawled. It read:

> *Here is antidote enough for all.*
>> *The Mongoose.*

He chuckled a bit as he looked at the four unconscious men on the floor. They would remain unconscious until the antidote was administered. Directions for giving it were on the back of the card. Dr. Wanberg would have no trouble restoring his patients.

NOW THE MONGOOSE took out other cards and fastened them to the coat lapels of his victims. Each read: *With the compliments of The Mongoose.*

He looked around the room again. For a moment, he listened at the hall door. He rushed back across the room, to the disk.

"Sister!"

"Yes?"

"I'm starting home."

"Careful!"

"I'll want some cold supper."

"Chicken and salad," she said.

The Mongoose was done in the library. He unlocked the door and opened it cautiously. There was nobody in the hall. Down in the living room, he could hear somebody talking—a guard and a servant, he supposed.

He went through the hall quickly, toward the front of the house, leaving the door of the library standing open. Another bottle came from his pocket. On the floor at the top of the stairs, he sprinkled a quantity of powder. He tossed it over a set of portières, threw it against the wall.

The Mongoose gave another quick glance around. He ignited a match, tossed it into the powder, turned and sped toward the rear of the house again.

A tiny flame sprang up, spread. It darted up the wall and to the top of the drapes. Chemical reaction began. A huge billow of black smoke rolled through the hall, down the stairs, obscuring vision. It was harmless, but it looked like a conflagration to the servant below who happened to glance up.

"Fire! The house is on fire!"

The Mongoose heard that cry as he rushed through the rear hall and toward the service stairs, almost tripping over the unconscious butler. He heard doors being slammed. Cries of alarm came to his ears. He heard the pounding of feet on the floor below.

THE GUARDS outside were attracted to the front of the house. The newspaper reporters watching at the gate rushed toward the door. And The Mongoose darted through the rear of the house on the lower floor, being compelled to use his vapor gun but once, and gained the service entrance.

He listened there for an instant, snapped out the lights in the hall, opened the door a crack. Nobody seemed to be outside. So he went out, closed the door, and crouched in the darkness at the side of the building.

There was a wild tumult in front. Smoke was pouring from an open window, attracting attention. Traffic was stopping out in the street. The Mongoose was smiling behind his mask as he went across the rear court and got over the wall into the next yard. He found the gate, let himself through and into the alley. There he discarded his mask and gloves and hurried to the street.

When he reached the first corner he glanced back. There was quite a crowd in front of the Donnibell house now. In the distance, sirens told of the approach of fire apparatus.

The Mongoose—Sidney Carleigh now—turned his back upon the scene. He went briskly along the street, and came to the theatre just as it was disgorging its audience. He mingled with the theatre crowd, to all appearances a man who had seen the show. And, if there was any question, he had the seat check in his pocket.

But there was no question. He got his car, drove slowly along the street, came to the garage, and turned the car in.

"Nice night, Mr. Carleigh," a garage attendant offered.

"It is, indeed," Sidney Carleigh replied. "A very nice night!"

Ten minutes later he was chuckling softly again as his sister closed the front door of the apartment after him.

"A nice profit," said he. "And some revenge. Those newspaper boys won't miss a thing. In the morning the town will learn how The Mongoose got in, made fools of the four, and got out safely again."

"You left the antidote?" his sister asked.

"Yes. The experience won't harm Flora Donnibell. Do her good. She's had a few hours of rest, one evening without a wild party."

"Did you destroy the black box on the wall?"

"No. Afraid the guard in the rear court might see it. But that box is loaded heavily. When it's opened it'll be destroyed immediately. The second air strikes the chemicals inside it— But let's forget that, Eleanor. We've settled another account for dad."

"For dad!" she whispered.

"And now—about that cold chicken and salad! You might add a cup of coffee. I'm not quite sure how The Mongoose feels—but Sidney Carleigh is hungry."

THE MONGOOSE STRIKES AGAIN

*Aboard Ship The Mongoose Followed His
Prey—and His Enemies Knew They Had Him.
To Get Away Now He'd Have to Swim!*

CHAPTER I

THE CLUTCH OF FEAR

THOUGH GENERALLY REGARDED by an unsympathetic public as one of the wolves of Wall Street, Harvey Blandale certainly was not acting wolf-like at the moment.

His present demeanor was more that of a frightened sheep. Instead of giving the impression of being a ferocious beast of prey about to slay and devour, he presented the picture of a cowering victim awaiting the roaring charge which would hurl him into oblivion.

In the luxurious seclusion of his private office, Harvey Blandale was pacing nervously from wall to wall. His eyes were wide, and his breathing was rapid and labored. Frequently he gulped, or licked at his lips as though they were parched. The stamp of fear was in his face.

Everything had been arranged. Everything had been timed to the second. If there was no slip, things were sure to work out correctly. If there was a slip—! But Harvey Blandale would not allow himself to think of such a contingency. It would mean disaster. There must be no slip!

In the outer offices, Blandale's clerks and stenographers, file girls and office boys went about their routine duties, not knowing that their employer was in a state of mental agony. For a great fear was clutching at Harvey Blandale. Despite his millions, his social position, business prestige, his influence and power, he felt helpless and alone—and in danger.

Now he glanced at his watch, and found that it was five

*Behind him came a
determined pursuit*

minutes after the hour of one. And the Bermuda liner sailed promptly at two. It had been given out that Harvey Blandale was rushing to Chicago unexpectedly on important business, and would leave on the Limited which departed at two-forty. But Harvey Blandale was not going to Chicago—he was going to Bermuda.

As he resumed his pacing back and forth across the room, the telephone buzzer sounded its warning. Its familiar soft buzz made Blandale flinch. He darted across the room to his desk, and seized the receiver.

"Yes?" he questioned.

"Mr. Graddon calling in person, sir," the switchboard girl in the outer office announced.

"Send him right in."

Blandale hurried across to the door, which he had locked

on the inside. He unlocked it, opened it, and admitted Detective Mark Graddon, a private operative who worked for certain prominent men in the financial district, and was known to be rather unscrupulous at times. The door was closed again swiftly, and locked.

"Graddon, thank heaven you're here!" Blandale cried. "I've been in agony waiting for you, man!"

The Mongoose
ran desperately

"Steady, Mr. Blandale!" the detective warned. "You're going to pieces. We can't be having anything like that, you know. Take a grip on yourself."

"It—it's my nerves, Graddon."

"I understand, Mr. Blandale. But we must be careful, sir. Nobody must think that there's anything wrong. I'll get you safely away from the city. There's nothing for you to fear. All our plans have been made."

"Do you suppose that fellow will suspect the trick?"

"Certainly not! Nonsense to believe it! That Chicago gag is good. It'll throw The Mongoose off the track."

"I hope so, Graddon. I certainly do hope so! This thing is breaking me up!"

"You're taking it too seriously, sir."

"Seriously? Great heavens, Graddon! Who wouldn't take it seriously? Here's a man who says that he's out for revenge—a criminal who calls himself The Mongoose. And he has threatened that he will—"

"Steady, Mr. Blandale!" Graddon interrupted. "You've got to play your part, remember. Try to act and look naturally."

"The fellow may be watching."

"Let him watch. There's no danger."

"Danger? Remember how he robbed Stephen Wazer! How he drugged all of us, made fools of us. It's unbelievable, Graddon, that one man could do all that. Why hasn't he been caught? Can the police do nothing? Can't you do anything?"

"It's because he's only one man, and not a professional crook using professional methods, that he's hard to catch," Graddon replied. "Don't worry—we'll get him. No crook ever lived who didn't make a little mistake, sooner or later. Now, about today. You haven't told anybody the plans, have you?"

"The president of the steamship company knows, but he's a personal friend of mine, and will keep it secret," Blandale replied. "I'm traveling incognito, as far as the passenger list is concerned. I sent my secretary, Craley, to buy the Chicago tickets openly."

"And I'm hoping The Mongoose saw him do it," Graddon put in.

"Jebbins, my valet, knows the truth of it, since he is to travel with me."

"We needn't worry any about Jebbins. He's the sort to keep his mouth shut about his employer's affairs," Graddon said. "We'd better be starting, Mr. Blandale. We've just about time to make it. If you'll please try to control yourself, so the folks in the outer office won't think there's something wrong—"

The telephone buzzer interrupted him. This time the call was over Blandale's private line. He hurried to the desk, picked up the receiver.

"Hello!" he snapped.

"So you're taking a little trip to Chicago, are you?" a man's voice asked.

"Leaving in a few minutes—yes. Who's talking?" Blandale demanded.

"Oh, pardon me! I thought you'd recognize my voice. This is The Mongoose."

"What?" Blandale cried.

"I just wanted to tell you that I know all about your Chicago trip. I know every move you make. You can't shake me off, Blandale. Good-by!"

CHAPTER II

THE SNEAKAWAY

HARVEY BLANDALE DROPPED the receiver as though an electric shock had passed through it. He whirled to confront Detective Mark Graddon again.

"It—it was that fellow—The Mongoose!" Blandale cried. "He says he knows all about the Chicago trip."

"Keep your nerve! He only thinks he knows all about it. You're the one who's going to have the laugh, only The Mongoose doesn't know it yet," Graddon said. "He's done just what we hoped he'd do, hasn't he? Thinks that you're going to Chicago."

"It's uncanny! The fellow seems to know everything."

"There's nothing uncanny about it," Graddon declared. "He's probably been watching you and your affairs closely. Your chief clerk bought the tickets for Chicago, and The Mongoose probably thinks that he's right smart to know it."

"Then you think he's being fooled?" Blandale asked, eagerly. "He really believes that I'm going to Chicago?"

"That's the way it looks to me. He's walked right into our trap. He'll probably be watching at the train. When you don't show up, he will think he's been fooled. Be too late, then, for him to get with you. You'll be on a steamer out on the briny, and he'll be here in town. Just the way we wanted it!"

"This situation—it's unbearable! That one man can do such a thing—"

"Steady!" Graddon warned. "There's nothing for you to be worried about. Let's be getting along, Mr. Blandale. We haven't any time to waste."

Blandale made a heroic effort to reduce his breathing to normal and appear his usual self. Graddon picked the traveling bag Blandale had ready. The door was opened, and they stepped into the front office.

Twenty pairs of eyes were turned upon Blandale as his employees scrutinized him. Word had been passed through the office that he was to make a rush trip to Chicago. Blandale compelled himself to forget his fear for a moment, and gave his usual parting jest:

"Be good children until papa gets back!"

They chorused wishes for good luck and a safe journey. At the front door Craley, the chief clerk, met the financier. Blandale handed him an envelope.

"Sealed orders, Craley," he whispered. "Open them at nine o'clock in the morning, and act accordingly. Obey to the letter."

"Certainly, Mr. Blandale! Good luck, sir!"

Then Graddon got Blandale out into the corridor and hurried him toward the elevator. On the ground floor, they went through the crowded lobby to the street, where Blandale's limousine was waiting at the curb.

"To the Grand Central Station," Blandale ordered his chauffeur. He spoke purposely in a voice that twenty passers-by must have heard.

The big car wheeled away from the curb, turned a corner, and fought its way through the traffic of a side street. The chauffeur had received prior instructions. He did not drive toward Grand Central Station. He went around a couple of blocks, and then piloted the car toward the pier from which the Bermuda liner would sail.

"Just be careful until the ship gets out into the stream," Mark Graddon was saying to Blandale. "If the fellow has taken the Chicago bait, he's fooled. But it won't do any harm to be cautious until you're safely away."

"And while I'm gone, Graddon—"

"Depend on me to do my best, Mr. Blandale. I'm as anxious as you to have that fellow in a cell. He's threatened me, too, remember."

"If he makes a crooked move while I'm gone, possibly you can catch him, and dispose of him. Please understand me, Graddon—I'm not afraid! It's my nerves. If I wasn't a nervous wreck, I'd stay in town and face it."

"I understand thoroughly, sir."

GRADDON MADE haste to ignite a cigar, to keep from smiling. The car went through the traffic-congested street toward the distant pier. Blandale was crouching back in a corner of the seat as though fearful of being recognized by somebody outside. His mind was racing.

That shady business deal ten years before… danger of being sent to prison for swindle… an innocent bookkeeper, William Cratch, framed… bogus evidence manufactured… a group of financiers saved by sending an innocent man to the big stone house up the river.

And then—after ten years—retribution! The sudden appearance of the victim's son, spending his time and an inherited fortune in having vengeance on the men who ruined his father's life… calling himself Guthrie Jayne… getting a position as private secretary to one of the guilty men… learning their business secrets.

The first blow... Stephen Wazer the victim... a directors' meeting and a huge robbery... Guthrie Jayne calling himself The Mongoose, saying the name is appropriate because he is attacking snakes—declaring that he will get them all, one at a time.

Queer threats... tricks of chemistry... messages sent on dictaphone cylinders... Jayne laughing at the efforts of the police to catch him... and utterly disappearing at the end of the chase!

And then—something more personal and terrible for Harvey Blandale—the announcement by The Mongoose that Blandale was to be his victim now!

As the limousine swept around another corner, Blandale drew in his breath sharply, and tried to shake off a feeling of apprehension. He had thought of this present plan himself, had arranged things so The Mongoose could steal nothing of great value from him while he was absent. He would go to Bermuda, take a vacation for a month. In the morning, Craley would read that letter and learn the truth. The clerk could be depended on to obey orders and run the office.

During his annual Bermuda vacations, Blandale always kept in touch with his office. He watched the market, and sent buying and selling orders by radio, using a code which only Craley knew. Business would not suffer through his absence.

But the great thought Harvey Blandale had was this—that The Mongoose, finding him missing, would select another victim from his list. And he might be caught in a criminal act. Then Blandale could return without fear, knowing that The Mongoose was powerless to strike.

The car reached the pier, and Blandale became alive to his immediate surroundings. It was almost sailing time, and there was a large crowd. Jebbins, Blandale's valet, hurried up to the car, got the traveling bag, and hurried away again. The other baggage already had been sent aboard.

Graddon went along with Blandale through the crowd. A brisk walk to the gangplank, a flash of tickets, and they were aboard. Blandale kept his head bent as though against the force of the strong wind which blew up the river, and had the collar of his overcoat turned up and his hat pulled down to his eyes. He hurried to his cabin.

"I have carried out all your orders, sir," Jebbins, the valet, reported. "Everything is as you requested it, sir." His tone seemed to say that he did not quite understand everything, and was pained because he had not been taken fully into his employer's confidence.

Blandale made a swift examination of the cabin and the adjoining bathroom. The windows had been closed except for an inch or so necessary for proper ventilation. The shades were drawn, in addition to the outside storm shutters being fastened. The lights were burning.

"Don't worry any more, Mr. Blandale," Graddon whispered. "I'm sure The Mongoose doesn't know you're here. He's swallowed that Chicago yarn. Good luck! I'll keep you informed if anything happens."

Detective Graddon shook hands and departed. Blandale closed and locked the door.

CHAPTER III

THE WARNING OF THE MONGOOSE

TAKING AN EXPENSIVE dressing gown from a suitcase, Jebbins deftly shook it out. He hung it on a hook against the cabin wall, where it swayed gently with the motion of the ship, which had backed into the stream and was commencing its voyage. As he reached for another garment, he glanced from the corners of his eyes at the man he served.

Being a valet of wide experience, Jebbins was not entirely unused to the eccentricities of employers. He had served several high-powered men in his time, including a Grand Duke whose amorous adventures often led him into serious trouble. He had seen various employers under severe nervous strains induced by business or social strife. And he realized that Harvey Blandale was under such a strain now.

Jebbins went on with his unpacking. Blandale paced around the cabin nervously, saying nothing, flinching at every unusual sound. Presently he spoke.

"Well, Jebbins, we're on our way," he said. His voice held a high strain of fright, and he dabbed at his face nervously with his handkerchief.

"Yes, sir. Pleasant voyage, sir!"

"I'm glad—very glad, indeed—that we've started."

"And I am glad for you, sir. I trust that the journey will be beneficial, sir. If you'll pardon me for saying so, you've scarcely been your usual self lately."

"So you've noticed that? It's a case of nerves, Jebbins. I need a rest from business—from a lot of things. I've been in—er—hell for the past ten days. Jebbins."

"Sir?"

"Afraid every moment that something terrible would happen. Bad at night as well as in the daytime. Terrible ordeal. I've been threatened, Jebbins. That fellow who calls himself The Mongoose—" Blandale concluded the sentence with a wave of his hand, as though further speech was beyond him.

"Oh, I understand, sir! I read about him in the papers," Jebbins admitted. "He robbed Mr. Stephen Wazer, your friend, didn't he, sir?"

"He did," Blandale replied. "And he has had the effrontery to send me word, Jebbins, that I'm to be his next victim. So I decided to slip away quietly, and take care of myself until the police catch the scoundrel. Absolutely no sense in running risks. The fellow is a dangerous crank."

"I quite understand, sir. Undoubtedly you have dodged him cleverly, sir. Now, I'd just try to forget the entire affair, get it off my mind, and enjoy my holiday—if I may be permitted a suggestion, sir."

"That's a sensible suggestion, too. You're a good man, Jebbins!"

"Thank you, sir!"

A measure of courage seemed to return to Blandale. He snapped off the lights and raised the window shades. He threw back the storm shutters and let the bright sunshine stream into the cabin.

Jebbins finished his unpacking and turned toward a small side table upon which several packages had been piled.

"I made the purchases you requested, sir," he reported. "Your usual brand of cigars—candy—fruit."

"Thanks, Jebbins."

THE RHYTHMIC quivering of the ship was soothing to Harvey Blandale's nerves. He felt that he was getting farther away from his trouble, leaving his fear further behind with every beat of the ship's engines.

Let The Mongoose go after one of the others on the list— and possibly get himself caught!... What was it that Jebbins had said? Oh, yes! To forget the whole affair, and enjoy his holiday. Jebbins was right!... No danger here on the ship... the fool Mongoose believed that he had gone to Chicago!

Jebbins was busy unwrapping a small box. He removed the lid. Inside, he found an envelope addressed to Harvey Blandale, and he handed it to his employer.

"I do not remember this package, sir," the valet said, as he continued unpacking the contents. "Pardon me, sir, but this—I scarcely know what it is, sir."

Harvey Blandale glanced swiftly toward the table. The next instant he gave a cry of fear and sprang to his feet, overturning the chair upon which he had been sitting. His face suddenly was ashen again. His breathing became labored once more. He seemed to be trembling from head to feet.

"Wrap that thing up again—quick!" Blandale cried. "Put the lid back on the box!"

"Yes, sir! Certainly, sir! Have I done something wrong, sir?" the startled Jebbins wanted to know. "Why, what is it, Mr. Blandale? Are you ill?"

Harvey Blandale certainly appeared to be ill. His face was white, and his eyes were bulging. Big globules of perspiration were standing out on his forehead. His short moment of courage seemed to have come to an end. The wolf of Wall Street was as a sheep again.

"That—that—" he mouthed. "Wait till I read this note, Jebbins. It may explain something."

He unfolded the sheet of paper he had taken from the envelope Jebbins had handed him. The note was both brief and instructive. It said:

> The purser has a dictaphone in his office. Use it!
> THE MONGOOSE.

"Are you ill, Mr. Blandale?" Jebbins was repeating. "Shall I send for the ship's doctor, sir?"

"It—it's The Mongoose!" Blandale said.

"Beg pardon, sir?"

"That thing in the box—it's a cylinder record for a dictaphone—an office dictating machine. That's the way The Mongoose sends his messages," Blandale explained. "And then the cylinder melts away—evaporates—utterly disappears—"

"Sir?" Jebbins gasped. His attitude was one of belief that his employer suddenly had gone insane.

"The cylinder is chemically treated—melts a short time after the open air strikes it," Blandale continued. "How did the thing get here?"

"Probably it was left to be delivered, sir, and some steward put it in the cabin. It could have been put there while I was ashore to meet you, sir."

"But, how did The Mongoose know? I—I thought he believed

I was on my way to Chicago. This is terrible, Jebbins! I wish Mark Graddon was here. You come with me to the purser's office. Bring that little box with you. Stand by me in this, Jebbins—be loyal!"

"Certainly, sir!" Jebbins suddenly was calm and collected, and in complete control of himself. "One moment, if you please, sir, till I arm myself."

"You have a gun?"

"Yes, sir. An automatic pistol, sir, and I know very well how to use it." Jebbins opened his own modest traveling bag and brought forth the weapon.

"And you are—er—somewhat capable in an emergency?" Blandale asked.

"If you'll pardon me for saying so, sir—I always had a gun ready for instant use while I was in the service of the Grand Duke. I was instrumental in saving his life twice, sir. There always was some jealous husband following him around."

A MOMENT later, Blandale was hurrying from the cabin with his valet at his heels. He was making a brave fight to regain his composure. He realized that he was well known by sight to many, and he did not wish to appear before the other passengers in a state of panic.

He tried to assure himself that he had nothing to fear here aboard the ship. There was nothing of value for The Mongoose to steal from him. Possibly this dictaphone message was only a threat of The Mongoose to get him when he returned.

A man of Harvey Blandale's rating had no difficulty gaining admittance to the office of the purser even at that moment, when the purser was a very busy man. Blandale asked permission to use the dictaphone. He explained that a record had been sent to him, and tried to give the impression that it was a sort of joke. The smiling purser waved him toward the machine, and turned to his duties.

Blandale sat down before the dictaphone, unwrapped the cylinder carefully, and put it on the machine. He was eager to hear the message the cylinder bore, yet was almost afraid to listen to it. He tried manfully to pull himself together. He steeled himself, adjusted the ear tubes, and started the machine. The message was not very long, but it was meaty:

> Hello, Blandale! So you are trying to run away to Bermuda. I have known every move you've made. That Chicago thing did not fool me at all.
>
> Running away will not save you, Blandale. You are to be my next victim. For your past sins, you must pay!
>
> Do not forget how you and some of your crooked business associates, caught in a shady deal several years ago, saved yourselves by giving perjured testimony and having my father, an innocent man, sent to prison, where he died.
>
> You cannot escape me, Blandale! I am almost ready to strike!
>
> I am here now, on this ship, watching every move you make!
>
> THE MONGOOSE.

With hands that were shaking, Blandale removed the tubes from his ears. He gulped as though choking. Jebbins quickly stood in such a manner that he shielded his employer from sight of the purser and those at the window of the office, so they could not see the expression of terror in Blandale's face.

"Look!… look!" Blandale whispered, hoarsely.

He was pointing at the cylinder. Little bubbles were commencing to appear on its surface. The cylinder seemed to be melting into nothingness.

"Into… thin… air," Blandale mouthed.

Jebbins was startled by what he witnessed, but he remained efficient. "Careful, sir," he warned, in a whisper. "We are not in private, sir. Somebody may observe your agitation."

Blandale was watching the disintegration of the cylinder record as though fascinated by the sight. Even Jebbins now failed to maintain his usual inscrutability. The bubbles seemed to be growing larger and working faster. A faint, pungent odor arose to assail the nostrils of the pair. And then—the cylinder was gone!

But Blandale could remember every word of the message it had carried. And one sentence of it, in particular, caused his heart to be clutched again by the icy fingers of fear—The Mongoose was here, aboard this ship!

CHAPTER IV

NO TRACES

IN HIS OFFICE back in the city, Detective Graddon shifted his cigar from one corner of his mouth to the other, settled himself comfortably in his desk chair, and ripped open a radiogram which had just been delivered to him.

An instant later, he was sitting up straight in the chair, and bellowing into the telephone.

Two of Mark Graddon's assistants happened to be in the office at the moment. They now beheld their chief in frenzied action. He dictated a reply radiogram. He talked to a distant airport. He ordered a high-powered livery motor car to be sent to the office building immediately for his use, and then he held speech with Police Headquarters, and arranged for motorcycle officers to clear a path for him through the heavy traffic.

After he had taken his somewhat feverish departure, one of his assistants picked up the radiogram from Graddon's desk, read it, and whistled. It said:

> Mongoose aboard skip. Get seaplane and come at once. Have arranged for you to be picked up.
>
> Blandale

There also was a certain code word which had assured Detective Mark Graddon, beyond all doubt, that Harvey Blandale had sent the message.

In record time, Graddon was in a seaplane and roaring over

the city and heading out to sea at a good altitude. He relaxed a bit, then, and did some thinking.

So The Mongoose, despite all precautions, was on the Bermuda liner, following Blandale, and undoubtedly intending to rob him or do him an injury of some sort. Blandale's getaway had not been secret.

Mark Graddon well knew the value of publicity of the right sort. It would mean considerable for him professionally, if he could catch The Mongoose. There would be rich reward, he would attract new clients—and once more he could thumb his nose at his friends on the regular police force, with whom he held constant rivalry.

If The Mongoose was on the Bermuda liner, he was in a trap, and Graddon had him! Graddon would return him to New York in irons, as soon as the necessary legal arrangements could be made. He wondered how the presence of The Mongoose aboard the ship had been discovered, whether he already was a prisoner.

They were soaring above the clouds now, and through rifts in them Mark Graddon could see the tumbling ocean. The pilot had informed him that it would not take them long to overtake the ship. Soon, Graddon could see the vessel in the distance, a tossing black speck which grew larger rapidly as they approached it at top speed, a plume of smoke trailing behind it.

They came up with the liner, and circled it until the ship was stopped and a boat lowered. Then the pilot of the seaplane dropped his craft to the water and made a perfect landing. The sea was calm, and the danger slight.

Graddon was transshipped. Passengers crowded at the rail to watch him board the liner, and for once Graddon had more publicity than he wished. An officer touched him on the arm, and conducted him to the captain's cabin....

"AND THAT'S all I know about it, Graddon," Harvey Blandale said, ending his long recital of what had occurred. "The confounded cylinder melted away, as usual. I've explained the whole thing to Captain Hanborne."

"I can't understand it," Graddon declared. "This Mongoose is supposed to be clever. Surely, he'd have sense enough to know that he'd be in a trap on this ship. The only way he can escape us is to jump into the sea."

"You must find him, Graddon—arrest him," Blandale said. "My life isn't safe."

"The Mongoose runs more to robbery than to murder."

"But I have nothing with me worth his trouble stealing," Blandale declared. "He must know that—since he seems to know everything. So he must be contemplating violence. You must protect me, Graddon!"

"Nothing for you to worry about, sir," Graddon replied.

Captain Hanborne, the grizzled commander of the liner, spoke up: "I'll give you every assistance, Mr. Graddon. If the man is aboard my ship, he must be found at once and put in irons. This vessel isn't an easy one for a stowaway. I'll detail an officer and a couple of husky men to help you."

Graddon took a couple of photographs from his coat pocket. "Here he is," he said. "I brought these along. Thought they might come in handy. This is the way he looked the last time we saw him. I'll show these to your officers, captain. With your permission, we'll search the ship thoroughly. Mr. Blandale, I'm sure that you'll be safe in your cabin with your valet."

"I'll send a steward along with you, Mr. Blandale, and have a man stand guard outside the door until the search is over," the captain added.

The ship was proceeding at full speed again. Blandale went back to his cabin with Jebbins at his heels, and with a couple of men to see that he got there safely. Graddon faced Captain Hanborne after they were gone.

"Far be it from me to criticize a good client," Graddon said, "but it looks to me like Blandale was scared."

"I don't wonder at it," the captain replied. "May have a guilty conscience—what?"

"Possibly," Graddon replied, smiling. "Most heavy financiers have, I'm told."

"Do you really think this Mongoose fellow is aboard?"

"I don't know what to think. He's clever. He disappeared mysteriously right under the noses of the police when he robbed Stephen Wazer of a fortune. He dabbles in gas and sleeping powders and that sort of stuff."

Captain Hanborne's eyes glittered. "I don't intend to have The Mongoose, or anybody else, playing such pranks on my ship," he said. "I'll call the men to help you, Graddon. Go over the ship from bow to stern. Get your man!"

GRADDON DID not get his man. He exhibited the photographs, and none of the ship's officers could remember seeing the original aboard. A methodical search was made of the ship. The Mongoose was not found.

Graddon went to Blandale's cabin.

"Have you found him?" Blandale cried. "Is the scoundrel in irons?"

"No, we haven't found him," Graddon admitted. "I don't think he's aboard. I believe, Mr. Blandale, that we've been the victims of a joke. The Mongoose sent that dictaphone cylinder to scare you. Wanted to make you think he was at your elbow. He's probably back in New York laughing about it—and planning to rob somebody else. And I—I'm on this confounded ship, and have to go to Bermuda and return from there. While I'm away, The Mongoose may commit another crime."

"You think that is it, Graddon? He may have guessed that I'd send for you."

"He certainly got me away from the scene," Graddon replied.

"But he may be here, Graddon. Please make another search."

"We've gone over this ship from one end to the other. Those men showed me places I didn't know a ship had, and we didn't find The Mongoose hiding in any of them. We've checked over all the passengers, and the crew has been vouched for. He's not aboard!"

Jebbins touched Graddon on the elbow. "Wh—what's that, sir?" he asked. The valet was betraying some agitation.

From Mark Graddon's coattail, he removed a bit of cardboard which had been fastened there with a bent pin. Graddon took a quick look at it, then roared his rage. Blandale experienced another spasm of fright.

The piece of cardboard was covered with fine writing in a hand evidently disguised:

> This is to prove, Graddon, that you can't see me when I'm near enough to brush against you. Welcome to our ship! I hope you had a nice flight from town.
>
> THE MONGOOSE

"He must have hooked that card to your coat, Graddon!" Blandale cried. "It proves that he's aboard. You've got to do something about it, Graddon! You've got to catch him!"

"I'll get him!" Mark Graddon declared. "We've got him trapped at last, Blandale! The only way he can escape from this ship is—to swim!"

CHAPTER V

THE MONGOOSE MAKES HIS PLANS

THE DELIGHTFULLY VIVACIOUS girl of twenty-five was smiling and dimpling as she stopped at the rail beside a man possibly a couple of years older and obviously her brother. The other passengers had been watching the pair. They seemed absorbed in each other's society, evidently not feeling the necessity of seeking companionship elsewhere.

Elderly ladies beamed upon this display of brotherly devotion and sisterly love. Younger ladies wished that the man would glance their way, and certain young gentlemen wondered whether there might be a chance of getting acquainted with the vivacious brunette with the dimples.

Sidney Carleigh and his sister, Eleanor, laughed as they looked out across the tumbling sea, as though at some jest they shared between them. Their conversation was confidential, and they were careful to stand where nobody could get their words as they traveled down the wind.

"You're a clown, Sid," Eleanor Carleigh was saying. "It wasn't necessary to pin that card to Graddon's coat—and it was running a risk."

"We must get some fun out of this," he replied. "It takes some of the bitter out of it. I caught a glance of Blandale—and he's a wreck."

"He should be!" she said.

"When I think of our father spending those years in prison, wasting away, I—I scarcely can keep my hands from the throats of the men who put him there."

"But what we have planned is the better way, Sid," she said. "We'll strip them of some of their wealth, and, when that is done, we can ruin them. The proofs you have, given to the proper officials at the proper time, will send them to prison, where they sent our father."

"Now, we have to deal with Blandale," Carleigh said. "Our plans are working out. Graddon is looking for Guthrie Jayne."

She laughed musically again, and he joined in her laughter.

"Guthrie Jayne!" she muttered. "Sid, you were a terrible looking thing as Guthrie Jayne."

To be The Mongoose, it had been necessary for Sidney Carleigh to suffer some. From an upstanding, not unhandsome man, he had become stoop-shouldered, pasty-faced, a thing of prominent ears and squinting eyes behind thick spectacles. He had worn a dusty blond wing on a head stripped of hair by a fever years before. He had been humble, servile.

And then, when he had struck the first time as The Mongoose, he had deliberately cast suspicion upon himself, made his escape, made it easy for the police to follow him. They had followed to a modest apartment house where he had a suite—and there Guthrie Jayne had disappeared.

Adjoining that apartment house had been a more pretentious one, owned by Sidney Carleigh. From a closet of the one, Carleigh had passed through a wall and into a bathroom of the other into the personal apartment of himself and his sister. The clever aperture in the wall had been closed.

Then Guthrie Jayne had removed the chemical pallor of his face, his dusty blond wig, had taken away bits of plaster which had changed the expression around his eyes, and tiny braces which had made his ears prominent. His shoulders straightened, a black wig went on his head, his skin became of a healthy appearance. Guthrie Jayne had disappeared forever, and only Sidney Carleigh remained.

And Graddon, and the police, were looking for Guthrie Jayne as The Mongoose.

"WHAT NOW, Sid?" Eleanor Carleigh was asking.

"We are simple passengers enjoying the voyage," he informed her. "When night comes, we do our work."

"Sometimes, I am afraid, Sid."

"That'll never do. You weren't afraid when we handled Wazer. Why be afraid now? It's going to be rich—for us."

"And Blandale thinks there's nothing we can take from him."

"He imagines we can't touch him because he isn't carrying a fortune in currency or jewels around with him," Sidney Carleigh said. "But we'll strip him of a share of his fortune, get some of it for ourselves, and turn his business associates against him."

"It'll be dangerous," she said.

"When I think of our purpose, I do not consider the danger. Blandale's cabin probably will be guarded—outside. Mark Graddon will be fussing around. Nevertheless, Blandale will be robbed. And the joke of it is—he won't know he's been robbed until he commences receiving indignant messages from New York. Let's get inside. The air's cold, and it's time to get ready for dinner."

Harvey Blandale ate dinner in his cabin with Mark Graddon. A second search of the ship had been made, and The Mongoose had not been found. Captain Hanborne had posted guards throughout the vessel, with orders to take into custody any man acting in an unusual manner.

"I don't understand why you can't find him," Blandale complained.

"I don't, either," Graddon confessed. "I know he's on this ship. But I tell you we searched so well a rat couldn't have hidden."

"This is terrible—terrible! I—I'm a wreck now. I can't endure much more. I had hoped to get to Bermuda safely, and have a good rest there."

"Let's get down to business and talk sense," Graddon begged. "Let's forget fear and all that sort of rot. Listen, Blandale! My professional reputation is at stake. The Mongoose wants to get me, too, because I had a hand in that case. Now—what's he after?"

"I can't imagine."

"You're not carrying anything valuable enough to attract him. And I don't believe he intends to harm you. If he did he'd have done it before this. If he could get close enough to me to pin that card on my coat, he surely could have got near enough to you to bump you off."

"Please don't talk like that!" Blandale begged.

"Moreover, if he wanted to bump you off, he sure would have too much sense to do it on this ship while at sea. How'd he escape? A murder at sea, and everybody on this ship would be investigated to the last of their life's history until the guilty man was found. He'd have bumped you off at the pier—or wait until the ship gets to Bermuda."

"Possibly that is what he intends to do," Blandale wailed.

"You're safe until we get to Bermuda, then. So try to take it easy," Graddon said. "You must brace up, or you'll be in the ship's hospital. I want to take The Mongoose back to New York in irons—not take you back in a box. You're dead sure you're not carrying anything—"

"Nothing," Blandale, interrupted. "I don't need to carry much money. I'm well known in Bermuda—can cash checks there whenever I please. I haven't enough stuff along to attract even a cheap sneak thief."

"Well, it's got me puzzled," Graddon admitted.

"WHAT PRECAUTIONS have you taken for tonight?" Blandale asked. "Captain Hanborne promised me protection."

"He'll give you plenty of that. He's scared stiff that something may happen to you on his ship. There'll be a man outside your cabin door, and another at the companionway. Since this cabin is on the promenade deck, there'll be a man on the deck, too. He'll be in hiding, watching. Another will fuss along the rail all night."

"Then I—I should be safe, shouldn't I?"

"Sure!" said Mark Graddon. "You can go to sleep, and Jebbins also."

"And what are you going to do, Graddon?"

"Stay awake. I'll talk to the guards and fuss around, and maybe spend part of the time here in the cabin, if it'll not disturb you."

"I wish you'd remain in the cabin all night, Graddon."

"We'll see what happens," Graddon said.

They finished their meal. Jebbins called the steward, and the soiled dishes were removed. Mark Graddon examined the cabin and bathroom carefully again, finding nothing unusual.

"If you'll pardon me for saying so, I have an idea," Jebbins announced.

"What is it, Jebbins?" Blandale wanted to know.

"I can remain awake in the dark cabin, sir, having my automatic pistol ready. When I was in the service of the Grand Duke

I once caught an intruder in that manner. I saw him enter, and was at him instantly."

"Might not be a bad idea, at that," Graddon said. "But don't shoot me by mistake."

An hour after dinner the ship ran into the fringe of a storm. Rain drenched the open decks, and passengers kept under cover. Lightning slashed the black night. The sea kicked up, and the Bermuda liner danced.

Sidney Carleigh and his sister left the salon and went to their cabin.

"The storm makes it better," he said. "It's going to be a fine night for crooks."

"Suppose Blandale isn't carrying what you think?"

"He always carries it, my dear. I know. You forget that Guthrie Jayne was once Stephen Wazer's secretary, and learned a lot of business secrets."

"And when you call the steward—"

"Are you worrying again? Keep it up, and you'll soon be as bad as our prospective victim," he said. "Please don't worry. When I remember our father, I can't fail."

"No, we must not fail, Sid! We owe it to his memory to succeed."

"Read something, and settle your mind," he advised. "I've got work to do."

He got a traveling bag, tumbled out its contents, and exposed a secret compartment in the bottom. From this he took several articles, which he put into his pockets. His sister did not read. She watched him carefully.

Sidney Carleigh finally entered the bathroom, carrying a bundle of clothes. When he emerged again he was dressed in a dark suit, and over this wore a dark raincoat. A dark cap was on his head.

"Sister, dear, kindly do not forget to keep your ears open," he said. "I may need your assistance."

"I won't forget my part, Sid."

"Come and kiss brother.... That's it!... Now, I'm ready. Behold, The Mongoose!"

CHAPTER VI

THE ATTACK ON BLANDALE

ELEANOR CARLEIGH SNAPPED out the lights in the cabin. Her brother went to the door, crouched there, listened intently. He could hear nothing except the noises of the storm.

He opened the door for a few inches, listened again, and then peered out. The deck seemed to be deserted. Billows of mist and fog were swirling around the deck lights and making vision uncertain. The storm was either abating, or the ship was running out of it.

"Good luck!" she whispered.

He stepped out and closed the door behind him. He thrust his hands down deep into the pockets of his raincoat, and went to the rail. For a moment he posed there as a person who loves to watch a storm.

Except when he was near one of the lights he was almost effaced in his dark clothing. But he knew that the members of a ship's crew have sharp eyes at night. So his manner was quite natural as he made his way slowly along the deck. There was nothing furtive or sneaking about him.

He knew well where to find the cabin of Harvey Blandale, and now The Mongoose made his way toward it, slowly and cautiously, stopping frequently to watch and listen. He found a companionway deserted, and descended swiftly.

Again he paced a storm-swept deck in the uncertain light. Somewhere along that deck, he knew, was a man on guard—and perhaps two men. And in the corridor were other men on guard. But that did not seem to be troubling The Mongoose. His advance was deliberate, his actions normal in every way.

The glow of a cigarette end betrayed the presence of the guard who was supposed to be keeping under cover. Head bent against the wind, so his features could not be seen, The Mongoose went on. He would pass within a few feet of the man.

He observed that the guard was in a little niche near a ventilator. The right hand of The Mongoose came from his coat pocket as he approached and swung at his side. The hand was dressed in a thin glove.

He noticed that the glow of the cigarette disappeared as the guard drew farther back in the recess. The Mongoose swayed slightly toward him as he passed. A tiny vial of thin glass was crushed in his hand. It fell to the deck with its contents, fell back in the little niche.

The Mongoose walked on for some distance, and then turned and retraced his steps. As he neared the recess again a peculiar odor came to his nostrils. He smiled slightly and quickened his stride.

Now his hand came from his raincoat pocket again, and this time it held a hypodermic needle. He stooped over the guard, to find him unconscious. But it was an unconsciousness which had been induced by the chemical released from that crushed vial, by the gas breathed into the lungs of the guard, and it would not endure long. The Mongoose seized the man's wrists and jabbed the needle home. His unconsciousness would last for an hour or more now.

He thrust the unconscious man as far back as possible, and turned down the deck again. Far forward, he spotted the other guard. He knew that these men had taken their positions only recently, and that relief for them was not due for some time. Once more The Mongoose crushed a tiny vial and walked on. Again, he used the needle.

And now he slipped quietly along the deck until he came to

the cabin of Harvey Blandale. The window in the bathroom was up for about an inch. Voices came to The Mongoose.

"Please go to bed, Blandale, and try to get some sleep," Mark Graddon was saying.

"How can I sleep, with this horror upon me?"

"Be sensible, sir! How could anybody, even this Mongoose, get at you? Men guarding on the deck outside, and out in the corridor. Jebbins sitting there in the corner with his automatic pistol ready."

"And you—?" Blandale questioned.

"I'm going to get out and prowl around a bit. Get me some coffee, possibly. I'll be back later, and stay with the guards in the corridor. You turn out the lights and get some sleep."

The Mongoose heard Graddon leave the cabin. There was silence for a moment, and then the valet spoke.

"If I may be allowed to make a suggestion, sir—no doubt it would do you good to get some sleep. Let me give you one of your powders, sir."

"Those things are powerful, Jebbins. In my present nervous condition they might be harmful."

"Pardon me, sir, but they'd not be. You'll be sound asleep inside a minute, sir. And I'll sit here faithfully while you're sleeping. Detective Graddon believes that you overrate the danger, sir."

"What do you think, Jebbins?"

"I do not believe that this—er—Mongoose, as he calls himself, would risk a move tonight. I'd say, sir, that he'd wait until about time for us to land."

"You may be right, Jebbins. It might be better for me to get some sleep and fortify myself. You may prepare the powder."

THE MONGOOSE heard Jebbins enter the tiny bathroom, and he went swiftly along the deck for a distance. The ship was rushing through another drive of rain. The Mongoose protected himself from the drifting downpour by keeping away from the rail.

After a short interval he returned to the window of the bathroom. Jebbins and his employer were talking again.

"There, sir! You'll be asleep immediately, sir."

"You'll stay awake and on guard?"

"You may depend upon me, sir."

"If—er—anything happens, do not hesitate to call out."

"I'll remember, sir."

"Jebbins, tell me—what would your Grand Duke have done in such a situation?" Blandale wanted to know.

"He'd have gone to sleep, sir, probably with the remark that if he didn't live to see tomorrow it'd undoubtedly be only another rotten day anyhow, sir."

Blandale muttered something that The Mongoose could not understand. Then there was silence. The lights were turned off in the cabin and bathroom.

The Mongoose deftly crushed a couple of the little vials and tossed them into the bathroom through that inch of open window. He glanced up and down the deck, seeing nobody. Crouching in the darkness, he waited.

Presently he heard Jebbins coughing, heard him moving around, knew that he had come into the bathroom and was running water. He coughed again. The Mongoose knew that he was taking a drink of water. And water would only hasten the action of the drug the valet had inhaled.

Then there came a groan—the sound of a body falling.

The Mongoose smiled in the darkness. He glanced along the deck again, made certain that nobody was approaching. From a pocket of his coat he took an instrument, with which he attacked the window. There was a soft snap, and the lock was broken.

The Mongoose raised the window swiftly, and squeezed through it. He closed the window again, save for that inch or so. To his nostrils he held a tiny sponge, saturated with a liquid which would counteract the effects of the gas with which the cabin was reeking.

He went into the cabin, found the light switch, and turned on the lights. And now he worked swiftly, using his hypodermic needle twice. Harvey Blandale was stretched unconscious in his bed. Jebbins was carried from the bathroom and propped up in a chair in a corner, where he had intended sitting on guard.

The gas drifted out of cabin and bathroom rapidly. The Mongoose got to work. He got the traveling bag Harvey Blandale had carried from his office, found it unlocked, opened it, went through it carefully. At the bottom he found a little book bound in fawn leather—a loose-leaf book with pages covered with typewriting.

He thrust this book into his pocket, left the bag otherwise as he had found it. And now he took half a dozen cards from a pocket, pinned one to the front of Blandale's pajamas, fastened one to the lapel of Jebbins's coat, scattered the others where they would be seen. Each card bore the same message:

With the compliments of The Mongoose

Hurrying into the little bathroom, The Mongoose listened at the window. A moment later he raised it and crawled through. He lowered the window again, went briskly along the deck, meeting nobody.

FIVE MINUTES later he opened the door of his own cabin and stepped inside.

"Sid?" his sister questioned.

"Yes. Snap on the lights."

Lights glowed an instant later. Eleanor Carleigh hurried to her brother's side.

"You got it?" she asked.

"Exactly as I expected. Not a hitch in the plans so far. We're half done, you might say."

She lighted a cigarette for him. Without removing cap or raincoat, he sat down at a table and studied the little book he had taken from Harvey Blandale's traveling bag. Then he pulled a sheet of paper toward him, seized a pencil, and wrote, often referring to the book.

"Can you do it?" his sister asked.

"Easy! Remember, my dear, that The Mongoose was once the private and confidential secretary to Stephen Wazer—and Wazer is a close friend of Blandale. Perhaps their friendship will not be so strong this time tomorrow night."

"The hardest part is coming now, isn't it?"

"Sending the messages won't bother me much," he replied. "I only hope there'll be no interference."

"Explain it to me again, Sid. I haven't much of a head for business."

"This little book, my dear, contains the private code with which Harvey Blandale communicates with his chief clerk, Craley, when he is away from town. When he sends Craley orders regarding business, Craley obeys them instantly and without question."

"I understand that."

"Good! Now, listen. Blandale and Wazer and Clark Donnibell, three financial rogues, are handling a certain stock called Transcontinental Copper. They're all set to fleece the public out of a million. It's a poor-value stock, but they've built it up until it's quoted at about three times its normal value."

"I understand that much, too."

"Fine! The one way they can put across their little deal is for them to stick together, hold on to their stock. Tomorrow when the exchange opens, there'll be fireworks. I'll send messages to Craley tonight. They'll tell him to dump Transcontinental Copper on the market at any price."

"And what happens then, Sid?"

"Wazer and Donnibell will be rather startled. They'll find that Blandale has slipped away from town. They'll naturally think that he's double-crossing them, dumping his stock for some reason. The only way they can protect themselves is to buy as fast as he sells. They've got to keep the price up."

"I—I think I understand, Sid."

"Fair enough! They won't be able to keep the price up, because there'll be too much stock offered. They'll find that out about the time they get in too deep. Then they'll lose a fortune in the crash. Transcontinental Copper will go down to almost nothing. Blandale won't know what's going on until it's too late to stop it. Our enemies will be at one another's throats. Blandale will tell the truth, and they won't believe him. There'll be no record of the radiograms being sent from this ship, though the receiving station will have a record of them being received."

"Let me get it straight, Sid—we make them all lose a lot of money."

"That's right! And they'll split up, thinking that Blandale has tricked them. Blandale will be the heavy loser."

"And do we get anything out of it? I mean money."

"Listen to the little innocent!" he said, grinning at her. "When Wazer and Donnibell start buying, a broker will sell me short. He'll load 'em up with all they want, to a certain amount. Then, when the stock breaks, he'll buy it in cheap. Understand, baby? I'll sell short points and points above what I'll have to pay to get the stock—and Wazer and Donnibell will have to pay!"

"It seems involved," she complained.

"They'll think that it's involved. We'll take out expenses and give the rest of the profits to charity. But the great thing is that those scoundrels will distrust one another after this. Mr. Blandale is going to upset the market—but he doesn't know it."

He got up and buttoned his raincoat, and into a pocket of it thrust the messages he had written.

"Lights out, please," he said.

She turned them off, and a moment later he slipped out of the cabin again.

The deck was still deserted. The Mongoose made his way cautiously along the rail. He did not want to be seen by anybody now, if such a thing could be avoided. What he had done so far this night was as nothing when compared to what he must do now.

Careful not to be observed, he hurried toward the wireless room. The Mongoose knew that the junior operator would be on watch at this hour. It was a quiet night, and probably nobody would be around the room except the man in charge. Getting control of the key was the only thing bothering The Mongoose. He could "send," and he knew the necessary call letters, signals and code.

Once he darted out of sight as a member of the crew passed. When he approached the wireless room, he was compelled to hide again. An officer was just leaving.

When he felt that it was safe to do so, The Mongoose went on. At the door of the wireless room, he stopped to listen. He could hear the operator fussing around inside, and whistling. The Mongoose guessed that he had just finished the night luncheon.

He disliked to use violence on an innocent man, but it was necessary now. The Mongoose assured himself again that there was nobody in his near vicinity, and knocked on the door.

"Come in!" the operator invited.

His invitation went unheeded. The Mongoose knocked again. His hand came out of his raincoat pocket as he heard the operator's muttered imprecation and quick step inside. The door of the wireless room was jerked open.

"I said to come in—"

The Mongoose struck once—swiftly and with accuracy—then caught the groaning operator as he toppled and started to fall. An instant later, The Mongoose had returned the blackjack to his pocket, had the operator inside, and had locked the door.

He resorted to the hypodermic needle again, made sure that the operator would have at least an hour of drugged sleep. Then he hurried to the key.

This was slow and cautious work, now. The Mongoose took his time about it. He did not want to do anything that would arouse suspicion. But soon the ether waves were being disturbed by his dots and dashes. The message he had written to Craley, Blandale's trusted chief clerk, was being hurled through the air.

He sent three messages, each related to the other. Those messages were in Blandale's private code. Craley would not hesitate to do as they commanded, though the orders might surprise him.

CHAPTER VII

PURSUED!

DETECTIVE MARK GRADDON prowled around the ship, hoping to surprise some lurking figure that would turn out to be Guthrie Jayne. On the promenade deck, he heard groans coming from a recess near a ventilator. Graddon flashed his electric torch, and observed a member of the crew, one of the men who had been on guard, just returning to consciousness.

"What happened to you?" Graddon demanded. "Hurry up and talk!"

"I—I don't know."

"See anybody? Somebody smash you on the head?"

"Think not, sir. I saw somebody coming along the deck, and got back out of sight. He passed, and that's all I remember."

"You're a fine guard," Graddon commented. "Where's the other man?"

"A little forward, sir."

Graddon rushed forward—and found another man just returning to consciousness, another who could not tell what had happened to him.

That was enough for Graddon. He rushed to the end of the deck, hurried quickly to the corridor, dashed along it to the door of Blandale's cabin. The door was locked, he found. He pounded upon it. Nobody answered his call, nor opened the door to admit him.

Graddon shouted to one of the guards not far away, and the man came running. He had seen nobody, he declared, had heard nothing suspicious. Graddon pounded on the door again, and thought he heard a low moan.

"I've got to get in there," he declared. "Here goes the door."

He hurled himself against the door, but it did not give. He sensed that it would not give easily. And so he raced around to the deck again, with the other man at his heels, and came to the bathroom window.

A moment later, Mark Graddon was inside. He snapped on the lights. Harvey Blandale was tossing and moaning in his berth. Jebbins seemed to be asleep in a chair in a corner. Nothing had been disturbed, as far as Graddon could see.

He rushed to Jebbins first, with the intention of shaking him awake and berating him for going to sleep. He saw a card fastened to the lapel of Jebbins' coat—and read the message of The Mongoose.

Then he saw the card pinned to Harvey Blandale's pajamas. He saw another on the table—another on a chair.

"The Mongoose! He's been here!" Graddon gasped.

He rang for the steward, and sent him for the ship's doctor. Throwing the windows wide open, Graddon let the cold air rush into the cabin. He shook Jebbins again, but Jebbins only muttered as though in delirium. His automatic dropped to the floor.

Graddon was shaking Blandale when the doctor arrived. The financier was regaining consciousness rapidly. They sat him in a chair, gave restoratives, waited for him to recognize them.

"What's happened, Mr. Blandale?" Graddon asked.

"Why, I—nothing, as far as I know."

"You've been doped! The Mongoose has been here!"

"The Mongoose here? How—"

"I don't know how. The guards on deck were drugged. Your valet is doped. Everything seems to have gone to pieces. You sure you didn't have anything worth stealing?"

"Certainly I'm sure, Graddon."

"Then the scoundrel must have been just showing off. He called and left his card." Graddon's voice was sarcastic. "You awake, Jebbins? What do you remember?"

"There seemed to be something in the air, sir. I—I began choking. And that's all I can remember."

"Drugged!" Graddon snapped. "But, why? Nothing stolen. Nobody assaulted. I'll get that devil! He's aboard the ship! I'll make another search as soon as it's daylight, and it'll be a search that'll go down in history! I'll get that Mongoose if it takes me the rest of my life!"

"This is terrible... terrible—" Harvey Blandale was muttering.

IN THE wireless room, The Mongoose finished sending his messages. He received the last acknowledgement. He made the unconscious operator comfortable, and then started for the door.

His work was done. Now he had to get out, get back to his own cabin, and go to bed. The Mongoose would disappear for the time being. Mr. Sidney Carleigh would enjoy a visit in Bermuda with his sister.

Somebody tried the door!

The Mongoose came to an abrupt stop. He knew that this might be a moment of peril. There came a knock on the door.

"Open up, Johnson!"

That was some officer, The Mongoose sensed. He would expect immediate obedience to the command. A moment's delay would make him suspicious.

The Mongoose darted silently to the light switch and turned off the lights. He pulled his cap down lower on his forehead, and turned up the collar of his raincoat.

"Johnson! Open up! Are you asleep?"

Suspicion rang in the voice of the man outside. The Mongoose slipped across to the door, holding his blackjack in his right hand. With his left he prepared to turn the key in the lock.

"Just a minute," he called.

"What's the trouble with you? The skipper wants to know—"

The Mongoose turned the key, turned the knob, opened the door a couple of inches. A gasp of astonishment came from the man outside. He lurched into the wireless room.

The Mongoose struck swiftly with the blackjack. The blow was intended to be a light one, just powerful enough to stun the other for a moment. But it was too light. The Mongoose darted through the door like a flash but with the alarm cry of the other ringing in his ears.

As he started to rush away a member of the crew appeared. A short distance behind him came a steward carrying a tray. The man in the wireless room bellowed another alarm.

The Mongoose whirled swiftly and fled. The steward dropped the tray and began pursuit. Out from the wireless room stepped the officer The Mongoose had struck—in time to have The Mongoose crash into him.

Down he went, and The Mongoose ran on. He felt sure that none of these men had got a good look at him. But they would not quit the pursuit now. They had been warned that possibly a criminal was aboard, that anybody acting in an unusual manner was to be investigated promptly.

"After him!" the officer was shouting. "Catch him!"

The Mongoose ran, darted along the deck, rushed down a companionway. There would be a score after him soon, he knew. Those on night duty would be attracted by the tumult. He had to beware being caught in a trap.

He could not fail now, he told himself. He had important work to do—take vengeance, and later clear his dead father's name. And there was Eleanor, waiting for him in the cabin.

RUSHING THROUGH swinging doors he bowled over another steward. On he went, and gained a deck. As he rushed along the rail there he began emptying the pockets of his raincoat, removing the articles which would be damaging evidence if found on him, and tossing them over the rail and into the sea.

Behind him came the determined pursuit. As he darted beneath a light there came a ringing command to halt. A weapon cracked, and a bullet whistled past The Mongoose's head. He rushed to the boat deck, darted through a sheet of driving rain, and got to cover again.

Another companionway was near him, and he hurried toward it. But he heard somebody coming up, and swerved aside in time to avoid being seen. He began to feel like a trapped animal.

Men were shouting above the howling of the wind and the churn of the sea. More members of the crew were coming. Passengers, awakened by the tumult, were coming from their cabins in all stages of dress.

The Mongoose got to the promenade deck again. But he found the way to his cabin blocked. He turned and rushed forward, trying to keep away from the scattered lights.

And suddenly the ship was ablaze with light. Some officer had thrown all the switches. There were few dark corners now. But The Mongoose was in one of them.

He jerked off his raincoat, and swiftly turned it inside out. It was a double coat, planned for just such an emergency as this. The side now exposed was gray, not black.

He fumbled at his belt, gave a quick jerk with each hand, and the dark trousers he wore fell to the deck in two pieces. The Mongoose tossed them over the rail. He tore off the coat and hurled it into the sea also. Beneath coat and trousers was a suit of light gray.

He had thrown his cap over the rail. Those who had pursued had seen a man in dark clothes. If they met The Mongoose now they would not believe him to be the man they sought.

The pursuit was coming nearer. Officers were shouting commands. The Mongoose strove to reduce his breathing. He stepped out into the light.

Then they were at him, volleying questions at him. One put hands on him, but the haughty glare of Sidney Carleigh made him desist.

"What's the row?" Sidney Carleigh demanded.

"Who are you?" an officer asked.

"Carleigh. I am with my sister—Cabin B-40. Came up here to watch the storm and do a bit of thinking."

"The man we're after had black clothes on," one of the others cried. "He probably dodged for the companionway."

"You see anybody rushing around here?" the officer asked.

"Matter of fact, I did," Sidney Carleigh answered, truthfully.

"Where did he go?"

"Can't say. What's the row? Chasing a thief? Might as well turn in, I suppose. A man can't do much thinking with all this racket going on."

Already, they were leaving him, rushing away, scattering to continue their search. Sidney Carleigh made his way slowly to his cabin. He entered and turned on the lights. Eleanor, in négligée, rushed toward him.

He motioned her for silence. He listened a moment, but heard nothing to indicate that he had been followed and was under surveillance. Nevertheless, he spoke in whispers.

"That was close, but I won out. Everything's fine, my dear."

"I heard the noise, Sid. I—I was terribly frightened."

"I think that fellow they call The Mongoose was up to one of his tricks. But it's nothing for us to worry about. Get to bed, and have a beauty sleep. Not that you need it!"

AS LATE as noon that day, Harvey Blandale was walking around with a puzzled expression in his face. For about the twentieth time, he made the same remark to Captain Hanborne.

"I can't understand it! Simply drugged everybody and left those confounded cards. Got away when he was chased, too. Beat up your wireless operator and assaulted one of your officers. And why? That's the question!"

"And he's still on this ship!" Detective Mark Graddon said.

"We'll keep searching until we find him," Captain Hanborne stated. "When we get to the end of the run, nobody gets off this ship until we're sure of their status!"

"Can't understand it at all," Blandale mouthed.

Nor did he understand, at first, the wild messages that soon began pouring at him out of the air. What did Wazer mean by calling him a double-crosser? What did Clark Donnibell mean by saying two could play at that game? And what did that ass of a Craley mean, reporting that orders had been carried out?

There were a couple of code words in Craley's message that Harvey Blandale did not remember. So he sought his little book to refresh his memory—and found that the little book was gone. And then he began to fear. But not for several days did he understand the full extent of the disaster, and guess what The Mongoose had done.

Before that time Mr. Sidney Carleigh and his charming sister had disembarked, no suspicion being attached to them, and were enjoying the delights of Bermuda—enjoying them still more because of the knowledge of a job well done, and because a radio message from his broker had informed Sidney Carleigh that the recent upheaval in Transcontinental Copper had netted him a nice profit.

SMOKE OF REVENGE

A Blond Woman, as Clever as the Mask of Sin, Helps
The Mongoose Avenge the Death of His Father

CHAPTER I

DAWNING TROUBLE

WAVES OF LAUGHTER swept through the theatre as the curtain fell at the end of the second act of the town's latest comedy hit. Men and women in the audience prepared to leave their seats and promenade or smoke during the intermission. And an usher went down an aisle and touched Mr. Henry Fabert on the shoulder.

Only a man who possesses a clear conscience can endure a touch on the shoulder without reacting to it with a thrill of apprehension. Henry Fabert betrayed his true character by flinching slightly.

Henry Fabert was an attorney of some prominence. He was also a bachelor, of the flashy and notorious variety. He lived in a gorgeously furnished penthouse atop a fashionable apartment building. Among persons of the better sort he was avoided as much as possible, and only tolerated when circumstances compelled a meeting.

When he felt that touch on his shoulder, Henry Fabert jerked his head around quickly. He vented a sigh of relief when he saw the usher's uniform.

"Mr. Fabert?" the usher asked.

"Right!"

"I was told to hand you this, sir."

The usher gave Henry Fabert an envelope, and withdrew up the aisle without awaiting monetary reward.

Those on the stage took a final curtain call for the act, and the house lights were turned up. Fabert glanced quickly at the envelope the usher had given him. No name or address was on it. He brushed it against his nostrils.

"Lavender!" he said.

The man who sat beside him chuckled. He was Bert Denwell, Henry Fabert's confidential secretary, and also his close companion in many escapades.

"I'm betting fifty bucks it's from a brunette," Denwell said.

"You're on, my lad! And you'll lose. Brunettes don't use lavender."

Fabert grinned, and ripped the small envelope open. From it he removed a card. He held the card so the light fell across its glossy surface. A few words had been hand printed on the card with pen and ink. They read:

> You are the next on my list!

Henry Fabert made a sound that was half an exclamation of surprise and half a grunt of speculation. He glanced around swiftly, but saw nobody who seemed to be watching him particularly. He examined the other side of the card, and found it blank. He passed it to Denwell.

"What do you make of this, Bert?" he asked.

"May be a joke," Denwell suggested.

"And it may not be one."

"Probably some fair lady is making an attempt to arouse your curiosity. You've got a reputation for being liberal. Next on the list—um!"

"I have a feeling it's nothing like that."

"A feeling? You mean a hunch? Got a guilty conscience about something?" Denwell asked, grinning.

"It's only a hunch to be cautious. So I'm the next on the list. But—what list? Whoever sent this card to me should have been more specific. I'm a lawyer, not a detective. Let's find that usher."

Fabert put envelope and card into a coat pocket, got up, and

*Graddon saw a
man in evening
dress rushing from
the penthouse*

led the way slowly up the crowded aisle. He located the usher
without difficulty, and drew him aside.

"Are you the boy who handed me a letter?" Fabert asked.

"Yes, sir."

"Who gave it to you?"

"I don't know him, sir—never saw him before. A gentleman handed me the letter just before the end of the act. He
pointed you out to me, and told me your name. Is there something wrong, sir?"

Fabert ignored the question, and asked one of his own. "What
did he look like?"

"He was middle-aged, sir—tall and well-dressed. Had a small
black mustache."

"That description probably fits a hundred men in the theatre.
Would you know him if you saw him again?"

"I'm sure of it, sir."

"Good! Try to locate him. If you do, let me know quietly
where he is. Say nothing to him about it. Understand? Here!"

Fabert slipped the usher a bit of currency that made the youth's eyes bulge.

Then Fabert and Denwell went on out into the lobby and consumed cigarettes. Fabert was betraying a measure of nervousness unusual for him. His famed inscrutability seemed shattered for the moment.

"Do you think it might be something serious?" Denwell asked him, in whispers.

"A man never knows, Bert. But I haven't been treading on anybody's toes lately, so far as I'm aware."

"Going to call off tonight's party?"

"Certainly not! This may be only a hoax. We'll go ahead as we've planned—pick up the crowd at the night club, and go on to the penthouse. Only, let's keep our eyes and ears open."

THEY RETURNED to their seats for the last act of the play. But Henry Fabert was no longer interested in the town's smart new comedy. He was thinking about the card he had received. It worried him. It might be nothing worse than a practical joke. It might be only the work of some unbalanced crank. But a guilty conscience whispered half a hundred unpleasant possibilities to Henry Fabert.

He tried to cast aside a feeling of premonition which came to him. He was a fool to let an anonymous card upset him so! He could not be in personal danger. He was not a weakling, and Bert Denwell was an athlete. And part of Denwell's job was to act as a sort of bodyguard for Henry Fabert.

The play ended. Through the jostling crowd, Fabert went up the aisle with Denwell toward the check room, nodding to acquaintances, searching for anybody who might be betraying an unhealthy interest in him.

They claimed their overcoats, and got into them, adjusted their mufflers, prepared for the street. The usher hurried up to them.

"I didn't catch sight of your man again, sir," he reported. "Sorry!"

"Very well!" Fabert replied. "You did your best, I'm sure."

"Pardon me, sir! There's something sticking to the back of your overcoat." The usher fumbled an instant.

"What is it?" Fabert asked.

"A small piece of paper, sir. Why, it's fastened to your overcoat with a bent pin! I'll have it loose in a moment. Here it is, sir."

Fabert accepted the bit of paper the boy offered him, and glanced at it. The usher went on toward the door.

"What is it—something else disturbing?" Denwell asked.

"A picture of some sort. Look!"

"Looks like the picture of a rat," Denwell commented. "No, it's a weasel! Isn't it? Small printed picture, probably cut out of some book or magazine."

"But what's the object of pinning a thing like that on my overcoat? That's a kid's trick," Fabert said. "And, who could have done it?"

"A hundred had a chance to do it. We were in that jam at the door of the check room," Denwell recalled. "Anybody who brushed against you there could have done it. The 'how' is easy enough to answer, but tell me the 'why' of it. Why should anybody go to the trouble of fastening such a thing to your coat? What's the significance of it? Picture of a weasel—"

Denwell was interrupted by a smothered exclamation from Fabert. The lawyer's eyes seemed to dilate, to glare for an instant. It was evident he was making a struggle to avoid showing agitation in public.

"What is it?" Denwell asked. "Are you ill? Your face is as white as—"

"Weasel!" Fabert whispered. "Don't you see it, Bert?"

"Don't know what you are driving at."

"That's not the picture of a weasel. Look at it again. It's the picture of a mongoose. Understand now?"

"The Mongoose!" Denwell gasped. "That fiend who's been running around robbing everybody!"

"Yes! And I'm the next on his list!"

CHAPTER II

TWO WOMEN

THEY WENT OUT to the street, and stood at the curb waiting for Fabert's chauffeur to bring the car.

"The Mongoose!" Bert Denwell repeated. "He'll probably try to rob you. We must warn the police."

"Wait till we get into the car, and I'll explain some things," Fabert said. "This isn't a case for the police. I've kept the truth of this thing from you, Bert. Didn't think that he'd ever come after me. But this means that—that he *knows!*"

"Pardon me, but you're rambling."

"I'll explain presently. We'll have to get busy—make some plans."

"I should think so! About that party tonight—"

"We'll go ahead with that. I don't expect The Mongoose to strike at me tonight."

"And there might be a chance that the mysterious and ravishing blonde—" Denwell hinted.

Fabert smiled nervously. "Exactly!" he said.

The car came, and they got in. Fabert gave the chauffeur instructions to drive to a certain night club. As they rolled along the street through the congestion of after-theatre traffic, Fabert spoke rapidly, and in low tones.

"The Mongoose isn't, as the general public thinks, merely a clever criminal who makes a specialty of running around and robbing wealthy men. He's a sort of avenger."

"How's that?" Denwell asked.

"I'd have told you about this before, Bert, but the secret wasn't mine alone. Now, however, you've got to know. You'll have to stand by me."

"You can depend on that—whatever it is!"

"Thanks…About ten years ago, some big financiers got caught putting across a gigantic swindle. They faced jail. Managed to save themselves by framing an innocent bookkeeper named William Cratch. He was sent to prison, where he died."

"It's been done before," Denwell commented, callously.

"A short time ago, a son of this William Cratch showed up. He called himself The Mongoose, saying he was attacking snakes, and began his work of revenge. He's already robbed three of the guilty men of large sums."

"I'm commencing to understand."

"The police haven't been able to get a line on him. The real reason for these attacks by The Mongoose has been kept secret— as you can imagine. The public has been allowed to believe that he's only a clever professional crook going after wealthy men."

"And now he's threatening to come after you—to rob you?" Denwell said. "But, why should he threaten you? Were you mixed up in the swindle?"

Fabert gave a sickly smile. "At that time, Bert, I was a poor and struggling lawyer—also honest," he replied. "Big financiers scarcely would have admitted me to one of their secret deals. I was named by the court to defend this Cratch, who was penniless."

"But, if you defended him, and for nothing, why should this son of his—" Denwell began.

"Don't be dense, Bert! My good fortune began from the date of that trial. I received money, market tips, protection in my investments. I had big legal business tossed my way. Can't you understand?"

"Not quite."

"Why, they got to me! I was the lawyer for the defense. In such a manner that the court did not suspect me, I—well, I didn't make out a very strong case for my man."

"You mean you threw him down?"

"Yes—betrayed him. Not pretty, is it? But I was tempted—and I fell. It wasn't difficult—and the rewards certainly have been heavy. The gang has taken care of me, all right! And this Mongoose, the son of the innocent man I helped trap and send to prison—he knows about it, somehow. That's the only possible explanation. So—I'm the next on his list."

"What are we going to do?" Denwell asked.

"When we get to the night club, I'll telephone Mark Graddon. He's a private detective who works for the gang, as you know. I'll have Graddon meet us at the penthouse. We'll go right ahead with our party, but meanwhile Graddon can make his plans."

"Where and when do you suppose The Mongoose will strike?"

"Who knows? He may work some trick. He's a fiend! Knows a lot about chemistry and electricity, and all that. Let's brace up now, Bert! We're almost to the club. We don't want our guests to think there's something wrong."

Henry Fabert was well known at this particular night club. He spent plenty of money there. The manager greeted him at the door.

"Evening, Mr. Fabert!" he said. "Your guests have gathered. I arranged for one vacant chair at the table, as you directed."

"Good! And the mysterious person?"

"She's here again, tonight—came alone. Got a table in the corner."

"Thanks! I want to do some rather private telephoning before I go in."

"Use my office, Mr. Fabert. Use my private line, and your call won't go through the switchboard."

AS SOON as they had handed coats and hats to the check room girl, Fabert and Denwell entered the manager's office. Fabert used the private line, and dialed a number. Presently a sleepy voice answered him.

"Hullo!"

"Graddon? This is Henry Fabert. Did I get you out of bed?"

" 'S all right, Mr. Fabert."

"I wish you'd struggle into a dinner jacket and hurry to my penthouse. My butler knows you and will let you in. I'll be along later with a bunch of friends—throwing a party."

"Thanks, Mr. Fabert. But I—I don't quite feel up to one of your parties tonight. I'm beginning to get bald and fat, and the girls don't like me. I've got to go easy on liquor—"

"Wait a minute!" Fabert interrupted, laughing. "This is business, Graddon. I've heard from our friend, The Mongoose."

"What?" Graddon cried.

"I thought that'd wake you up. Got a notice from him. He says that I'm next on his list."

"Where are you now?"

"At the Rainbow Club. I had a party arranged—didn't want to change plans at this late hour. Can't explain to my guests, as you very well know. We're coming on to the penthouse."

"I'll go right to the penthouse and wait for you," Graddon said. "We'll have a conference as soon as you arrive. I'll get a couple of my best men up there."

Fabert ended the conversation, then telephoned his butler and told him of Mark Graddon's impending arrival. Then he went out into the Club with Denwell.

A special table had been arranged for the Fabert party, and twelve guests were at it now. There were three vacant chairs. It was a flashy gathering, with Clarice Hayle, a musical comedy star, trying to star here also.

Fabert and Denwell were greeted by cheers. Cocktails were thrust toward them. There was a moment of babble, then the majority of those at the table went on the floor to dance.

Henry Fabert sat at the end of the table, with Clarice Hayle beside him, looking around the semi-dark room across which colored lights were flashing.

"Where've you been, bad boy?" Clarice Hayle demanded.

"Denwell and I took in a show—that new comedy. Didn't want to get here till the clan had gathered."

"I noticed an extra chair. Who belongs to that?"

"That's a secret, Clarice. Maybe somebody—and maybe nobody. Might not come."

"Male or female?" she demanded.

"You're hoping that it's a very eligible male, eh?" Fabert taunted.

Her pretty eyes grew narrow. "Wrong! Hoping that it's not a female," she corrected.

"Jealous?"

"Try me, and see," she said.

Fabert laughed, but it was a nervous effort. He imagined that the fair Clarice might be uncomfortable in a jealous rage. She was taking their little affair too seriously to please Fabert. She wasn't going to be as easy to shake off as others had been.

The crowd returned to the table. In the confusion, Fabert escaped. He motioned Denwell to take care of Clarice and keep her occupied. Denwell understood and began an argument with her. Clarice was the sort that likes to argue.

Passing among the diners at the edge of the dance floor, Fabert approached a table in the corner of the room. A short distance from it, he stopped to view and again appraised a woman who sat there. She was the ravishing blonde Denwell had mentioned.

HERE WAS one woman who puzzled Henry Fabert. He had brushed against her accidentally in the Club. He had seen her half a dozen times in other places, had spoken to her. She was always alone. He could learn little of her. She was not the usual type of unaccompanied woman to be found in such places.

She had repulsed all his advances, though she did it laughingly, almost teasingly. Fabert, wise in such things, had believed at first that she was trying to arouse his curiosity and lead him on to an infatuation. Now he was not so sure. She had dropped the hint that she was English, was a writer of fiction, and was studying American types.

Now Fabert went on to the table, and she glanced up as he approached, and smiled.

"So we meet again," he said. "You know, you're very exasperating. I can't understand you. You seem to know me, and a lot about me, and I don't know even your name."

"You're a prominent person, and I'm not," she replied, laughing. "You may call me Sonia Kews."

"Thank you! See that gang over there? My guests. Notice the vacant chair? Waiting for you."

"How nice? You mean that you want me to join your party?"

"Please! It's a large party, so you needn't be afraid."

"Oh, I'm never afraid!"

"We're going to leave in a short time and go to my penthouse. Going to finish the party there. I'd like to have you come along. Want to get better acquainted with you."

"Go to the wicked Mr. Fabert's naughty penthouse?" She pretended horror.

"But you're not afraid—you said so."

"So it's a challenge! I think that I'll accept your kind invitation."

"Great!" Fabert said. "Come and meet the gang."

He led her back to the big table, and to the black glares of Clarice Hayle and introduced her around. He gave her only the share of attention due a strange guest. But not even Henry Fabert could completely hide his interest in this girl.

Clarice Hayle bent toward him. "She's beautiful, this Miss Sonia Kews," she whispered. "Such beautiful eyes and skin—to scratch! Beautiful blonde hair—to pull! Better not get me started, Henry!"

"Behave yourself! I'll tell you all about her later," Fabert promised.

He nodded to Denwell, and the latter planted the suggestion that it was time to move on to the penthouse. There was a moment of confusion around the table while the women got into their wraps. Fabert was paying special attention to the mysterious Sonia Kews. A glowering Clarice Hayle watched him from the near distance. Denwell took charge of the new girl, to allay Clarice's mounting rage. They started toward the exit, talking and laughing. Across the room, the famous orchestra was commencing another dance number. Fabert allowed the others to go ahead, beckoned the head waiter, scrawled his name across the check.

"Beg pardon, Mr. Fabert! You're about to lose something from your waistcoat pocket, sir," the head waiter said.

It was a small piece of paper, folded. Henry Fabert knew that he had not put it into his waistcoat pocket. He kept from betraying his astonishment.

"Thanks!" he muttered.

He unfolded the scrap of paper as the head waiter moved away. On it were a few scribbled words, in a handwriting which was obviously disguised:

Enjoy yourself while you may, Fabert! Nero fiddled while Rome burned. The English officers danced on the eve of Waterloo. You are following historical precedent.
THE MONGOOSE.

CHAPTER III

POSSIBLE SWAG

CLARICE HAYLE, SONIA Kews and a couple of guests rode with Fabert and Denwell in Fabert's car. The others made the journey to Fabert's penthouse apartment in taxicabs.

During that short ride, Fabert's mind was busy. That note

had been slipped into his waistcoat pocket in the club. Either of the women could have put it there. One of the men in the party might have done so. But Fabert knew them all well, with exception of Sonia Kews, and could suspect none of being associated with The Mongoose.

Nor could he bring himself to suspect Sonia Kews. He tried to remember whether she had been close to him, and could not think of a time when it would have been possible for her to put the note in his pocket. He had not danced with her. He really had not been close to her except while helping her on with her cloak.

It must have been done while he was checking his things, he decided. Only another trick of The Mongoose or somebody associated with him. It was not known whether The Mongoose worked alone. In fact, little was known except that he worked.

At the apartment house, they gathered in the lobby and ascended in a large elevator to the roof. Henry Fabert's penthouse was a real house constructed in the center of the roof, and with verandahs and gardens around it.

They rushed inside, making themselves at home. Sonia Kews was the only one who had not been there often before. Fabert had a moment alone with Denwell, and instructed him to attend Sonia Kews for the time being, and allay Clarice Hayle's jealousy. He must disappear for a short time, for his conference with Mark Graddon. The party would run itself.

"Mr. Graddon is in your study, sir," the butler reported, in whispers. "I'll see to it that you're not disturbed."

Fabert hurried to the study. Though his character was not all that could be desired, Fabert was a shrewd and hardworking lawyer at times. In this study, he worked out many legal problems.

Detective Mark Graddon was waiting for him, pacing back and forth and chewing savagely at a cigar. Fabert told him swiftly of the card at the theatre, the picture pinned to his coat, the note which had been slipped into his waistcoat pocket.

"Easy enough—that stuff," Graddon declared. "So he's after you now, eh? I expected it. He'll be after me, too. He knows that I faked the evidence that sent William Cratch to prison."

"What do you suppose he'll try to do?"

"May try almost anything. Don't get frightened at any of his tricks. Remember, The Mongoose is only a man. He's nothing supernatural. He'll make some mistake yet, and then I'll have him. I've got to get him!"

"What are you going to do, Graddon?"

"Protect you. Stick right with you. I've got a couple of my men here, in hiding. We'll guard your office. But I'm working in the dark. Where can The Mongoose strike? You don't keep a fortune in your office safe, do you?"

"I have plenty of money there—at times. But not an amount that would attract The Mongoose," Fabert replied. "He goes after big stakes."

"It's something else, then," Graddon declared. "He may try some new sort of game on you."

There came a discreet knock on the door. At Fabert's call, the butler entered.

"Pardon me, Mr. Fabert, but this package came for you about nine o'clock," he reported. "It was sent up from the office. I'd not bother you with it now, sir, except that it's marked important."

The butler put a small package on the desk, and retreated at Fabert's gestured command. Mark Graddon sprang forward as soon as the door was closed.

"Now we'll get at it!" he said. "I've been waiting for this. You got a dictaphone machine here?"

"There in the corner. I often dictate stuff here. But what do you want—"

"I'm betting that there's a dictaphone cylinder in this package," Graddon interrupted. "That's the way The Mongoose sends his messages. Remember? He sent dictaphone cylinders to the others."

Mark Graddon unwrapped the package swiftly.

"And you'll have to work fast," he added. "These things are treated chemically, so they'll melt and evaporate after they've been exposed to the open air for a short time. You listen to the thing—and then let me listen. Yes—here it is, as I thought."

The package was unwrapped. From a box Graddon took a dictaphone record carefully protected with cotton. Fabert put the record on the dictaphone and adjusted the ear tubes. He started the machine.

"Be sure you get it!" Graddon barked at him. "Don't miss anything."

Fabert was bending forward, his eyes mere slits, listening intently:

Hello, Henry Fabert! This is The Mongoose talking to you. It isn't necessary for me to tell you why I am giving you attention. You are one of the worst of the lot! You betrayed the trust of a man you were supposed to defend. You are a disgrace to your profession!

These first blows of mine are to strike you scoundrels in the purse. Later, I may take a more terrible revenge. But now I seek only to take a share of your ill-gotten wealth, to give to charity. I do not need your money for my own use.

I am going to strike at you tonight, Fabert. I'll make one of your wild parties wilder. The fire of revenge is burning, and where there is fire there is smoke.

THE MESSAGE ended. Fabert got up quickly and motioned for Mark Graddon to take the ear tubes. The detective heard the message through.

And then they sat and watched the cylinder record. Almost instantly, little bubbles began appearing on its surface. The record seemed to be melting. A pungent odor was in the air.

"There it goes!" Graddon said. "But we both heard the thing."

"He said that he'd strike tonight—during the party. That means here, in the penthouse. What do you suppose he'll do?"

"Yeah! And he also said that he'd grab a share of your ill-gotten wealth. How can he do that here?" Graddon wanted to know. "Got a safe?"

"Right behind that panel in the corner," Fabert replied.

"Is it a safe, or just a tin box?"

"It's a good safe."

"I'll look at it later. The question is—what can The Mongoose steal around here? As you remarked, he plays for big stakes. Any money in that safe?"

"Possibly six or seven hundred dollars."

"He wouldn't go to the trouble of trying to get that. The Mongoose spends time and coin in his preparations, as we know. He's looking for big profits. Better come clean with me, Fabert."

"What do you mean by that, Graddon?"

"Better tell me what there is here that The Mongoose would want to steal. He seems to know more along those lines than I do. Got any valuable art objects?"

"Nothing to speak of."

"Got something that's a sort of pet of yours—something that it'd break your heart to have stolen?"

"Nothing like that, Graddon."

Mark Graddon lighted his cigar and blew a cloud of fragrant smoke toward the ceiling. "I can't force you to tell me," he observed. "But I sure can work a lot better when I know the facts in a case. You needn't be afraid to talk to me, Fabert. I'm in the pitch as much as you."

"All right!" Fabert bent forward and spoke in lower tones. "In that safe, I've got unset jewels that'd be worth two hundred thousand in the retail market."

"What?" Mark Graddon almost shrieked the word. "Are you mad?"

"I bought the lot for a hundred thousand cash, about a month ago," Fabert explained.

"Didn't know you were a jewel merchant."

"I was approached by an old client of mine. He made the deal for—er—somebody else. Diamonds, emeralds and rubies. All unset, understand."

"And you bought them for about half price? There's only one answer," Graddon said.

"You've guessed it, of course. It's stolen stuff. That big wholesale jewel robbery three months ago. I helped out the men who got the stuff—they were afraid to market it. And I did myself a good turn. I can sell 'em to some of my friends and make a nice profit, and also save them some money. They can have 'em set any way they like."

"And the stuff is in that safe?"

"Yes. But how could The Mongoose know it?"

"Don't ask me," Mark Graddon said, "how that baby knows anything. He just knows. He may have had the jewels planted on you. You're out a hundred thousand—and you may be out the jewels, too—if he can get them."

"How can he get them—if they are what he's after?"

"If he tries, we'll get him!" Graddon promised. "Fabert, I brought a couple of my best men with me. Before you came with your guests, we searched the penthouse and the roof, thoroughly. You may be sure that The Mongoose isn't here at present."

"If he comes—"

"I've got one of my men posted at the elevator entrance, and another by the only fire escape that runs down from the roof. Those are the only two ways anybody can get up here. So, there you are, Fabert—The Mongoose can't get in."

But The Mongoose was in already!

CHAPTER IV

TAPPED TALK

HENRY FABERT LEFT Detective Mark Graddon in the study and went out to his guests. He knew that he could not remain away from them longer without his absence causing comment. Fabert was always an active host.

Denwell hurried up to him as soon as he appeared. "You'd better watch yourself with that blonde," he whispered. "Clarice is sure suspicious. And she's keeping sober."

"I'll take care of that," Fabert replied. "You go into the study and have a talk with Mark Graddon. Ask him what he wants you to do. He'll tell you what it's all about. And keep your eyes and ears open."

"About this Mongoose thing—there's no danger tonight, is there?"

"There might be. The Mongoose sent me one of those dictaphone records. Said that he'd strike tonight and make my wild party wilder."

"You'd better call the cops."

"I don't dare do that, and you know it. Graddon has a couple of his men here, and they should be able to do the work. Nothing may happen until after the guests have gone. The Mongoose would be a fool to pull off anything in a crowd."

"What do you suppose he's after?" Denwell asked.

"Have you forgotten my little deal in unset jewels? They're still in the safe in the study."

"You'd better get those things into a safe deposit box."

"Can't do that tonight, can I? And I want 'em here. Can't market 'em while they're in a safe deposit box."

Denwell went to the study, and Henry Fabert mingled with his guests. Those guests, used to the penthouse and such parties, were scattered through the house and out on the verandahs, making themselves at home. Servants were busy passing trays of drinks. Food went untasted.

Even with the menace of The Mongoose hanging over him, Henry Fabert did not forget Sonia Kews, the mysterious blonde. He did not see her now, and began searching for her. But Clarice Hayle intercepted him.

"Where've you been, bad boy?" she demanded. Fabert was commencing to hate that phrase.

"Had to attend to a little business, in my study," he explained.

"Yes? Anyhow, I know you haven't been with that Sonia Kews. I've been watching her. Bert Denwell has been with her all the time."

"Possibly Bert is interested," Fabert suggested.

"And so are you! I'm not being fooled a bit. Who is she?"

"Just a woman a friend of mine introduced to me," he said. "She's new to the town—doesn't know many people. English. I'm only trying to be decent to her."

"Yes?" Clarice lifted her arched brows. "Remember that you're not speaking to an infant, Henry. She's smooth, that girl! I know the type. And you're just about fool enough to fall for her work."

"Jealous again?" he taunted.

"Just behave, Henry—that's all! Little Clarice is a terror when she gets real mad."

"I've got to hunt up Miss Kews, and be decent to her. She'll think I'm a rotten host."

"Pay a little attention to me, first," Clarice urged. "She's probably talking to somebody."

Henry Fabert knew better than to refuse the request. He decided that he would humor her. But he'd get away as soon as possible, and find where Sonia Kews had gone....

AT THAT instant, Sonia Kews was walking toward the end of one of the verandahs, where it was almost dark. She stopped at the railing, and looked out across a sea of twinkling lights. She had managed to get away from everybody for the moment.

She sat on the railing, and made herself comfortable. Some of the guests were laughing and talking at the other end of the verandah, but nobody was near her. From somewhere she brought forth a gold pencil, and with it she began tapping gently on the corner of the verandah.

She stopped. Another tapping replied to her. It seemed to come from beneath the floor. Her pencil began tapping again—tapping dots and dashes:

"I am all right. Everything is going fine."

"Good. I have everything ready."

"Graddon and two of his men are here."

"Okay! I made the connections. Think you will be able to carry out the plans?"

"I'll do my best. But be careful, brother."

"Do not worry about me. You be careful yourself," the taps came in answer.

"Do not make a move too soon," she signaled. "I'll try to let you know more later."

Then she put the pencil away. She smiled faintly. This was a perilous game, but worth the playing. There was keen satisfaction in it, as well as a thrill.

In another section of the city, she was known as Miss Eleanor Carleigh. She lived with her brother, Sidney Carleigh, in an apartment house he owned. The men who had conspired to send innocent William Cratch to prison knew that he had left a son who called himself The Mongoose and exacted vengeance. But they did not know that The Mongoose had a sister.

Together, they had planned their campaign. For several years, they had been preparing for it. A fortune unexpectedly inherited in England had provided ample funds for their purpose. And brother and sister had dedicated their lives to punishing the men who had wronged their father.

But Eleanor Carleigh was acting the part of Sonia Kews now,

and she acted it well. A great deal depended on that. Each step
in their plan had to be carried out according to schedule. The
Mongoose, hidden beneath the verandah in a place previously
prepared, would be depending on her to do her share.

SHE WALKED slowly back along the verandah toward an
open French window which gave into the spacious living room.
She was watching, observing. Liquor already was dulling the
wits of the guests. But one—Clarice Hayle—was alert enough.
And Fabert and Denwell were patterns of sobriety. Then there
were Mark Graddon and his two men, and some servants to be
considered.

She stepped through the window and into the living room.
Not far away, Fabert was talking to Clarice Hayle. He turned
Clarice over to another man, excused himself, and hurried across
the room to the alluring blonde.

"All alone?" Fabert asked.

"Deserted! Mr. Denwell was very charming, but he finally
drifted away."

"Sorry! Had a bit of business that claimed my attention. A
lawyer can't call his time his own you know. It's always office
hours with me."

"Something seems to be disturbing you," she said. "You look
worried."

"Mean to say that I'm showing it? Only a little business trouble, such things as pop up every day."

"You haven't shown me your wonderful house," she suggested.

Her eyes were twinkling as she spoke. She seemed to be issuing a challenge. Fabert guided her through the rooms of the
lower floor. They seemed to be getting better acquainted rapidly.

She proved as charming as Fabert had anticipated. He forgot
the menace of The Mongoose.

"And your study—" she questioned. "Where does the big wise
lawyer sit and think out his problems?"

Graddon and Denwell were in the study, but that did not

deter Fabert, who was growing infatuated. He took her into the room, and Graddon and Denwell obeyed his delicate hint and left, Denwell to mingle with the guests again, and Mark Graddon to sit a short distance from the study door, on guard.

But the ravishing blonde was as elusive as before, Fabert found. If he had expected love-making, he was disappointed. He seemed unable to understand her. He told himself that she was a type entirely different from anything he ever had encountered before.

"I'd like to make you a present," he said, finally, "in token of your kindness in coming here."

"A present? That depends," she said. "I'm rather particular about accepting presents."

Fabert laughed, and went to the wall. He pressed a spring, and a panel slid back. The front of a safe was exposed.

"Oh!" she gasped. "Trick panels, and everything! Is this a house of mystery?"

"I swear this is the only trick panel," Fabert replied.

He knelt before the safe on one knee. She drifted toward him, still talking. A wave of perfume seemed to engulf him. He closed his eyes an instant, opened them, began working the combination. She stepped back as he pulled open the door.

Fabert glanced at her, to find that she had turned her back and was inspecting a picture on the wall. Opening a drawer, Fabert took from it a magnificent unset diamond.

"With my best regards," he said, smiling at her.

"Oh! Isn't it a beauty?"

"I'll have it set for you, any way you like. Or you do it, and have the bill sent to me."

"I couldn't—really," she said. "At least not now. Perhaps some day—when we're better acquainted—"

"Then you'll allow me to get better acquainted with you?"

"Perhaps. But Miss Hayle may object. Lock your safe, please, and let's join the others."

Fabert replaced the diamond and re-locked the safe. He slid the panel back into place. She had crossed the room and was standing at the door.

"As far as Miss Hayle is concerned—" Fabert said, as he joined her.

But Miss Hayle, at that instant, opened the door and confronted them. Her eyes were blazing.

"I'd like to speak to you, Henry!" she snapped. "Miss Kews will excuse you, I'm sure."

"Why, certainly!" Miss Kews was very polite about it.

Fabert began a remonstrance, but Clarice Hayle cut him short. Miss Kews swept out of the study, smiling faintly, and went toward the living room. The study door slammed behind her.

She evaded those in the living room, and went through the French window and out upon the verandah again. Once more she went to the end of it, and made herself comfortable on the railing. And again the pencil began its tapping.

"Brother… first plan worked… watched him and got combination of safe… behind panel under big picture… spring at top of wainscoting."

"Okay!"

"Listen to combination." Slowly, she tapped it out for him. "Understand?"

"I have it," he tapped in answer.

"No indication of party breaking up. Almost two o'clock. Graddon hanging around study."

"How about the Hayle woman?"

"She is getting jealous. Think I can start trouble at any time."

"Make it as near two-thirty as possible. Okay!"

CHAPTER V

SMOKE AND FLAMES

HENRY FABERT PROBABLY would have been greatly surprised had somebody told him the truth about the mysterious blonde who called herself Sonia Kews.

He was under the impression that he had caught sight of her in a night club, had been attracted, and cleverly had got to meet her. And now he was entertaining her in his penthouse, and hoped to ripen the acquaintance.

But it was the lady who had cleverly brought herself to Fabert's attention. It was a part of The Mongoose's plan for her to do so—for her to be in the penthouse tonight—and it was a part of that plan, also, to have Clarice Hayle grow jealous and create a scene.

Sonia Kews walked along the verandah again, and once more entered the living room through the French window. The radio was playing. Two couples were dancing. In a corner, somebody was telling a story to a group.

The butler was fussing around, keeping an eye on things. Detective Mark Graddon, a look of disgust on his face, was sitting near the door of the study. That door was closed, and high voices came from behind it.

She did not see Bert Denwell. Dropping on the end of a divan, Sonia Kews formed her lips into a pretty pout and got a pained expression around her eyes. Puffing languidly at a cigarette, she waited.

The door of the study was opened presently, and Fabert and Clarice Hayle emerged. The actress evidently had been angry, but now was mollified to a degree. Fabert's face was inscrutable.

He looked into the room and beheld his ravishing blonde alone on the divan, plainly angry at being thus deserted. Fabert was the sort to be ever turning toward a new face. And he was growing tired of Clarice Hayle and her scenes off stage.

He brushed past Clarice and went straight toward the divan, as Clarice stopped to say something to Mark Graddon.

"Alone again, my dear?" Fabert asked.

"It seems to be a habit of everybody to leave me alone this evening," she said. "I have been wondering just why you asked me here to your house, Mr. Fabert. Your other guests appear to have interests in common, and that leaves me rather out in the cold."

"A million pardons!" he said. "You'll have no further cause for complaint, I assure you." He sat down beside her on the divan. "When the party breaks up, I'll take you home. And I'd like a luncheon date, please."

Clarice Hayle descended upon the divan like a tornado.

"What did I tell you, Henry?" she screeched. "I told you to stay away from this blonde, didn't I? Want me to scratch her eyes out?"

She shrieked the words so that they rang through the house. Her shrill voice silenced the hilarity. Everybody hurried to see what was happening. Mark Graddon, in the door of the study, turned to look back. Denwell came hurrying from another room.

"You're forgetting yourself, Clarice!" Fabert cried. "This lady is my guest."

"You stay away from her, I said! If you don't—"

Sonia Kews got to her feet, slowly and in a manner somewhat regal. An expression of loathing was in her face as her eyes swept Clarice Hayle.

"Mr. Fabert, I must be leaving," she said. "Really, when you asked me to join your party, I scarcely expected a scene like this."

"Clarice doesn't know what she's saying or doing. She's had too much to drink," Fabert declared.

"Not on your life, Henry Fabert! I've been careful to stay sober. You don't get tired of me and toss me over for the first baby blonde who comes along. Who is she, anyway?"

Fabert made frantic motions to Denwell, who hurried forward and touched Clarice on the shoulder. Clarice was another who could not endure a touch on the shoulder without flinching. She whirled upon Denwell like an enraged tigress.

"Take your paws off me, Bert, or I'll scratch your face open!" she cried. "Trying to help your boss, are you? Why doesn't he handle his own women?"

"That's enough!" Fabert roared. "Clarice, you're going too far! I'll not endure a scene like this!"

Sonia Kews touched him on the arm. "I seem to be the innocent cause of it all," she said. "Please, I'd better go."

"I'll escort you," Fabert told her.

"You'll do nothing of the sort!" Clarice cried. "You'd like that, wouldn't you?"

"Don't bother, Mr. Fabert. I'll call a taxi," Sonia Kews offered.

"At least, I'll escort you to the taxi." He motioned to the butler. "My hat and coat! Bert, see if you can control that wildcat until I get back. The rest of you, go ahead with the party. You've seen Clarice's tantrums before. Don't let her spoil the fun."

CLARICE DECIDED to indulge in hysterics. She flopped in a chair, and Denwell and one of the women hovered over her, while a servant hurried for smelling salts and water. Sonia Kews got her cloak, and Fabert his hat and coat, and they went through the French window and to the verandah.

"Please—I think I dropped a handkerchief over there by the corner," Sonia said.

Fabert followed her. "You don't know how I feel about this," he apologized. "I know how it must look to you."

"I've seen jealous women before."

"I'm afraid I must place Clarice firmly outside my circle of friends hereafter," Fabert said.

"Here's my handkerchief." She bent and picked it up. Her voice was raised for an instant. "Now, if you'll take me down and get me a taxi, Mr. Fabert—" And The Mongoose, in his hiding place beneath the verandah, heard that.

It was only a short distance from the end of the verandah to the gate in the wall around the penthouse. Just beyond that wall were the elevators. The Mongoose waited a moment and then slipped cautiously from his hiding place. He was in evening dress, without hat or coat.

In the shadows at the end of the verandah he crouched for an instant, watching and listening. All the guests were inside the house enjoying Clarice Hayle's fit of hysterics. The Mongoose walked quickly toward the gate, where one of Mark Graddon's assistants was on guard.

The Mongoose was chuckling, as though at a good joke. He pretended a slight inebriation, also.

"What a night!" he confided to the guard. "Did you hear that dame howl?"

"Thought somebody was bein' killed," the guard replied.

"Only a jealous woman, buddy! Fabert has a lot of trouble on his hands. His old girl got jealous of his new one. I've got to get down and give him an earful before he comes back and walks into some hot water. Remember me when I come back, and don't keep me out and away from the drinks."

"Okay!" the guard said.

That guard had been warned to watch for anybody entering, had been told nothing about anybody leaving. To the guard, The Mongoose was one of Fabert's guests, who was going to descend in the elevator and would soon return.

The Mongoose got into the cage, and went down three floors. There, he left the elevator and hurried along the hall as though going to one of the apartments. When he reached the rear stairs, he descended rapidly for a distance of five floors more.

On each floor there was a hall ending in a wide window which fronted on the avenue. Careful that he was not observed, The Mongoose opened the window for a distance of six inches. From beneath his coat he took an object which looked not unlike a hand grenade. He pulled the pin, put it in a corner near the window, went to the stairs and began a swift ascent.

On the next floor above he went through all this again, and on the next floor, and so following. He was continually alert against discovery, especially careful as he neared the top of the building. When he came to the roof, he saw that all the elevators had descended.

The guard was pacing around just inside the open gate. The Mongoose fumbled in a pocket, then stepped forward and called to him softly.

"Fabert come back yet?"

"Not yet."

"He's having a sweet time to square himself. I stopped in a friend's apartment long enough to get back to normal. Has that jane in there been doing any more screeching?"

"There's been considerable racket," the guard replied.

"If you ask me— Why, what's this?" The Mongoose's voice held a sudden note of alarm.

The Mongoose darted to a dark spot near the wall. The guard sprang after him, bent to look. And then the guard found himself thrust back against the wall and half throttled—and the sting of a needle was in his wrist.

"Take it easy!" The Mongoose whispered. "A nice long sleep, and you'll be all right again. And tell your boss Graddon his operatives should be more alert."

There was a sharp struggle. But the drug already was at work. The guard's strength ebbed from him almost immediately. His body sagged. The Mongoose chuckled and stretched him comfortably against the wall.

Now he passed swiftly through the gate, kept to the shadows and hurried to the parapet on the avenue side of the building. From another inside pocket of that strange coat he wore he took a small but powerful electric flashlight. He held it over the parapet, directed it at the nearest street corner, and flashed a series of signals.

Down on that corner, where she had left the taxicab, The Mongoose's sister saw those flashes, and hurried into a convenient drug store and into the telephone booth there.

The Mongoose darted back against the building again, went toward the rear of it, keeping always in the dark spots. He stopped beneath an open window. Just inside that window was the telephone, and he could hear if anybody answered it.

But, before the telephone bell jangled, a red glow crept up the side of the apartment house. Puffs of smoke came from half a dozen hall windows. Far down in the avenue, people began giving shouts of alarm.

Inside the penthouse, the telephone bell rang. The Mongoose listened. Presently, the butler answered the call.

"Yes?" he intoned.

"Building on fire," a woman's voice informed him. "Everybody out! Waste no time! This is the switchboard calling!"

CHAPTER VI

LOOT

BEFORE THE BUTLER could relay that information to those in the penthouse, some woman on the verandah screamed. The hoarse voice of a frightened man roared in alarm.

"Fire! Fire!"

The cry that always terrifies.

Fabert's guests rushed to the doors and windows and saw smoke curling up over the parapet, saw a red glow which made it look as though the building was enveloped in flames. Their shrieks and cries pierced the night. They rushed for the gate, toward the elevators, thinking only of getting away. Some of them darted down the stairs for a couple of floors, to be turned back there by billows of pungent smoke.

The great apartment house was in a turmoil. The switchboard

girl was warning tenants in earnest now. It was after two o'clock in the morning. Men and women came from sound sleep to face the horror. They rushed into the corridors, ran to elevators and stairs.

Fire alarms were turned in. A score of telephone messages flashed to Police Headquarters. Nobody stopped to think that this was a new building, as fire-proof as it was possible for a building to be. Leaping flames and billowing smoke furnished evidence enough for eyes.

On the roof there was an immediate exodus. The guests had fled at the first alarm, save three half overcome with intoxicants, and the servants were helping those. Graddon's man, who had been guarding the top of the fire escape, came running to the house, shouting for his chief.

Graddon was bellowing at the butler, demanding to know whether everybody was out. He rushed from the house himself, seemed to hesitate, and then hurried to the elevator. A white-faced boy was waiting for him. The elevator was packed with frightened men and women.

Smoke was curling up the stairs to the roof now. It half filled the elevator shaft. The cage dropped swiftly out of sight.

Crouching beside the building on the dark side, The Mongoose indulged in a chuckle. He had been watching the gate carefully. He knew that everybody was gone, and that he was alone on the roof. And now he rushed to the gate in the wall, slammed it shut, put up the heavy bar and turned the big key in the lock. The wall was one that could not be scaled readily, the gate something that could not be opened without effort.

Into the house The Mongoose rushed, and to the study. He hurled open the door, darted to the corner, worked the sliding panel. The door of the safe was before him.

He worked as swiftly as possible. None knew better than The Mongoose how long the contents of his little bombs would continue to pour forth pungent smoke and a red glare. He knew, too, that the smoke would hang in the halls heavily for some time, and that it was a throat irritant.

He knew that fire apparatus was clogging the streets down below. Trained fire-fighters would be charging into the building. The fleeing tenants and guests would hamper them for a time. But it would not be long before they realized that they could not locate the source of the flames. Then there would be an immediate investigation—and the possibility of somebody guessing right.

The Mongoose had slipped on thin rubber gloves. Now he knelt before the safe and worked the combination as his sister had given it to him. He failed the first time, probably through haste and nervousness. He tried again—and succeeded.

He opened the door, jerked open the drawers inside. In one he found what he sought—glittering jewels, diamonds and rubies and rare emeralds. The Mongoose was a man who appreciated good gems, but he wasted no more than a single glance at these. He dumped them into two small chamois bags he had ready, thrust the bags into his pockets.

Then he got out a small card, and placed it on the floor of the safe he had ransacked. In hand-printing were the words:

With the compliments of The Mongoose

He did not hesitate now. He fled from the study and across the big living room, and out upon the verandah. He stopped there for an instant to listen. From the street far below came a roar as of a mob. Fire engine whistles were screeching. Gongs were clanging.

The smoke was still rolling out of the windows and toward the sky in sluggish clouds and there remained the red glare. But The Mongoose knew it would not last much longer. His bombs were about burned out. The smoke would remain hanging for a time, but the glare of flames would be gone.

And experienced firemen would take a few sniffs and report

that chemicals had been burning, instead of materials from which the building had been constructed.

From the hiding place beneath the end of the verandah, The Mongoose got his hat and coat and put them on. Then he started toward the top of the only fire escape that came up to the roof.

"Hey, you!" a stentorian voice shouted.

The Mongoose whirled. Somebody was pounding at the gate. And a man's head was showing above it. The man was Detective Mark Graddon....

GRADDON HAD succumbed to the panic as had the others. He did not doubt the evidence of his eyes. He saw smoke and thought he saw flames. He heard the butler shouting that the switchboard girl had given an alarm of fire and ordered everybody out.

Graddon thought of nothing in that instant except making sure that nobody was being left behind, and then getting out himself. Henry Fabert's jewels were in a good safe, and the safe was closed and locked. Graddon was in the elevator with a crowd of others and being shot to the ground before he realized quite what had happened.

The lobby of the apartment house was a scene of bedlam. In all stages of dress and undress, men and women were charging through it to the street, fleeing the scene. There was no semblance of order.

Graddon had lost track of his men. He had seen but one, and supposed the other had fled. He did not know that the gate guard was indulging in a drugged sleep.

He watched an elevator being emptied, ordered the operator to go up again, and got into the cage. The shaft was half filled with pungent smoke. Halfway to the roof, the boy stopped the elevator and opened the door.

Graddon had no opportunity to order him to go on up. Men and women charged into the cage, shrieking to be carried down. Graddon managed to get out, and the elevator shot down without him.

The smoke and flames seemed to be only in the front of the building. Graddon ran toward the rear, found the stairs there, and went to the next floor above. Conditions there were the same. Knowing something of fires, Graddon commenced wondering a bit.

And suddenly it flashed upon him that this was a trick of some sort—and a trick of The Mongoose! He remembered that The Mongoose was supposed to be an expert in chemistry and knew a lot about electricity.

Mark Graddon did not waste time waiting for some frenzied elevator operator to answer his signal. He began mounting the rear stairs toward the roof. Two flights caused him to slacken speed. Graddon was overweight, and not in the best of physical condition for this sort of thing. His progress became slower.

Panting and half exhausted, he came to the top. He stumbled over the unconscious body of the gate guard, made a swift examination.

"Drugged!" Graddon muttered. He darted to the gate, to find it locked and barred. His suspicion became certainty now. He pounded upon the gate, howled demands that it be opened. Springing up, he caught the top of the gate with his hands, and pulled himself up until he could peer over.

He saw a man in evening dress rushing from the penthouse, and called to him. The man darted to a patch of shadow, and kept going. Graddon could not continue holding himself to the top of the gate. He dropped back.

Raging, he sought for some way to get the gate open, to get over the wall. He punched the button calling the elevators. He howled down the stairs for help, thinking some of the firemen might hear him. Mark Graddon sensed that it was The Mongoose he had seen on the roof, running from the penthouse.

He stood back, rushed, sprang to the top of the wall, caught it and clung. Inch by inch, he drew himself up. His muscles strained in agony. Perspiration broke out on his forehead. The top of the wall was cutting into his palms.

But finally he managed to throw a leg over. He gathered his remaining strength, made a last supreme effort, and got to the top, to stretch there panting.

Somebody inside sprang and caught him by the leg, and jerked him down. Graddon crashed to the hard pavement of the court, and it half stunned him. He realized that somebody was straddling him, felt a sharp sting in his wrist, knew that he was being drugged.

He tried to fight, but the effort availed him nothing. He could see, dimly, a man with a mop of shaggy blond hair, a mustache, a man who wore spectacles. And then he ceased to see anything.

"You'll be all right in half an hour, Graddon.... This is The Mongoose talking to you.... I'll deal with you personally one of these days. You're on the list!"

Then the voice, too, faded away, and Mark Graddon was in oblivion.

THE MONGOOSE scurried across the roof to the top of the fire escape again. He had delayed to render Graddon helpless, for he feared Graddon might give an alarm which would prevent him doing what he wished to do now.

Down the fire escape he went rapidly, past three floors. He kicked in a window, got inside the building. He found the rear stairs and rushed down them, until he came to where firemen were going through the halls.

They gave him scant attention. Only another frightened tenant rushing to get out of the building, they supposed. They could tell nothing afterward except that he was a man with a mop of blond hair which fell over his eyes.

The Mongoose came to the last flight, descended, and lost himself in the milling crowd. It was the place of greatest security at the moment. Gradually, slowly, he made his way out to the street. He drifted along the walk, and allowed a policeman to hustle him through the fire lines.

Down the street he went through the crowd which had gathered. Around the corner, he met the woman who had called herself Eleanor Carleigh.

"Everything all right?" she whispered.

"Very much all right!"

They walked half a block, hailed a taxi. They rode for half a mile, and got out at a corner. Near the corner, Mr. Sidney Carleigh's roadster was parked, and had been for hours. But it was a street where parking was permitted. He had made sure of that.

Eleanor Carleigh drove. Her brother divested himself of blond wig and mustache, removed wads which had dilated his nostrils, erased make-up which had made him look yellow under his eyes. Then he chuckled.

"Had to handle Graddon at the last," he said. "You mailed those letters?"

"Yes."

"Then every city editor in town will know in the morning just what happened. Graddon will be a joke. And Henry Fabert may have difficulty explaining where he got a fortune in jewels that I found in his safe."

"He'll probably say that The Mongoose got nothing."

"The Mongoose," Sidney Carleigh said, "knows better. Now for a short rest, Eleanor, and then some more planning. There are plenty of others on the list."

He ignited a cigarette, puffed with relish. Eleanor Carleigh increased speed a little and they hurried home.

JEWELS OF THE RAJAH

*Behind Triple-locked Doors in the Inner
Sanctum of Bahadur Lal, The Mongoose Wreaks
a Vengeance That Is More Deadly than Death*

CHAPTER I

BAHADUR LAL

THERE WAS AN unholy gleam in the eyes of the man who called himself Bahadur Lal, as he relaxed in a heavy carved chair banked with cushions, in the quiet seclusion of his innermost private room.

Deftly he loosened the roll of silk with which his throat was swathed and gave a touch of adjustment to his turban, on the front of which glittered valuable jewels.

Then his hand went out languidly to touch a button concealed beneath the edge of the huge Oriental desk before which he sat. Immediately a door was opened on noiseless hinges and a Hindu servant in native costume glided snake-like into the room, with scarcely no more noise than a shadow would have made.

The servant made a deep salaam and stood waiting, with his head bowed and his eyes upon the floor. Bahadur Lal was toying with a dagger encrusted with gleaming gems, as he looked at the man.

"The American Lady—she is waiting?" Bahadur Lal asked.

"The memsahib has been waiting for more than half an hour, Excellency."

"It is written that waiting tauts the nerves and spurs the imagination."

"Your humble servant informed her that Bahadur Lal was in deep communion with the higher powers, and that he could not be disturbed in his meditations."

Bahadur Lal smiled, almost grinned, and his gleaming eyes

*Out of nowhere came the
soft voice of The Mongoose:
"I'll be at your lecture"*

narrowed a trifle more, seeming to send forth flaming flecks of steel.

"The meditations are at an end," he said. "The memsahib has waited long enough, and you may admit her at once. It is written that seeking after knowledge is a virtue in a man, but in woman, only opens the door to devilment."

With that bit of questionable wisdom ringing in his ears, the servant backed to the door and retired. Bahadur Lal rose and straightened his neckcloth, then walked across the thick carpets to a window, which was barred with a network of steel on the outside, and curtained with heavy drapes inside. He looked down upon an ocean of roofs, and at the crisscrossed dark streaks which were streets.

"Excellency!"

It was the soft voice of the servant again. Bahadur Lal turned from the window slowly, gracefully, his head uplifted, his nostrils dilated, and in his face the dreamy expression of one who has been contemplating lofty things.

The servant again was making a deep salaam. Beside him stood a fashionably-gowned young woman, her face flushed and her eyes bright with excitement.

Bahadur Lal waved a hand. The servant withdrew silently and closed the door softly behind him. Then Bahadur Lal approached his guest, and himself salaamed, though an expert might have detected a trace of sarcasm in the gesture.

"Welcome!" he said. He spoke in voice that was deep, rich, vibrant. "It is written that a beautiful woman can make radiant the darkest day."

"You are flattering," she accused.

"You are modest, and in a woman modesty is the fairest flower in the garden of virtues," he said. "Sit here, please, where the light will fall upon your face."

He gestured toward a wide couch heaped with silken cushions. He bowed yet again, as she passed in front of him to sit on the end of the couch. He followed her, but did not offer to sit beside her, taking instead a chair a few feet away.

"I feel greatly honored, Bahadur Lal, to be received in your private study," she said.

"FEW ARE welcomed here," he admitted. "Generally, they create a disturbing influence. But I have sensed, Miss Carleigh, that you are a genuine seeker after the truth and the light, and do not come to me—as do so many others—through curiosity or in pursuit of what some persons call a thrill."

"Your philosophy is wonderful. Oh, if you had nothing to do but think, and teach!" she said. "It is to be regretted that you must mingle your philosophy with more material things."

"You mean my business?" His white teeth flashed in a smile. "Money is so necessary in this Western world, if one is to have comfort. So I am an importer, and a jewel merchant. Thanks to my business, I do not lack for funds. But often I am in sore need of that rare companionship which can come only from another human being in perfect accord."

"I understand," she said. "I did so want to see this room where you meditate. And it is beautiful!"

She got up and roamed around the study with apparent eagerness, while Bahadur Lal followed close behind her. She looked at the rare objects of Oriental art, the massive carved furniture, the silk draperies. Finally she stopped beside the desk and picked up the jeweled dagger.

"This must be worth a fortune," she said. "I never saw anything like it before."

"It was a gift from a rajah," he explained. "Beneath one of the largest jewels, which may be removed easily by one who knows the secret of so doing, there is a tiny cup filled with deadly poison. One but touches the tip of his tongue to it, and his span of life is at an end."

"Oh, how terrible!" She dropped the dagger on the desk, shuddered a bit, and wiped her hands swiftly on a dainty bit of handkerchief. "Why don't you take the poison out of it, Bahadur Lal?"

"It was a gift from the rajah," he reminded her. "Perhaps he thought I might have need of it some day."

"Except for that terrible dagger, I love this room. There isn't a modern touch in it."

"The necessary modern touches are here, but hidden," he explained. "A very necessary modern safe, behind those heavy curtains in the corner. And some pieces of office equipment behind those drapes."

"But you have a regular business office, haven't you?"

"At the front of the building, yes. Here I have only a dictating machine and a filing case in which I keep papers I may wish to peruse privately."

"I understand—a sort of auxiliary office. Thanks for allowing me to see this beautiful room, Bahadur Lal. And now I must leave."

"So soon? Stay yet awhile," he begged. "Let me have you served."

"Not this afternoon, please. I had to wait so long before seeing you, and I have a rather important engagement."

"You will delight me by attending my lecture tomorrow evening?" he asked.

"It will be a privilege."

"And perhaps, after the lecture, we may talk again—in this room?"

"Perhaps," she agreed.

Bahadur Lal pressed the button, and the servant appeared immediately. The jewel merchant bowed before his guest once more as she followed the servant from the room.

Perhaps it was just as well, for his peace of mind, that Bahadur Lal did not see the expression in Eleanor Carleigh's face as she descended in the elevator. And it might have disturbed him a trifle if he had known that she now had, inside her pretty head, a fair map of his private study, and had noted especially the location of the safe.

Bahadur Lal walked to the window again, and looked down over the sea of roofs. His eyes were glowing.

"She is rich, and eager to listen to my philosophy," he muttered. "To her and her friends I shall sell many valuable jewels at a profit. What fools these American women are! And some of the American men, also. Only a few more years, and I may return to my native India and live like a nabob!"

CHAPTER II

THE THREAT

THE SERVANT SOON returned.

"The memsahib has descended in the elevator, Excellency," he reported.

"That is well."

"And here is a small package the memsahib said to give to you. It seems that she picked it up from the floor of the corridor, where undoubtedly it had been dropped by some careless and unworthy person. The package is addressed to you, hence the memsahib handed it to me."

"Put it there on the desk."

The servant obeyed, and retired. Bahadur Lal turned from the window, back to the desk, and picked up the package. He saw that his name and address were indeed written on the wrapping. He tore away a layer of paper, and exposed a small pasteboard box, which he opened.

Inside the box, he found what looked like a roll of cotton. He took it out, unwrapped it, and held in his hand a small cylinder. It was a record for a dictaphone.

Bahadur Lal paled slightly. He drew in his breath with a little hissing sound. His eyes glistened like those of a cobra. And then an ironic smile played around the corners of his mouth.

"So it has come to me," he muttered, "even as it came to some of the others. Perhaps, this time, the result will be entirely different. It is written that a well may become dry, if visited too often."

Now he stepped briskly across the room and drew aside some of the silk draperies, exposing a dictaphone, a desk and chair. Bahadur Lal seated himself in front of the machine, into which he often dictated notes for his lectures on philosophy.

He seemed to hesitate for a moment, as though gathering courage for an ordeal. Then he slipped the record on the dictaphone, adjusted the ear tubes, and started the machine.

With his face an inscrutable mask, he listened to the message of the record:

> Hello, Bahadur Lal, as you call yourself! This is The Mongoose speaking. I am sending you this to warn you that you're the next man on my list. And I strike soon!
>
> Ten years ago when certain rich men were caught perpetrating a swindle and faced prison terms, they saved themselves by giving perjured testimony and sending an innocent bookkeeper, William Cratch, to prison, where he died.
>
> You accepted money to give false evidence, and so helped convict, him. You helped blacken his name and send him to a living hell, for money!
>
> William Cratch was my father. I am avenging him. I have

struck at several of the guilty men. You are the next! For your sin, you must pay!

The record came to an end. The ringing voice of The Mongoose was still.

Bahadur Lal removed the tube from his ears. Then he bent forward and watched the little cylinder.

According to what he had been told, these cylinder records sent to prospective victims by the man who called himself The Mongoose soon melted and disappeared, leaving no trace. There was nothing so very remarkable in that—the cylinders simply had been treated chemically, so that they disintegrated after being exposed to the open air for a certain length of time.

GETTING SLOWLY to his feet, Bahadur Lal stood over the dictaphone and watched closely as the little bubbles formed on the record's surface. The bubbles grew larger, and spread. The cylinder seemed to be melting away. Soon, it was gone. The last damp spots disappeared.

Bahadur Lal sighed. "So it is with man," he observed. "For that which we receive, we must pay. But at times it is delicious to postpone payment as long as possible."

His mind flashed back a decade, to the time when he had committed perjury for profit, and without thought of the consequences to the helpless victim. Now, an avenger was abroad. Regardless of the merits of the case, Bahadur Lal felt it his duty to put up what fight he could.

He walked across the room to the big desk and reached for a telephone concealed in the cabinet at the end of it. Swiftly he dialed a number.

"Hello," a gruff voice said.

"Is this Detective Mark Graddon?"

"Right."

"It is Bahadur Lal talking, sahib."

"Howdy, Bahadur Lal! Haven't heard from you in a long time. What can I do for you?"

"If it is possible, sahib, I wish you would do me the honor of coming to my place immediately. I have received something which calls for your attention. A little box, sahib, with a dicta-phone record in it."

"What?" Mark Graddon cried. "You've been sent one of those things?"

"It is so, sahib. I have listened to it, and it has disappeared, as did the others. It spoke rather harshly of me, sahib, and informed me that I am the next on the list."

"I'll come right over there," Graddon said. "Watch yourself till I arrive. Get some of your trusted men around you. Keep your eyes open."

"In my private room, sahib, nobody can reach me."

"Yeah? I've seen this Mongoose work before. Don't take any chances. He can get through a keyhole, or maybe through a solid wall."

Bahadur Lal replaced the receiver on its hook and returned the telephone to the cabinet. He sat down in front of the desk, and seemed to meditate. If he felt even a modicum of fear, he did not reveal it in face or actions.

In less than twenty minutes, Detective Mark Graddon came bustling into the room. Big, burly, florid of face, raucous in speech and decisive in action, Mark Graddon was the sort of man to give anyone assurance.

"So you got one of the things, huh?" Graddon asked. "We'll get right down to business, Bahadur Lal. I want to catch this Mongoose. I'm in this here thing personally, understand. I was in that deal ten years ago—framed some of the fake evidence. The Mongoose'll be comin' after me next."

"In an evil moment, years ago, I accepted money for bearing false witness," Bahadur Lal said. "For that which we receive, we always must pay. My business was tottering at the time. Since then, I have prospered. Those I served evilly sent much business my way, as they promised. If the time now has come for me to pay—" He ceased speaking, and waved a perfumed cigarette in gesture.

"Are you goin' to lay down and give up?" Mark Graddon snapped at him.

"No, sahib. You misunderstand me. I shall fight, naturally, with you to aid me. The Mongoose, sahib, is of my native India, as is also the deadly cobra which it attacks. Who should know better than I how to deal with the mongoose?"

"THAT'S THE stuff, Bahadur Lal! We'll land this baby, and put an end to him runnin' around wild and robbin' folks. Now— what is there here for him to steal?"

"Sahib! I have a fortune in this establishment."

"The Mongoose doesn't play for small stakes, remember. He goes after big stuff."

"Small stakes? For one thing, I have now in my safe, sahib, jewels worth the ransom of a king."

"Yeah? Then they go into safety deposit the first thing in the mornin'—too late today."

"They are perhaps all right here, sahib. I have certain means of guarding them."

"Yeah, and The Mongoose probably knows all about the means you've got. Your servants and clerks—"

"Four men—my own people."

"You trust all of them!"

"Absolutely!" Bahadur Lal said.

"Well, you're here on the fifteenth floor of the building. You've got all the floor north of the corridor. It's an easy place to watch and guard. I'll scatter some of my men around."

"But business must go on as usual, sahib. There must not be a hint of anything wrong. I refuse to flatter this Mongoose by revealing the slightest timidity. It is written that the brave man walks with his head erect and his face lifted to the sky."

"Yeah? I'll bet it's also written that, if he doesn't watch his step, he might trip over a stick. Business as usual, then—we can watch your customers."

"And I am giving a small lecture on oriental philosophy tomorrow evening, sahib, in my private hall here."

"Put it off."

"Sahib! And have this Mongoose think that I fear him and his works? That is impossible!"

"Then give your confounded lecture! How many people will be here, and who are they?"

"Not more than twenty, sahib. All ladies and gentlemen of position."

"We can check on them, and watch 'em. Maybe The Mongoose will try to pry his way in here then," Mark Graddon said. "I'll have some of my men get over here right away. We can't make a move until The Mongoose comes here and starts somethin' himself, but we'll be ready for him."

"A state of preparedness is always commendable."

"You can be prepared for a few shocks," Mark Graddon told him. "Don't forget that The Mongoose is a shark on chemistry and electricity. He's full of tricks."

"Then the conflict should be interesting, sahib. I also, am full of tricks. Oriental tricks, sahib. I have them scattered all around this place."

"Maybe you'd better put me wise, Bahadur Lal."

"It is written, sahib, that when a trick is explained, it is no longer a trick."

"Uh-huh!" Mark Graddon grunted. "Anyhow, I hope this stunt will be The Mongoose's last."

"It is written, sahib, that we do not know what is being held for us in the storehouse of fate."

"Yeah? Have it your own way, Bahadur Lal! All I'm achin' for is a fair and square chance at The Mongoose! If he comes prowlin' around me, I'll give him a dose of fate out of the business end of a gun! That's written, too!"

CHAPTER III

A DISTURBING VOICE

MARK GRADDON WENT to the telephone and called his office. He gave certain orders about men being sent to him immediately. Then he faced Bahadur Lal again.

"Where's your safe?" he asked. "I don't mean the one in your front office, either. I mean the safe where you keep jewels hidden away?"

"What leads you to believe I have a second safe, sahib?"

"You're with friends, Lal! We're tarred with the same brush, Bahadur, old pal! I know damned well that you sell many a gem that never paid an import duty, and you can bet you don't keep stock like that in the safe in the front office. You come clean with me! If I'm goin' to protect you from The Mongoose, I've got to know what I'm protectin'. Where's that safe?"

Bahadur Lal flashed his teeth in a grin, and then started to make reply. But, instead, his lower jaw sagged and he looked at Mark Graddon from bulging eyes. From somewhere had come a soft, even voice:

"The safe you're talking about, Graddon, is in the northeast corner of the room, behind those heavy silk draperies."

Mark Graddon whirled around swiftly, darted to the draperies and pulled them aside, ran to some more and pulled them aside also. He would have made a wager that somebody hiding behind those drapes had spoken.

"Sahib—"Bahadur Lal began. He was as yet unable to control his facial expression. "That voice, sahib?"

"Yeah, that voice! Where did it come from?" Graddon asked.

"It seemed to be in this very room."

"And did it give the right dope about the safe?"

"Yes, sahib. The safe is where the voice said. But, consider!

That voice answered you, which means that whoever spoke has been hearing our talk."

Again the voice came to them: "I hear everything you say. I know everything you do. This is The Mongoose speaking! Graddon, your efforts will be futile. Bahadur Lal, you might as well submit to fate. I have a debt to collect."

"Can you hear me, Mongoose?" Bahadur Lal asked the question in an ordinary tone.

"I hear you well, Bahadur Lal. It is written that your very thoughts are loud cries in my ears." The speech was followed by a series of chuckles.

"Then hear me, Mongoose!" Bahadur Lal cried. "I am not as the others you have attacked. I am not the plain, matter-of-fact, material man of the West. I sense, I feel! Mysteries are solved for me."

"Giving a lecture on philosophy, Bahadur Lal?" The Mongoose asked.

"I'll match you, trick for trick, Mongoose!"

"Good hunting!"

Mark Graddon got into this queer conversation. "Me, I'm one of them matter-of-fact men of the West," he said. "There's one of that devil's queer machines around here some place, and I'm goin' to find it and rip it out!"

"Wasting your time, Graddon," the voice of The Mongoose assured him. "You'd do a lot better to think of protecting yourself. You're on my list, Graddon, and I'll be coming after you soon! You were one of the fiends who sent an innocent man to die behind stone walls!"

"Come after me any time you're ready, Mongoose!"

"Now we all understand one another," The Mongoose's voice said.

GRADDON CLUTCHED Bahadur Lal by the sleeve.

"Let's get into some other room and talk," he said.

"It is uncanny, sahib, this being overheard by somebody we know is present but cannot see."

"Nothin' uncanny about it!" Graddon exploded. "He's got a wireless dictograph planted around here somewhere, and when my men arrive I'll have 'em find it. He used that stunt before."

Again, a sarcastic chuckle came out of nowhere to smite their ears.

"Making a wild guess, aren't you, Graddon?" The Mongoose asked. "Perhaps I am using something new. Go ahead with your arrangements. They don't interest me. Nothing you can do will prevent me from making Bahadur Lal pay, when I'm ready to do so."

"When are you goin' to come after him?" Graddon asked.

The Mongoose chuckled again. "It is written that uncertainty keys the nerves," he said, in imitation of Bahadur Lal.

Mark Graddon beckoned Bahadur Lal, and they left the private room, carefully fastening the door. They went along a hall toward the showroom of the establishment.

Bahadur Lal had living quarters here for himself and his four Oriental servants and clerks. He had the little lecture hall, and a consultation room. He had a couple of private rooms for the showing of fine jewels, and the front office. The showroom was large. Oriental art objects and furniture were on display.

In one of the private rooms they sat down at a table and bent across it.

"I'm having three men come here at once," Graddon said. "I'll keep that many here day and night till this thing is over. You see that they get fed from your kitchen."

"Certainly, sahib."

"I want a list of the folks who are comin' to your lecture tomorrow night—if you know."

Bahadur Lal took a slip of paper out of his pocket. "Here is the list, sahib."

And out of the nowhere came the soft voice of The Mongoose

again: "Put my name at the bottom, Bahadur Lal. I'll be at your lecture."

Bahadur Lal gave a cry of rage and sprang to his feet. For a moment, he was a picture of Oriental fury. His hand darted to his waist and grasped the jeweled hilt of a knife that had not before been visible. Then he smiled faintly, and relaxed.

"It was foolish of me to be startled," Bahadur Lal said. "I forgot myself for a moment, and paid the fellow a compliment. We shall ignore him, sahib, as one unworthy of attention."

"So he can hear us in here, too," Mark Graddon said. "Maybe we'd better get up on the roof and write notes back and forth. If I ever get my hands on that rogue—"

"Graddon," the voice of The Mongoose interrupted. "Your men have arrived. Better get busy and give them orders. They're in the front room."

"How do you know that—if it's true?" Graddon cried at the bare wall in front of him.

"I hear them talking to one of Bahadur Lal's clerks. Give them my regards, please."

The Mongoose chuckled again. But Graddon did not wait to hear the chuckle. With Bahadur Lal close behind him, he darted from the little room, ran along the hall, and went into the front room. His men had arrived, as The Mongoose said!

"So he knew!" Bahadur Lal spoke in a whisper.

"Don't get worked up about it," Graddon told him. "Hearin' us talk is one thing, but comin' here and gettin' away with swag is somethin' else again. He's got me mad now, Bahadur Lal. I'm goin' to land that Mongoose! He won't make a monkey of me again!"

CHAPTER IV

DOABLE PREPARATION

MARK GRADDON'S ASSISTANTS were tried and true men who had followed him through cases which called for a mingling of brain power and physical strength. He posted one in the corridor outside the door, one in the showroom, and left one to roam around the place, making his rounds like a watchman.

"I'll have 'em relieved every four hours," he told Bahadur Lal. "You go right ahead with your business and your work, and leave the rest to me."

"I place myself in your hands, sahib."

"Thanks, but that ain't enough," Graddon said. "Use your own wits, too. You said something about tricks."

"I have a few little traps, sahib, that I have devised in my odd moments."

"See that they are in workin' order." He stepped close to Bahadur Lal and whispered: "I'll be back some time this evenin'. We've got to catch this Mongoose. We've managed so far to keep from the dear public the real reason for his work, but it may leak out. Then there'll be fireworks!"

"I understand, sahib."

"We haven't been able to get a line on The Mongoose. We haven't set eyes on him since he pulled off his first stunt. No two ways about it—he's a slicker! And we'll be still slicker if we catch him!"

Graddon's men were changed at intervals, but the night passed without incident, save that Bahadur Lal did not rest as well as usual. In the morning he showed the strain under which he was laboring.

Graddon came and went as much as he could without causing comment. Bahadur Lal's shop did the usual amount of business, but there were no suspicious customers. Graddon and his men searched the place, but located nothing unusual. If The Mongoose had special contrivances hidden there, they could not be found.

Again, the shop was closed for the day. Gates of metal shut off the showroom from the remainder of the floor. The front office was locked. Bahadur Lal retired to his private quarters. Graddon had five men there to keep a sharp vigil.

The lecture was to be at nine o'clock in the evening. The guests would enter by the front door, pass along a hall, and go into the little lecture room. Graddon made a close examination of this lecture room.

It seemed quite ordinary, except for some Oriental decorations. In half a dozen places there were huge incense burners, and the lighting effects were unusual. But Graddon failed to see anything of which The Mongoose could make use.

Half an hour before the guests were due to arrive, he made his final arrangements. One man was stationed in the corridor. One was in the dark showroom. One was in the little hall that ran to Bahadur Lal's study. And two were to be in the lecture room to deal with any situation that might develop there.

"We're ready, Bahadur Lal," he reported. "If that Mongoose starts anything around here tonight, he's goin' to get the worst of it. He may try some fancy stunt. But we'll have our eyes on everything, including your guests. Got all the arrangements made."

"I thank you, sahib."

They were in the little lecture room. Bahadur Lal was lighting the incense. He already had ignited it in the pots out in the hall, and the exotic fumes were being wafted throughout the place. Bahadur Lal was a good stage manager. But others were making arrangements, too.

IN A luxurious apartment some distance away, Eleanor Carleigh, looking wonderfully attractive in a gorgeous evening gown, and an evening wrap inside the lining of which several unusual articles were stowed, was looking with admiration at her brother, Sidney.

"The plan is great, Sid," she said. "Hope nothing goes wrong."

"Nothing will go wrong," he replied.

"I'm always so afraid for you."

"And never for yourself? You do as much as I, Eleanor."

"We won't argue about that again, Sid. I hope you get every jewel that fiend's got. He's a snake! He's got the meanest eyes!"

"You are speaking of Bahadur Lal, the great philosopher?" Sidney Carleigh chuckled.

"The great faker!" she corrected. "Oh, Sid, to sit there and have him smirk at me, and try to take my hand! And to remember he was one of the men who sent our father—"

"Heads up!" he said, quickly. "Keep your mind on the night's work, honey."

"I will, Sid."

"I certainly startled Bahadur Lal and Graddon yesterday afternoon when I talked to them out of the air. It took us some time to get those wireless dictograph disks planted, but we did a good job."

She broke in: "It's time to be going, Sid."

"I'm ready. Got everything."

"Sid, you act like a boy starting out to play a prank. Don't you ever realize your danger? If they could catch you, they'd stop at nothing. They're afraid you'll tell everything. Graddon never would take you to jail. Why, he'd—"

"He'd probably shoot me down, and say he did it while I was trying to escape," Sidney Carleigh supplied. "I refuse to let myself think of the risk. Let's get along! Don't forget your part in the night's show. Got everything?"

"I'm ready," she said.

They went down in the elevator, and got into a coupé waiting at the curb. Sidney Carleigh drove. At their destination, they parked the car in the side street, walked around to the entrance of the building and went up to the fifteenth floor. They were alone in the elevator, arriving a bit late purposely.

"No danger of him starting the lecture before I arrive," Eleanor had said. "The beast thinks that he's working me to buy jewels."

"Don't forget about the private room."

"I'll not, Sid. I watched the servant yesterday and I know how to open the door."

"And the antidote—"

"I'll have it ready."

Graddon had taken his man out of the corridor and placed him just inside the front door of Bahadur Lal's establishment. He eyed the pair as they entered. Bahadur Lal was waiting a short distance down the hall. Another of Graddon's men was not far away. The other guests had gone on to the lecture room.

Carleigh never had met Bahadur Lal personally, and now he accepted an introduction rather coldly.

"I'll call for you, Eleanor," he said.

"Will you not honor me by remaining for my poor lecture, sahib?" Bahadur Lal asked.

"Sorry, but I've got a date more interesting—for me. Some other time, perhaps. My sister seems interested in your line of stuff."

"I intend giving her special private lessons," Bahadur Lal explained. "She has a receptive mind. I'll take good care of her, sahib, until you call for her."

Eleanor Carleigh had moved aside during this conversation. She had brushed against the pedestal, on top of which was the incense pot. For a moment, her hand hovered over the pot and her fingers drifted back and forth through the streaming smoke.

Sidney Carleigh went out and descended in the elevator. He knew that Graddon's men had overheard that conversation, and that they saw him leave.

And Eleanor Carleigh, forcing herself to smile, accepted the arm of Bahadur Lal and allowed herself to be escorted to the lecture room, where the others were waiting.

She remained standing a moment, while Bahadur Lal went forward to the platform. She seemed to be adjusting her wrap. But her hand again hovered for an instant over an incense pot.

CHAPTER V

SLUMBERING FOES

DETECTIVE MARK GRADDON felt slightly uncomfortable in that select company. But he told himself that he was there strictly on business. Catching The Mongoose was imperative. Graddon's clients were commencing to wonder what he was going to do about it. They were tired of being robbed.

They could not call in other detectives without revealing the truth about what happened ten years before. And unless The Mongoose was captured, and dealt with violently, greater trouble might come. The Mongoose had in his possession documents which would expose that old swindle.

Mark Graddon had been promised certain rich monetary rewards if he caused The Mongoose to cease his activities. Then, too, he had a very personal interest, For that reason he was doubly alert tonight, as he had urged his men to be.

Two of the men were in the lecture room with him. The door was closed. One was in the hall, one in the showroom, and one, now, in the front office. Bahadur Lal's four Hindu clerks and servants were in their quarters in the rear of the building.

Bahadur Lal began his lecture. He talked in a crooning voice that lulled the senses. The incense fumes permeated the room. The lights were low, and colored, making grotesque shadows.

Mark Graddon knew a stage setting when he saw one, so he only sniffed a bit at this. He was watching Bahadur Lal. If he watched Bahadur Lal, he reasoned, he would see The Mongoose if the latter appeared. If The Mongoose tried to strike elsewhere in the building during the lecture, Graddon's men would get him!

However, Graddon was leaving nothing to chance. He sat near the door. He decided that he would slip out presently and have a look around. He wanted to get away, anyhow. He didn't like the confounded incense. The place reeked with it.

The soft voice of Bahadur Lal droned on. His guests, both men and women, relaxed in their easy chairs and tried to follow the speaker's line of reasoning. If the voice of Bahadur Lal grew softer, weaker, they did not notice it. For their sense of hearing had grown weaker, too. They ceased following the speaker's words.

Heads drooped, arms relaxed. One elderly gentleman slipped out of his chair and sprawled on the floor. Mark Graddon, sitting near the door, noticed that one of his men looked as though he were asleep. He decided to slip over and shake him, whisper a rebuke. But he found he was weak and sleepy himself. He could not get out of the chair. He tried to cry out, call for help, and his lower jaw sagged and only a little meaningless mutter came from his lips.

"That… incense…" Mark Graddon guessed. Then he ceased to be concerned about it.

Miss Eleanor Carleigh had been holding a handkerchief to her face continually, to her nostrils the greater part of the time. Concealed in the handkerchief was a tiny sponge, saturated with a pungent liquid. It was this liquid which brought tears to her eyes, and not the incense smoke.

She watched those in the room. She saw them fall asleep. She watched Bahadur Lal as he sagged forward on the desk beside which he had been standing to lecture, and saw him drop to the floor. Then she got up and moved swiftly to the door, and opened it cautiously.

She glided silently into the hall. The hall, too, reeked of

incense. She kept the handkerchief to her nose as she hurried along.

One of Graddon's men was sprawled unconscious in the hall. Afraid that he might be noticed through the door by anybody passing in the corridor, she tugged at the unconscious man and got him back in the shadows. Through the metal gate, she could see the detective in the showroom, where he had dropped to the floor. She hurried on to the glass door of the front office, which was standing partly open. Graddon's man, who had been stationed there was also unconscious.

Hurrying to the corridor, Eleanor Carleigh opened it and peered out. Nobody was in the corridor. The elevator indicator told that a car was ascending, an express car. She smiled a bit, and drew back into the room.

Sidney Carleigh got out of the elevator and hurried along the corridor toward the door. His sister opened it.

"Everything all right?" he asked.

"So far, Sid."

"Let's hurry, honey!"

They sped to the lecture room, and Sidney Carleigh stooped and lifted the unconscious form of Bahadur Lal. His sister going ahead to show the way, he carried the Hindu to his innermost private room. Eleanor opened the door, working a little catch as she had seen the servant do it the day before.

They made another trip to the lecture room, and this time Carleigh picked up Mark Graddon, which was an entirely different matter. Graddon was heavy.

"Put more stuff in the incense, and close the door," he directed. "More in the pot in the hall, too. Give me a whiff of that handkerchief, or the stuff'll be getting me!"

Graddon was carried to the private room and stretched on the floor beside Bahadur Lal.

"Stay in here till I knock," Carleigh said.

"Where are you going, Sid?"

"Four Hindus in the rear. Want to be sure they won't come bothering around."

"Be careful, Sid!"

"I'm not Sid now," he objected. "This is The Mongoose you see before you."

HE HURRIED out again into the other narrow hall and slipped along it toward the rear. The Mongoose had a map of the place in his brain. He knew where the four Hindus would be found, unless Bahadur Lal had given them special orders.

At a certain door, he stopped to listen. Voices came to him from the room beyond. The Mongoose fumbled in a pocket and brought forth a little blowpipe. He inserted the end of it in the keyhole. Gently, he blew a fine powder into the room where the four servants were talking.

Then he stood back, waited. He wanted to be sure that the stuff did its work, that the powder became a choking gas which would be even more potent in that closed room than the incense smoke, charged with the same drug, had been elsewhere.

Presently he heard the thud of a falling body. There was a jabbering of talk. Another thud! A strangled cry! A hand fumbling at the doorknob.

The Mongoose whipped an automatic out of his hip pocket and held it ready. As the door was opened, he threw his left arm across his face, to hide his features. He prepared to strike with the gun, rather than shoot.

But he was not compelled to resort to such force. The servant who opened the door swayed and crashed to the floor as he started to leave the room. The Mongoose tossed him back into it, glanced in at the others, then closed the door and locked it on the outside, and threw the key away.

Now he hurried back to Bahadur Lal's private room and gave his signal. Eleanor Carleigh opened the door. The Mongoose darted inside.

"Everything okay," he said. "Now, to get to work here."

"They haven't moved, Sid?"

"Not with their lungs filled with that stuff," he said.

He put on thin rubber gloves. From beneath his coat he took a coil of fine, strong twine. Deftly, he bound Mark Graddon's wrists behind his back, and tied his ankles together.

"Got the sponge, Eleanor?"

"It's ready, Sid."

"Hold it a moment till I get this corner of the room fixed up."

The corner he meant was the one opposite that which held Bahadur Lal's private safe. He pushed the silk draperies aside, parted them and left them so.

"How about the sheet of glass?" Eleanor said.

"Here's the package behind the file case," The Mongoose replied. "Getting that in here was the worst part of the job. The seals aren't broken, so nobody has been prying. No evidence against you."

From behind the file case, he brought a flat package about four feet long and two wide. It was wrapped in heavy paper. Without breaking the seals, The Mongoose removed the twine which bound the package.

Inside that package was a dainty water-color painting, in a light frame. And, behind the painting, was a sheet of glass the same size. The Mongoose removed the glass, did the package up again, and replaced it behind the file case.

All very simple! Eleanor Carleigh had left that package there a few days before, asking Bahadur Lal to put it in his private room and keep it for her. It was a water color she wished to give a friend, she had said, after tonight's lecture. And Bahadur Lal, were he to look at that package now, would swear that it had not been touched.

The Mongoose had propped the sheet of glass up between the parted draperies.

"Hurry!" Eleanor was urging.

"Nothing to worry about, honey. They won't wake up for another hour or more. Turn that light this way, please."

Obediently, she turned the desk lamp, the only one burning in the room. And she saw The Mongoose doing a strange thing.

From beneath his coat he took a mask. Not an ordinary false mask, but a mask expertly made, a thin affair that fitted snugly to the face and throat. He put it on, after stuffing his soft hat into a coat pocket.

Then he brought forth a turban, and put it quickly on his head.

"Well?" he asked.

"Perfect!" she said. "So perfect that it makes me shudder. Two of you is too much!"

She turned the light away so that it did not strike him directly. He got down behind the sheet of glass. The mask was that of Bahadur Lal. In the dim light, it seemed the face of Bahadur Lal that leered in the corner.

"Use the sponge," The Mongoose directed. "Turn that little desk light the other way. We're ready for the last act."

CHAPTER VI

GLITTERING SWAG

ELEANOR CARLEIGH HELD the sponge first beneath the nostrils of Detective Mark Graddon. She allowed him to inhale some of the vapor, and then squeezed a few drops of the liquid on his mustache. Then she went on to Bahadur Lal, who was stretched, unbound, on the thick carpet at the end of the desk.

"It won't take them long to come back to life," The Mongoose warned. "I'd better not talk any more now. Don't forget your part, honey."

"Trust me!"

"Be a fine little actress now!"

Then, The Mongoose was silent, crouching behind the sheet of glass in the darkness. With the desk light turned as it now was, he could not be seen at all.

Eleanor Carleigh left Bahadur Lal, presently, and went to the other side of the room, where she sprawled on the end of the divan. She waited until she heard one of the men moaning and moving a bit, and began uttering low moans herself.

Mark Graddon was the first of the two men to return to full consciousness. He struggled with the twine which bound his wrists and ankles, vainly trying to work free. He rolled over on the floor and saw Bahadur Lal stretched at the end of the desk in the dim light.

He heard moans, and twisted his head and saw Eleanor Carleigh sprawled on the end of the divan, acting as though she was trying to sit up.

"Wh-what happened?" Graddon mouthed. The full strength of his voice had not returned. "Where—"

Eleanor Carleigh moaned again, dropped back on the divan as though exhausted from her efforts to move. Mark Graddon tugged at his bonds once more. He rolled to the wall, propped himself up against it, tried to see better.

And now Bahadur Lal felt the effects of the reviving vapor he had breathed into his lungs. He began moaning feverishly, and presently rolled over against the desk.

"Bahadur Lal!" Graddon cried at him. "Wake up, and help me! Get these ropes off!"

Bahadur Lal sat up on the floor, holding his hands to his reeling head. Without speaking, he pulled himself erect, clung to the desk.

"What—what—" he gasped.

"Snap out of it!" Graddon begged. "Get me untied! Help that woman, whoever she is! She seems to be sick."

Eleanor Carleigh raised herself again, sat up on the divan, pretended to be ill and weak, but really was watching them closely. She lurched to her feet as Bahadur Lal started weakly across the room, staggered against him, clung to him so he could not go to Mark Graddon's aid.

"What has happened, Bahadur Lal?" she asked. "We're here in

your private room. There's some other man here, too. I—I grew sick in the lecture hall—"

"It's that Mongoose!" Graddon roared. "Help me, Bahadur Lal! Young woman, if he ain't sensible yet, come here and untie me! No time to lose!"

"The Mongoose!" Bahadur Lal exclaimed. He thrust Eleanor Carleigh aside, rushed to the corner and pulled back the draperies, exposing the front of the safe. "But he hasn't been here!"

"My wrists and ankles are tied!" Graddon bellowed. "Wake up! Get me loose! If that devil is at work around here—"

BAHADUR LAL seemed to come to a full realization of the situation. Once more, he started across the room. But a voice came out of the darkness, seemed to fill the room. Bahadur Lal and Mark Graddon heard that voice again, as they had heard it in this room the day before—the voice of The Mongoose.

"Stop, Bahadur Lal! Touch Mark Graddon now, and you die! You little know the trap I've arranged. All your guests, and servants, and Graddon's men are unconscious. Worrying about your jewels, Bahadur Lal? The rajah's jewels? Perhaps they are gone already. A bad thing for you, if they are!"

Forgotten, as far as Bahadur Lal was concerned, was Mark Graddon and his plight, and even Eleanor Carleigh. The rajah's jewels! They had been smuggled into the country to him. He had orders to sell them slowly, and get the best prices he could. The funds were to be sent to the rajah secretly. He desired to use them in fomenting an uprising in the hills. And the rajah would accept no explanations if anything happened to those jewels! Their loss would be the same as a death warrant for Bahadur Lal.

He gave a wild cry and rushed across the room. Somebody laughed mockingly—The Mongoose. Bahadur Lal did not doubt for a moment but that the voice of The Mongoose had come to him mysteriously as it had the day before. He did not dream that The Mongoose was in the private study.

Down before the safe, Bahadur Lal went to his knees. He worked feverishly at the combination knob. The perspiration was standing out on his forehead. Mark Graddon continued to howl for release, but Bahadur Lal ignored him.

"You—young woman!" Graddon shouted. "Come here and help me! Get this rope off!"

"I—I'm afraid!" Eleanor Carleigh said. "Oh, I want to get away!"

She acted in such a manner as to allay any suspicion Graddon might have felt. She turned deaf ears to his begging. Going to the divan again, she dropped on the end of it as though exhausted.

Bahadur Lal concluded working the combination, and pulled open the heavy door of the safe. Inside was a series of strongboxes, each with its special combination, Bahadur Lal worked one of these knobs, and pulled a strongbox open. He jerked it out and carried it to the desk beneath the light. He dumped the contents on the desk, opened chamois bags, spilled beneath the light a brilliant, scintillating shower of rare gems—diamonds and emeralds, rubies and pearls.

"They're here—not gone!" he cried. "They're safe! The rajah would never have forgiven—"

Out of the darkness came a voice in interruption:

"Stand back. Bahadur Lal! Quickly, or you die! At once!"

Bahadur Lal sprang backward, startled. Soft laughter filled the room.

"Thanks, Bahadur Lal, for opening the safe and getting the jewels out for me," the voice of The Mongoose said. "You kindly solved a very difficult problem."

With a cry of alarm, Bahadur Lal started for the desk again. In a corner of the room, a gun barked, flame split the darkness. A bullet whistled past within inches of Bahadur Lal's head, and thudded into the wall.

"Back!" The Mongoose cried.

Bahadur Lal recoiled. From the dark corner slipped the form of a man. A choking sound came from Bahadur Lal's throat. It was not caused by the fact that the intruder held a menacing automatic, or that Bahadur Lal's own evening cape was wrapped around his shoulders.

The face! Bahadur Lal saw that the face was his own. The sight of it made his brain reel.

"What cussed trick—" Graddon began.

The Mongoose was chuckling again. He rushed to the desk, and began scooping up the jewels. He menaced Bahadur Lal with the gun again when he started forward. The jewels disappeared beneath the cape somewhere.

Despite the menace of the gun, Bahadur Lal would have dashed forward then, risked death to recover those jewels. It meant death if they were taken away. The rajah—Bahadur Lal knew him well—knew some of the men the rajah would probably send after him.

But Eleanor Carleigh was waiting for that. She sprang forward and clutched Bahadur Lal around the neck.

"Take me away!" she begged. "Get me out of this awful place. I—I can't stand it!"

In the instant when Bahadur Lal's eyes were turned toward her, The Mongoose disappeared.

CHAPTER VII

THE BOOK IS CLOSED

"GET ME LOOSE!" Mark Graddon howled again, as he tugged at the twine which held his wrists lashed together. "Watch yourself, Bahadur Lal! Get to the door! Call somebody to help! The Mongoose is in that corner. He can't get out of this room except through the door."

Soft laughter came from the corner. A light glowed as The Mongoose used a tiny electric torch. The beam struck the mask, making a ghostly replica of Bahadur Lal's countenance behind the sheet of glass.

"Give me your attention, please!" The Mongoose said. "I have taken the rajah's jewels, Bahadur Lal. That is the price you pay for what you did ten years ago."

"It is written," said Bahadur Lal, "that fowls come home to roost."

"It is fortunate that you can apply your philosophy to such an emergency," The Mongoose replied. "I could have harmed you while you were unconscious, but did not. I only wanted the jewels. I'll dispose of them and give the money to some worthy charity."

"I have but to rush upon you—" Bahadur Lal began.

"And die!"

"And what matters that? You have slain me already. I know the price the rajah will exact."

"The Mongoose never killed anybody yet. I don't want to commence with you. Mr. Graddon!"

"Well?" Graddon snarled.

"I brought you here and restored you to consciousness because I wished to tell you something face to face. I know what would happen to me, if you caught me. You'd never turn me over to the police. You'd simply slaughter me, to seal my lips and protect yourself and your employers. I just want to warn you, Graddon, that it would not do any good. Certain documents would be handed to the district attorney, in case of my death."

"Yeah? It'd be a weak case, without you to back it up with testimony. Don't bank on that, Mongoose. I'm goin' to get you, if it takes a lifetime."

"Meanwhile, I shall go ahead with my work of vengeance," The Mongoose said. "Tonight's work has been profitable. I have the rajah's famous jewels."

"But you're not out of here with 'em yet!" Mark Graddon cried. "Now, Mongoose, we'll see what's what!"

Mark Graddon had not worked in vain. He had continued tugging at the twine which bound his wrists. One of the strands had slipped. Graddon had continued his work, though the twine cut into his wrists and brought blood.

AND NOW his wrists were free. He did not have a chance to free his ankles also. But he could get at the gun he wore.

He lurched to one side and his hand darted to his shoulder holster. The movement was seen plainly even in the dim light. Eleanor Carleigh screamed, sudden fear for The Mongoose seizing her.

As swiftly as he could work the gun, Graddon emptied it straight at the mask across the room. The pencil of light which illuminated it went out. There came the sound of a glass crash.

Eleanor Carleigh screamed again. Laughter came from the dark corner—the laughter of The Mongoose.

"Your gun is empty now, Graddon," he said. "And it may interest you to know that I had a sheet of bullet-proof glass before me."

"Charge him, Bahadur Lal!" Graddon cried.

Graddon had courage. Knowing that The Mongoose was armed, he untied his ankles and hurled himself across the room. And Bahadur Lal, a sentence of death upon him already if he did not recover the rajah's jewels, rushed after him.

There came another laugh from The Mongoose. He sprang away from the corner, and let them charge past him. As they passed, he fired.

But he did not shoot bullets to cut them down. From the muzzle of the weapon he held now came a stream of vapor. It engulfed them, got into their eyes and nostrils and mouths, blinded them, choked them, sent them reeling back against the wall, to grow weak swiftly and slump down to the floor.

The Mongoose watched a moment, and then darted to the fallen men. From the head of Bahadur Lal, he took the jeweled turban, and put it on in the place of the one he wore. He adjusted the cape about his shoulders.

"Come!" he whispered to Eleanor Carleigh.

They let themselves out of the private room and hurried along the hall. In the establishment of Bahadur Lal was the stillness of death.

"I was so afraid for a moment," she whispered.

"I had the glass to soften the mask," he whispered in reply. "Getting the bullet-proof variety was a happy thought."

"I don't hear a sound."

"They're all probably asleep. Due to come awake before long, though. Remember all the rest of it, now?"

"I'll not forget."

"Keep up rapid conversation in the elevator and the lobby of the building. According to schedule, the elevator man who brought me up has been relieved. When I come up again, there won't be any check back."

They hurried to the corridor and went to the elevator, where The Mongoose rang.

"Look all right?" he asked.

"Keep the cape up around your face," she said. "You scarcely can tell it's a mask, except that the lips don't move when you talk."

"That's why you're going to do the talking," he said.

The elevator came up, stopped, the door was opened. She stepped inside first, and he followed her, his head inclined. The elevator operator, who knew Bahadur Lal by sight, scarcely gave him a look.

Eleanor Carleigh kept up a rapid conversation, as she had been instructed. When they reached the ground floor. The Mongoose bent his head again as he followed her out. The elevator man yawned and picked up a magazine, to continue a story where he had left off.

Nobody was in the lobby of the building. They went through it briskly, and turned up the street. Around the corner they went, and toward where the coupé was parked.

"Start back now," he whispered to her. "Nobody in sight."

Eleanor Carleigh went back around the corner, walking swiftly. As she neared the entrance of the building, she began running. Into the lobby she dashed, calling to the elevator operator.

"Get help!" she cried. "Bahadur Lal has been robbed. Get some men upstairs."

"But he just—" the elevator operator began.

"That wasn't Bahadur Lal! That was a man wearing a mask of Bahadur Lal's face. He forced me to come down in the elevator with him, so he'd not have to talk. Didn't you notice how fast I was talking, and how silly? He had a gun. Please—get help!"

The night elevator man had a police whistle. He dashed out to the street and blew it lustily.

IN THE coupé, The Mongoose stripped off the mask, took off the cape and turban and put his own hat on his head. He started the machine and drove rapidly down the street, turned a corner, and went for a distance along a tree-bordered boulevard. At a convenient spot, where he was sure he was not observed, he tossed mask, turban and cape into the street, and drove on.

He doubled back toward the building again. On a corner where there was an all-night drug store, he stopped the car. Taking the rajah's jewels from his pocket, he hid them in a secret pocket of the coupé. Then he got out and went into the drug store.

The Mongoose was gone again. A nonchalant Sidney Carleigh approached the drug store counter and purchased a package of his favorite cigarettes. He chatted with the clerk while he broke open the package, got a cigarette out, and lit it.

"Nice night," Sidney Carleigh observed.

"Fine!" the clerk agreed.

"What's all the racket down the street?"

"Sounds like police cars," the clerk replied. "Maybe there's a raid somewhere."

"Might be," Sidney Carleigh said.

A little later, he got into the coupé and drove to the building, to enter upon a scene of excitement. There had been a big robbery in the establishment of Bahadur Lal, jewel merchant, somebody said. Carleigh mentioned his sister, and hurried to the elevator.

The victims of The Mongoose's attack had returned to consciousness. Police were questioning them. Two detectives were listening eagerly to a recital by Eleanor Carleigh.

She glanced up and saw her brother, and ran into his arms, words rushing from her lips as she tried to tell what had happened.

"And when I became conscious, I was in his private study," she said. "Bahadur Lal was there, and that detective, Mr. Graddon.

"They were shooting, and—it was terrible, Sid!"

"But why did he take you to the private study?" Sidney Carleigh asked.

"He thought that Bahadur Lal was—well, interested in me personally," she replied. "Just imagine! And he was going to threaten to kill me if Bahadur Lal didn't open the safe."

Eleanor Carleigh quickly hid her face against her brother's coat lapel. She was afraid she might laugh after telling that one.

"Fearful mess!" Sidney Carleigh declared. "I'll get you home out of this. I suppose you'll have a fit of nerves. Please don't go into hysterics."

The dawn was breaking as Bahadur Lal stood once more in front of the window in his private study, looking down upon the sea of roofs. He was thinking of the rajah, and the rajah's certain vengeance. Bahadur Lal was not the man to wait for that.

"Greed has caused me to live a life of evil," he muttered. "From boyhood, I have been a thief. There is no lower thing in all the world. Scales always must be balanced. It is so written!"

He was holding the rajah's gem-encrusted dagger in his hand. And now he removed a certain large jewel, and lifted the hilt of the dagger to his lips.

"It is written!" he said.

And the book was closed.

RANSOM FOR VENGEANCE

*The Mongoose Uses a Box of Cigars, a Masterpiece
in Oil and the Nerve of a Burglar to Wrench
the Ill-gotten Wealth from a Perjurer*

CHAPTER I

MR. FANSHAW FAINTS

A LEONINE CHARACTER was Mr. Homer Fanshaw in the business world, and now he was the same in the library of his palatial residence, as he paced back and forth over the expensive rug.

His head was held high, his eyes blazing, his thick shock of gray hair seeming to bristle.

Detective Mark Graddon, sitting on a divan and puffing at a costly cigar which Mr. Fanshaw had given him, watched his client with admiration. Mark Graddon knew power when he saw it. He was a rather unscrupulous private operative, who worked at times for unscrupulous men of big business. He had encountered many dominant personalities in his time, but never one more dominant than Homer Fanshaw.

Back and forth Mr. Fanshaw paced. Once he paused to kick angrily at a hassock, and at times the hands swinging at his sides became fists. Mark Graddon waited patiently, puffing at the cigar and sensible to the fact that this was not a time to speak. Mr. Fanshaw would do the speaking, when he was ready.

Presently, Fanshaw came to an abrupt stop in front of the divan and fixed his angry gaze upon the detective.

"The scoundrel must be captured!" Fanshaw declared, in stentorian tones. "He should have been caught long before this. Why is it, Graddon, that you are seemingly so helpless in this matter, when you are so capable in others?"

"The Mongoose," Detective Mark Graddon asserted, "is a clever man."

"Granted! Nevertheless, he must make mistakes at times; leave clues behind, and all that sort of thing."

"He hasn't yet," Graddon replied. "He uses unique methods, Mr. Fanshaw. If he used the ordinary tactics of professional crooks we'd have him."

"You've got to get him! He's robbed half a dozen men already, the most of them my close associates," Fanshaw pointed out.

"He's made fools of them and of the police—and he's made a fool of you, Graddon!"

"It burns me up," Graddon confessed.

"And what are you going to do about it? I got that message from him an hour ago, as I informed you. One of his confounded dictaphone cylinder records. The thing melted and evaporated after I had listened to the message. And the message was certainly short enough."

"Tell me again, please, and try to remember the exact words," Graddon requested.

"He said that he was The Mongoose and that I was to be his next victim, and that it was on account of that old Cratch case ten years ago."

"He's the son of William Cratch, that bookkeeper we framed and sent to prison."

"I know all that. He's out for both revenge and profit, this Mongoose. He told me that he'd strike within forty-eight hours."

"We'll get him," Graddon promised.

"I believe you've said something similar on several other occasions," Homer Fanshaw said, witheringly, as he glared at the detective. "You get busy, Graddon. Make your arrangements."

"Yes, sir. The Mongoose is after a profit, as you say, and undoubtedly a big one. Now—what could he steal from you?"

"How do I know what the fellow might go after? I'm a rich man, as the world knows."

"Yell for the butler, Ladman!" Mark Graddon cried

"But, what could he get at?"

"Well, I've always a small fortune in money and negotiable bonds in my office vault. But he'd have to be an expert cracksman to get at it when the vault's closed. It's the best vault obtainable, and fitted with alarms."

"He probably wouldn't try to go at it like a cracksman," Graddon said. "He'd try some clever stunt. In the daytime, when the vault isn't locked—"

"PLACE SOME of your men in my office immediately," Fanshaw directed. "It is now eight o'clock in the evening. He may try to do something tonight. Within forty-eight hours, he said. Your men can easily guard the office. Call in the police to aid you."

"We'd better keep the cops out of this," Graddon suggested, quickly. "We don't want the world to know exactly why The Mongoose is attacking certain men. It's been my hope to catch him and—er—fix him so he couldn't talk too much."

"Catching him is the main thing, Graddon. Nobody will believe anything he says. To the public, he's only a common thief who uses spectacular methods. My associates and I control several newspapers. We'll see that public opinion is formed as we wish it. He's got to be caught!" Mr. Fanshaw smashed a ponderous fist down upon a table.

"We'll get right at it," Graddon promised.

"He's not up against a weakling this time," Fanshaw continued. "I'm not saying anything against the others he's robbed—please understand—or questioning their judgment and courage, but I'm telling you this, Graddon—he can't scare me with his devilish electrical contrivances and his puffs of smoke. Got some sort of a wireless dictograph he uses, has he? Let him have it! Let him listen in to what we're saying. I don't care! But, if he comes around me, he's going to have a fight on his hands!"

"That's the spirit," Graddon complimented. "Now, Mr. Fanshaw, in addition to the office vault—"

"There's a safe here in the library—behind that tapestry," said Fanshaw.

"Anything in it that might attract The Mongoose?"

"Always some money—say a thousand or so. Some old jewelry, mostly heirlooms, stuff my family never uses. Documents and account books of no value to anybody but me."

"That's not enough to attract The Mongoose, unless it's some of the documents he's after," Graddon said.

"I understand what you're insinuating, Graddon. But the papers in that safe are harmless—don't refer to any important business deals, shady or otherwise."

"Then it isn't the safe he'll go after. But we'll put men here to guard the house."

"Get all your men at work on the thing. Hire some extra ones, if you wish. And I still think that we should notify the police and let them help. They could comb the city—"

"They've done that," Mark Graddon interrupted. "My old friend and enemy. Detective Sergeant Tim Ladman, handled The Mongoose case exclusively for a couple of months—and couldn't get a line on him."

"He's got to be caught!" Fanshaw repeated vehemently. "It's unthinkable that such a man can run around robbing people."

"I wish I had some idea of where he might strike," Graddon said. "This safe here doesn't seem probable—and your office vault would be too risky for him. He'd know that it would be guarded."

"Guarded!" Fanshaw roared. "Graddon, you and your men guarded other places, after he'd threatened to strike—and what came of it? He simply struck—and got away! We've got to catch the rogue. The police must help."

"I'm against calling them into it, sir. If you'd consult with some of the others interested, I'm sure they'd agree with me."

"When The Mongoose comes after me, I'm the one interested," Fanshaw exploded. "I'll consult with none of them. This is my affair."

There came a discreet tap at the door, and at Fanshaw's command a butler entered.

"There's a gentleman to see you, sir," the butler said. "He is from Police Headquarters. His name is Ladman."

"Tim Ladman!" Graddon exclaimed. "What's he doing here?"

"We'll find out immediately," Fanshaw said. "Show him right in here."

The butler disappeared. A moment later he was back and Detective Sergeant Tim Ladman was ushered into the library.

"So you're here, too, Graddon," Ladman said. "The Mongoose, I suppose."

"What about The Mongoose?" Graddon growled.

"I got a message from him."

"You did?"

"Sure!" Tim Ladman grinned. "He told me that Mr. Fanshaw is the next man on his list, and that he's going to strike at him inside forty-eight hours. And he said he wished that the police would try to catch him, because Mark Graddon and his men couldn't make it interesting enough for him."

"Oh! He did, did he? We'll make it interesting enough for him this time! Well, Ladman, since he notified you, we might as well work together."

"WE'D HAVE had results, maybe, if we'd worked together before this," Ladman rebuked. "You've been keeping me in the dark about The Mongoose. This campaign of his smells like revenge to me. You don't want the cops to know what's behind it. Catching him is the only thing that interests me, Graddon."

"I've been talking to Mr. Fanshaw, and we can't decide what The Mongoose will try to steal. There's a safe here with little in it, and the office vault is well protected. And The Mongoose doesn't run to plate and toilet articles. He always goes after something big."

"Let's plant a few men here, and at the office," Ladman suggested.

"We'll do that, and right away."

"What's in there?" Ladman pointed to a closed door.

"That is a sort of anteroom," Fanshaw explained, leading them toward the door. "I keep some art objects there. Nothing that could be stolen and sold. You perhaps have read in the newspapers about the painting I am presenting to the museum?"

"Sure!" Graddon said.

Fanshaw had opened the door.

"It's on an easel over there, with that drapery over it," he explained. "Tomorrow evening, a few of my friends are coming here to view it. And the next afternoon it will be presented to the museum."

"Cost almost a quarter of a million, didn't it?" Tim Ladman asked.

"Yes. It's a Michelangelo, discovered by accident last year. I had a lot of negotiating to do before I could buy it. If it'd been found in Italy, they wouldn't have let me bring it out of the country. It was found in Spain."

"It's a lot of coin to pay for an old painting," Tim Ladman offered.

Fanshaw laughed a bit.

"Worth the price," he declared. "Art lovers will worship it.

I'm glad to be able to present it to the museum. It's getting me a lot of publicity, too."

"For that much money, you can buy a lot of publicity," Tim Ladman said. "If The Mongoose—"

Fanshaw's laughter interrupted him again. "The Mongoose won't steal the painting, if that's what is worrying you," he said. "What would he do with it? You can't peddle a thing like that as you would a string of pearls. The art world knows all about it. Nobody would touch it. The Mongoose, if he stole it, couldn't get rid of it anywhere."

"We can hide some men in this room, and they can watch the library," Graddon said.

"Good idea!" Ladman agreed. "We can plant men around Mr. Fanshaw's office, too. But The Mongoose wouldn't be fool enough to try to get info the vault. If he had the proper tools, and plenty of help, and wasn't interrupted, it'd take him hours."

"Somehow, I can't think he'll go after either the office vault or the safe here," Graddon declared. "You're sure there's nothing else he could get at, Mr. Fanshaw?"

"He plays for big stakes only, you've told me. I can't imagine what he'd go after here in the house. Valuable art objects in this room, as you can see—but he couldn't sell them, as I explained about the painting of Michelangelo."

"Our men will guard the painting, anyhow," Ladman said, "and the other stuff in this room."

"Please," Fanshaw said. "If anything happened to the painting, it'd be a calamity. I don't mean only the money it cost me. But everything is arranged for turning it over to the museum. There has been reams of publicity about it. Would you care to look at it?"

"Sure," Ladman said, quickly. "Any daub that cost that much jack is worth looking at."

"You and Graddon stand here," Fanshaw directed. "I'll snap on the lights over the easel—there! Now, I'll remove the drapery. Where you're standing, you can get a good view."

Side by side, the detectives watched and waited. Homer Fanshaw walked across to the easel, grasped the drapery, and whipped it aside. The next instant the two rushed toward him, as he gave a cry of mingled pain and rage.

The frame remained on the easel, but the painting was not in it. It had been cut out along the edges of the frame. And tacked to one corner of the frame was a card which bore the words:

Removed by The Mongoose

"Yell for the butler, Ladman!" Mark Graddon cried.

For Homer Fanshaw had fainted.

CHAPTER II

THE MONGOOSE'S DEMAND

THEY CARRIED FANSHAW back into the library and stretched him upon the divan. The butler and a maid hurried with restoratives. The financier opened his eyes and moaned, and managed to sit up.

"I'm all right," he announced. "It was the shock of the thing. Bowled me over. Now, we'll go ahead and make our plans."

"Shall I call your physician, sir?" the butler asked.

"Don't need him. You and the maid clear out of here. We've got some business to transact."

The servants withdrew and closed the door. Fanshaw was on his feet again, pacing back and forth across the expensive rug. Graddon and Ladman sat on the divan and waited for him to speak.

"Well, he did it!" Fanshaw said, presently. "He stole the famous Michelangelo. But what's he going to do with it? How does he expect to cash it in?"

"You'll probably hear from him again soon," Graddon said.

"This is terrible. I was going to have a private showing tomorrow evening. And the next afternoon, the ceremony of presentation to the museum. Something must be done! The painting must be recovered."

"The Mongoose thinks he's hurting you by stealing it," Mark Graddon said. "It's probably his idea of revenge."

"He did hurt me," Fanshaw admitted. "I must get that painting and give it to the museum. It's a matter of honor with me."

"He couldn't sell it," Graddon said "You don't suppose he'd destroy it?"

"Good heavens! That would be sacrilege," Fanshaw cried. "And how would he profit if he destroyed it? Don't even have such a thought!"

"Your vault and safe—needn't worry about them now," Ladman said. "The Mongoose's got what he wanted, evidently. And when did he get it? How could he get into the house? He cut the painting out of the frame. Must have rolled it up and carried it away somehow."

"Let's take a look at the room," Graddon suggested.

They went into the anteroom and turned on all the lights. The two detectives made a swift investigation. One of the windows was unlocked, and Fanshaw said that the catch was always supposed to be on. Beneath the window on the outside there were shoe tracks in a flower bed.

"He got in through this window," Graddon reported. "The catch has been snapped—jimmied, probably. The chances are that he got the painting inside the last couple of hours. He may have been in here while we were talking in the library."

"Can't you—er—find fingerprints, or something of that nature?" Fanshaw asked.

"The Mongoose isn't the man to leave his fingerprints scattered around," Graddon replied.

"What are we going to do?" Fanshaw wailed. "We must do something."

"Can't do anything but wait and see if he communicates,"

Graddon answered. "We don't know where to look for him. I'll use the telephone and get some of my men out here."

"And I'll have a picked squad of cops ready," Ladman added.

They returned to the library. Fanshaw sank weakly into a chair.

"The butler will show you where to telephone," he said. "I haven't a phone in the library. I—I'll wait here. Feel a bit faint yet. But I'm not frightened, understand. I'm mad! I'll fight The Mongoose to the end. We'll get that painting back, and we'll get him, too!"

Graddon and Ladman went out to find the butler and use the telephone. Homer Fanshaw relaxed in an easy chair at the end of the reading table. The theft had infuriated him. He disliked to think of the publicity. He felt that it would be a reflection on him, that he had not guarded the painting better.

And all this because he had joined with others, some ten years before, and had framed an innocent man and had him sent to prison. It had seemed a clever thing at the time. A group of financiers, caught putting through a gigantic swindle, facing arrest and conviction, simply had cast the blame upon another man, had made it appear that a bookkeeper had perpetrated the swindle in their names.

How were they to know that years later a son of the victim would appear and exact vengeance? Was this Mongoose to be allowed to do as he pleased? Was he to make fools of them all, rob them, play with them, use his diabolical tricks?

"Fanshaw!"

The name was spoken softly, almost sibilantly. Fanshaw whirled to face the door, thinking one of the detectives was trying to attract his attention.

"**THIS IS** The Mongoose speaking to you, Fanshaw. I'm using the wireless dictograph. If you search, you may find the disk in your library. But you'd better not bother it. I may want to communicate something important at any time. If you speak, I can hear you, the same as you are hearing me now."

The thing was uncanny, that voice coming from nowhere and filling the library. But Homer Fanshaw was not afraid. He had heard of the many strange devices used by The Mongoose. He had decided that he would let nothing startle him.

"Did you get that painting, Mongoose?" he demanded. His voice was not that of a frightened man, either. It was the voice of a man angry and determined.

"I got it."

"And what are you going to do with it?" Fanshaw asked.

"I'm holding it for ransom, Fanshaw."

"You're—what? Holding it for ransom?"

"Exactly! The painting can't be turned into money on the market. So you'll have to ransom it, and at my price."

"Have to, eh?" Fanshaw said. "Suppose I don't?"

"Then two things are possible. I may destroy it, and it'll be lost to the world forever."

"You couldn't do that, man!" Fanshaw cried. "It's supposed that you're a man of culture and education, Mongoose. If you are, you simply couldn't destroy an old work of art like that— kill a masterpiece."

"But," The Mongoose said, "I could ship it to the Italian government. It belongs in Italy."

"I bought it—"

"And you've promised it to the museum. Oh, I understand, Fanshaw! You're buying a lot of publicity. You want the country to think you're a patron of the arts, that your sordid soul isn't entirely wrapped up in tainted money. You'd look considerable of an ass, if you fell down on the deal. You've got to present this painting to the museum to save your face."

"What kind of a deal can we make. Mongoose?"

"Now you're talking like a business man, Fanshaw. I can't sell the painting, so I'll let you ransom it with something that I'll be able to market."

"What's your price?"

"I don't want cash from you, Fanshaw. I want that diamond necklace you gave your wife last Christmas."

"What?"

"I know all about that necklace. If you tried to hand me a bogus one, I'd know it instantly—and you'd never see the painting. I can market the stones easily, Fanshaw. You paid about a hundred and fifty thousand for the necklace, didn't you? You can buy your wife another."

"Can't we make the deal for cash?"

"No, thanks! You're a clever man! Currency can be traced sometimes. I took cash from another of my victims, but I knew he was a coward, and would be afraid to try to trick me. I do you the honor to say that I consider you a worthy opponent."

"Thanks!" Fanshaw said, sarcastically. "So you want the necklace?"

"I demand it!"

"You won't get it!"

"Then the painting will be sent to the Italian government. You'll lose face. And I'll strike at you yet again, and take my profit. Get that necklace out of your safety deposit box in the morning, Fanshaw, and have it ready."

"Where'll you get it, and when?"

"I'll let you know that later," The Mongoose told him. "I've done all the talking I care to for the present."

"Wait, Mongoose! How can I communicate with you?"

"I'll do the communicating—and when I please. All you have to do is obey orders. We won't have any argument, or any dickering. There'll be no change in my terms. I'll trade the painting for the necklace—that's all!"

"But if—"

"Good-by, for the present!" The Mongoose interrupted.

Homer Fanshaw sprang to his feet and looked around the room foolishly. It made a man feel foolish to conduct a conversation at a wall. He hurried across to the door and opened it, to find that Mark Graddon and Tim Ladman were coming along the hall toward him, having concluded their telephoning.

FANSHAW BECKONED them into the library.

"He's been talking to me," he reported. "That trick two-way wireless dictograph of his. Told me not to destroy the disk, if I found it, for he might want to communicate again."

"What did he say?" Graddon asked.

"It's simple enough. He's holding the painting for ransom. He'll trade it for my wife's diamond necklace."

"Then—"Tim Ladman began.

Graddon motioned him to silence. He indicated that he wished both of them to step out into the hall. There, he whispered to them:

"The Mongoose probably can hear everything we say in that room," he said. "And probably in other parts of the house. Let's get outside before we talk any more."

They hurried through the house, went outside, and upon the lawn. Through the moonlight they walked toward a tree beneath which there was a bench. There, they sat down.

"When The Mongoose communicates again," Mark Graddon said, "he'll probably explain how and when he'll trade the painting for the necklace. Our only chance is to catch him then."

"We must trick him," Fanshaw declared. "I've no intention of turning that necklace over to him."

"He'll probably know whether you get it out of the safety deposit box," Ladman said. "The Mongoose seems to know pretty much of everything."

"I'll let you gentlemen in on a little secret," Fanshaw said. "Wealthy women, and wives and daughters of wealthy men, have fortunes in fine jewels. But nine-tenths of them have paste duplicates which are generally worn instead of the real thing. The genuine jewels are seldom worn except on very special occasions."

"And you've got a duplicate of the necklace?" Graddon asked.

"I have. A rare job, too. Take an expert to tell the difference. And the joke is this—the bogus necklace is in the safety deposit box with the genuine one. So, if The Mongoose is watching, he'll think I got the real necklace out of the box. If he arranges to transfer the painting for the necklace, we'll use the bogus one. By the time he discovers it's paste, we'll have the painting—and possibly The Mongoose. I'm not fool enough to risk the real necklace in an attempt to trap him."

"Great!" Ladman said.

"We've got to trap him this time," Mark Graddon put in. "If he gets away with this, we'll be the laugh of the town—especially if news of it gets out."

"News of it must not get out," Fanshaw said, in determined fashion. "I couldn't endure the ridicule. We must trick him with the bogus necklace, recover the painting, and capture him if we can."

They were silent for a moment, while Mark Graddon struck a match and touched it to the end of a fresh cigar. And suddenly soft laughter came to their ears, mocking laughter. They sprang off the bench, looked around wildly. Nobody was near.

"Mongoose speaking," came a voice. "There's a wireless dictograph disk in the tree above you, gentlemen. I anticipated that there might be a conference on the lawn."

Fanshaw gave a groan of despair.

"Thanks for letting me know about that bogus necklace, Fanshaw," The Mongoose said. "I'd advise you not to try to trick me with it, if you hope to recover the painting. I am an expert on jewels, and you may be sure that I'll examine the necklace well before I restore the painting. Also, regarding news of this exploit getting out—I've already informed the city editors of two newspapers that I've taken the painting and demanding that you ransom it."

"You fiend!" Fanshaw cried.

"And those newspapers, Fanshaw, are not ones you and your

associates control," The Mongoose added. "Good night, gentle-men!"

"Wait, Mongoose!" Fanshaw shouted. "Can you hear me?"

He got no reply. If The Mongoose heard, he did not see fit to say so.

"Well, there we are!" Ladman said.

"What in the world are we going to do now?"

"I'm not licked!" Fanshaw snapped. "We'll trap him! But we must be careful. The painting must be recovered and presented to the museum as arranged."

"We can't do anything until he communicates again," Mark Graddon said. "Can't make any plans until we know how he wants to trade the painting for the necklace. And, what about that necklace, Mr. Fanshaw? You going to get it out of the safety deposit box in the morning?"

"I'll have to think that over, and decide between now and morning. I'm in a tough spot," Fanshaw admitted. "I simply must recover the painting. But we must outwit The Mongoose, too."

CHAPTER III

LADMAN GETS A SHOCK

AT NINE O'CLOCK the following morning, Homer Fanshaw reached his office suite to find both Mark Graddon and Tim Ladman awaiting him.

"Haven't heard from the fellow," Fanshaw reported.

"Are you going to get the necklace from the safety deposit box?" Graddon asked.

"What do you advise?"

"I don't like to say," Graddon admitted. "I hate to see you lose the necklace, and I'd hate to have you miss getting that paint-ing back."

"Which means that you're as good as admitting that we're licked," Fanshaw remarked. "Graddon, I'm growing ashamed of you!"

"I'm thinking of your interests, Mr. Fanshaw. My paramount idea is to catch The Mongoose. But I've got to consider my clients."

"Come into my private office," Fanshaw said. "We'll wait till we hear from him. My private office may have one of his confounded trick disks in it, for all I know."

They went into the private office, and Graddon and Ladman made themselves comfortable and smoked, while Fanshaw attended to his early mail.

A secretary entered.

"Package for you, sir," she said.

"Where'd that come from?" Mark Graddon demanded, springing to his feet.

"It was left by a messenger a moment ago."

"Regular messenger?"

"As far as I know, sir. He wore the usual uniform."

"We won't waste time looking for him," Graddon said, bitterly. "I've tried to catch The Mongoose's messengers before. I'm betting, Fanshaw, that package is from him."

"It's larger than the other I received, and heavier," Fanshaw said.

He motioned the girl out of the office, then cut the string which bound the package, and unwrapped it. He found two boxes inside. One was a pasteboard box, which evidently contained one of The Mongoose's dictaphone records. The other was a small steel box, which was empty.

"It's from The Mongoose, all right," Fanshaw said, as he took a dictaphone cylinder from the pasteboard box.

"Better listen to the message before the cylinder is destroyed," Graddon advised.

"I'll repeat the message as I hear it, and you and Ladman can help me remember it."

Fanshaw hurried to the dictaphone, put on the cylinder, and adjusted the ear tubes. He started the machine, and listened, and began repeating what he heard:

Hello, Fanshaw! This is The Mongoose speaking again. Listen carefully to these instructions.

Get the diamond necklace from the safety deposit and put it into the little steel box I am sending you with this record. At three o'clock this afternoon, put the box containing the necklace on a small table in front of the north wing in your private office. Open the window wide, and leave it so.

You may remain in the office, sitting at your desk, if you have courage enough, and watch me get the box and necklace. Nobody else must be in the office, except that you may have Mark Graddon with you, if you desire.

If you do not follow these orders exactly, or if you put anything other than the genuine necklace in the box, you'll never see your precious painting again.

The voice of The Mongoose ceased, and Homer Fanshaw removed the tubes from his ears and looked at the two detectives.

"Get all of it?" he asked.

They nodded in the affirmative.

AND WHAT do you suppose it means?" Fanshaw continued. "Why put the necklace in that confounded box? How can he get it, if I do so, and put it by the open window? This office is on the twentieth floor of the building. There's no fire escape at that window, not even a ledge in the masonry. It'd be utterly impossible for a man to get at the box through the window."

"That may be a trick," Ladman suggested. "Possibly he wants you to concentrate on the window while he enters the door."

"We can stop that," Graddon said. "We'll have a dozen men in the outer office. Nobody will get into this room. I'll be in here with Mr. Fanshaw. You, Ladman, camp right outside the door with some of your men and mine, and be ready for business. I'll have my service revolver ready."

"And I'll be sitting here with an automatic in my hand," Fanshaw added. "I don't know what The Mongoose intends trying, but he'll not get away with it!"

"Then you'll get the real necklace and put it into the box?" Graddon asked.

"That's my present intention. I don't want that painting lost. I'll get the real necklace and put it into the confounded box— and let's see him get it! But, if he does get it; he won't have any kick coming, and will have to return the painting."

"Is the daub worth it?" Ladman asked. "Why not let him take the thing and go to blazes with it?"

"I've promised to present it to the museum. I bought it for that purpose," Fanshaw explained. "I can afford the price of a diamond necklace better than I can afford a flood of ridicule. And I've arranged for a private showing of the painting at my house tonight, as you know. A flock of art critics will be there. Graddon, you go with me to the bank, and I'll get the necklace. Mr. Ladman can remain here on guard."

"We've got men scattered out in the corridor, and a couple in your front office," Ladman reported. "I'll have one sit in here while you and Graddon are gone."

"Fine! We're not licked yet," Fanshaw declared. "If you're asking me, this time The Mongoose has bitten off more than he can chew. I'd like to see him get the box containing the necklace with a couple of us sitting in this room holding guns and ready to use them!"

"You needn't expect him to walk in and put up a fight," Mark Graddon said. "We must watch out for a trick of some sort. Whatever it is he tries, you can bet it'll be some new stunt. If you're ready, Mr. Fanshaw, I'll go with you to get the necklace. And we'll have a couple of my men trail us, too."

"If it was me, I'd use the fake necklace," Detective Sergeant

Tim Ladman said. "It'd be just as good as a decoy. Then, if he got away with it, he wouldn't get away with much."

"And the painting would be gone forever," Fanshaw reminded him.

"For the price of that necklace, you could buy enough good pictures to fill this room," Ladman said. "Who was this Mike Angelo that his stuff is worth so much?"

Homer Fanshaw smiled a bit.

"You probably wouldn't appreciate the work if you saw it," he said. "It's the picture of a fat old saint."

"I like landscapes best myself," Ladman acknowledged. "Sea pictures, too. But I've never seen a picture yet that I'd trade a diamond necklace for."

Fanshaw and Graddon departed, and Tim Ladman made himself comfortable in the private office, after giving orders to his men outside. He sat in Fanshaw's desk chair, and helped himself to one of the financier's cigars, ignited it, puffed in evident content.

A lot of foolishness, Tim Ladman thought. All this fuss about an old picture!

"Ladman!"

HIS NAME was spoken softly, and Detective Sergeant Tim Ladman guessed that The Mongoose was communicating with him. He looked wildly around the room. Somewhere, he guessed, there was a little disk, which The Mongoose had put there in some manner.

"Yeah?" Tim Ladman said.

"I've been listening to your conversation. This is The Mongoose. So you think I can't get that necklace, do you?"

"It looks like a tough job to me," Ladman said.

"Think you can catch me?"

"I'll be doing my best, Mongoose!"

"It won't be good enough, Ladman. You little realize the

power I have at my command. I'll demonstrate. Light up one of Homer Fanshaw's fat cigars. You'll find them in the humidor."

"I'm smokin' one already."

"Good! Now, relax in the desk chair, and smoke and rest."

"I'm doin' that, too," Tim Ladman said. "What kind of a game is this, anyhow? What do you want me to do next? Tryin' to have some fun with me?"

"I only want to show you what power I possess, Ladman, show you how futile it is to pit your wits against mine."

Ladman started to say something taunting, but he did not. His throat felt tired, and he lost all inclination to speak. He waited, instead, for The Mongoose to do some more talking.

"Ladman!"

"Uh!" Tim Ladman grunted.

"Repeat after me: 'I am a sergeant of detectives.'"

Ladman started to say that this was rank foolishness. His lips moved, but no sound came from them. The detective sergeant felt sudden alarm.

"Can't speak, can you?" The Mongoose said to him, out of the void. "You can't move much, either. Try to get out of the chair."

Ladman tried. His muscles refused to function. Perspiration popped out on his forehead. His heart hammered wildly. His lower jaw sagged, and his eyes bulged. He gurgled a bit, tried to grip the arms of the chair, realized that he was helpless.

The soft laugh of The Mongoose came to him. It was as though The Mongoose was there in that room, witnessing his helplessness.

"You see?" The Mongoose asked. "Ladman, I'm more than two miles from you at this moment. I'm speaking from my laboratory. Yet I'm able to make you helpless, so you can't move, can't talk, scarcely can think. You'll be all right in a few minutes, so don't be alarmed. Good-by, for the present."

Then there was silence. Ladman tried to move again, but could not. And this had happened to him, with his men and

Fanshaw's clerks and stenographers only a few feet away, in the big outer office!

He closed his eyes a moment, tried to collect his scattering senses. Suddenly he felt strength returning to his body. The cigar had slipped out of his mouth long before. He was not thinking whether it might be burning Fanshaw's expensive rug. He was thinking only of getting to his feet, getting out of that private office.

But it was that cigar which had been his undoing—a doped cigar, as all in the humidor were doped, had been doped by The Mongoose late the night before, when he had entered the Fanshaw suite stealthily and made his final preparations.

CHAPTER IV

SPEEDY WORK

IN AN EXCLUSIVE apartment house two miles away, which he owned, Mr. Sidney Carleigh threw a few electric switches and removed head phones which he had been using. He got out of his chair and stretched, then went across the tiny room filled with apparatus and cabinets of chemicals, and pressed against the wall.

A sliding panel opened, and Mr. Sidney Carleigh passed through and closed it behind him. Along the rear hall of the apartment he went, and presently emerged into the spacious living room.

"Been having some fun, Sid?"

His sister, Eleanor, asked the question. She was curled up on the end of a couch; reading and munching candy. Sidney Carleigh bent and kissed her.

"Throwing a scare into Tim Ladman," he replied. "Fanshaw and Graddon went to get the necklace, and Ladman remained in the private office. Over the dictograph amplifier I heard him open Fanshaw's humidor and knew he'd helped himself to one of the drugged cigars. He thinks I worked some charm on him."

Eleanor Carleigh laughed a bit.

"You ran a risk doping those cigars last night," she protested. "We mustn't run unnecessary risks, Sid."

"I had to get into the office anyhow, to set the dictograph disk."

"We must never let anything happen to stop our work," she said seriously. "Oh, Sid! When I think of our poor father, wasting away in prison, dying by inches, an innocent man sent to that awful place—"

"Don't, Eleanor!" He sat beside her quickly, put an arm around her. "I'm not forgetting it for a moment. We're making the guilty ones pay. Fanshaw will pay this afternoon."

"If anything should go wrong—" she began.

"Nothing's going wrong, honey. This stunt is a simple one compared to some."

"You'll have to get out of the building, and with that necklace."

"It'll be easy."

"Fanshaw was one of the worst, according to the evidence we found," she said. "His perjured testimony did as much as anything else to condemn father."

"You're a bundle of nerves," he complained. "Cool down, or I'll not let you help me this afternoon. Can't have a nervous person on this job. You made that appointment with the modiste?"

"Yes. For two-thirty."

"Good! I'm to call for you at three, remember."

"I understand," she said.

"And, after I arrive, you'll continue looking at gowns until I signal you that everything's all right. Then we simply come away, with the necklace."

"It sounds so easy, the way you say it."

"I won't allow myself to think of it being difficult," he told her.

It was two o'clock that afternoon when Miss Eleanor Carleigh descended in the elevator and had the doorman call her a taxi. She made a delicious picture as she waited at the curb—an attractive young woman, becomingly gowned. The chauffeur was directed to drive to the huge building wherein Homer Fanshaw had his palatial suite of offices.

It was a few minutes after two-thirty when Miss Eleanor Carleigh entered the shop of an exclusive modiste on the twenty-second floor of the building. She was greeted with polite enthusiasm. Foreseeing the campaign against Homer Fanshaw, Eleanor Carleigh had become a good customer of that gown shop during the past three or four months.

It appeared that Miss Carleigh wished to purchase, but she scarcely knew what. Models paraded before her, wearing the latest creations. Miss Carleigh praised some and rejected others, bought an evening gown, asked to see some street costumes.

"I'm expecting my brother to call for me, as usual," she said.

"You have a wonderful brother—so attentive," the modiste told her.

"He's always willing to call for me here, at any rate," Miss Carleigh replied. "Perhaps it's because you have such pretty models."

"**HE NEVER** gives them a second glance. But I've seen the girls looking at him often enough. You'll be losing your handsome brother one of these days—or he'll be losing his beautiful sister. I hope we have the pleasure of making your wedding trousseau."

"No prospects," Miss Carleigh declared.

She allowed them to continue their flattery, killing time, waiting for her brother to arrive. He came promptly at three o'clock. In this distinguished-looking man of middle age, who always was sartorially correct, nobody would have expected to find The Mongoose. In the public mind, The Mongoose was a hawk-faced demon, or something of the sort.

"I haven't finished, Sid," Eleanor Carleigh said. "You go into the wailing room and smoke a cigarette until I am ready."

"Take your time," he replied, giving her a meaning look. "I'm in no hurry. I'll sit by the window and look over the roofs. Great way to get inspiration."

He walked into the little waiting room through the doorway which was curtained with heavy portières. The window was open, and Mr. Sidney Carleigh stood before it, looking down. Presently he bent out. Two floors below there was another open window—the one in the private office of Homer Fanshaw.

He glanced back at the doorway. He did not anticipate interruption. None of the shop people would bother him. If any started to enter the waiting room, Eleanor would signal him with talk that would sound ordinary to others.

He glanced out of the window again, looked down at that other open window. From beneath his coat he took a coil of fine, strong cord, to the end of which a peculiar-looking object was fastened. Swiftly, he let out the cord, let the peculiar-looking object descend against the wall of the building.

He stopped it just above the top of that other open window, waited an instant, then lowered it quickly for a few feet more. A moment later, he was pulling in the cord swiftly, coiling it as he did so.

The end of the cord came in. Sidney Carleigh detached something, and stowed the cord away again beneath his coat. A few seconds later, something fell and clattered on the floor of the court far below.

And, a few seconds after that, Sidney Carleigh, smiling, went back into the other room and looked questioningly at his sister.

"All right, Sid! I've finished," Eleanor Carleigh said. "You're a dear to wait for me. I didn't quite know what I wanted. We'll go, now."

Through the shop they went in the wake of the charmed modiste, who had made a good sale. They were towed into the corridor, and started toward the elevator.

"Get it?" she whispered.

"Got it!" he replied. "Didn't take time to examine it, but I can do that after we get home."

"We are not out of here yet, Sid."

"Worrying again? Stop it!"

"Where are you carrying it, Sid? If anything happened—if we were stopped and searched—"

He chuckled. "Remember, you're speaking to The Mongoose," he whispered. "The Mongoose—whose plans are always perfect and always work out, thanks to the fact that he's got a pretty sister to help him plan. If we're stopped and searched, which isn't likely, nothing'll be found."

"The place is swarming with policemen."

"Too many. They get in one another's way," he replied.

CHAPTER V

STRANGE ROBBERY

DETECTIVE SERGEANT TIM LADMAN never thought that the cigar he had been smoking had been drugged. It had come from Fanshaw's humidor, which always held only the finest cigars. Ladman was of the opinion that, in some peculiar manner, he had been subject to a paralyzing gas.

He did not tell anybody of his experience. Tim Ladman was a sensitive soul, and did not care to be laughed at. He got busy giving orders to the men under his command, and was calmed by the time Mark Graddon and Fanshaw returned from the bank.

Fanshaw carried the diamond necklace. He went into the private office with Graddon, put the necklace into the metal box The Mongoose had sent, and placed the box on the end of his desk.

"There it is," Fanshaw said. "It's what The Mongoose

demanded of me. We'll carry out his instructions to the letter, Graddon. But we'll be waiting for him."

"Don't hesitate to shoot, if you think such a thing's necessary," Graddon said. "If the mouth of The Mongoose is shut forever, it might be a lot better for some of us."

"I won't hesitate," Fanshaw declared. "We'll put the box into the vault, and lock it while we go to luncheon. And you can have a couple of your men stay in this office while we're gone."

Graddon's private operatives and Tim Ladman's policemen remained scattered in the corridors on that floor, and the floors above and below. They loitered near the elevators and stairs. Half a dozen were in the Fanshaw offices, eyed by the half-frightened clerks and stenographers.

The necklace was locked in the vault, and two of Ladman's men were left in the private office on guard while Fanshaw took Mark Graddon to lunch. Ladman spent considerable time in the private office himself. He watched his men closely, half expecting something to happen to them.

As the hour of three approached, Fanshaw and Graddon were alone in the private room. Fanshaw put a small table in front of the window, and opened the window wide. He got the metal box containing the necklace, and put it on the desk.

Mark Graddon got a service revolver out of its holster, made an examination of it, and held it ready. Fanshaw took an automatic pistol out of a drawer of his desk. The expression on his face was that of a grim and determined man.

"Might as well smoke up and soothe our nerves, Graddon," he said, opening the humidor. "Help yourself."

They lit their smokes. Fanshaw took the metal box across the room and put it on the table in front of the open window.

"We won't take our eyes off the thing," Fanshaw said. "Just smoke and watch. If we talk, don't even glance at each other, but continue watching that box."

"Right!" Mark Graddon agreed.

"How does The Mongoose expect to get the thing? Come

down in a parachute? Fly past in an airplane and hook it through the window? Graddon, it's like I told you—this time he's bitten off more than he can chew."

"Hope so," Graddon said.

"You don't sound very confident."

"All I'm asking is to get my hands on him—or get him in front of this gun," Mark Graddon declared.

"It's unthinkable that he could come here in broad daylight and steal that box and what it contains with officers scattered all over the place, and the two of us sitting here, fifteen feet away, and watching. And there's no trick to the box. I examined it carefully—just a plain metal box with a hinged lid that fastens with a metal pin. No chance for double bottom or top, or anything of that sort."

Homer Fanshaw rambled on in his conversation. Graddon puffed at his cigar and watched the box. Fanshaw ceased speaking to express a few syllables now and then. It was a couple of minutes after three.

They continued to watch and wait, relaxed in their chairs. Nothing happened. They could hear the hum of voices in the outer office, and knew everything was all right there. There was nothing unusual in the private office, as far as they could see. Yes, it was unthinkable that The Mongoose could get that necklace under the circumstances.

THERE CAME a sudden tapping on the upper half of the window. Graddon and Fanshaw glanced there quickly. Something was being lowered from above on a cord. It swung against the glass and thus caused the tapping.

Mark Graddon's eyes narrowed and gleamed. He understood, now. He knew the thing fastened to the end of that cord. He started to raise the revolver, started to get out of the chair and creep toward the window—that is, such was his intention.

But when he tried it, he realized suddenly that he was helpless. There was no strength in his body. His arms and legs would not obey the commands of his mind. He could not get out of the chair. He could not lift the weapon he held, and try a shot at that dangling cord.

He glanced toward Fanshaw, trying to speak to him. A series of vague mutterings came from his lips, and nothing more. And that glance told him that Homer Fanshaw was in the same predicament. He was trying to speak, and could not, nor could he move.

Perspiration streamed down Mark Graddon's face as he fought to get control of himself. His effort was mental only. His body was like a dead thing.

He looked at the window, watched. The cord was let down more, the swinging object at the end of it came to the open half of the window.

And suddenly that little metal box seemed to be alive. It twitched, slid along the surface of the table—and jumped to meet the object at the end of the cord. A moment later, it had been lifted out of sight. It was gone, and Homer Fanshaw's diamond necklace with it.

"A magnet," Mark Graddon was trying to mutter. "Lifted it with a magnet!"

Graddon felt strength returning after a short time. But it was Fanshaw who returned to activity first. A cry of rage came from his throat. The door was hurled open, and Ladman and a couple of his men tumbled into the room.

One glance was enough for Ladman. He guessed what had happened—the same thing that had happened to him. He had kept quiet about it, and he dare not tell them now. He would be blamed for not putting them on guard.

Ladman rushed to Graddon's side, shook him, tried to lift him out of the chair. Two of the officers managed to get Fanshaw to his feet and lead him toward the door. A moment later, Graddon was on his feet also, leaning weakly against the end of the desk, shaking his head at Ladman to say that he did not wish to leave.

"What happened, Mark?" Ladman was asking.

Graddon found his voice. It was scarcely more than a whisper, but it could be understood.

"Quick… he lowered magnet on rope and caught up box… stop everybody… descending from above."

Tim Ladman understood. He rushed from the office, bellowing orders to his men, throwing the office staff into the confusion of fright. The orders were relayed to the men on duty in the corridors, to those at the elevators and stairs.

Tim Ladman himself rushed to an express elevator and descended to the ground floor. Graddon staggered out of the private office, and motioned toward a water cooler. One of the clerks handed him a drink.

"What was it?" Fanshaw was demanding.

"Didn't you catch on? He lowered a powerful magnet from some window above, and it caught up the box. Fool never to think of the possibility of that. Well, he's done it again! He got your necklace, Fanshaw."

Homer Fanshaw raved.

"Get him! He can't have left the building."

"Ladman's attending to that. But there's little hope," Mark Graddon confessed. "It's a safe bet The Mongoose had his plans made perfectly."

CHAPTER VI

RECOVERY

SIDE BY SIDE, Sidney Carleigh and his pretty sister walked to the elevator, rang, waited for the car.

"I'll be glad when we're out of this building," she said.

"Growing afraid again?" he taunted. "Don't look so concerned. You'll make people suspicious. Let's see you smile."

"You didn't tell me where it is, Sid."

"Secret! But it's safe."

"And the painting?" she questioned.

"You'll be surprised—but no more so than Homer Fanshaw. I anticipate that Mr. Fanshaw will be on the verge of a stroke when he learns the truth."

The elevator stopped, and they got into it. Down to the ground floor they shot, and walked through the lobby of the building to the street. They were ahead of the alarm. A dozen uniformed police officers were around the entrance, and perhaps as many more officers in plain clothes. But they had not yet received word from upstairs to stop all persons descending. And the lobby was thronged with men and women hurrying in and out of the great building. It would be difficult for anybody to say afterward whether any suspicious characters had passed.

Sidney Carleigh and his sister did not look like suspicious characters. She was babbling about Paris gowns, and he was chaffing her about a woman's extravagance As they started to step out upon the street, Mr. Sidney Carleigh managed to bump rather heavily against a policeman.

He did it in such a manner that the policeman believed the fault his own. Mr. Carleigh dropped a small package he was carrying for his sister. A shower of small purchases flew to the walk.

"Beg pardon, sir! Sorry, sir!" The policeman stooped to gather up the articles. He handed them to Carleigh.

"My fault, I think," Carleigh said. "Just hold my stick a moment, please, while I stuff these things into my pocket."

The policeman obligingly held the stick. Mr. Carleigh disposed of the small packages, thanked the policeman and took his stick, and went with his sister to the curb, where he engaged a taxicab. A moment later they were rolling along the avenue, homeward bound.

"Would you mind telling me, Sid, what made you become so awkward suddenly?" his sister asked.

"Beg pardon?"

"You know what I mean. You bumped against that policeman purposely. You dropped those things purposely. You'd loosened the string on the package. I saw you do it, and wondered what you were up to."

"Tell you in a few minutes, when we get home," he said in low tones.

She was compelled to be satisfied with that. They reached the apartment house, stopped in the lobby a moment to speak to friends, then ascended to their own apartment. Mr. Carleigh made a swift examination, to assure himself there were no intruders present—a precaution he always took.

Then he sat down beside Eleanor on the couch, and smiled at her. It was a peculiar sort of smile.

"Sid, don't look so silly!" she ordered. "Now, you tell me the things I don't know. Why did you bump against that policeman and spill those things?"

"It was all a trick," he said, with mock seriousness. "The purpose was to make the policeman hold my cane for a moment."

"And what was the sense in that, Sid?"

"A sort of self-satisfaction, my dear. Bravado, and all that sort of thing. I wanted to get a chuckle out of this affair. I know what that cop never will know—that he held the Fanshaw diamond necklace for a moment, while he was talking to The Mongoose."

"The necklace?" she gasped. "Where is it?"

He reached for the cane. It was in two sections, hollow for about half its length, yet with the halves joined together so cleverly that the bisection never would be guessed, and with its weight balanced. Sidney Carleigh pulled the sections apart, and from the hollow space spilled the diamond necklace.

"Oh!" she cried.

"Beauty, isn't it?" he said. "You can have some of the stones, if you want them, mounted any way you like. We'll sell the rest and put the money into the expense fund."

AT SEVEN o'clock that evening, Homer Fanshaw sat in his

library like a man wrecked. His secretary had been frantically calling numbers and informing important gentlemen that there would be no private showing of the famous Michelangelo that evening. Mr. Fanshaw was indisposed.

Fanshaw really was indisposed. He looked helplessly at Mark Graddon, whom he had compelled to go home with him.

"He—he got the necklace, but he hasn't returned the painting," Fanshaw wailed. "Do you think he'll ever return it? Perhaps he's angry because we tried to catch him."

"If The Mongoose runs true to form, he'll return the painting," Mark Graddon declared. "He always keeps his word."

"The newspaper reporters have the whole thing."

"Can't be helped, Mr. Fanshaw. All your office staff babbled about it, and some of the cops. None of my men did, you can be sure. Shouldn't have called the cops in on this."

"The Mongoose called them in," Fanshaw reminded him.

"And a lot of good it did them!"

"What happened to us in the office?"

"I have an idea we'll know that when we get the chemist's report on those cigars," Graddon said, wisely.

"But they were my own private stock."

"That wouldn't prevent The Mongoose getting at them and doping them," Graddon said.

Fanshaw opened his mouth to speak again, but a third voice stopped him. The Mongoose was speaking over his wireless dictograph, as he called it.

"Hello, Fanshaw! Howdy, Graddon! Greetings! I'm speaking to you from my comfortable quarters a few miles away. I've been listening to your conversation. You're right, Graddon, in saying that I always keep my word. Sorry you called off your party tonight, Fanshaw—not that I care a cuss about your feelings, but it deprived some excellent gentlemen of the chance to make a close examination of a masterpiece."

"The painting—where is the painting?" Homer Fanshaw

barked at the wall from where the voice seemed to be coming. "You got the necklace. You said it'd be ransom for the painting."

"It isn't very far from you," The Mongoose said. "I didn't take the trouble to carry it away from your house."

"What?" Fanshaw cried.

"I cut it out of the frame, rolled it carefully into a large tube, and took it through the window with me. Just outside the window, Fanshaw, is a big drain pipe running from the roof, to carry off surplus rainwater. The lower joint is loose and can be unscrewed. You'll find the painting inside the pipe. Remove it carefully, if you don't wish to damage it. It's a rare painting, Fanshaw. I'll be glad to inspect it when it's hung in the museum. I'll probably chuckle some as I look at it—but nobody will know why."

SIX SACKS OF GOLD

*With Loaded Guns, Detective Graddon and Milton
Lanniger Sat Before a Safe Containing $50,000 and
Listened to the Mocking Threats of The Mongoose*

CHAPTER I

A LETTER IN CODE

AS HE WAITED impatiently for the telephone call to be put through his private switchboard, Milton Lanniger tapped nervously on his mahogany desk with the end of a gold pencil, kicked at the almost priceless oriental rug beneath his feet, frowned at the valuable tapestry which adorned his office wall, and in other ways betrayed a state of irritability.

It was within a few minutes of five in the afternoon. Ordinarily, Mr. Lanniger would have been gone. But he had experienced a hard day and his clerks were working overtime. Business affairs had gone against him, as they had steadily for the last several months. Unseen and unknown enemies seemed to be sniping at him on the commercial battlefield.

Rated as a wealthy man, nevertheless he found himself now approaching the end of his liquid resources. Soon, he would have to commence raising cash—and then his business foes would know that he was on the toboggan.

That would not do at all. It would mean the beginning of his ruin. He always had been rather ruthless in business affairs, and sometimes even downright unscrupulous. He had made many enemies, and scores would rush in to the kill when they learned that he was wounded.

But Milton Lanniger thought with some satisfaction of a certain little private hoard which he had gathered against just such an emergency as this. Not much, to be sure, but it would tide him over the week-end, and by Monday he could arrange a counterblow. He wasn't licked yet! Even his worst enemies said that he was a great fighter, and that, if he ever was vanquished, he would go down fighting.

Take this letter, now! It had been delivered to the front office by special messenger. Most men, Milton Lanniger told himself, would have wilted and gone to pieces under the circumstances. But it only made him mad, and wanting to fight.

"Here's your party, Mr. Lanniger," said the switchboard operator.

"Hello!" Lanniger barked into the transmitter. "This Mark Graddon? Milton Lanniger talking. I want you to get over to my office as soon as you can, Graddon.... Tell you when you get here.... Very important, yes.... Damn it, man, I'd not waste time calling you if it wasn't.... Drop everything else and get over here!"

He slapped the receiver on its hook and jumped up from his desk chair. Back and forth from corner to corner of the private office he paced, like a man either walking off a fit of rage or trying to walk one on. He kicked at the almost priceless oriental rug a few times more, picked a valuable statuette up off a filing cabinet and slammed it down again and yanked at the corner of the rare tapestry as though he meant he to tear it off the wall.

He glanced at his watch, and tried to estimate how long it would take Mark Graddon to get there. Graddon's office was about a dozen blocks away, but the traffic would be congested at this hour, with everybody leaving business and hurrying to get home. And Graddon moved slowly at times.

But Graddon was a good man at his job. Formerly a police department detective, and a good one, he had opened his own agency some fifteen years before.

He worked almost exclusively for big financiers, could keep secrets both business and personal, and was at all times discreet. Graddon could be trusted by the men who employed him—and they paid him well for his services.

Stopping beside his desk, Milton Lanniger picked up the

He peered through the window and smiled to find that his plans were working out as he hoped

letter and looked at it again. He tossed it down, curled his lips in a sneer.

"Can't scare me!" he muttered. "Damned schoolboy tricks! About twenty years in jail would do the fellow good! Digging up an old dead-and-gone thing like that! Preposterous! Made asses out of some of the fellows, but he'll not make one out of me! I'll—"

The buzzer sounded.

"Well?" Lanniger snapped. "Oh! Send him right in. And don't let us be disturbed."

A moment later, Detective Mark Graddon was in the private office. Graddon was a massive man, but snappy in action, stolid looking, but alert. There was an active intelligence behind the dull mask of his face.

"Thought I asked you to get here quick," Milton Lanniger gruffed, glancing at his watch again. "Must have walked, and done a lot of window shopping on the way. Stop in to see a friend somewhere? Sit down there at the end of the desk—your feet must be tired."

Mark Graddon grinned, and sat down. As a matter of strict truth, he had made a record-breaking trip the dozen blocks between the two offices, as several traffic cops would have testified.

"Pardon me, Mr. Lanniger, but you seem to be all steamed up about something," Mark Graddon said.

"**I DO?** You have wonderful powers of perception, Graddon. Yes, I'm all steamed up about something. Here's a letter. It was left in the front office a short time ago—came by special messenger. Look at the envelope first. See that queer little mark down in the corner?"

"Yeah!" Mark Graddon said. "Looks like a fish worm all tangled up. What is it?"

"It's a private mark, known only to a few. When a letter is shoved under my nose and the envelope has that mark, I drop everything else and get at the letter. Understand?"

"I get it!"

"Good! So, when I saw that mark, I naturally ripped the envelope open and jerked the letter out. Here's the letter. Take a look at it."

Mark Graddon did so. "Looks like a mixture of Greek and something else," he offered.

"It's in code," Milton Lanniger explained. "A very special private code, Graddon, supposedly known to about six persons. Used by me and a few close associates at times when nothing else will do."

"I understand," Graddon said. "You got a letter written in your private code, and it's got you all steamed up. What's the trouble? Anything I can do to help?"

"Think I sent for you to discuss the weather?" Lanniger barked. "I translated the thing right away, naturally. Thought it had something to do with a business deal—had every reason for thinking so. Lot of tricky stuff going on lately in the market. Well, Graddon, take a cigar out of that humidor you're looking at so hard, light up, settle back in your chair, and prepare for a shock. Here's the translation—read it."

Graddon grinned again, took a cigar and lighted it, settled back in the comfortable chair, and took the sheet of paper Milton Lanniger offered him. He began reading the translation of the code letter.

An instant later, he was sitting up straight, and had put the cigar on an ash tray. He read:

> My dear Milton Lanniger:
> As I always warn before I strike, I am taking this means of warning you.
> You are the next scoundrel on my list. For your sins, you must pay, and for the suffering you caused others you now must suffer. I do not need to go into details. You understand.
> The Mongoose

"Gets you, huh?" Milton Lanniger said. "And in my own private code—don't forget that!"

"Oh, that's not very remarkable!" Mark Graddon replied. "Don't forget that The Mongoose, before he began doing his work was the confidential private secretary of one of your close business associates."

"Anyhow, to blazes with the letter! Let's get right down to business," Lanniger suggested. "He's threatening me, it seems. Says that I'm the next on his list. Graddon, that fellow must be caught!"

Mark Graddon sighed. "We've been trying to catch him," he replied. "We haven't stopped trying for an hour since he broke out. But he uses unusual methods—"

"I know all about that," Lanniger interrupted. "I know what happened to the others. But I don't want it to happen to me. Why, it's preposterous!"

"He's after swag—and revenge."

"Rot! Ten years ago, a few of us almost got caught in a tricky business deal—some people called it a swindle. What the hell of it? Everybody was doing it. If we didn't get the suckers somebody else would. To dodge jail we framed a bookkeeper named William Cratch—"

"I helped to do the framing—arranged for a lot of fake evidence and witnesses," Graddon interrupted.

"Yes, you know all about it. Cratch was sent to jail. He died there, if I remember rightly. Now this fellow shows up, says that he's Cratch's son, and begins riding all of us. Robbing us right, left and center. Making fools of the gang. Calls himself The Mongoose, because he says he's attacking human snakes. Damned foolishness!"

"He's a bad actor," Mark Graddon offered. "I give him credit for being clever."

"It's got to stop!" Lanniger thundered. "Suppose we did frame the old man? Can't touch us now—statute of limitations, and all that. So let's get after this fellow. The rest of the gang have been afraid of publicity. This Mongoose is trading on that. Well, I'm not!"

"If the public knew the facts—" Graddon began.

"To hell with the public! It praises or raves today—and forgets tomorrow. I've no compunctions at all. We saved ourselves at the expense of another man—all right! Who the blazes was he? If he lived to get out of prison we'd have fixed him for life and sent him away somewhere. Just taking the rap for us, that's all. Nothing for this son of his to cut up about."

Graddon, hardboiled though he was, didn't exactly get this line of reasoning. But he said nothing, only picked up his cigar again.

"No compunctions whatever!" Lanniger continued. "Why should I have gone to jail? Every man for himself at a time like that! I had everything to live for. But, enough of that! What are we going to do about this?"

"We'll try to catch him," Mark Graddon replied. "You want to understand, Mr. Lanniger, that The Mongoose isn't an ordinary burglar, or anything like that. He's one smooth customer. One reason we haven't caught him before this is that he doesn't use any of the old methods. He's an expert in electricity and chemistry—plays all sorts of tricks."

"I know all that. He's probably listening to us now," Milton Lanniger said. "Got some sort of wireless dictograph, I've been told. To hell with him and his tricks! Graddon, you get busy! We've got to land this Mongoose, and land him hard! I'm itching for a fight, anyhow. They've been getting at me in the market lately. I need something to stir me up."

"THE MONGOOSE," Graddon said, "is no piker. He plays for big stakes, and he always knows what he's going after. He'll try to rob you. Where can he get loot?"

"Well—I've got a vault here in my private office, and another in my apartment uptown," Lanniger said.

"How much stuff in 'em?"

"Not one whale of a lot just now," Lanniger said. "I've been using up collateral. Got a few negotiable bonds here—say about fifteen thousand."

"Not enough to attract The Mongoose, under ordinary circumstances," Graddon said. "He tackles the stuff in fifty thousand dollar lots—and up."

"Fifty thou—" Milton Lanniger ceased speaking, and seemed to choke. "Just happened to think of something, but never mind!" he continued.

"Anything else he might go after?" Mark Graddon asked.

"I don't see how he can tap my bank account or get into my safety deposit boxes," Lanniger replied.

"Got anything in the vault at your apartment?"

"Stuff that would gladden the heart of a burglar, possibly—but not The Mongoose."

"What have you there?" Graddon persisted.

"Got a vault in one of the rooms—a sort of home office of

mine. I own the apartment house, Graddon, if you'll remember—had it built. Had my personal apartment specially constructed. It takes the entire third floor of the house—I like to be near the ground."

"What's in the vault?"

"Always a little cash. Some old jewelry that isn't worth a hell of a lot except as keepsakes, and some other stuff like that. My butler puts the plate there. Had a small dinner last night, and had the gold plate out. Left the vault open when I came away, so he could put it back."

"Left it open?" Graddon asked. "You sure must trust your butler."

"Jepson? Sure! He's been with me a long time. But you don't understand, Graddon. It's a double vault. The butler can get into only the front part. Inner door—understand? Have to unlock that to get at the valuable stuff. Only plate and stuff like that in the front part."

"And what's in the back part?" Graddon asked.

"What the hell makes you think that I have got anything of value there?"

"The Mongoose only goes after big stuff. If he's out to get you, he knows exactly what he's after. There's not enough here in your office to attract him—not worth the risk. He can't get at your bank balance or safe deposit boxes, as you said yourself. So, he must be after that vault in your apartment."

Milton Lanniger dropped suddenly into his desk chair like a man from whom strength has fled. "Sufferin' snakes!" he ejaculated.

"What is it, Mr. Lanniger?"

"But he couldn't do it, Graddon—he couldn't get into that inner vault. How the hell could he? He'd have to get into the front part first, and he couldn't even do that. Then he'd have to have the key to the inner compartment. And the thing could be guarded—"

"If I'm to do anything, I've got to have the facts," Mark Graddon said.

"Can I trust you, Graddon, to keep your mouth shut about something? Beg pardon! Shouldn't have said that! Know you're to be trusted."

"You can trust me," Graddon said.

"Fair enough! Graddon, I've always had a horror of being caught some day without necessary resources. Afraid I'd get pinched for ready cash. Afraid currency might depreciate, and bonds go wrong, and all that. Holy horror of being flat broke."

Graddon smiled. "A lot of us are like that," he said.

"I've prepared for it—guarded against it. Gold, Graddon—gold! It's always of value, anywhere and at any time. Hard times may come, governments may fall, bonds and stocks may crash, but gold is always gold!"

"True enough!" Graddon agreed.

"So I—well, I gathered a little gold together. It's in the vault at my apartment. Six sacks of double eagles, Graddon—about fifty thousand dollars in gold."

CHAPTER II

THE MONGOOSE MAKES A DATE

MARK GRADDON SAT up straight in his chair as though a shock of electricity had burned him, and his cigar almost dropped from his mouth.

"Fifty thousand—gold!" he gasped. "That's what The Mongoose is after. I'll bet on it!"

"But how could he know I have it?" Lanniger asked. "I've gathered it a little at a time."

"You've probably dropped a hint sometime or other," Graddon told him. "I don't know how The Mongoose learned about it, but I'll bet that's what he's got his eyes on."

"But, how could he possibly get it?" Lanniger demanded. "It's in the inner vault, I tell you, and the vault is in my apartment. How could he get into the room, and then into the vault, get the gold and carry it out and get away with it, without being nabbed?"

"I'm not saying he can," Graddon pointed out. "I'm saying that he'll probably try it. The place should be easy to guard. I'll have my men scattered all around. If you're asking me, The Mongoose has bitten off a mouthful this time. Six sacks of gold, huh? They'll weigh something. He can't carry that away like a handful of diamonds in his hat or a hollow cane."

"Better use plenty of men, Graddon. Call in the cops."

"We don't want the police mixed up in this," Graddon said quickly. "They'd only be in the way—and ask a lot of questions. I want to get hold of The Mongoose myself—and maybe fix him so he won't be able to talk."

"If the fellow comes with a gang—"

"As far as we've been able to find out, The Mongoose always works alone," Graddon said. "That's one reason he's hard to catch. Now, Mr. Lanniger, how many persons in the apartment?"

"I've three servants: Jepson, my butler, and Pierre and Marie. Pierre is the chef, and Marie is his wife. The three run the place. Marie and Pierre are off today, so nobody's there except Jepson."

"When did Pierre and Marie leave, and when will they return?" Graddon asked.

"I suppose they left as usual this morning after the work was done. Probably they'll be back late tonight or early in the morning. They go out into the country sometimes, I believe. Pierre has a brother who raises vegetables, or something like that."

"Then nobody'll be at the apartment this evening except Jepson. That's fine," Graddon said. "We don't want a lot of people in the way. There's no telling when The Mongoose will strike. It may be tonight, or tomorrow night, or even in the daytime. He may hold off and try to wreck your nerves with the suspense. But, when he strikes, we'll be ready for him."

"That's the spirit, Graddon!" Lanniger cried. "You've got to catch the fellow! I certainly won't forget you, if you can land him."

"I don't need any spur," Mark Graddon replied. "He'll be after me soon, too, if he isn't landed. I was in on that deal ten years ago, and The Mongoose knows it."

"You're in charge of the thing, Graddon. Use your own judgment. What do you want to do?"

"I'd sure like to get that gold into a safe deposit vault," Graddon said.

"It's too late to do it today. And I want the gold right where it is," Lanniger declared. "I've kept it where I can get my hands on it quick, in case of emergency. Matter of fact, I was planning to use some of it over the week-end. But don't let a hint of that get out, Graddon!"

"Certainly not!" Graddon said.

"I'M PINCHED financially, Graddon, and don't want my business enemies to know it. They've been after me. I'll use that gold tomorrow, and by Monday I'll plan something to put 'em on the run. Graddon, I—I've *got* to have that gold to use tomorrow! If anything happens to it—"

"We'll take care of it," Graddon promised. "We'll guard it tonight. And, if you remove it and use it tomorrow, we'll have the laugh on The Mongoose."

Milton Lanniger opened his mouth to say something more, but a buzzer sounded. He reached across the desk and grasped his private-line telephone.

"Yes?" he barked. "This is Lanniger."

"I know it," came a smooth male voice in reply. "There's nobody else can bark into a telephone quite as nastily as you, Lanniger."

"Who's this, and what do you want?"

"This is The Mongoose speaking, Lanniger."

"What's that? Mongoose? Trying to kid somebody? Make it snappy, whoever you are—I'm busy."

"Yes, I know. You're busy with Mark Graddon. Talking about your private gold reserve."

"Why, how did you—" Lanniger began.

"I'm the all-seeing eye and the all-hearing ear, Lanniger," The Mongoose told him, and Lanniger heard a soft chuckle come over the wire. "I see everything you do, and hear all you say. It is really very amusing sometimes."

"Damn you—"

"Don't swear, please. It may pay you to listen to me for a moment. I'll give you a chance to save your precious gold."

"Speak your piece!" Lanniger said.

"Get fifty thousand in small bills, and have them ready for me to collect, and I'll not touch your gold."

"I'll see you in—"

The Mongoose chuckled again. "Lanniger, you couldn't get hold of fifty thousand in the morning without exposing your financial weakness," he said. "I know all about it. You're due to be broke, Lanniger! Your little gold reserve is your only hope—and even that can't save you. You're going to be wrecked financially, Lanniger! I'm doing it! That's the thing that'd hurt you most. And I want you hurt, you crook!"

"Why, you— Listen, you! If I ever meet you face to face, I'll—"

"You'd do nothing, Lanniger. I know you well. I could break you with my bare hands."

"So you think that you can get the gold, do you?" Lanniger asked.

"I know it!"

"When are you coming after it?"

"That's something for you to worry about," The Mongoose said. "Good-by, until later, Lanniger!"

The connection was broken. Mark Graddon had hurried from

the room and to the switchboard. And now Lanniger called the operator himself.

"Where'd that call come from?" he demanded. "How'd it get on my private line? Did the man who called give you the code word?"

"The call didn't come through the switchboard, sir," the girl replied. "Mr. Graddon, that detective, was just here, and I told him the same."

Graddon came hurrying back into the private office as Lanniger replaced the receiver.

"That call—" Lanniger began.

"I went out to trace it," Graddon said. "It never came through the switchboard. Another of The Mongoose's tricks. Probably tapped the wire some way."

"He said he could see and hear."

"I doubt the seeing part—that's probably another of his jokes. But he may be able to hear us," Graddon said. "He's probably got one of his wireless dictograph disks hidden around here somewhere."

"Why, in that case he's been able to listen to business conferences—hear my instructions to brokers and secretaries! Now I understand how I've been beaten in every move."

"That's probably it," Graddon said. "We'll go through the offices and look for the confounded disk. Meanwhile, you'd better telephone your apartment, Mr. Lanniger, and tell your butler to be alert till we get there. Ask him if any strangers have been about the place."

Lanniger put through the call, waited, fussed and fumed. There was no answer.

"He isn't there," Lanniger reported. "I'll have his hide! He's sneaked away to a picture show, I suppose. Knows I won't be home for dinner tonight, since Pierre's off."

MARK GRADDON sprang to his feet. "Let's get out there," he said. "You may be blaming your man Jepson unjustly."

"What do you mean, Graddon?"

"Maybe The Mongoose is at work already. He may have done something to Jepson. Let me have the telephone, sir, and I'll call my office and have a couple of my best men hurry out to the apartment to meet us."

Graddon did his telephoning, and then Lanniger ordered his car.

They hurried down in the elevator and went out into the wintry night. It already was dark, the street lights were burning, the wind was cold, and there was the sting of sleety snow in the air.

The chauffeur rushed them through the streets, along a broad avenue where the car skidded on the icy pavement, and finally drew up and stopped in front of a huge apartment building.

Into the building they hurried, shot up in the elevator to the third floor, and hurried along a corridor there, and Milton Lanniger used his latch key.

"Jepson!" he bellowed, as soon as they had entered. "You hear me, you rascal? Where are you, Jepson?"

He got no reply. They searched swiftly through the big apartment of some twenty rooms, an entire floor of the building. Jepson, the butler, was not in the place. He wasn't even bound and gagged and tossed into some closet, as Mark Graddon had half feared they would find him. And everything in the apartment seemed to be in order.

"He's sneaked away to a picture show," Lanniger declared. "He's crazy about pictures. I'll have his hide this time! Told him never to leave the apartment entirely without protection."

"Where's that vault?" Graddon asked.

"Come along, and I'll show you."

They walked along a cross hall and turned into a small room which had been fitted up as a sort of ornate office. Lanniger pulled aside a wall hanging, and the door of the vault was disclosed.

"Safe so far, Graddon," he said. "Now, tell me—how can The

Mongoose get into this room, unlock that vault, get the inner compartment open, get six heavy sacks of gold, and get away with them? Especially if you and your men are watching, and I'm here prepared to help?"

"Seems utterly impossible," Graddon remarked. "I told you he'd bitten off more than a mouthful this time. Makes me suspicious. May be a trick. He may not mean to carry away the gold, but set us to watching it while he strikes somewhere else."

"The way he talked, I think it's the gold he's after. Like to see him try to get it!"

Graddon's two men arrived. He stationed one in the big living room of the apartment, and the other out in the corridor of the building, and gave them strict orders. They had been after The Mongoose on other occasions, and were as eager as their chief to catch him. Graddon had offered a special reward.

Then the detective returned to the apartment, where Lanniger was pacing around the living room like a wild man.

"You can't get to the den except through that hall," he explained. "Only one window in the den, and it's three floors up, and no fire escape landing. He can't do it!"

"We'll get him if he tries it," Graddon promised.

"You've got to protect that gold, Graddon!" Lanniger said, in a voice so low that Graddon's man would not hear. "You don't know what it means. If I can't have that gold to use in the morning, I—I'll be busted! Got to cover certain investments. If I can manage to hang over the week-end, I'll be all right."

"Don't worry," Graddon said. "Getting into a double vault and carrying away six sacks of gold is a tough job for only one man when he's got determined opposition."

"And that's exactly what he's going to have—determined opposition," Lanniger declared.

He started to turn back across the room again, but came to an abrupt stop. Soft, mocking laughter had reached his ears. Lanniger and Graddon and the latter's man looked at one another in surprise.

Then they heard a voice, and from whence it came they could not tell:

"Lanniger.... This is The Mongoose speaking.... Be in your den exactly at nine tonight.... Be sure.... I'll speak to you again then, and tell you something of importance."

CHAPTER III

THE MONGOOSE LISTENS IN

THE FLOOR OF the building directly above Milton Lanniger's sumptuous personal apartment was cut up into small suites, each of two rooms, kitchenette and bath. The rentals were moderate for the neighborhood, and the small apartments always filled.

But there had been a vacancy about a month before and the vacant suite had been leased immediately by a little old woman who was known as Mrs. Sarah Timpen. She was supposed to be wealthy, and almost a recluse. She seemed to spend the greater part of her waking hours reading and listening to the radio.

Mrs. Sarah Timpen was regarded by the employees of the apartment house as somewhat eccentric. But she was quiet and reserved, and attracted little attention. It was noticed that she had certain peculiarities. For instance, she always wore thin black gloves, saying that they prevented an escape of personal magnetism.

She owned a small coupé of cheap make, and had a license to drive it. Almost every day she took her car out for an hour or so. Her eccentricity extended to the car, also. She did not want to keep it in the garage. She wanted to park it in the little court adjoining the alley, four floors below and directly beneath the window of her living room. The superintendent, having received a generous tip, allowed her to do so.

There was a closet in her bedroom into which she would not

allow the chambermaid to go. Mrs. Timpen had a special lock put on the door. Since her reputation for eccentricity already had been established, this caused little comment. A timid old lady, perhaps afraid of having some of her personal belongings stolen, the employees supposed.

But there were some queer things in that closet—electric batteries, pieces of delicate machinery, headphones, a microphone, an extension telephone, jars of chemicals—queer things for a little old lady to be owning.

As far as the employees of the apartment house knew, she had only one caller. He was a stoop-shouldered man with a pasty face, large nose, protruding ears, whose watery eyes were almost obscured by thick spectacles. He called on Mrs. Timpen regularly, about three times a week, always bringing her a box of cheap candy. Mrs. Timpen explained that he was her first cousin, and that they were the last remaining members of their family.

On this particular day, the stoop-shouldered man came to the apartment house about seven-thirty in the evening. He used the desk telephone and called Mrs. Timpen's suite.

"This is Jeremy, Sarah," he said, in a cracked voice. "I came a bit early, so we can read that book. It'll take us until almost midnight. I'll come right up to the apartment—yes."

The desk clerk overheard that. Mrs. Timpen and her cousin were going to be busy reading a book, until almost midnight.

The stoop-shouldered man ascended in the elevator to the fourth floor, and shuffled along the corridor there, to ring Mrs. Timpen's bell.

"Hello, Cousin Sarah!" he greeted, as the door was opened.

"Welcome, Cousin Jeremy! Come right in! Going to be cold tonight, isn't it?"

The stoop-shouldered man stepped inside, and the door was closed. Then they looked at each other and indulged in spasms of silent laughter, and she took him by the hand and led him to a couch on the opposite side of the room, where they talked in low tones.

"How goes it, Sid?" she asked.

"Everything's lovely, Eleanor. I called Lanniger's butler from a suburban drug store about three o'clock. Imitated Lanniger's voice and manner, and told Jepson to take the roadster and go at once to the country place and get everything ready—that I'd be out tonight with a couple of friends for a secret business conference. Then I watched. Twenty minutes later the faithful Jepson drove past."

"And the other two servants are having their day off," she added.

"Right! I came back and slipped into the apartment and finished my work there. Then I hurried home and went to the laboratory. The letter was delivered on time. I listened in and heard Lanniger call Graddon. I spoke to him in his office over his private wire. They came to the apartment, and I spoke to them again here, over the wireless. Then I made up and got here as quickly as possible. It's been one busy afternoon."

"And everything's ready now in the Lanniger apartment?" she asked.

"Everything. I went there this morning, posing as a radio expert sent by Lanniger, and Jepson let me go all through the place. I pretended to be fixing the radio, trying to find the cause of some interference. Got a chance to have some time alone in the den, where the vault's located—and fixed everything there. Good piece of luck, too—the vault door was unlocked. The butler was getting ready to put some plate back—they had a party there last night."

"That's great, Sid!" she said.

"Not a hitch anywhere along the line. Plans working out perfectly, as usual. That's the result of using care, taking time, and giving attention to minor details. Everything's ready."

"I've been worried sick, Sid," she said.

"You're always worried more or less, just before we finish one of our little schemes," he told her. "That's only nerves, my dear sister. Compose yourself. Everything will be all right."

He got up and walked around the room as though trying to quiet his own nerves, still acting the stoop-shouldered old man. It was a masterful make-up. For, when he was Sidney Carleigh, he was tall and straight, with regular, manly features belonging to a man of perhaps thirty-five, with an athletic swing to his body. And his sister, Eleanor, now playing the part of Mrs. Sarah Timpen, was an attractive, vivacious woman who caused many heads to turn for a second look.

"WE'RE RUNNING a big risk to get that fifty thousand, my dear," Sidney Carleigh said. "But it means more to us than that amount of money—of which we have plenty, thank heaven! That beast of a Lanniger, who helped send our father to prison—"

"Hush, Sid!" she said.

"Don't worry, Eleanor. I'll not let my rage wreck my judgment. The moment I become The Mongoose, I'm as cold as ice. This man Lanniger is one of the worst. He doesn't even feel remorse for what he did. If we can get that gold, he'll be ruined. I've smashed him to pieces in the market, by listening over the wireless dictograph to his plans, and then tipping off his business enemies as to what he planned. I've got him where he needs that gold to keep from being ruined. If we get it tonight, Lanniger will be a bankrupt by noon next Monday."

"You want to go into the closet now, Sid?" she asked.

"Yes. I'd better check up."

They went into the bedchamber, and Eleanor Carleigh opened the closet. Her brother entered. He put on the headphones, worked dials on a panel in front of him. He tuned in the wireless dictograph on the disk he had secreted in Lanniger's living room, and listened.

Lanniger and Mark Graddon were talking down there.

"I've sent down to the café for something to eat," Lanniger was saying. "Sorry Pierre isn't here. I'd planned to eat at the club. Can't imagine what's keeping Jepson away so long. Take his hide off in strips when he gets back."

"Jepson's absence is worrying me," Mark Graddon confessed.

"He's had plenty of time to see a show and get back. He'd be afraid to stay away too long—afraid you might telephone the apartment after office hours, or come here right after dinner."

"Where can the rascal be?" Lanniger asked. "We've looked all through the apartment, and we know he isn't here—not even in a closet. He's helping himself to a night off, that's what!"

In the closet on the floor above, Sidney Carleigh spoke into the microphone: "Lanniger! You'll learn about Jepson at nine o'clock."

Down in his living room, Milton Lanniger sprang to his feet, his face purple with wrath.

"Graddon, I can't stand much more of this!" he cried. "That damned Mongoose—he hears everything we say! It's uncanny—gives me a creepy feeling. It's like somebody peeking at you from behind a curtain."

"Only his wireless dictograph," Graddon said. "We haven't time to look for the disk now. It's only about the size of a quarter, and might be stuck around almost any place. Just be careful what we say."

"Graddon, you catch that fiend. You've got to do it. Better send for more men."

"I've got half a dozen here now," Graddon said. "This man here, one in the hall, one by the elevator, one on the floor above, one on the floor below, and one downstairs in the lobby, camping right by the desk telephone, where he can get a call quick in case of trouble."

"Then The Mongoose's game is blocked," Lanniger declared. "He can't even get into the apartment, let alone into that vault in the den. Unless he shoots his way in—lays us all out—"

"He's never resorted to that kind of violence yet," Graddon said. "But he'll play plenty of tricks, possibly. Keep your eyes and ears open. And we're not sure, Lanniger, that he's going to strike tonight. If he doesn't, we'll use double precautions tomorrow."

Out of the void the voice of The Mongoose came to them:

"I strike tonight, gentlemen!"

Milton Lanniger sprang up again and brandished a fist over his head. He shouted at the wall:

"Come on and try it, Mongoose! Let me get a sight of you, and I'll empty my automatic into you!"

"You'll not be able to see me," the voice of The Mongoose said. "You'll hear me, know that I'm near, possibly, but you won't see me. For you'll be blind!"

"What's that?" Lanniger cried. "Be blind, huh? If I can hear you near me, I'll put a few slugs of lead in you just the same."

The mocking laughter of The Mongoose came again, and again he spoke: "You'll be powerless to move a muscle. Your brain will be active, but your body dead. You'll not be able to call for help—not even able to speak. At nine o'clock, in the den, I'll tell you more."

Lanniger would have spoken again, indulged in a profitless tirade, but Mark Graddon motioned him to silence. Graddon beckoned, and Lanniger followed him out into the corridor.

"He probably can't hear us out here, but speak in whispers, anyhow," Graddon said. "Don't let that stuff he said wreck your nerve. It's a part of his game to make us afraid of him. We'll refuse to be scared."

"Be blind and unable to move!" Lanniger said, sneering. "Does he think we're going to stand still and maybe let him shoot us in the arm with a needle, and dope us?"

"We'll go to the den, and remain there," Graddon decided. "We'll just be quiet, and smoke and wait. He can't get the gold unless he goes into the den and gets into the vault. And we'll be ready for anything—anything at all."

CHAPTER IV

THE MONGOOSE DROPS A HINT

AT TEN MINUTES before the hour of nine, Eleanor Carleigh put on her hat and a heavy coat and prepared to leave the apartment. Her brother emerged from the closet and went with her to the hall door.

"Heads up—and be careful!" he said.

"You be careful, Sid," she replied. "The car's spotted just right, isn't it?"

"Yes. I parked it there when I came back today after my usual drive."

"Don't worry. Everything will work out all right. Got that sharp knife? Good! Cut the rope—don't waste time at trying to untie the knots."

"I understand, Sid."

"You're talking to The Mongoose now," he whispered. "Here's where we strike another blow of vengeance."

He kissed her, then opened the door. A quick glance revealed that no one was in the corridor. Eleanor Carleigh slipped out, and made for the rear of the building.

When she came to the rear service stairs, she went down them slowly, careful not to be observed, cautious as she passed each floor. She did not stop at the ground floor, but went through a door and down into the basement.

She listened there for a moment. The superintendent had his apartment there. The door was closed. She could hear him talking to somebody. Quietly, she slipped along the hall and went to the outside door. An instant later, she was through it and out in the cold night.

She hurried around the corner of the building and into the little court where her coupé was parked. It was so dark there that nothing could be seen. Eleanor Carleigh unlocked the door of the coupé and opened it. She got in, started the engine, let it run to get warm. The howling wind, forerunner of a blinding snowstorm, drowned what noise the motor made.

She looked up. On the third floor she could see a lighted window, which she knew was in the den of Milton Lanniger's apartment. Directly above that was another lighted window—in the living room of the apartment she had been occupying as Mrs. Sarah Timpen.

As she watched, this window grew dark. Then she saw three flashes of an electric torch. Eleanor Carleigh took a tiny torch from her coat pocket, and flashed it three times in reply. Then she waited.

Having turned out the lights in the room, The Mongoose had opened the window and given the torch signal. He kept the window open. From beneath the couch, he took a coil of light, strong rope, the end of which was fastened securely to the base of a radiator.

He let the rope through the window and down to the ground four floors below. Presently a jerk on it assured him that it had reached bottom, and that Eleanor had secured it there.

The Mongoose hurried back to the closet, put on the headphones and adjusted them, and again reached for the dials with his rubber-gloved hands. He manipulated them swiftly, and tuned in on the den of the apartment below....

"Well, it's nine o'clock, and we haven't heard anything from The Mongoose," Lanniger was saying. "Promised he'd tell us something about Jepson. Said he'd strike tonight, too. Are your men ready, Graddon?"

"They're all at their stations," Graddon replied. "Best men I've got—and all my operatives are good."

"Graddon, it's impossible for that fellow to get in here and steal that gold, isn't it?" Lanniger asked. He wanted to be reassured. "Here we sit, and both of us armed and ready to shoot. One of your men in the living room and another out in the hall.

The vault closed, and the door to the inner compartment closed and locked, and the key in my waistcoat pocket."

"You haven't looked into the vault since we came from your office," Graddon said.

"And I don't want to open it now," Lanniger said. "The vault's going to stay closed until I take the gold out in the morning. When I do take it out, you and your men will guard it all the way to the bank. Nothing must happen to that gold, Graddon. I've told you how serious the situation is."

"I understand," Graddon said.

HE TOUCHED a match to his cigar, and started walking around the little room. He opened the door and looked into the hall, and could see his man in the living room. Closing the door again, he paced back to the desk beside which Lanniger was sitting.

"Five minutes past nine," Lanniger said. "The Mongoose doesn't keep his engagements. Maybe he's given it up as a bad job. Trying to catch us off guard, possibly."

"Listen!" Graddon barked.

From the living room came sounds as of a dozen guns being fired. His service revolver held ready, Graddon sprang to the door and opened it. He could see his operative standing in the living room, looking around wildly.

"What is it?" Lanniger cried, rushing to Graddon's side. "Gang shooting their way in?"

Graddon was howling to his man, who did not answer. He whirled to confront Lanniger.

"Stand right here in the door," he said. "Keep your gun ready. Watch the door of the vault. Shoot if you see anybody."

Graddon rushed along the hall and into the living room.

"What happened?" he howled. "Why didn't you answer me?"

The man stationed in the corridor was pounding on the front door, and Graddon rushed across and let him in. Pungent smoke was swirling through the room. Graddon opened one of the windows and let the cold night air rush in and dispel the smoke.

"I don't know what happened, Graddon," his man was reporting. "I thought somebody was shooting at me. Sounded like it—and there's the smoke."

"Mongoose trick," Graddon judged. "Can't see why he did it, unless to decoy us from the den." He glanced along the hall, and saw Lanniger standing in the doorway. Everything seemed to be all right there. "Keep that window open. Don't get a whiff of that smoke—might put you to sleep. You two men stay right here at the end of the hall. Watch the door of the den, and watch this room. And be ready to shoot!"

In the closet on the floor above, The Mongoose touched a row of tiny buttons. Electric sparks flashed.

Down in the living room of the Lanniger apartment, there was another series of minor explosions, and again puffs of pungent smoke swirled across the room.

"It's coming from the moulding," one of Graddon's men said.

"Coming from the baseboard, too," the other added.

"Watch, as I told you," Graddon snapped at them. "And don't drink in any of that smoke. Better open another window, maybe."

He hurried back along the hall toward the door of the den, where Lanniger was waiting.

"Mongoose trick," he reported. "Trying to get our attention off the den, probably. We'll fool him there. We'll go into the den and lock the door."

"And then let's see him get in," Lanniger added.

"Nothing to do but watch the door and window."

"That window's three stories from the ground and fifteen from the roof," Lanniger pointed out.

"We'll watch it, nevertheless," Graddon said.

They stepped into the den, after a last glance down the hall had assured Graddon that his men were in position and were all right. Lanniger locked and bolted the door. Then they went to sit beside the desk.

"Schoolboy tricks!" Lanniger stormed. "How do you suppose he made all that noise—and why?"

"He's exploding chemicals by electricity," Graddon said. "May have been working around this apartment for months, getting ready. That smoke—probably make a man unconscious if he breathed in any of it."

"Then his game isn't working," Lanniger declared. "The open windows and cold air spoiled it. Think we'd better open this window, too, Graddon?"

"Leave it closed—and locked."

"But he couldn't get in there. It's three—"

"I know," Mark Graddon interrupted. "But it's safer to keep it locked, safer to put every obstacle possible in his way."

"It's a quarter after nine now, and he hasn't spoken to us, as he promised. Bet his plans have gone wrong. He may have said that just to get us to be here in the den."

"Here's where we belong," Graddon said. "We're protecting the gold in that vault. Do it better here than anywhere else."

In the closet above, The Mongoose turned another dial, and spoke softly into the microphone. The two in the den heard his voice:

"Hello, Lanniger…. Hello, Graddon…. This is The Mongoose…. Can you hear me?"

"Yes, we can hear you," Lanniger growled. "Speak your piece, Mongoose."

"You haven't looked into your vault since you came home, have you, Lanniger?"

"No, I haven't."

"Perhaps you'd better do so. You might find something interesting there. I'm not saying so, understand, but—Jepson, your butler, may be in the vault, Lanniger—and your gold gone already."

Then came that soft, mocking laughter again.

CHAPTER V

THE MONGOOSE STRIKES

THE LAUGHTER CEASED. On the floor above, The Mongoose left the closet and hurried to the open window in the dark front room. Through it he went swiftly, grasped the dangling rope, and began a slow and careful descent.

Running along the side of the building at the floor below was a narrow ledge of masonry. The Mongoose stopped on this ledge, stood upon it, holding to the rope and bracing himself against the force of the wind. By stepping a few feet to one side, he could peer through a window and into Lanniger's den.

He looked in cautiously, and smiled when he found that his plans were working out as he had hoped. That hint about Jepson possibly being in the vault, and the gold gone, had startled both Lanniger and Graddon. They had jumped to their feet, Lanniger clutching at the detective's arm.

"It can't be, can it, Graddon?" Lanniger cried. "He couldn't have got the gold! Tell me he couldn't!"

"If he did, he got it before we came here," Graddon said. "Safe enough to look and see, if you want to do it."

"That's what I'll do, Graddon. I'll open the vault. If he's put poor Jepson in there—"

"If he has, Jepson's probably a dead man," Mark Graddon declared.

Lanniger knelt before the vault door and began working the combination. His nervous, trembling fingers fumbled over the knob. He compelled himself to be calm, and began again.

Mark Graddon stood behind him, revolver held ready. He watched the door, the window, listened for any sounds that might come from the living room beyond. But he heard nothing to indicate that trouble of any sort was there.

Lanniger finished working the combination, and pulled the door of the vault open. Graddon peered over his shoulder. Light from the den poured into the vault.

The first glance was satisfying, for it failed to reveal the body of the butler stretched upon the steel floor. Everything seemed to be in order. There was nothing to indicate that the place had been entered and ransacked. Bundles of documents on the steel shelves remained untouched. Lanniger's plate was there, glistening in the light.

"I'm going to open the inner compartment," Lanniger said. "I've got to be sure the gold's there. Then we can close the vault again, and guard it. The Mongoose was lying to us."

"Hurry it up," Graddon begged. "I'll feel better with the vault closed and locked. This all may be a trick just to get you to open it."

Lanniger took a key from a waistcoat pocket, inserted it in the complicated lock, turned it forward and back. There came a soft click.

"Almost afraid to look—" he mouthed.

He pulled the door open, and gave a glad cry. There were six sacks, side by side. Lanniger lifted one of them a bit, dropped it, heard the chink of coins.

"Lied to us," Lanniger said. "He's failed, and he knows it. Tried to shock us—another schoolboy trick."

"Lock it up," Graddon begged. "Let's get out of here… watch till morning…."

Graddon's voice seemed to grow weak, die away. Lanniger turned quickly toward him. Graddon had reeled back against the wall of the vault. His hands were clutching his collar, trying to rip it off his throat. There was a wild look in his face.

"Graddon!" Lanniger cried. "What is it, man?"

"Gas… odorless… get out… out…" Mark Graddon muttered.

An overpowering gas. Another Mongoose trick, Lanniger

thought. He'd have to lug Graddon into the open room, get out himself and close the vault. Graddon was starting to slip down to the floor. His head was rolling from side to side. He seemed to be making an ineffectual effort to speak.

"Graddon!" Lanniger cried.

He started to spring to him. Then Milton Lanniger felt suddenly as though strong hands were at his throat and trying to choke him. He, too, tried to tear off his collar. He tried to get past Graddon and out of the vault, into the den, having some vague idea of opening the window and letting in the cold fresh air.

But his legs refused to move for him. He could not communicate to them the orders of his mind. His arms commenced to feel like leaden weights. His heart was pounding. A film seemed to be growing over his eyes.

Then he remembered what The Mongoose had said—that he would be blind—could hear, but could not see or move.

Lanniger thought of his precious gold again. He wanted to close the door to the inner compartment. He managed to turn toward it, and tried to take a step. But his legs sagged beneath him. Slowly, he collapsed, and finally sank to the floor beside Graddon. His lips were moving, but no sound came from them.

But his brain remained active. He sensed everything. He knew where he was, and under what circumstances. And he was wondering what the next act in the drama would be.

THE MONGOOSE had been watching through the window. And he did not hesitate now, when he saw both men helpless. Holding to the protecting rope with his left hand, he searched a pocket with his right, and brought out a glass cutter.

Working swiftly, he cut around the window pane. He gave a sharp tap, and the glass crashed inside the den. An instant later, The Mongoose was through the window and into the room.

He rushed to the door, and found it locked and bolted. He hurried into the vault, holding a tiny sponge to his nostrils, and keeping his eyes almost closed.

"Hello, Graddon!" he said, speaking in low tones. "How do you feel, Lanniger? Thanks for opening the vault and the inner compartment for me. When you opened the outer door, Lanniger, you released the gas. I arranged that this afternoon, after decoying your butler to your country place. He's out there waiting for you now, Lanniger, expecting you to be there with some friends for a conference."

The Mongoose laughed, brushed past the helpless men, and entered the inner compartment. He picked up a sack of gold and carried it out.

"The first sack," he told them. "Your gold reserve is getting cut down rapidly, Lanniger."

The Mongoose hurried to the window, and flashed his electric torch. Down on the ground, he saw Eleanor's answering flash. From around his waist, The Mongoose took another fine, strong rope. He fastened one end to a radiator, tied the sack of gold to the other end, and lowered it gently.

Down it went through the night, past dark windows and through the snow that had started to fall. It came to rest. Eleanor Carleigh cut the rope just above the knot, and The Mongoose drew it up swiftly, while his sister below put the bag of gold into the coupé.

The Mongoose hurried back into the vault, using the sponge on his nostrils again. The gas was clearing out, he knew, but there was some danger remaining. Some of it might cling inside the vault, and a whiff of it would be enough to do the work. Lanniger and Graddon would be helpless for half an hour or more.

"Here goes the second sack, Lanniger," The Mongoose said. "You won't be able to cover your shortage tomorrow. You'll be ruined, Lanniger—as you've ruined so many others."

The Mongoose carried the second sack to the window, lowered it, reclaimed the rope after it had been cut, and hurried back to the vault again.

Milton Lanniger was experiencing mental agony. He could not move. He could not see. He sensed The Mongoose passing and repassing him, carrying out the precious gold, realized that this would mean ruin for him. The Mongoose had struck at the right time and in the right manner, and his vengeance would be complete.

Graddon was passing through a spasm of mental agony also. He knew well what was happening. He tried to move, to bring life to his seemingly dead limbs, but could not. A film was over his eyes, and he could not see.

Graddon had guessed that the gas had been stored in the vault, and had been released when the door was opened. He wondered how The Mongoose had managed that, not knowing that the butler's carelessness in leaving the vault door unlocked had given him the chance.

The Mongoose made the last trip with a sack of gold, and sent it down through the night. He got the signal that it had been cut free by his sister and stowed away in the little coupé. He dropped the rope, with which he had been sending down the sacks. He would use the other, heavier rope in his descent.

But he was not done. He went back to the vault again, and looked down at the helpless men.

"I've done it, Lanniger," he said. "This will hurt you worse than anything else I could contrive against. You'll be ruined. Your enemies won't miss this opportunity to jump on you, and you have a host of enemies. Lanniger, many men, standing as I am now, knowing you were instrumental in sending their innocent father to prison, wouldn't hesitate to kill you! I could do it now, and make a getaway. Nobody knows where to find The Mongoose."

There was venom in the voice, and Lanniger flinched mentally. For a moment, he felt a horrible fear. He was absolutely helpless to offer a defense, if The Mongoose decided to attack. The fear of violent death was heavy upon him.

But The Mongoose was speaking again:

"I'll deal with you later, Graddon, for your part in the affair. You'll be about the last man I'll handle. Until I do, you can go right on making a fool of yourself trying to catch me. I'll be leaving you now. *Au revoir,* gentlemen!"

There was a wealth of sarcasm in that last word. The Mongoose chuckled, mockingly, and left the vault. In the den, he stopped an instant to take a deep breath. Then he started for the window and the rope.

There came a sudden pounding on the door of the den. One of Graddon's men had grown suspicious, evidently.

"Chief!" he cried. "You there, chief? Open up!"

"Your chief is asleep," The Mongoose cried in answer. "Lanniger's asleep, also. If you'd got a whiff of that smoke in the front room, you'd have been asleep."

"Who's talking in there?" the man in the hall demanded.

"This is The Mongoose talking. Your chief will come back to life in about ten or fifteen minutes. He'll be able to explain to you all about the action and effects of my new gas. It'll be quite interesting, I assure you."

"Let's smash in the door!" one of Graddon's men cried at the other.

As they hurled themselves against it, The Mongoose laughed again, loudly, then dashed to the window. An instant later, he was descending the rope, hand under hand.

CHAPTER VI

CHOP SUEY FOR TWO

DOWN THROUGH THE swirling snow he went, his gloved hands slipping on the wet rope at times. Below, he saw the continual flashing of Eleanor's electric torch.

Above him, frantic men crashed against a door, hurled their bodies against it until the hinges splintered and the door flew inward. They sprawled into the room, weapons ready.

They saw the two unconscious men on the floor of the vault,

and, what attracted them more at the moment, the window with the pane cut out. They rushed to the window, looked below, flashed their lights.

The Mongoose glanced up and saw them when he was yet a floor from the ground. He descended more rapidly. Below, his sister was crying for him to hurry.

At the window above, a gun barked. A bullet screeched past the head of The Mongoose and sang away into the stormy night. Another followed.

"Halt! Stop, down there!" one of the men at the window was shouting.

He emptied his gun into the air as a signal. Both of them began screeching for help. The rushing wind carried their voices to oblivion.

But the shooting had been heard. At the mouth of the alley, a passing police patrolman got the sound of rapid gunfire, and looked up in time to catch sight of the flashes. He got out his own weapon and started along the alley slowly, cautiously.

The Mongoose struck the ground. Eleanor clutched him by the arm.

"Hurry! Into the coupé!" she said. "A bullet may hit you, Sid. I'll drive, as we planned."

"Gold safe?" he asked.

"Stowed in the back. Hurry, Sid!"

They got into the car, and she worked the gears. The engine had been running continually, and was warm. Eleanor Carleigh guided the coupé out into the alley, and turned toward the nearest street.

Ahead of them, a flashlight gleamed. A stentorian command to stop rang at them through the storm.

"Step on it!" Sidney Carleigh said, grimly. "And keep your head down."

The car sprang forward like an animated thing, lurching and skidding on the wet pavement of the alley. Another command to stop roared at them. The light flashed again, and in its beam they caught sight of a policeman's badge. Its wearer darted aside just in time to escape the wheels.

The coupé rushed on. Behind, a gun cracked. A bullet ripped its way through the back of the car and passed between brother and sister. Another followed.

The policeman was pursuing them afoot, and firing as he ran. The coupé came to the end of the alley, and went skidding in a sharp turn into the street, almost overturning, lurching sickeningly and missing the opposite curb by inches.

"Step on it!" Sidney Carleigh commanded again.

"Leave it to me, Sid. You go ahead with your part of the program," she replied.

Behind them, the policeman had charged into the street. He fired again, but missed. Around the corner beyond him came a sedan making for the avenue.

"He's grabbing that car and coming after us!" Sidney Carleigh said. "You'll have to dodge 'em."

"I'll dodge 'em, Sid."

"And double back to where my car's in parked."

Despite the lurching of the vehicle in which he rode, Sidney Carleigh was transforming himself. The stoop-shouldered old man was disappearing.

From his nostrils, he took wads which had distended them. From behind the ears, he took plugs which had held them in a protruding position. A wig came off. Padding came from beneath the back of the coat. From a pocket in the car, he took a rag saturated with a greasy substance, and with this he washed his face free of the make-up.

"Dodge 'em!" he said, again. He had glanced through the rear window of the car. The sedan was pursuing them, and gaining slightly.

ELEANOR CARLEIGH took the light coupé around another corner, seemingly on two wheels. Again the car lurched and skidded and threatened to overturn, but she righted it, pressed down on the accelerator, and flew on. The sedan took the corner a moment later, and came after them.

Around another corner she went at a terrific rate of speed. A policeman on the walk howled at them, saw the pursuing car with a brother officer standing on the running board, and whipped out his service revolver. But Eleanor Carleigh sent the coupé around still another corner as he fired.

"Slow down, and cut through that alley," her brother instructed.

She managed to make it before the pursuing car came into view. She stopped the coupé, snapped off the lights. They watched the sedan roar by. Then she backed the coupé swiftly, made sure that the sedan had rushed on, and turned back in the direction from which they had come. Turning into a broad avenue, she drove at an ordinary rate of speed.

"That wasn't so good," her brother said. "Made even The Mongoose shiver for a moment. Better get off the avenue as soon as you can, and cut through the side streets. That sedan will be coming back, and there'll be an alarm out about this coupé. With this storm and not very many cars out, we'll be spotted."

Eleanor drove through a cross street, and came to a boulevard that ran down to the theatre and restaurant district. On this brilliantly-lighted thoroughfare, there was considerable traffic, and she drove into it.

"Safer this way, Sid," she said.

"Good enough! Follow the boulevard till we have to cut through. We're not done yet, remember."

Presently she turned the car into another cross street, where there was scarcely any traffic at all, and sent it along at a better rate of speed.

She slowed down as she approached a corner where a gaudy restaurant had a front covered with glaring signs. Turning the corner, she ran slowly along a line of parked cars.

"There!" her brother indicated.

He pointed to a powerful sedan, which was his own. Eleanor Carleigh parked the coupé deftly beside it.

"Get into the sedan," he whispered. "I'll transfer the stuff."

She left the coupé and got into the back of the sedan. The Mongoose watched until he was sure he was not being observed, and handed her a bag of the gold. She put it beneath the rear seat, in a place that had been made for the purpose.

Working swiftly and cautiously, he transferred the six bags. Then he got into the front of the sedan, and behind the steering wheel. He started the motor, backed slowly into the street, and drove away.

"My poor, little coupé," his sister wailed. "I'll never see it again."

"I'd not advise you to go to Police Headquarters and put in a claim for it," he said, laughing a bit. "They might ask you some embarrassing questions."

"It was a good little car, Sid."

"I agree with you. Did its work well. Responded nobly when called on, and all that sort of thing. Are you changing?"

"Yes," she replied. "I'll be changed by the time you get there."

It was Eleanor Carleigh and not the old eccentric lady who was beside him now. She, too, had removed a wig. A few pulls at hidden strings, and her old-fashioned gown fell from her, revealing her dressed in a costume suitable to her youth and attractiveness. Make-up came off a moment later. A little light was snapped on in the rear of the sedan, and she powdered her face, applied lipstick, beautified herself. From a pocket she took a chic turban, and put it on.

"All right, Sid," she said.

He swung the sedan into a semi-dark side street. Eleanor opened one of the doors a bit as he slowed down, and tumbled out dress and wig and old hat.

"Done, Sid!"

"Fair enough. Now, we'll go home," he said. "Curl up in a

corner and make ourselves comfortable. Tell me later how it feels to be sitting over a fortune in gold."

SIDNEY CARLEIGH was also the sole owner of an apartment house.

It was an estate inherited in England that enabled him to live comfortably and devote his time to having vengeance on those who had wronged his father. What loot he took in so doing was used for expenses, and the remainder given to charities.

He drove the sedan behind the building and into a basement garage. Waving the night attendant aside, Sidney Carleigh backed the car into its position.

Eleanor got out and hurried to the elevator.

"Bad night," Carleigh said to the attendant. "Pavements slippery."

"Very bad, sir."

"Leave orders to have the car washed."

"Yes, sir."

"I wish you'd do me a favor."

"Anything at all, Mr. Carleigh."

"Take the roadster and go to that chop suey palace about ten blocks down the street. Know the one I mean? Good! Get me a mess of chop suey and some Chinese noodles, chow mein— anything at all. Got a notion it'd go good tonight. I'll sit around here and smoke and tend to business for you—if any."

The attendant grinned as Carleigh handed him a bill. "Be right back, sir," he said.

"Take your time, my boy."

The attendant got into the roadster and went out into the night. Sidney Carleigh lowered the garage door—which would be opened only at signal.

Then he got one of the sacks of gold and carried it through a hall to where there was a series of dumb-waiters. He signalled, and his sister answered the signal. Carleigh sent up the sack of gold.

Three more trips he made to the dumb-waiter, and each time he sent up gold. By the time the attendant had returned with the chop suey Sidney Carleigh was done, and was smoking a cigarette and looking bored.

He thanked the attendant, tipped him, and ascended in the elevator. His sister let him into the apartment.

"I'll stow it away, while you dish up this stuff," he said, grinning. "Then come into the laboratory."

At a certain place in the rear hall, Sidney Carleigh pressed against the wall.

A hidden panel slipped back noiselessly, and revealed a short hall with a room at its end. Carleigh carried the bags of gold through the hall and into the room, and stowed them away in the wall behind another secret panel.

In this hidden room, too, were delicate pieces of machinery, batteries, dials and disks. Carleigh sat down in front of the bench and adjusted the headphones. His sister came hurrying in to him.

"Tuning in on the Lanniger apartment," he told her. "Wait a moment! Here it is!"

They could hear Lanniger talking:

"I'm ruined, Graddon—ruined! That damned Mongoose! And you and your men did nothing! Let him do as he pleased and get away!"

Sidney Carleigh twisted a dial and spoke into a microphone on the bench:

"Hello, Lanniger.... This is The Mongoose.... When your enemies are selling you out Monday, remember the innocent man you helped frame and send to prison. And you, Graddon— I'll be attending to you later!"

Then Sidney Carleigh turned the switch and cut off all the apparatus, and went into the dining room to eat his chop suey.

PROFIT FOR THE MONGOOSE

*A Withered Old Lady and a Bogus Cosmetic
Factory Are the Tools of The Mongoose in
a Diabolically Clever Vengeance Plot*

CHAPTER I

THE COSMETIC FACTORY

WITH JUST A hint of furtiveness in her attitude, the little old lady with the mass of dirty-looking gray hair bent over the bench again and picked up a bottle.

Her face was the color of parchment. Thick spectacles almost obscured her eyes. But, behind those thick spectacles, the eyes were twinkling merrily as she spoke. Her voice was quick, high in pitch, strident, and a vocal expert probably would have said that it was disguised. Her manner was that of a person saying one thing and meaning another.

"It's the best face lotion on the market today," she was declaring to the well-dressed, prosperous-appearing man of middle age who stood beside her at the end of the bench. "Manufactured after our own private formula. It will make the toughest skin a thing of rose-petal loveliness."

"Indeed? May I offer the suggestion, madam, that you make use of some of it yourself?"

"Sir? I'd have you know that I'm past the age where I'm concerned with the beauty of my face."

"My error! I didn't know that a woman ever got past that age," he replied. "Seriously, madam, if this new lotion is all you claim it to be, there should be considerable money in marketing it."

"It's profits we're after," the little old lady admitted. "Can't I interest you in buying into the business? A return of a hundred percent—"

"I regret to say that I'm not very much interested in face

311

lotions," he interrupted. "However, I'm vitally interested in profits."

The little old lady chuckled as she put down the bottle she had
been holding, as though she had found some humorous double
meaning in his remark about profits. She blinked at the bright
sunshine that streamed through a window and advertised that
it was a pleasant afternoon outside.

They were in a suite of offices on the tenth floor of a prominent building in the heart of the city. The front room was of the
ordinary office variety, but the two big rear rooms formed a sort
of combined laboratory and factory. There were numerous jars
of messy stuff scattered around—bottles, heaps of labels, packing cases.

The little old lady bent over a bundle of labels and lowered
her voice a bit as she continued speaking and praising the face
lotion. But that was for the benefit of the window-washer, who
was just finishing the work in the front office.

As she talked, the well-dressed man busied himself at the end
of the work bench, where there was a mirror not more than two
inches square imbedded in the wood.

He was bending over until his eyes were but a short distance
from this little mirror, and regarding its surface carefully.

"The window-washer's gone," the little old lady said, after a
time.

"Good! Now, we can get down to the real business. The
mirror shows me that our man is in his private office now. If the
messenger boy does as he was instructed, our man will receive
the package inside a few minutes."

"I'm almost sorry that we're so near the end. It's been a lot
of fun preparing for this," the little old lady said. "I've certainly
learned a lot about cosmetics. May think of going into the business seriously. What's to become of all this stuff—afterward?"

"This stage setting? Who cares?" the man asked. He laughed
a bit. "There'll be a profit—and a big profit—in this cosmetic
factory, though it's been run for only a month and no goods

"Listen to me, Mongoose!" Mark Graddon barked at the empty room. "You can't nab this jack and you know it"

whatever have been sold. A lot of real factory owners would like to know the secret of that."

"If there should be some slip—" she began.

"NOW—NOW! THERE you go again! Never dare to think of such a thing!" he admonished. "Do we ever make slips? Have we ever been known to make a mistake—in this affair?"

"One mistake would be enough," she warned. "Even if we managed to escape the consequences, it would put an end to our work. And that must go on—it must! Discovery at this time would wreck everything." She, too, glanced at the little mirror in the table. "Can you see him now? What's he doing?" she asked.

"Mr. Chester Kempter is inspecting documents of some sort. Take a look," he replied.

He stepped back, and the little old lady went to the end of the bench and bent over to peer directly into the square of glass. In that mirror, portrayed by electrical connection and transmission, was depicted the interior of the office room immediately below the bogus laboratory. The little old lady could see a man sitting at a desk and looking at some papers.

"Oh, how I hate him!" she breathed.

"Naturally," the man beside her said. "But you don't want to think about that too much. It's in moments of anger that a person gets careless and makes mistakes."

"I'll not get careless. Don't worry!"

He patted her gently on the shoulder and smiled down at her. "I'm not much afraid of your committing any serious blunders," he said. "Now, I'd better be getting out of here, for I have my own share of the work to do, remember. You can manage your end?"

"I'm ready."

"Turn on the dictograph and listen in. Watch everything in the mirror. Did you make a test of the air machine today?"

"Yes, during the noon hour. It worked perfectly."

"And you've been careful about fingerprints?"

She smiled up at him. "I've been very careful to leave a lot of fake ones scattered around—but none of my own," she replied.

"They probably will go over this suite of rooms pretty well, when they learn that it had been abandoned—especially after what'll happen downstairs."

"Let them! They'll find nothing but a lot of trash when they do," she replied. "Gallons of harmless mixtures, and tubs of vaseline. Plenty of empty bottles, and heaps of pretty labels. An empty desk, empty safe, and empty filing cabinets."

"It'll give them another mystery to occupy their minds," he said, laughing lightly. "It'll be something for them to think and talk about. Well, I'd better be going now."

The well-dressed man allowed her to usher him through the front office and to the corridor door. Standing in it, hat in hand, he spoke for the benefit of anybody who might happen to be passing on the way to the elevator.

"I'll think the proposition over carefully, madam, and give you my decision in a few days," he said. "I believe that the goods would prove profitable, if marketed properly in huge quantities. Good afternoon!"

Swinging his stick, his face an inscrutable mask, he paced off down the corridor, and presently was standing in front of the elevator cage. He descended in an express elevator a moment later, got out at the ground floor, emerged into the street, and walked briskly along it.

He was known as Mr. Sidney Carleigh, an English gentleman of means who had settled in the States, owned a couple of apartment houses, dressed well, liked to attend the races, theatre and opera, and in general lived as a gentleman should.

What the public, and particularly the police, did not know, was that Sidney Carleigh was also The Mongoose, a clever avenger who had struck at several men of prominence recently.

Nor was it known that the little old lady puttering around her cosmetic shop was really Miss Eleanor Carleigh, his clever sister. And, when she left the shop, she would go to a modest suite in a quiet hotel, remove her wig and perfect make-up, change her attire, and then go on to the elegant apartment she shared with her brother—not as a little old lady at all, but as a radiantly beautiful young woman who caused many a man to turn and look after her.

CHAPTER II

CRIME COMES HOME TO ROOST

IN HIS PRIVATE office directly beneath the bogus cosmetic factory, Chester Kempter perused an abstract of title and a realty company's estimate regarding a certain piece of property. He was considering buying the piece, but he was a slow buyer and a cautious man regarding values.

Mr. Chester Kempter was feeling quite pleased with himself. Recently, he had sold for one hundred thousand dollars' cash some property which he had acquired ten years before for twenty-five thousand. And even the twenty-five thousand he had paid for it had come to him as a sort of gift. Now, if he could handle the hundred thousand to such an advantage, he would be on the way to becoming rich.

The door opened, and his secretary appeared.

"A package for you, sir," she announced.

"Put it there on the desk. Can't you see that I'm busy? What is it?"

"I don't know, Mr. Kempter. It was brought by an ordinary messenger boy."

"Box of cigars, probably. I won a bet from Hawkins yesterday at the country club. Put it down! Get out! Don't let me be disturbed!"

The secretary put the box on the end of the desk and retired from the private office as though glad to do so. Chester Kempter continued reading the abstract of title. He was little and fat, with furtive eyes and a mean disposition, the sort a knowing man would not have trusted very far.

Finishing with the abstract of title, he tossed it aside, bent forward to scribble a note—and happened to notice the package. It was only a small package, and now that he looked at it closely he saw that it could not be a box of cigars, as he had supposed.

His name and office address had been printed on the wrapper with pen and ink. As he continued thinking about the business problem with which he was confronted, Chester Kempter got out his gold penknife and snipped the cord which bound the package, and removed the wrapping.

He uncovered a pasteboard box, and opened it. A wad of cotton was before his eyes. He bent forward still more, wondering, took something from the box, and unwrapped it.

An instant later, Mr. Chester Kempter was leaning far back in his desk chair like a man from whom all strength suddenly had fled. His face had gone ashen, his eyes were bulging, and he was breathing in quick gasps. Chester Kempter was badly frightened, and plainly showing it.

The thing he had removed from the little box was a cylinder record for a dictating machine. He guessed instantly what this meant—a visit from The Mongoose, the terrible avenger who always seemed to work his will on his victims. It finally had come to him, as it had to others who were guilty. And he had been hoping that The Mongoose did not know.

He managed to conquer a measure of his fear, and carried the cylinder to the dictaphone in a corner of the office. Beads of perspiration were standing out on his face, and his hands were trembling, as he put the cylinder on the machine and adjusted the ear tubes.

He had heard considerable about this method of communication used by The Mongoose. It was said that these records were chemically treated, and melted and disappeared a short time after being exposed to the open air.

Though he disliked to listen to the thing, Chester Kempter feared to refuse. There might be disastrous consequences for him, if commands and instructions were on that record, and he neglected to acquaint himself with them.

He started the machine, braced himself both physically and mentally, and listened:

> Hello, Chester Kempter! This is The Mongoose speaking to you. About ten years ago, a man named William Cratch was tried on a charge of perpetrating a swindle. He was an innocent bookkeeper, made a cat's-paw by a band of wealthy men who brought about his conviction by unscrupulous means to save themselves.
>
> But you know all this, Kempter, without me telling you. For you were on the jury, planted there for a purpose. You accepted money to help swing that jury to a verdict of guilty, and ruin an innocent man!

There it was! The Mongoose knew!

Chester Kempter scarcely could hear the words which were

coming into his ears, because a spasm of fright was choking him. There could be no escape from this, he told himself. Half a dozen of the guilty men already had felt the weight of The Mongoose's vengeance.

THE POLICE had been unable to catch The Mongoose, or even find his trail to follow. He worked in original ways, used none of the usual methods of criminals. He seemed to have terrible devices and devilish contrivances at his command. He was known to be expert in chemistry and electricity, and brought to his aid strange forces of which other men seemingly could not avail themselves.

Chester Kempter straightened a bit in his chair. The words of The Mongoose were still striking into his ears:

> With the money you received for your share in this dastardly crime, you bought a piece of property at a bargain price. A short time ago, you resold the property for one hundred thousand dollars cash. You still have this cash in your bank, waiting until you can find another good investment.
>
> William Cratch, the innocent man you helped send to prison, where he died, was my father. I am avenging him. I have struck at several of the guilty ones, and now your time has come. You are the next on my list!
>
> Because you have an innocent family depending on you for support, I'm not going to strike at your business at this time. I require at present only the hundred thousand cash, the fruit of your infamy. I'll communicate again later, and in a different manner.

The deep, monotonous voice of The Mongoose ceased. Weak and trembling, Chester Kempter sank back in the chair as the message was finished. He stared at the little dictaphone cylinder as though fascinated by it. He saw little bubbles begin forming on its surface, and rapidly grow larger. The record was starting to disappear into nothingness.

But Chester Kempter did not remain sitting there to witness the destruction of the cylinder. He hurried to his desk, seized the telephone, and into the transmitter barked a number. Presently, a gruff voice answered his call:

"Yeah?"

"Is this Mark Graddon?"

"Right!"

"Chester Kempter speaking. I wish you'd come over to my office at once, Graddon. I've received one of those records sent by The Mongoose. He said that my time had come, and that he'd communicate again later."

"What's that? I'll sure be right over there! Take care of yourself till I arrive. Keep somebody near you."

"Please hurry, Graddon!"

"I'll hurry—don't worry about that!"

After he had replaced the receiver on its hook, Chester Kempter got up and paced around the room, trying to work off the fit of nervousness that had seized upon him.

That was Detective Mark Graddon to whom he had just been speaking, a private operative none too scrupulous, who worked principally for a group of financiers no more scrupulous than himself. Mark Graddon was vitally interested in this Mongoose affair. He had been instrumental in building up the bogus evidence which had sent the innocent William Cratch to prison, and was a potential victim of The Mongoose himself.

So, The Mongoose was demanding of Kempter that hundred thousand dollars he had in the bank, was he? How did The Mongoose expect to get it? Was he foolish enough to think for an instant that Chester Kempter would draw it out of the bank and hand it to him?

Kempter tried to tell himself that it was preposterous to feel afraid. True, The Mongoose had worked his will with some of the others. But, perhaps this time he would be caught and punished. Mark Graddon, spurred on by lavish offers of reward, and having a personal interest also, would get him!

"Kempter!"

The name was spoken in a deep voice that seemed to fill the

private office. Chester Kempter whirled around, an ejaculation of surprise escaping him. Nobody had entered the room. Nobody was there. Yet he would have taken oath that his ears had not failed him, that his name had been spoken.

"Kempter! This is The Mongoose speaking! Sit down in your desk chair—quick!—or you die!"

CHAPTER III

PLANS ARE MADE

CHESTER KEMPTER WAS not made of especially heroic stuff. That deep voice from an unseen speaker weakened him. He dropped into the chair because he did not have the necessary strength to stand. His eyes were bulging again, his breath coming in quick gasps, his heart was hammering at his ribs.

"I hear everything you say, and see everything you do," the voice of The Mongoose continued. "Dare to disobey me in the smallest thing, Kempter, and you may expect the worst. I can blast you and your entire establishment from the face of the earth in an instant. You understand?"

Chester Kempter did not reply. He did not see anybody to whom he could speak, and speaking was beyond him at the moment anyway. His lips moved, but no sound issued from them. He wanted to spring out of the chair, rush to the door, open it and dash into the front office. But fear held him there as though he had been chained.

"I know that you've sent for Mark Graddon. He can't do anything to help you. Was he able to help any of the others?" The Mongoose asked. "Nor will Mark Graddon be able to help himself, when I decide to strike at him. Now, pay close attention to instructions."

There was a moment of silence. Kempter waited fearfully for what was to come.

"Tomorrow morning, draw one hundred thousand dollars from your bank—in fives, tens and twenties only,"The Mongoose went on to say. "At exactly four in the afternoon, tomorrow, put the currency in the middle of your desk, after clearing away everything else. Put the bills in loose piles, with no bank bands on them. Then go out of your private office and close the door, and I'll get the money."

Chester Kempter was giving close attention. Every word rang in his ears. He did not miss a syllable of The Mongoose's instructions.

"That's all you have to do,"The Mongoose said. "But—listen carefully to this: If any of those bills are marked, or if I learn that their numbers have been listed—if you fail to do exactly as I've said—you'll receive punishment that'll be the talk of the town. I'm not bluffing, Kempter! You know some of the things I've done."

Yes, Chester Kempter knew—the almost unbelievable things that The Mongoose had done. Fear continued to grip Kempter and hold him in the chair. The perspiration was streaming down his face. He felt that he was about to faint.

"Tell Mark Graddon of my orders, if you like,"The Mongoose continued. "He'll probably tell you not to obey. Follow that advice, if you think it best. But you can imagine what'll happen if you do, or if you try to trick me with bogus money, or anything of the sort. That's all now, Kempter. You're getting off easy. A crooked juror! Helping send an innocent man to prison. Taking twenty-five thousand dollars for doing such a thing! You'll notice, Kempter, that what I'm demanding of you is that twenty-five thousand and the profits it's made for you, and nothing more."

Chester Kempter made a heroic effort to speak, as though he wished to hear his own voice. "Wh-wh—" he began.

"I hear you,"The Mongoose interrupted. "There's no need for conversation. You heard *me,* and you understand. All you have to do now is obey. Good-by, for the present."

The voice died away. Kempter moved slightly, then got out of the chair like a sick man. He remembered every word The Mongoose had spoken. He wondered where that voice had come from, and how The Mongoose could hear him muttering.

Lurching past his desk, Kempter went across the room to the door, and pulled it open. Nobody was in the front office except his secretary. She glanced up at him from her typewriter, then sprang quickly to her feet.

"Mr. Kempter! Are you ill?" she cried.

"I—it's all right," he stammered.

"But, your face— You look terribly ill. Shall I call a doctor?"

"No. I—I don't want to see anybody. Mark Graddon, the detective, is coming here. I want to see him—nobody but Mark Graddon."

"Very well, Mr. Kempter."

He pulled himself together and went to the water cooler in a corner of the office, and drank deeply, knowing that the eyes of his secretary were upon him, and that she was wondering what had shocked him so.

As he turned to go back to his private office the corridor door opened, and Detective Mark Graddon hurried in.

"Ah, Graddon! Waiting for you," Kempter said. "Come inside, please."

He tried to smile, for the benefit of the secretary, but it was a sickly attempt. Inside the private office, and the door closed, Kempter dropped weakly into his desk chair again, and waved Graddon toward another.

"Tell it," Graddon said.

Kempter told it—told of receiving the dictaphone cylinder and what it had said, and of what the voice of The Mongoose had told him.

"Cool off!" Graddon advised. "Nothing to be scared about. That cylinder—it's old stuff. And his voice—we ran across a contrivance of his in another case. He's got some sort of a wire-

less dictograph. Probably a tiny disk around this office somewhere. He can talk to you, and hear what's said."

"Then let's search for that disk, and destroy it"

"Take it easy," Graddon suggested. "I hope he's listening now,
for I want to tell him this—I'm going to land him if he tries to
put through this job! He's been lucky so far. But here's something he can't pull off!"

DETECTIVE MARK GRADDON smashed his fist down
upon Kempter's desk by way of emphasis, and made the desk
set jump. As the echoes of his stentorian voice died away, soft
laughter came into the room. It grew in volume until it seemed
to ring back from the walls—mocking laughter.

"Laugh!" Graddon cried. "We'll see who laughs last,
Mongoose! Just wait till I get my hands on you!"

Chester Kempter was shaking with fear again. It was uncanny,
that laughter which came from nowhere and seemed to be all
around them.

"Please—please," Kempter begged. "Let's go somewhere else,
Graddon, and have our talk."

"Nonsense! Who cares if he does hear it? He may as well
know it now as later, Kempter."

"Know what?"

"That we're going to tell him to go to blazes. You draw out
a hundred grand and put it here on the desk for that ass of a
Mongoose to try to gobble? Certainly not! And, if you don't
draw it out and bring it here, how's he going to get it? Tell me
that! Why play his game, play right into his hands? Leave your
coin in the bank, Kempter, and give him the laugh!"

"Graddon!" Kempter sat upright, horror in his face. "If I do
that, he may—may—"

"Oh! Afraid of him, are you?"

"Yes," Kempter admitted, "I am."

"Nonsense! He's never hurt anybody yet. Done a lot of bluffing. Stolen some stuff. Played his devilish games with his new-

fangled machines, and all that. But he hasn't actually resorted to violence. And I don't think he'll ever do that. Not his style."

"Let's call in the police, Graddon."

"Better leave the cops out of this. If The Mongoose is captured, he may talk and spill a lot of stuff."

"But—aren't you going to try to capture him?"

"That's different." Mark Graddon smiled knowingly. "If I and my men catch him, Kempter—well, something may happen to him, to prevent him ever talking."

"Graddon!"

"That's just a hint, Kempter. The Mongoose might cause a lot of trouble for certain gentlemen, if allowed to do so. So—he won't be allowed to do so. Understand?"

"He—he may be hearing you," Kempter said.

"Probably he is. Hope so," said Graddon. "He knows what to expect. It's war between me and The Mongoose! War to the death!"

"I don't want any trouble. I've got a family. I'd rather let him have the hundred thousand—"

"So that's how you're built!" Graddon interrupted, witheringly.

"Yes!" Kempter was brave enough to admit it. "He's got me scared."

"And you want to draw out that money and put it on your desk here tomorrow afternoon?"

"Yes. I'll play fair with him, Graddon. I'll get the money as he said, and put it here. If he's a fair man, he can't punish me, can't harm me, when I carry out his instructions like that. I'll put it here, Graddon, as he said—then it's up to you to protect it."

"Um!" Mark Graddon got up and walked around the office. "It might not be a bad idea, at that. Two windows to this office, nine floors up, no way of reaching them from the outside. Only the one door, opening into your front office. I can put men all around here, and out in the hallway."

"And how could he get in here and get the money, Graddon? Why, he can't!"

"He's done a lot of impossible things—but this certainly seems beyond even The Mongoose," Graddon said. "All right, Kempter! Get your money and put it on the desk as he directed. If he comes to get it, we'll nab him! If he doesn't, we'll guard the money all night, and put it back into the bank the next morning—and have the laugh on him. Say—you're quite sure you understood his directions correctly?"

"Quite sure, Graddon."

"Seems funny! Come to think of it coolly, how the deuce could he get here and get that money, when we're waiting for him? And in the middle of the afternoon, too! Kempter, I think The Mongoose has gone and set himself an impossible task this time. But we'll take no chances. I'll telephone now for some of my men. I'll have them planted here inside fifteen minutes, and more tonight. The Mongoose will work none of his funny games around here. You got only that girl in the front office working for you?"

"That's all at present."

"Go out and tell her to take a vacation until day after tomorrow—say you're going on a trip, anything. We don't want her around here in the way, and we don't want her to see our preparations. I'll telephone for my men."

Chester Kempter got up to hurry to the front office, to do as Graddon requested. And, as he moved across the room, soft and mocking laughter filled it again.

"Laugh ahead, Mongoose!" Mark Graddon roared at the blank wall. "We'll see who laughs tomorrow. You can't pull off this stunt! If you try it, you're my meat!"

CHAPTER IV

MONEY FOR BAIT

WITH TWO OF Mark Graddon's trusted assistants to guard him, Chester Kempter went to his bank the following day about noon and drew out one hundred thousand dollars in small bills, as The Mongoose had instructed, to the astonishment of the bank officials. He turned aside successfully their somewhat inquisitive remarks.

To a man of Kempter's nature, this was an act of agony. He had the fear that the money never would be returned to the bank. But he kept telling himself that it would be impossible for The Mongoose to get it. Perhaps he'd be captured in the attempt. And Kempter might even get a lot of credit for being instrumental in his capture.

One moment Kempter feared, and the next he felt indignation. At times, a guilty conscience assailed him. He remembered the white, drawn face of William Cratch when the verdict of guilty had been announced on that day ten years before. He had helped send an innocent man to prison!

And this money—this hundred thousand he had hoped to make the nucleus of a great fortune—had come to him as a result of that dastardly act. But Kempter did not want to lose it. He had made great plans. He had handled this dirty money for ten years, and might as well go on handling it!

He reached the office with the money in a small satchel, and the two men walking on either side of him. Mark Graddon had scattered operatives through the hallways on the ninth floor, and had stationed a couple on the eighth. The front office of the Kempter suite held more of his men. One was in the lobby downstairs to watch for suspicious persons, one guarded the stairway on the ninth floor, and one remained near the elevators continually.

But it was a furious Mark Graddon who rushed at Chester Kempter when he entered the office after his trip to the bank.

"What's all this about the cops?" Graddon demanded.

"I—I don't know what you mean."

"Yes, you do! You went to the cops," Graddon accused. "The Inspector's just had me on the telephone. He's sending half the force over here, to listen to him tell it."

"Well, I—I thought—" Kempter began.

"Didn't I tell you that we didn't want the cops in on this? The Mongoose must be handled in a certain way if he's caught. He's got evidence—documents. Suppose the cops get him? He'll spill everything, in an effort to vindicate himself. Tell how his father was ruined, and all that—play for sympathy. He may get John Public riled up, and a grand jury busy."

"I—I'm going to protect my property," Kempter blustered. "The Mongoose has got away every time. You haven't been able to catch him. It's right that the police should know what The Mongoose intends doing. Yes, I went to them, and told the Inspector everything."

Graddon glared at him.

"All right!" he snapped. "It was a fool move! For a plugged dime, I'd take my men and walk right out of here—"

"Don't do that, Graddon! Don't leave me alone, with this money. The Mongoose might come—"

"Serve you right if he did. Went to the cops behind my back. Sergeant Tim Ladman will be coming in charge of the squad. We've fought each other for years."

"I thought that—the more officers we had around here—"

"I know what you thought—that I couldn't handle the job. Now I'll have the cops as well, keep them off to one side. And Tim Ladman is no fool."

"Maybe you can catch The Mongoose."

"Oh, shut up!" Graddon exploded. He did not show, to Chester Kempter, the respect he exhibited toward his millionaire clients. "Sit down in the corner, and wait. I want to think, and I can't do that while I'm blabbering to you."

Kempter sat down—and thought. If this thing got out, there would be some questions at home from Mrs. Kempter. From her, her husband had kept all knowledge of the original twenty-five thousand and its increase. Mrs. Kempter was not the sort of woman to condone an offense like sending an innocent man to prison.

The more Kempter thought, the more miserable he became. And the more he feared. It was fear that had sent him to the police to ask for aid. He wished that he might not be here at the hour The Mongoose had said he would come for the money, yet he did not want to go away.

Sergeant Tim Ladman came in charge of the police squad, as Graddon had predicted. They had been rivals for years.

"Well, Graddon, what's the dope?" Ladman asked. "Had to call on us for help, huh?"

"I didn't do the calling. Kempter got a hint that The Mongoose might pay him a visit this afternoon, and got scared and ran to you cops. I'm after The Mongoose, for what he did to some of my clients."

"I thought The Mongoose went in for big stakes," Tim Ladman said. "Why is he playing around a piker like Kempter? Only a small time real estate man and business broker."

"Oh, he's got some coin, and The Mongoose learned about it somehow."

"Yeah? Well, what are we going to do about it?"

"Not much to do, except stand guard," Graddon said, pretending a yawn. "The Mongoose threatened to rob Kempter's office at four o'clock this afternoon. We'll be here to see that he doesn't."

"Rob it of what?" Ladman persisted.

"Search me! What's in the safe, I suppose."

"You come clean with me, Graddon!" Ladman demanded.

"I know what's generally in the safe of an establishment like this—a bunch of documents, deeds, receipts, contracts, a couple of bonds maybe, and possibly some small change."

Graddon took his aside. "Tim, go easy," he begged. "There's something behind all this. It has to do with some of my clients. Kempter is only small fry. I think The Mongoose wants to get some papers out of the safe. Maybe some old contracts—I don't know what. That's all."

"Well, what do you want to do?"

"I've got my men planted in here," Graddon pointed out. "Got a few in the halls, too. Suppose you put your men in the halls and down in the lobby. I'll have the telephone here connected with the lobby phone. If anything happens, an alarm will be telephoned down there at once."

"Suits me," Ladman said. "But I was assigned to this job by the Inspector himself. I'm not playing shut-eye."

"That's all right, Ladman. Everything's all right."

"There are several thousand persons in this building," Ladman pointed out. "Going and coming all the time."

"If there's an alarm, you can stop everybody in the lobby until we look 'em over. Have the other exits guarded, too."

"All right!" Ladman agreed. "You have those phones connected, and I'll place my men."

Mark Graddon gave a sigh of relief as Ladman hurried away. The police would not be in the Kempter offices, at least, to see what happened, if anything did—or to hear The Mongoose if he spoke. Graddon made the rounds and cautioned his men again. Then he went into the private office with Kempter, and closed the door. Kempter put the satchel containing the money on the desk.

"It's after three o'clock," Kempter said. He was weak and shaking again.

"Brace up!" Graddon told him. "I advised against drawing the money and playing The Mongoose's game, remember. But you knew it all. You even ran to the cops."

"Graddon! You—you don't suppose that The Mongoose can get away with it?"

"For once, I think he's planned a little too big," Graddon replied. "The money's here, for bait. We'll do exactly as he instructed you. But he can't get through those windows, and he won't get in at that door. Tomorrow, you can put your money back into the bank. My regret is that The Mongoose probably won't attempt it, with all these cops scattered around, and so I won't have a chance at him."

CHAPTER V

GRADDON MAKES A BET

IN THE COSMETIC factory on the floor above, the little old lady was smiling and her eyes were twinkling behind her thick spectacles. She glanced at an old-fashioned watch she wore, and saw that it was a quarter after three.

She was puttering around the shop, but managed to keep in the vicinity of the work bench the greater part of the time. Now and then she touched a button, and heard voices coming from the Kempter offices below. Frequently, she glanced into the little mirror, and viewed the scene.

If she was at all nervous, she did not betray it in her manner. She even hummed as she fussed around the rooms. At times, she journeyed to the corridor door and listened there for a moment.

It was about half past three when the corridor door opened, and the little old lady hurried into the front office to greet her caller.

"Ah, Mr. Carleigh!" she cried. "I knew that you'd return. I felt sure you were interested."

"In your face lotion, madam?" he asked, as he drew off his gloves and put aside his stick. "Your complexion tells me that you haven't been using it since my last visit."

"If you'll come back into the laboratory, there are some more things I'd like to explain," she said. "I'll lock the door to the front office, so we'll not be disturbed."

He smiled at her, and they went into the room behind, and locked the door. The little old lady threw a tiny electric switch hidden beneath a packing case. That turned on a sensitive dictograph in the front office. Nobody could enter, however carefully, without the knowledge being relayed to the rear room. In that amplifying dictograph, the slightest rustle would sound like a crash.

"How's everything, Eleanor?" he asked.

"Just fine, Sid. I'm growing excited."

"Never do in the world!" he cautioned. "Can't afford to be excited on a job like this. Keep cool."

"Not excited enough to hurt," she defended.

Sidney Carleigh had gone to the little mirror, and was looking at the scene in the office below. Mark Graddon and Chester Kempter were sitting beside the desk, upon which the satchel had been placed.

"He drew out the money, as I happen to know," Carleigh said. "Thinks he's keeping faith with me, so I'll not punish him. And also thinks, undoubtedly, that I can't get at the money. There are cops scattered all around the building, as well as Graddon's men."

"Sid! It won't interfere?"

"Certainly not!" he told her. "Now, sister mine, I cease to be your brother for a time, and become The Mongoose. You may not notice the change in me, but there is one. Everything ready?"

"Yes. I've been working the dictograph—listening, but not talking. I tested the air machine again."

"You mean the face cream mixer," he said, chuckling. "We're using a lot of machinery on this job—it's worth a hundred thousand."

"When I think—" she began.

"Now!" he warned. "Keep cool! I know what you're thinking—that the fiend who goes by the name of Kempter helped send our father to prison. Eleanor, I know the man! Taking that money from him will hurt him worse than shooting him down. He's built his whole hopes for the future on it. His regular business gives him only a comfortable living. He wants to be rich. And we'll take from him what he expected to make him rich."

He turned toward the end of the bench again, and pressed a button there. The dictograph began working. The Mongoose listened as he watched in the little mirror. The words came distinctly, though in soft tones. They could not have been heard in the front office.

"It's ten minutes of four," Kempter was saying.

"What of it?" Graddon asked.

"Better get the money ready, hadn't I?"

"Go ahead! It's your money," Graddon said. "I told you to leave it in the bank, remember, and defy The Mongoose."

In the mirror, The Mongoose saw Chester Kempter sweep his desk clean of everything. Then he opened the satchel and took out the bundles of currency. He removed the bank bands and put the bills in neat piles in the middle of the desk.

KEMPTER PATTED the money lovingly, and his eyes grew moist as he fondled it. He regretted that he had drawn it from the bank, that he had not defied The Mongoose as Graddon had suggested, and run the risk. But his fear of injury had been greater even than his love of money.

"There it is," he said, finally.

"It'd be quite a haul if The Mongoose could get it," Graddon said.

"But, how could he?"

"He can't," Graddon replied. "Only way he can, is to get rid of all of my men first. He might dope those in the outer office, but he couldn't get at all of those in the halls. And the cops are scattered downstairs, too. No chance! This is once that The Mongoose is stumped."

"He—he sounded so certain—" Kempter began.

"Don't be an ass!" Graddon exploded. "He thought that he was scaring you. Probably didn't think you'd even call me into the game. Now, he'll have to call quits on this deal. Two windows—nine floors up, and no way to get at them from the outside. They're closed and locked. One door—and half a dozen men watching it. How could he, or anybody else, get through the hall and into your outer office, even, without being grabbed? Man—I only wish he'd try it!"

"The walls—"

"Thinking of sliding panels and all that cheap truck?" Graddon interrupted. "I've examined the walls, Kempter. I've gone over every square foot of them. The walls in this private office are sound. This is a new budding, remember. And there's a paneled ceiling that's solid, too. No need to examine that."

"He simply can't do it!" Kempter said.

"You're right! He worked one of his games by doping everybody with some kind of gas. Can't work that here. If my man in the front office doesn't speak over that telephone every few seconds to the cop in the lobby downstairs, it'll mean that something's wrong.

"If another of my men doesn't put his head through the corridor door and signal to the man near the elevator every few seconds, it'll mean the same thing. Result—swift action! I only hope The Mongoose tries it! We'll have him!"

"It is five minutes of four now," Kempter said.

"Okay! Kiss the money good-by and come along."

"Please don't talk like that, Graddon—about kissing it good-by."

"I meant for just a little while," Graddon said, laughing. "It's all nonsense, leaving this room."

"But The Mongoose said to go out and leave the money on the table."

"All right, Kempter! We'll do exactly as The Mongoose said. Then he won't have any excuse for getting rough with you."

Mark Graddon had gone across to the door, and now

Kempter followed him, glancing back at the heaps of currency on the desk. One hundred thousand dollars! The foundation of a fortune, if used properly! Kempter almost sobbed at thought of losing it.

As he joined Mark Graddon at the door, as Graddon reached out to turn the knob and open it, a voice came to their ears.

"The time has come! Leave the private office! If you have not done exactly as I instructed, Kempter, you'll regret it!"

There was no question—it was the voice of The Mongoose. Graddon accepted the challenge.

"Listen to me, Mongoose!" he barked at the empty room. "You can't nab this jack, and you know it. Better make some new plans. There's the stuff on the desk, waiting for you. Let's see you get it!"

"Like to make a little bet?" the voice of The Mongoose asked.

"What's the bet?"

"A hundred even that I get that money today."

"And, if you win, I suppose you'll drop around to my office to collect?" Graddon said, sarcastically.

"Don't worry, Graddon—I'll collect!"

"It's a bet!" Graddon snapped. "But—how am I going to collect from you?"

"If I lose, I'll mail you the hundred. But I'll not lose, Graddon. Get out of the office now, you and Kempter."

"How'll you know whether we do?"

The soft laughter of The Mongoose came to them.

"I can see you," he said.

"Bluff!"

"Want proof, do you? You're holding a cigar in your right hand. You're knocking off the ashes on Kempter's fine rug. Now you're shoving your hat to the back of your head, as you do when you're nervous. And you're certainly nervous now, aren't you, Graddon?"

"Not because of you!" Graddon growled. "You're bluffing—and guessing?"

"Yes? Look at Kempter. He's twisting that ring on his little finger."

A cry came from Kempter.

"Graddon! He can see us! He's watching us. How can he be doing that? Where is he?"

"Another of his freak stunts," Mark Graddon growled. "Come on—let's get out, if we're going."

They stepped into the front office and closed the door behind them. The others in the office immediately became alert. The man at the telephone was speaking to the policeman down in the lobby, telling him that everything was all right. The one at the door opened it and signaled to the other down the corridor, according to agreement.

"Now, Mongoose—let's see you do your stuff!" Mark Graddon growled. "You may talk over freak dictographs, and you may have some way of seeing a room from a distance, but I'd like to see you get the money off that desk!"

CHAPTER VI

THE MONGOOSE LAUGHS

IN THE OFFICE above, the little old lady spoke.

"Exactly four o'clock, Sidney," she said.

"They've left the private office and closed the door," he told her. "Detective Mark Graddon has defied me to do my stuff, as he calls it, and it'd be a shame to disappoint him. Everything ready?"

"Yes, Sid."

"Careful, now! Watch in the mirror and watch that door particularly. We don't want to be caught in the middle of this, and let them learn how it's being done. And we don't want to delay an instant, either."

The Mongoose knelt beside the peculiar machine which was supposed to be a mixer for face creams. He threw a lever, touched an electric switch, and a queer buzzing sound filled the room, a soft hum which presently caused a vibration.

Next, The Mongoose rolled back a small rug, pressed several buttons concealed in the flooring beneath it—and a section of the floor, about a foot square, slipped to one side. Below there was an aperture, and below that the ceiling of Chester Kempter's private office.

"All right?" he asked, in a whisper.

"All right, Sid!"

The Mongoose pressed another button, and a section of Kempter's ceiling, about six inches square, folded inward neatly. The Mongoose reached back to the machine, which was vibrating steadily, and unfolded an arm of metal.

He extended this metal arm into the opening. At the end of the arm was a sort of cup about three inches square. As though this had been the muzzle of a gun, The Mongoose aimed it at the heaps of currency on the table in the room below.

"Ready!" he said.

The little old lady darted to the end of the work bench, reached beneath it, and threw a lever there. A coughing sound was heard. Down on Kempter's desk, the piles of currency were agitated gently. A few of the bills began drifting up toward the ceiling of the room in a crazy fashion.

"Full power!" The Mongoose whispered.

Immediately, the low hum increased to a minor roar. There was a terrific suction of air. The currency on the desk below shot up toward the ceiling, and into the mouth of the cup on the metal arm of the machine. A steady stream of it poured upward—until the desk was bare.

That machine was working after the principle of the vacuum

cleaner. The air suction drew up the bills, passed them through the arm, and into a receiving bag inside the machine.

"Quick!" The Mongoose said.

She sprang to his side to help. The hole in the ceiling, then that in the floor was closed, and the rug put back into place. While he put the arm of the machine back as it had been formerly, she pulled out the receiving bag.

Near at hand was a large container of metal. Into this, they dumped the currency from the receiving bag of the machine.

"Finish that while I set off the fireworks," The Mongoose directed.

"Is that necessary, Sid?"

"Got to keep them excited down there," he explained. "And I spent nights fixing the electrical connections. You rush that part of the job."

The Mongoose darted to the work bench and began throwing tiny switches and touching buttons.

In the corridor just outside the door of Kempter's suite a puff of smoke and a flash of flame came from the wainscoting.

One of Mark Graddon's men gave a cry of alarm. The door of the office was jerked open.

At that instant, in a corner of the office, there was a tiny explosion. A small section of wall was torn away, and flames and smoke shot out. The man at the telephone sprang away from the instrument. Chester Kempter gave a screech of fear.

"Steady, everybody!" Graddon cried. "Stand by! Keep your eyes open! This may be some of The Mongoose's tricks!"

A pungent odor seemed to be filling the room. Those in it began coughing. Their eyes started smarting. They suddenly seemed to be choking.

"Into the corridor!" Graddon cried. "All of you—quick! Close the door, and stand in front of it!"

HE DROVE them before him, Kempter included, rushed them out into the corridor, and closed the door.

"Stuff might put you out—gas," he explained. "The Mongoose can't get into the suite if we guard this door. Now, what the—"

Down the corridor there was another flash of flame. Cries of alarm came from the floor below, where another had occurred. Chemicals released by The Mongoose pressing buttons and throwing switches in the bogus cosmetic shop flooded the hallways.

Somewhere in the big building, a bell jangled its startling alarm. A puff of smoke rolled down the stairway, and the scent of pungent vapor was in the elevator shaft.

Graddon called to his men to stand steady. He opened the door of Kempter's office again, rushed into the office and across it, and kicked out a window. Fresh air poured into the room and cleared away the smoke and fumes.

"In here!" Graddon called.

They rushed back into the office, and closed the corridor door. Coughing and gasping, they gulped the fresh air, struggled to speak.

"Keep your eyes open!" Graddon howled. "The Mongoose was behind all that, you can bet. But it didn't work. Thought that we'd run away and let him have a chance to get into this office, probably. Have your guns ready, you men! If he comes through that door, get him! Watch out for a gas bomb, or something like that."

Tense, alert, they waited. But the hall door did not open. Nobody sought entrance to the office. In the corridor, the tumult subsided. The smoke had cleared away, and there were no more bursts of flames.

"Fooled him!" Graddon told the others. "The Mongoose didn't work it this time. Sorry we didn't get a chance at him."

"You think he won't come, now?" Kempter asked.

"Not with us waiting for him like this. He's not a fool—I'll say that much for him," Graddon replied. "He probably was hiding somewhere near, perhaps in another office. Thought everybody would skip when he started those fireworks, and he could rush in here and get his swag."

"I'd better put the money back into the satchel," Kempter whispered.

"Sure!" Graddon agreed. "I'll detail a couple of men to guard it until the bank opens tomorrow."

Chester Kempter felt a glow pass through him. His precious money was safe. The Mongoose had been outwitted.

He went across to the door of the private office, with Mark Graddon a step behind him. Kempter opened the door. The next instant, his wild cry startled them all.

"It's gone—gone!"

Graddon hurled him aside and sprang into the private office. One glance was enough to assure him that the currency which had been piled on the desk was indeed gone. The top of the desk was bare. Neither of the windows was open—both were still locked on the inside. And he knew that nobody had passed into the office from the front room through that door.

"Gone... gone!" Kempter was groaning.

Graddon darted back to the other room.

"Telephone the alarm!" he shouted to his man. "Tell them down in the lobby. The Mongoose's been here and done his work. I sure don't know how, but he's done it!"

He sent others rushing into the corridor to stop anybody they met. He darted back into the private office again, where Kempter had dropped weakly, helplessly into the desk chair, and slammed the door behind him.

"I'll go over every square foot—" he began.

He ceased speaking. A chuckle had sounded. The chuckle grew into a laugh which filled the room. And then they heard the voice of The Mongoose:

"Greetings, Graddon! I've won a hundred from you, I believe. Small change, compared to what I've just taken from Kempter, but every little helps. I'll come to collect it one of these days—and more along with it!"

CHAPTER VII

GREASY BILLS

IN THE BOGUS cosmetic factory above, the little old lady had been working furiously while The Mongoose had been making his fireworks display. The currency had been stuffed into the container. The remainder of the container had been packed tightly with face cream, to the brim, smoothed, and a sheet of glazed paper pasted over the top.

Now, the little old lady put the metal lid on the container, and swiftly pasted two labels on the lid where it overlapped the can.

"All done, Sid!" she said.

"Now for the rest of it!"

"Hush!" she warned, suddenly.

The sensitive dictograph had brought a sound to their ears. Somebody had opened the corridor door of the front office.

The Mongoose darted to a corner of the room, where he would not be seen when the connecting door was opened. The little old lady went to the door and unlocked it softly, pulled it open and smiled.

"Oh! A policeman!" she gasped. "You startled me."

"Sorry, ma'am," the policeman told her.

"I was expecting a salesman," she went on, advancing toward him. "You aren't interested in cosmetics, are you? We don't retail our goods here, you know. This is where they are made. I can give you a list of stores—"

"No face dope for me," the policeman interrupted. "There's been some trouble in the buildin', and we're just checkin' up around here."

"Trouble?" she questioned.

"Yeah! That man they call The Mongoose has been tryin' to

rob somebody. Queer lot of fake fires, too. We're checkin' up on everybody in the buildin', and I've got this wing on this floor."

"Oh, you frighten me!" she complained.

"Nothin' to get scared about. I'll have to go through your place and see that nobody's there. Here's a man's hat and cane—"

"My nephew's," she said, quickly. "He went away somewhere. Perhaps he heard the noise, and went to see what it was all about. You say there's been a robbery?"

She had been leading him slowly toward the connecting door. The Mongoose was prepared for an emergency such as this, she knew. And now the little old lady stepped aside, and smiled, and indicated that the policeman was to enter the rear room. He did so, turning halfway around to smile back at her.

A cloud of pungent vapor shot from somewhere and assailed him. He gasped—and drew it deep into his lungs. As though he had been struck a heavy blow, his eyes glazed immediately, his vision was wrecked, the strength was sapped from him. The Mongoose sprang from behind the door and caught him as he started to fall, eased his body to the floor.

"Don't breathe that stuff, Eleanor," he warned. "We've got to hurry now. You'd better change, while I pull this laddie inside and make him comfortable."

He tugged at the unconscious policeman, got him into a corner, and left him there. He would be unconscious for fifteen minutes or more.

The little old lady had rushed to the washroom in the corner of the laboratory. She pulled off her gray wig and tossed it aside, rapidly removed her make-up. A few tugs at hidden strings, and her dress slipped from her. Beneath was a modish gown such as Miss Eleanor Carleigh would be expected to wear.

She opened a hand bag and brought out a small vanity case. Working deftly, rapidly, she touched up her brows, peach-bloomed her cheeks, resorted to a lipstick. Then she took a stylish turban from a box and put it on over her black curls, and hurried back into the other room.

"All ready, Sid!" she said, smiling at him.

"Sid's right! The Mongoose is gone for the time being," he replied. "Eleanor, you're a beauty!"

"Coming from a brother, that's a real compliment."

"If the right man ever comes along, and you decide to leave me—"

"Never, brother, until we've wiped the slate clean!"

He clasped her gently, kissed her, then put her aside. He picked up the metal container and carried it into the front office, and she followed.

"It'll look better if we had something to wrap it in," he said.

"But might not be so convincing," she added. "Let's hurry, Sid!"

They went to the corridor door and opened it. Nobody was near.

Side by side, Sidney and Eleanor Carleigh went to the elevator and rang. They waited for some little time, and finally the elevator ascended.

"Rotten service!" Sidney Carleigh muttered.

"HAVE TO pardon it this time, sir," the operator said, as he started the cage downward. "We've had some excitement around here, and the cops are checking up on everybody."

"Excitement? Cops?" Sidney Carleigh lifted his brows a bit, as though the thought of excitement and policemen were distasteful to him.

"You and the lady'll probably be questioned when you get down," the boy informed him.

"And just what has happened?"

"Some crook they call The Mongoose, I heard. He robbed some office—shot four men."

Eleanor Carleigh gasped, and her brother managed to refrain from grinning.

"Nervy fellows, these crooks," Mr. Carleigh observed. "Did this fellow—er—have a gang with him?"

"I suppose so. They generally run in gangs," the boy stated.

The car reached the street level, the door shot open, and Mr. Sidney Carleigh and his sister stepped out into the arms of the police. Detective Mark Graddon seemed to be in charge.

"Who are you, and where did you come from?" he demanded.

"Sir?" Sidney Carleigh expressed extreme disapproval in his voice and manner.

"I'm an officer." Graddon exhibited a badge.

"Ah! Possibly that explains your rather brusque manner," Sidney Carleigh said. "Just what is the trouble? I'm Sidney Carleigh, owner of the Manchester Manor and Metropolitan Arms apartment houses. This is my sister."

"And what's that you're carrying?" Graddon demanded.

"It is a big tin of face cream. Fact, I assure you. You see, my dear sir, a little old lady has a cosmetic factory in this building, and she wants me to put some money into it."

The building superintendent came up.

"Looks all right, Mr. Graddon," he said. "An old lady does have a cosmetic shop in the building. And I've seen this gentleman before, I believe."

"Go along," Graddon growled.

Sidney Carleigh bowed somewhat sarcastically, and went on to the street with his sister by his side. They hailed a taxi, got in, and started home.

"If he only had known what was in the bottom of that can," Eleanor whispered.

"Some greasy bills." Her brother smiled again.

"Close shave, eh, Sid?"

"Nothing of the sort!" he protested. "One thing I regret—I should have made Graddon carry this can out to the taxi for me."

"Well—that's over!" She snuggled closer to him.

"Another score settled," he whispered. "A little rest, now—and then to settle yet another!"

TRAP OF THE MONGOOSE

*In the Rôle of Mephistopheles, The Mongoose
Spreads Sulphur and Brimstone to Collect
$50,000 in Vengeance Money*

CHAPTER I

MR. GARSELL'S FRIGHT

THE LETTER WAS in an envelope of the kind favored by ladies who are inclined to be fashionable rather than refined. From it came a scent so strong that it must have permeated other epistles with which it had been intimately associated in its passage through the mails.

Such letters were so numerous in Robert Garsell's mail, and of such a personal tone, that his private secretary generally put them aside on one corner of the desk unopened. That is where Garsell found this one, on a bright morning when everything seemed pleasant and peaceful.

He did not recognize the handwriting on the envelope. He rather hoped that this was the initial correspondence of a certain lively little brunette he had met recently, and who had intrigued his fancy to an extent. So he ignited a perfecto, leaned back comfortably in his easy desk chair, and slit the envelope open with a flourish.

From it he extracted a folded sheet of paper which was tinted, as was the envelope, with lavender. It exuded an aroma that spoke eloquently of boudoirs and beauty. Mr. Garsell hesitated a moment, to allow the pleasure of anticipation to thrill him. Then he unfolded the sheet of paper, bent his head forward, and prepared to read.

But this was no glowing epistle which promised a further interesting acquaintance with a lady, brunette or otherwise.

In the center of the sheet of paper letters had been printed with a pen, and purple ink had been used. The thing looked rather mysterious:

E-SO-OG-NOM

"What the—?" Mr. Garsell began, sitting up straight in his chair and putting his cigar aside in an ash tray. He told himself that this might be some new sort of advertising dodge, though he scarcely believed it. The thing seemed to have a personal touch. He read it a dozen times, puzzled over it, turned it upside down and looked at it sideways. But there seemed no solution of the enigma.

Then he read it backwards, scribbling the letters on his desk pad to see if he could make anything out of them. And, an instant later, Mr. Robert Garsell had jumped to his feet and away from the desk as though a cobra had been coiled there ready to strike.

His face suddenly had grown pale and he trembled like a man unable to control his nerves. He extracted a handkerchief from his pocket and wiped a perspiring brow which had been dry a moment before, not realizing that he did so. He glanced swiftly around the private office, as if expecting to behold some enemy crouching in a corner, ready to open fire on him.

Then Robert Garsell made a heroic effort to regain control of himself. He was a man among men, he reminded himself emphatically. He was Robert Garsell, who had fought his way up in the world against opposition that had been formidable at times. He had wealth, and large holdings of real estate, political pull, and had his hands in a dozen batches of financial dough. He had disposed of enemies often before—so why not now?

Squaring his shoulders he walked back to the desk and reached for the telephone.

"Get Mark Graddon for me at once," he ordered his switchboard girl.

Turning to the heap of papers which were awaiting his attention, he made an effort to get down to business. But he was

"Careful! Don't make a sound or this little toy I'm holding is liable to bark and bite"

unable to concentrate. His thoughts strayed. Real estate was not paramount in his mind at the moment.

He was remembering a little affair of some ten years before, when he had combined with some other unscrupulous financiers to send an innocent man to prison on a trumped-up charge—when it had been a case of the financiers either doing that or going behind bars themselves. And now—

A buzzer sounded, and Garsell turned to the telephone.

"Mark Graddon speaking," a strong masculine voice said.

"This is Robert Garsell, Graddon. Come to my office at once, please."

"Something important?"

"Very! Lose no time getting here. If you're pinched for speeding, the fine is on me."

Garsell snapped the receiver back into place and got up to pace the room. No sense in trying to work! Here was something that called for immediate attention. After proper disposal of it, he could handle such affairs as real estate sales and purchases, appraisals and loans.

Mark Graddon was not long in getting to the spot, for his own office was less than a dozen blocks away. He was admitted immediately, and took a hasty glance at his client, noticing his highly nervous condition.

"What's the trouble?" Graddon asked, as he sat in a chair at the end of the desk.

"Take a look at this!" Garsell tossed him the sheet of lavender paper.

Mark Graddon picked it up, sniffed at it, smiled slightly, and unfolded it. Probably another attempt at extortion, Graddon thought. He handled such cases a dozen times a year. He was a private detective who served men of means, and many of them grew careless when some woman attracted their fancy.

"Wh—what—?" Graddon gasped, when he saw what the letter contained.

"I'll save you time," Garsell said. "Just read the thing backwards."

Mark Graddon did so. "The Mongoose!" he cried.

"You've got it, Graddon. That's what the confounded thing spells backwards. I suppose it's a gentle hint that I'm to be his next victim."

GRADDON SMASHED a fist down on the desk. "This time we'll get him!" he declared. "I've been waiting for him to make the next move. I've got certain plans laid. He's made a fool of me for the last time!"

"I hope you're right," Garsell said. "The Mongoose has done pretty much as he's pleased, seems to me. He's tapped half a dozen of the boys, and tapped 'em hard. What does he do with all his money?"

"Uses some of it for expenses, and gives the rest to charity, so he informed me once," Mark Graddon replied. "I hate to disappoint the worthy charitable institutions, but contributions from The Mongoose are about over."

There came a knock on the door.

"Come in!" Garsell cried.

His secretary entered, carrying a small package. "Pardon me, Mr. Garsell, but this was left with word that you were to have it at once. Thought it might be something important."

She placed the small package on the end of the desk, and turned to leave. The package was wrapped in heavy brown paper, and liberally daubed with red sealing wax. Mark Graddon's eyes bulged when he saw it.

"Wait a moment!" he snapped at the departing secretary. "When did this come?"

"A few minutes ago. I brought it in as soon as I'd finished giving the clerks their instructions for the day."

"Who brought it?"

"Ordinary messenger. I scarcely noticed him. He wore the usual uniform."

"Did he have a receipt book for you to sign?"

"Yes, sir. Quite the usual thing."

"Think so, do you? Tell me now—were there any other signatures on the page of the receipt book he handed you to sign?" Graddon asked.

"I believe it was a fresh page, with this delivery entered at the top of the sheet."

"Thought so," Graddon said. "Fake receipt book. Fake messenger, probably."

"Is something wrong? Have I committed an error?" the secretary asked, frightened.

"Nothing you could avoid," Graddon assured her. "It's all right."

Garsell motioned for the secretary to quit the office, then turned to face Graddon. "What is it?" he asked.

"Straight from The Mongoose, probably—box looks like it. He generally sends a prospective victim a dictaphone record, telling him what's what. The thing is treated chemically, and melts into nothingness in a few minutes after being exposed to

the open air. Swing your dictaphone machine around in front
of the desk. I'll unwrap the package."

"But, what's the idea? And that queer letter—?"

"Wants to get on your nerves," Graddon explained. "Boasts
that he always warns his victims before he strikes. One way of
showing he holds me in little estimation."

Graddon removed the brown paper and disclosed a small
pasteboard box. He opened it cautiously. Wrapped carefully in
a sheet of cotton, he found a dictaphone cylinder.

"Here we are! Letter from The Mongoose," he said. "Put it
on the machine, and listen to the thing. Then give me a chance
at it before it melts away."

Garsell accepted the cylinder and handled it as though it had
been red hot. He slipped it on the dictaphone, shivered a bit,
adjusted the ear tubes, and bent forward to listen to the message
The Mongoose had sent:

> Hello, Robert Garsell! This is The Mongoose talking to you.
> You know what happened about ten years ago, and how you
> were concerned in the affair. The time has come for you to pay.
> You are the next on my list.
>
> Because you did not play such an active part as some of the
> others, I am disposed to be more lenient with you. All I require
> from you is fifty thousand dollars cash. Have it ready, for I shall
> call for it very soon.

Without speaking, Robert Garsell got out of the chair and
motioned Graddon to take his place and listen, which the detective did. Then they both bent forward to look at the record.
Almost at once, large bubbles began forming on its surface. It
seemed to melt and run, to evaporate. Before their eyes, it disappeared rapidly, utterly, the last few damp spots faded away—and
there was nothing to show there ever had been a record.

"**FIFTY THOUSAND—LENIENT!**" Robert Garsell
muttered. "Graddon, you've got to do something about this! It

isn't only the money, please understand. The Mongoose must be caught, stopped, an end put to his nefarious work."

"I understand all that," Graddon replied. "You listen to me now, please. Garsell, you go right ahead with your business and your social affairs as though this thing hadn't happened. Try to look and act naturally."

"What's the idea?"

"From the moment you step out of this office, you're going to be watched and shadowed by some of my best men, and I'll be near you myself, too, as much as possible. Day and night, every second, we'll be near you. We don't know The Mongoose, and so can't watch him. But he'll have to contact you in some way to go through with the deal. When he does that, we'll get him!"

"Good scheme!" Garsell said.

"Don't let anything startle you. The Mongoose uses a lot of tricks in his work. He's expert with chemistry and electricity. For instance, don't go wild and throw a fit if he speaks to you out of nowhere."

"Out of nowhere?" Garsell gasped.

"He's done it before. He's got some sort of wireless dicto-graph," Graddon explained. "All he has to do is plant a little disk—say here in your office, or in your den at home—and he can talk to you from a distance, without the use of wires. He also can hear everything that's said near the disk. He may be listening to me now."

"In that case—"

"He knows what I'm planning, huh? Let him! Maybe he won't have the nerve to go after you, if he knows we're watch-ing. Now, you just forget all about this, and go right ahead with your business, and live your life as usual. Don't mention the affair to anybody."

"I'd expected to attend the Bohemian Ball tonight," Garsell said.

"Well, why not? The Mongoose isn't an assassin. He's only after money. He won't appear at the ball and shoot you down.

Enjoy yourself as though you hadn't received word from him. I can't imagine his working on you at the Bohemian Ball, in that mob. Leave everything to me. And stay in this office until I send you word that my men are on the job."

"I've a luncheon engagement—"

"Keep it. You'll be under shadow before lunch time. Keep all your engagements," Graddon told him. "Don't change anything because of this. Let The Mongoose do his stuff. And this time he'll walk into a trap!"

CHAPTER II

AT THE BOHEMIAN BALL

FEELING UNCOMFORTABLE IN evening attire, Detective Mark Graddon leaned against the wall and critically surveyed a throng that probably would not have been out of place on a motion picture lot.

His keen eyes appraised a bewildering array of devils and monks, clowns, ballet girls and bareback riders, knights in armor, Indians, men and women garbed in the native costumes of almost every country under the sun; men who proudly revealed their athletic forms in leopard-skin garments, and others who concealed their skinny anatomies under the voluminous robes of Arabian sheiks.

A man garbed in a blue domino brushed lightly against Graddon, and paused to glance around as though searching for somebody in the crowd. Graddon spoke to him in whispers from the corner of his mouth:

"Nelson! Keep on tailing him."

"I've got my eyes on him, chief. The others are watchin', too. He's easy to keep sight of, in that military uniform—nobody else seems to have one like it."

"Don't forget that The Mongoose is a smooth article. He may

not even be here, but we can't take the chance of thinking he isn't. Keep close to Garsell, but not near enough to tip off what you are. Get a line on anybody who speaks to Garsell and seems to annoy or startle him."

Nelson, one of Graddon's best men, moved away through the crowd. Graddon continued to scrutinize the passers-by. A masked ballet dancer waltzed up to him and danced back and forth.

"Naughty man! Ought to be in costume," she taunted.

"Somebody has to keep sane, sister!"

She danced past him again, closer, made sure that nobody was watching her particularly, and spoke in whispers: "Had a dance with Garsell, chief. He doesn't seem worried. Don't believe he's been contacted by our friend. No suspicious females have been near him. He's cutting up like the rest, flirting and dancing a little and moving on."

"Keep at it," Gradden ordered.

The ballet dancer danced away through the crowd, eluding a pursuing male. Three other men approached Graddon and reported in whispers. Graddon glanced through the crowd. He could see Robert Garsell, who wore the uniform of an officer of hussars.

"Probably a lot of work for nothing," Graddon muttered. "Chances are The Mongoose isn't even here."

But The Mongoose was there.

Just now he was dressed as a clown, wearing a white clown suit with huge red spots on it, a conspicuous figure wherever he moved. He danced and partook of the gayety as did hundreds of others who had been attracted by the Bohemian Ball, the annual charity affair open to almost anybody who wore a costume and had a twenty-dollar bill.

And now the clown sauntered through the throng and approached Garsell as he ceased dancing and stepped back toward a wall.

"Hello, Garsell!" the clown greeted in a low voice.

Garsell whirled to face him. "Who are you? And how'd you know me?"

"I'd know you anywhere, even in a mob like this. You stand out so from the others." There was a trace of sarcasm in the clown's voice.

"You've got me. I can't place you," Garsell said.

"You don't know me personally, Garsell. That'd never do. It might prove embarrassing for me." The clown stepped closer as the crowd suddenly surged around them, and chuckled. "Remember ten years ago? I'm The Mongoose!" he said.

Garsell was staggered an instant. And, in that instant, he heard the clown's mocking laugh, and then the clown was gone as though the crowd had swallowed him. Garsell plainly betrayed by his agitation that he had been shocked by what the other had said.

Nelson, who was within a few feet of Garsell, signalled, and another man hurried up. Garsell found himself gripped by the arm.

"I'm Nelson, Graddon's man! Did that clown bother you?"

"He said he was The Mongoose," Garsell whispered.

"The Mongoose? We'll get him!"

Nelson signalled again, and two other men saw the signal and started to fight their way through the crowd after him. Graddon saw, and hurried forward. But the clown was gone.

"After him!" Graddon said. "Everybody watch for that clown. Pass the word. Nab anybody who's wearing a costume like that, and bring 'em to me, no matter who he is or how loudly he squawks!"

The clown had darted into the big corridor, also jammed with guests, had hurried to an elevator and ascended to the tenth floor of the fashionable hotel, where he went rapidly down a hall and entered a room. A few minutes later, he emerged—and now he was a monk arrayed in sober-looking robe and cowl.

Down in the ballroom, Garsell had got over his momentary fright. He was not sure whether he had been addressed by The

Mongoose, or one of his own business associates who wanted to startle him. Nor was Graddon.

The music was commencing again, the crowd was surging as dancers tried to get on the floor, and Garsell started through it in pursuit of a woman he imagined he knew. He thought little of it when he suddenly collided with a monk. Garsell stepped aside and muttered the conventional apology. But the monk seemed to resent the minor collision out of proportion to its importance.

"Who do you think you are, bumpin' into everybody?" the monk barked. "You're not the only person on the floor. Give somebody else a little room."

"Why—why—" Garsell stammered in astonishment at the unexpected attack.

The monk raised his voice so that it attracted the attention of the mob of persons jammed in the corner. "For less than ten cents I'd smack you down!" he cried. "Come out into the hall and I'll do it!"

"Why, you—" Garsell began.

"Don't give me any of your lip! I know all about you—you home-wrecker and wife-stealer! Ought to beat you in the beezer right here in front of the crowd, then tear off your mask and let 'em see your face!"

GARSELL WAS not accustomed to having men address him in such a manner. He was rendered both motionless and speechless for a moment by the attack. The crowd surged, and in some mysterious manner the monk disappeared.

"What a monk!" somebody said.

Garsell moved away from the scene quickly. He was masked, but somebody might remember his costume, and, at unmasking time, learn the identity of the man who had been called a home-wrecker and wife-stealer. Suddenly he found Graddon at his side.

"What was the trouble?" Graddon whispered.

"Some fool dressed like a monk bumped into me, then bawled me out as if it had been my fault. Intoxicated, probably."

"Nothing to suggest?" Graddon hinted.

"Not a thing. He just sassed me for bumping into him. It made me boil over, though. I think I'll take a stroll in the corridor and cool off."

"We're after that clown," Graddon whispered. "If you see him again, make some sort of fuss and some of the men will come running."

Making an effort to control his rage, Garsell went out into the broad corridor, where the crowd was a little thinner, and where couples were sitting on the divans resting. He walked along slowly, looking for an empty seat in some secluded nook. He wanted to be alone for a time, slip off his mask and enjoy a cigarette.

Garsell glanced toward one of the nooks, and saw a double seat, half of which appeared to be filled with a delicious and fluffy bit of femininity. Robert Garsell was susceptible to such. He saw two eyes gleaming a flirtatious welcome at him through holes in a mask. Shapely ankles were crossed as though for his inspection. A well-modeled arm was hanging over the end of the seat.

Here was something that promised to take away from Garsell the bitterness of his recent encounters with the clown and the monk in the ballroom. He sauntered across to the divan.

"Do you mind if I sit here?" he asked.

"Do! I like your looks," she said.

"Thanks! You're not more than half bad yourself, as far as I can see," Garsell replied. "Blue-eyed blonde, anyhow. I can tell that much. How come that such a beautiful damsel languishes here alone? Been deserted by some cruel boy friend?"

"There's no boy friend," she replied, laughing musically. "I came to the ball alone."

Garsell sat down beside her. "Possibly you'll let me be your boy friend for a time, then," he said.

"I don't know about that. I've heard that you have a naughty reputation, Mr. Garsell."

"You know me?" he asked in surprise.

"There's nothing very wonderful about that," she said. "I happen to know you by sight. And I was near the motor entrance when you arrived tonight. You removed your mask to tighten the cord, and I had a glimpse of your face."

"So I did," Garsell remembered. "You have the advantage of me then."

"Few persons get that, I understand," she said. "You'll have to do some guessing, if you learn my identity.

"I don't think you can guess. We've never met formally."

"Why not just tell me, and end the suspense? All I have to do is follow you around until unmasking time."

"You might see my face then, but that wouldn't give you my name and address," she replied. "And I may be missing when unmasking time comes. Possibly I'm another Cinderella."

"Why not team up with me and have some fun? You say you have no escort, and I came alone, too."

She started to reply, but gave a little cry of annoyance and bent forward quickly, grasping at something. She had been fumbling at the front of her costume, and now something fell, to miss the edge of the rug and strike on the marble floor. Garsell saw that it was a key with a little metal tag attached.

"I'll lose that yet," she said, as he bent to recover the key for her. "That makes twice I've dropped it. Haven't a proper place to carry it in this costume."

"Let me take care of it for you."

"Let you have the key to my apartment? Why, how dare you, sir?" She giggled.

There was mockery in her voice. Garsell glanced swiftly at the metal tag. One side was stamped with letters which read: Worthington Arms. On the opposite side was the number of the apartment: 345.

"I have your address, at least," Garsell said. "Now be kind, and tell me your name. And then let's dance."

"I'd rather keep your curiosity aroused."

"Let's dance anyhow."

"Sorry, but I must go upstairs in the hotel and visit a friend," she told him, rising. "You're supposed to be a man of brains, Mr. Garsell. If you're so eager to learn more about me, get busy and do it."

"That's a challenge," he said. "I'll see you again, a little later?" He was walking beside her toward the elevators.

"How do I know?" she asked, laughing again. "Cinderella goes home a moment before midnight, doesn't she? Can she help it if the Prince follows and learns her identity? Only, I'm not leaving any slipper behind."

Once more she laughed, and darted into an elevator about to ascend, leaving Garsell looking after her foolishly. But Garsell's eyes were glowing.

She was not leaving a slipper behind. But she was leaving her key!

CHAPTER III

BROTHER AND SISTER

LEAVING THE ELEVATOR at the tenth floor, the woman with whom Robert Garsell had enjoyed the little scene hurried swiftly along a hall and entered one of the rooms.

She closed the door behind her, and locked it when she saw that a man already was there, sitting in an easy chair near a window and smoking.

"Hello, Sid!" she said.

"Greetings, Eleanor. You know, I don't like this Bohemian Ball. Under the circumstances, I can't dance with you, and I want to do it."

"There are a few hundred other girls downstairs."

"Ah! But none like my Eleanor."

"A person would think I might be your sweetheart, instead of your sister."

She removed her mask and sat down beside a table. The man looked at her admiringly. Eleanor Carleigh was a beautiful young woman. And Sidney Carleigh himself was rather handsome, in a manly way.

They were close together, this brother and sister, devoted to their life work of avenging their father's memory, punishing the unscrupulous men who, ten years before, had framed him and sent him to prison, where he had died.

Inheriting an estate in England, they had spent several years making their plans, with ample funds at their command. Sidney Carleigh and his sister were persons of culture and means. They owned two large apartment houses, in one of which they lived. They lived like educated, refined persons.

Yet, at times, Sidney Carleigh was The Mongoose, attacking the human snakes who had ruined his father. One by one, he was striking at the men responsible. Nobody but his sister knew his secret, shared his thoughts, aided him in preparation and in carrying out his plans.

"Everything seems to be going well tonight," Eleanor Carleigh said.

"Yes. I brushed against Garsell in my clown costume, and whispered that I was The Mongoose. Had no difficulty in getting away, though that ass of a Mark Graddon and several of his men were near."

"And the monk episode—?" she questioned.

"That was easier. It worked splendidly, Eleanor. I howled my denunciations at him where a hundred persons or more heard. Made my getaway easily enough, through the crowd, too. Graddon and his men are looking for the clown—and also for the monk, I suppose. Now, how about your part?"

"Not a hitch so far, Sid. I watched Garsell for more than an hour, dodging men who were trying to dance with me—dodging one of Graddon's woman operatives, too. I was commencing to think I'd never be able to attract Garsell's attention in a natural manner, and then he decided to stroll in the corridor. I got ahead of him and planted myself on a divan."

"And attracted him?"

"Yes. Only empty seat was beside me—I saw to that. He sat down and got into conversation. I aroused his interest and finally dropped the key—and he has it now."

"Think he'll walk into the trap?"

"He's that sort of man, isn't he, Sid? And are you doubting my personal appeal?" She laughed a bit.

"I suppose some of Graddon's people saw him talking to you."

"No doubt. We walked to the elevator, and I dodged into one just as the door was being closed. Nobody got in after me, so none of Graddon's operatives saw me come here. They may question and learn what floor I got off at, but I doubt if the elevator operator could remember. Some jam tonight. Even so, there are more than a hundred rooms and suites on this floor, I fancy. And probably all occupied tonight."

"Fair enough!" Sidney Carleigh said. "If our plan doesn't work, we have others. But I'm hoping Garsell takes the bait. He isn't worth wasting more time on. Perhaps you'd better leave now, Eleanor. Be sure you dodge him downstairs."

"Trust me, Sid. But the end, as we've planned it—isn't it dangerous for you?"

He lowered his voice. "The Mongoose must be prepared to face danger," he answered. "When he fights the cobra, he takes a chance. But he generally wins."

"Oh, Sid, be careful!"

"Be careful yourself," he said.

She got up, walked across to him, kissed him on the forehead.

"See you later," her brother called after her. "I'll spot our man and whisper in his ear as arranged."

She put on her mask again, opened the door and darted into the hall. Sidney Carleigh got up and locked the door behind her, then crossed to a closet in a corner of the room. From it he took the clown costume he had worn earlier in the night. And now he stripped off his monk's costume and stood forth as a scarlet Mephistopheles. He put on his Satan's cap and shoes, and a red mask he had ready.

Making a bundle of the other two costumes, he went to a window and opened it silently, snapped out the lights, and hurled the costumes far out into the night. The wind caught the garments and scattered them, drove them down toward the earth in half a dozen different places.

"So perish a clown and a monk," Sidney Carleigh muttered. "Now, The Mongoose is the devil himself!"

HE CLOSED the window, drew down the shade, and snapped on the lights again. He had engaged this room, using an assumed name, for the purpose of dressing for the ball—as scores of others had engaged rooms, those who did not wish to dress in fancy costume at home. Neither he nor his sister had touched a thing in it without having gloves on their hands. There was no danger of fingerprints.

And in the Worthington Arms there was an apartment, No. 345 to be precise, the key to which Eleanor Carleigh had dropped for Robert Garsell to pick up and retain, which had been engaged almost a month before in anticipation of this very night.

But the landlord of that apartment house knew Sidney Carleigh under another name, and had an idea that the gentleman had rented the place to be used as a rendezvous with the apparently delightful lady who visited it about once a week, always heavily veiled. The tenant himself, the landlord noticed, appeared only that often also.

Now, Sidney Carleigh no longer, but The Mongoose for the time being, he snapped off the lights, opened the door and stepped into the hall, a red devil about to descend to the ground floor and ballroom again.

He went slowly toward the elevator, smiling behind his mask. For he saw two men he felt certain were attached to the private detective agency of Mark Graddon, and did not doubt they were hoping to catch sight of a clown or a monk. He hoped that Eleanor had escaped their scrutiny.

Descending in an elevator, The Mongoose went toward the ballroom, and began a search for his quarry. He finally located Garsell standing back against a wall and looking through the crowd. The Mongoose made his way as speedily as possible to Garsell's side. He walked with a sliding motion, totally unlike his usual snappy stride. He knew how a man's manner of walking could betray him to experienced eyes.

"Ah, a soldier!" he said, in Garsell's ear. "A leader of armies, and a slayer of men! I'll get you in the end!"

"You'll probably get a lot of folks who're here tonight," Garsell said, taking in the devil's costume.

"I have words for your ear, general. Maybe it's a joke, and maybe not. That's for you to judge. If not, undoubtedly it is sin, hence in my province. The little lady seemed in earnest."

"Lady?" Garsell queried.

"She was over by the door, unable to get through the crowd, and grabbed me by the arm and asked me to do her a favor.

"Who can refuse a lady, eh? She pointed you out, so I'm not mistaken in the man. And she asked me to use my satanic strength and fight through the crowd and give you a message."

"What sort of lady?" Garsell asked.

"Ah! Delicious! A golden blonde, unless she's wearing a wig. Dressed in some sort of fluffy stuff."

Garsell betrayed interest. "What was the message?"

"She said to tell you that she couldn't see you now, but that you had something belonging to her, and would you please bring it to her between one and two o'clock this morning. She said you'd know what I meant. I hope so, for I do not."

Garsell slapped him on the shoulder. "You're a kind devil!" he said. "I know what she meant, all right. If I had a chance, I'd buy you a drink for bringing me that message."

"I drink only molten brimstone, with sulphuric acid for a chaser. Glad to have been of service. So long! See you in hell!"

CHAPTER IV

THE SHOCK

UNMASKING TIME FOUND Robert Garsell greeting friends and acquaintances and making merry in the usual manner. He had a feverish desire to get away, but could not do so too early without causing comment.

Graddon and his operatives had kept Garsell in sight continually. They had noticed the Mephistopheles speaking to him, but had thought nothing of it, hearing Garsell laugh during the conversation.

Nelson joined Graddon in the corridor.

"Didn't find the clown or monk, chief," he reported.

"The clown may have been one of the crowd, knowing the secret about The Mongoose, and wanting to startle Garsell," Graddon said. "Or, he may have been The Mongoose himself, trying to scare him. He didn't contact him again, and he didn't give Garsell any orders, or Garsell would have said so."

"That woman he was talking to disappeared somewhere upstairs."

"Ordinary flirtation," Graddon decided. "Probably nothing to do with our business. Garsell's known for his flirtations. May have been some woman he knows."

"Want him still tailed?"

"Day and night, and no orders to the contrary unless they come from me," Graddon said, emphatically.

Nelson hurried away to communicate with the others, and

Graddon continued to watch Garsell, following him along the corridor as he walked toward the door with some friends, and finally getting near enough to overhear the conversation.

"Sorry, but I must refuse," Garsell was saying. "No speakeasies for me tonight."

"He's probably got an important date," one of the men said.

They laughed and went on, and Garsell turned aside to dodge another group of acquaintances. Those words interested Graddon. An important date!

He waited for a chance to speak to Garsell, "Going home soon?" he asked.

"Not for some time, possibly. It's quite all right, Graddon. No sense in you and your men bothering any more about me tonight. If you'll just have my place guarded—"

"We'll do that," Graddon said. "Please understand, Garsell, that there are two angles to this affair. Keeping The Mongoose from robbing you is one of them. Catching him is another. He has said you're to be his next victim, so he'll come after you sooner or later. If you don't mind, I'll have my men continue to shadow you."

Garsell stepped nearer and lowered his voice. "I have an engagement with a lady," he said.

"My men won't interfere with it, but they'll know where you are all the time, and see that The Mongoose doesn't contact you. And they don't talk, so be reassured."

"Confound it, I'm under espionage as if I were a criminal," Garsell complained. "I don't like it. Let your men pick me up when I get home."

He went on through the hotel lobby, and finally drifted toward the motor entrance. Mark Graddon, his face grim, issued certain orders. He had no wish to interfere with Robert Garsell's love affairs and intrigues, but he was going to catch The Mongoose!

Garsell had his car called, and drove away. Half a dozen

blocks up the street, he ordered the chauffeur to pull up at the curb, and got out.

"Go on home, and put up the buggy for the night," he told his driver.

The chauffeur smiled slightly and drove away. It was not the first time Garsell had done this. He kept certain of his affairs a secret even from his trusted chauffeur.

Garsell signalled a passing taxicab and got in. He gave the address of the street corner nearest the Worthington Arms. Then he leaned back against the cushions and toyed with the key the mysterious girl had dropped.

The Worthington Arms, Garsell knew, was a huge apartment house on the outskirts of the select residential district.

The atmosphere was Bohemian rather than exclusive. Garsell had been in the building before, and did not hesitate to enter it now.

He left the cab at the corner and walked to the entrance, glanced through the glass doors to see a scattering of persons in the lobby, and strode inside. He wore a long overcoat over his masquerade costume. But the fact he was in costume attracted little attention. Many of the tenants of the Worthington Arms had been to the Bohemian Ball.

Garsell glanced at the key tag again and checked up on the number. He entered an elevator and ascended to the fourth floor, then walked down to the third. He found No. 345, walked past the door, and for a time watched from the end of the hall.

Presently, he returned to the door of No. 345. He listened, but heard nothing. He touched the bell button, stood back to wait. The ring was not answered.

He rang again, and again waited in vain, and then he knocked, thinking that the bell might be out of order. But nobody came to the door.

GARSELL WONDERED about it a bit. He disliked entering with the key he held. But he remembered the atmosphere of the place, and the manner in which the key had come into his

possession. Between one and two, had been the word the red
devil had carried to him. It still lacked fifteen minutes of two
o'clock.

Garsell did not want to loiter in the hall, and perhaps be seen
and recognized. Perhaps, he thought, she had intended for him
to enter and wait for her, if he got there first. So he inserted the
key, unlocked the door and opened it carefully. He saw a short
hall, and beyond it a living room of the ordinary sort, with one
floor lamp burning.

"Anybody home?" Garsell called.

There was no reply. Leaving the door open, he walked inside
and to the living room. There was nothing unusual about the
room. The furnishings were such as are generally found in such
a place. There did not seem to be many intimate things scattered around.

Garsell came to a swift decision. He would wait. He retraced
his steps and closed the door, came back and sat down on a
couch, lit a cigarette and made himself comfortable. On a small
table at his elbow were glasses and a couple of bottles of liquor.
Garsell sniffed at the liquor and decided that it was passable,
and poured himself a drink.

He began to grow nervous because of inaction. Two o'clock
came, but the lady he expected did not. He got up and moved
around the room, examined a couple of silver statuettes, and a
picture in a nickeled frame, inspected a queer sort of metal ash
tray, dropped the remnant of his cigarette into it and ignited
another.

Through a partially-opened door, he could see another little
hall, and went toward it, pushing the door open wider. There
was a bathroom, and across from it a room which he thought
probably was a bedchamber. The door of the bedchamber stood
open a few inches, and faint light came through it, as though a
night light had been left burning.

Garsell had a measure of curiosity. He decided to peer into
the bedroom, then return to the living room and wait a few

minutes longer. If his fair charmer had not returned by that time he would leave and consider the evening wasted.

He walked to the bedroom door and opened it wider, and looked inside. Then he gave a cry of mingled surprise and fright.

A night light was burning on a table beside the head of the bed, casting its dim radiance over that corner of the room. And what it revealed brought a shock to Robert Garsell.

Sprawled on the floor was the lady of the key, still dressed in her masquerade costume. The bosom of the fluffy costume was drenched with blood. A knife protruded from her breast. Her head was twisted to one side, and Garsell could not see her face. A dark pool on the rug beside her spoke eloquently of lifeblood ebbing away.

It flashed into Robert Garsell's mind that here he was in a strange apartment where he had no real business being, alone with a woman undoubtedly murdered, and that it would be difficult for him to explain. Panic came to him. He fought to regain control of himself. He started to take a step forward, to have a closer look at her.

Then he heard a masculine voice: "Garsell! Into the living room, quick!"

CHAPTER V

THE TRAP

THAT VOICE ACTED upon Garsell like an electric shock. He whirled and darted from the room, through the little hall, and into the living room. There, he came to an abrupt stop. He had expected to find himself facing somebody—but the room was empty.

"Wh—what—" he stammered.

"Sit down! There on the end of the couch!"

Garsell could not tell from whence the voice came. It seemed to be right in the room, near him, but he could see nobody. He sat on the couch as he had been ordered, but principally because a feeling of weakness had come to him.

"So you killed her!" the voice said.

"What do you mean? I haven't killed anybody! Where are you?" Garsell asked.

"You killed her, and you'll go to the electric chair."

"Who are you?" Garsell cried. "I can't see you."

Laughter reached Garsell's ears—soft, mocking laughter. It seemed to fill the room.

"I'm The Mongoose, you fool!" the voice came again. "I'm the son of the man you condemned to a living hell, the innocent man you humiliated and shamed and caused to die in prison. And now I'm going to send you to that same prison. And you'll die there, too, Garsell—but in the chair! You'll burn in the hot seat!"

"That woman! I—I never—"

Suddenly it came upon him that this was absurd. He could see nobody, and felt sure nobody was in the room. Where was the voice of The Mongoose coming from, then? What was to prevent him from leaving the apartment, getting away from the scene? He started to get up.

"Sit down!" the voice ordered promptly. "Better listen, Garsell."

"Where are you?"

"In a place where I can see you, Garsell. But I'm speaking to you over a wireless dictograph. I can watch you and direct your movements, but you don't know where I am and couldn't tell anybody else that little fact. Listen! Tonight, at the Bohemian Ball, you had trouble with a man in a monk's costume."

"He bumped against me—"

"A hundred witnesses heard him denounce you for something. He threatened to beat you up. He called you a home-wrecker and wife-stealer, and raved like a man who had reason for hating you."

"He was drunk—"

"Keep quiet, and listen!" The Mongoose ordered. "I want you to appreciate how this affair will look to the world. You have trouble with this man. A little later, you are sitting on a divan in the hotel corridor, carrying on a flirtation with a pretty girl. Later, you are found in this apartment, and the girl dead in the bedroom—murdered! What are you doing here?"

"I flirted with the girl. She hinted I was to come here. She sent word to me to do so between one and two this morning."

"Sent word by whom?"

"A man at the dance—a man in a Mephistopheles costume."

"And you know him, and can get him to testify in your behalf?" The Mongoose asked.

Garsell suddenly realized that he did not. He had no proof of that detail. And he realized, also, that he was carrying on a conversation with somebody he could not see, was talking into the air. And once more he started to get up, with the idea of rushing from the apartment, getting out of the building.

"Don't move—unless you want to go to the chair," the voice of The Mongoose said. "Pay close attention. I want to show you the situation you're in. Why did you come to this apartment?"

"I—I had her key. She left it with me accidentally. An ordinary affair—"

"You call it an ordinary affair? Listen closely, Garsell. The man in the monk's costume, with whom you had trouble at the ball—let us say that he's the husband of the lady who gave you the key, and who now is dead in the bedroom."

"What?" Garsell cried.

"You come here with the key and let yourself into the apartment. You quarrel with the lady, attack and kill her—"

"Don't say that! I didn't kill her. I just looked into the bedroom and saw her there."

"Use your brains, Garsell. How does it look? You've been carrying on an affair with a married woman. You had a key to the place. A hundred persons heard you denounced tonight as a home-wrecker. Plenty of witnesses saw you talking to the woman in the corridor."

"I never saw her before—don't know her—"

"Would anybody believe that, do you think? And you're here in this apartment—"

"I've never been here before."

"GARSELL, YOUR fingerprints are on that picture frame on the table, on that metal ash tray, and on those statuettes. In the ash tray is the butt of a cigarette—the sort you smoke, with your monogram on it. On every side—evidence!"

"I'll soon—"

"Don't move!" The Mongoose warned. "I can blow you and that apartment to bits by merely touching a button."

"What do you want? I—I've got to get out of here! How do you know about the fingerprints?"

"I was watching when you put them there, Garsell."

"Then this—this is a frame-up?"

"Call it that if you like."

"But that dead woman—! Do you mean you killed her just to set a trap for me?"

"Perhaps she was taken for a ride, for talking too much, and we just worked two deals together," The Mongoose said.

"You can't get away with this!" Garsell cried. "You're not fighting an idiot! I'll call the police and tell my story. They'll soon find who killed that woman in the bedroom. All the public will ever have against me will be that I flirted with a woman and went to her apartment."

"Go ahead, Garsell! Call the police, and give the town a new sensation. Call Graddon's men. They trailed you to this apartment house."

"What?" Garsell cried.

"Watching you all the time, in an effort to catch me, the fools! Even they will have to testify about the trouble you had with the monk, about being with the woman on the divan in the corridor.

Graddon and his men will drop you quick enough, when they find you're mixed up in murder."

"Don't say that!" Garsell begged. I'm innocent! I can't afford a scandal. Let me get out of here! How much do you want? Can't we talk business?"

"That's better," the voice of The Mongoose told him. "We'll get right down to business. This murder affair is nothing to me, except I use it to further my own ends. I want fifty thousand dollars, Garsell."

"Fifty thou—"

"That's it! Get me that amount, and I'll get you out of this. Nobody will think but what you've merely been in this building to one of the many parties that are being held here tonight."

"But that woman—! She's in that costume. They may remember I was talking to her at the hotel."

"She won't have on that costume when she's found, Garsell. And she may not be found here."

"You—you'll fix everything?"

"Everything!" The Mongoose said.

"But—that amount of money—"

"You have it in your safe in your own apartment, Garsell. You're holding it ready in preparation for a shady deal you're planning. I happen to know."

"What do you want me to do?"

"Go home and get the money, and bring it back here," The Mongoose said.

"Back here?"

"Don't shiver. Bring the money right back here. You can change into regular clothes when you go home. Let Graddon's men, if they're trailing you, think you've come back to keep an engagement. Why not drive your roadster, as though you were going to take the lady on a trip? That'll do, fine! Bring the money in a suitcase, and that'll carry out the trip idea. Since this is Saturday morning, it'll look like one of those week-end affairs."

"I—I—" Garsell stammered.

"And don't hesitate!" The Mongoose said.

"How do I know you'll keep your word?"

"I've never broken it to any of you scoundrels yet, have I? And you'll keep faith with me, too, Garsell! I've everything arranged. You don't know where I am, or who I am. Try any tricks, and you'll face a murder charge!"

"If I go away now, and don't come back with the money—"

"Do it, if you feel that way. Remember, your fingerprints are scattered all over the place; Graddon's men know you came here. The police will connect this with the quarrel you had with the monk, when they find he's the lady's husband. If they question you, and you tell the truth—well, you know how silly it will sound."

"I—I'll do as you say."

"Good!" The Mongoose said. "Hurry home, change clothes, come right back with the money in a suitcase. And one thing more. Once away from here, you may decide to risk not coming back. You may think it advisable to take Mark Graddon into your confidence and lay a trap for me, even risk scandal and a possible trial for murder."

"I promise—"

"Your promises are worth nothing!" The Mongoose interrupted. "I depend on something stronger. Garsell, you took a drink of liquor out of that bottle at the end of the couch when you came to the apartment."

"What of it?"

"The liquor was poisoned, Garsell."

"Poisoned?" Garsell sprang to his feet, his face livid.

"Sit down! Be quiet and listen. It was all prepared, Garsell. A slow poison. You don't know its identity, or the antidote—but I do. You'll be all right, if you get the antidote within a couple of hours. If you don't—"

"You're lying to me!"

"Sure of that?" The Mongoose asked. He laughed again. "Go on thinking it, Garsell—until it's too late. As soon as you're back here with the money, you can have the antidote. I promise that."

"I'll get the money—I'll be right back."

"And be careful not to tell Graddon's men anything. You must carry this off right under their noses. That poison is stirring in your blood already, Garsell. Be glad that I don't let it finish you!"

"I'll go—go right away!"

"Pull yourself together. Try to look and act natural when you leave. You don't want to arouse suspicion, do you?"

"If somebody comes here while I'm gone, and finds—"

"Don't worry about that. I'm on the job, Garsell. Don't waste any time, if you want that antidote to work."

CHAPTER VI

TO CATCH THE MONGOOSE

ROBERT GARSELL PULLED himself together and got out of the apartment. He walked up to the fourth floor, called the elevator, and descended. A few minutes later, he was in a taxicab and on his way home.

Before he had reached the elevator, the voice of The Mongoose had spoken again in the apartment Garsell had left.

"All right, Eleanor. Get going!"

The "dead" woman in the bedroom got up from the floor, and made a wry face as she contemplated the pretty costume, now ruined by red ink. That rug would have to be sent to the cleaner, too, but the landlord would receive anonymous compensation for that expense.

Working swiftly, Eleanor Carleigh removed the masquerade costume and got into a natty, fashionable suit. She went swiftly through the apartment, and walked down the rear stairs and to a side entrance, quitting the building.

In a room across the narrow court, The Mongoose was peering beneath a lowered shade. He could see both the bedroom and the living room of the apartment. He had been able to watch Garsell from the moment of his entrance, and by means of the wireless dictograph had heard and talked to him.

Now, The Mongoose made himself comfortable, and waited, puffing at a cigarette. He knew that Graddon's men were trailing Garsell. They might prove a menace at the last moment, but The Mongoose was prepared for that. Nor could he expect to carry on his campaign of vengeance without running into some tight corners.

So he smoked and waited, while Garsell sped across town to the apartment where he lived, a prey to emotions that he could not describe. He was trying to think of some way out of the trap without paying the amount demanded, but could not.

As The Mongoose had told him, the evidence all would point to him. Though he escaped conviction, he could not stand a scandal. His business affairs were shaky at the moment. His personal reputation was at the breaking point. And—the poisoned liquor!

He did not know whether The Mongoose had spoken the truth about that, but he dared not question. It seemed to him that he had a peculiar taste in his mouth. Panic descended upon him again, and he fought it off.

At his destination, he tried to act in a natural manner as he left the cab. In the lobby, he saw a man he supposed was from Mark Graddon's agency. Garsell did not address him. He hurried to the elevator and ascended to his suite.

He changed clothes quickly, then got a small bag and carried it to his den. He had an excellent safe there, hidden behind the paneling in the wall. The money was there, though he wondered how The Mongoose knew it. Garsell had more than the fifty thousand on hand, prepared to make a deal where cash must pass. And it was in small bills.

Working swiftly, he got the money out of the safe and stuffed it into the bag. A surge of anger passed through him as he did so.

He felt the ignominy of proving such an easy victim. If he had not spoken to the woman on the divan, fallen for the key trick, gone to the apartment— But he had done those things. And it did not add to his self-estimation to realize that The Mongoose had known he would do them.

He closed the safe and moved the panel back, picked up the bag and hurried into the living room. The front door buzzer sounded.

The sound startled Garsell. He wondered who could be calling at almost three o'clock in the morning. Quickly hiding the bag behind a couch, he went to the door.

"Who is it?" he asked.

"Graddon! Want to see you a moment."

Mark Graddon! Garsell certainly did not want to see him then, but had no reason for refusal. He opened the door, and Graddon strode in.

"Thought you might be going to bed," Graddon said. "But you've dressed."

"I'm going out," Garsell said.

"My men reported that you'd gone to the Worthington Arms. I know the reputation of that place."

"Well?"

"Understand it's some of my affair if you go there to a party, or to see some member of the feminine sex. I'm interested only in The Mongoose. I was wondering if you'd heard from him."

"How could I? Your men have been near me all the time, haven't they?"

"Thought he might have got word to you—possibly a threat," Graddon said, watching him closely. "May I ask where you're going now?"

"See here, Graddon! I—I can't tolerate interference in my personal affairs."

"Don't mean to meddle. But, under the circumstances—"

"I'm returning to the Worthington Arms. I'm going away for the week-end. Just a little—er—trip."

"With a lady?"

"Possibly."

"Going to give The Mongoose a chance to get at you? Have some sense, Garsell!"

Robert Garsell had stood about all he could endure. His nerves had been keyed to the snapping point. Graddon's eyes seemed to be boring into him.

"Tell me the truth!" Graddon snapped, suddenly.

And Robert Garsell broke down and told him.

"What can I do, Graddon?" he cried, when he had finished. "I shouldn't have told you. He's got me in a trap!"

"Quiet!" Graddon said. "Garsell, remember the truth about this Mongoose business. Several prominent men are involved. One reason we haven't gone after him harder, with the police called in to help, is because we don't want him to talk if he's caught. He'll spill that agony story about his father, get the sympathy of the public."

"But what else—"

GRADDON LOOKED straight at him. "He can be caught—and then shot while trying to escape," Mark Graddon said.

"Graddon! That's—"

"That's something for you to forget," Graddon said. "Understand, Garsell, you're only one small corner of the affair. I'll handle this thing."

"How, and protect me? I demand protection! I'm willing to pay my share, the fifty thousand. Lay a trap for him when he takes on the next man."

"If I kept doing that, I'd never nab him," Graddon said.

"What can you do?"

"Catch him. Maybe he can explain that murder. Expose the trap. You'll take the money there—so we'll have evidence of extortion. Make it look like we'd been watching and trailing him, caught him with the goods."

"But the murder thing—"

"Don't worry. The worst you'll get out of it will be a laugh because you flirted with some woman and got decoyed. That won't hurt you much."

"You're forgetting that poisoned liquor."

"We don't know The Mongoose was telling the truth about that. Be another charge against him, if he is."

"But I may die."

"I'll have a doctor ready to pump you out. But we'll go through with the deal. Give him the money, and let him give you the antidote. Extortion, attempt at murder—we'll have all sorts of charges against him in this, in addition to his other pranks. So there won't be much regret on the part of the public if he's shot while trying to escape. Understand? We'll make a monster out of him! May even make it look like you'd let yourself be decoyed, to set a trap for him. Make a hero out of you!"

"What must I do—and what are you going to do? I must know. And that antidote—"

"You take the money there as he ordered, and get the antidote. We won't make a move until we know you have it, and are safe. I'll have the place surrounded. He'll have to be in the building to get the money. And nobody'll come out of it, believe me, without being stopped and put over the jumps. As soon as you have the antidote and are safely out of that apartment, we'll be in."

"It's the poison I'm worried about," Garsell said.

"That may be only a trick. Maybe the liquor wasn't poisoned," Graddon said.

"But we aren't sure. And my throat—it seems dry now, full of acid."

"May be only imagination, but we won't take a chance. I'll have a doctor waiting, in case anything goes wrong and you don't get the antidote. Leave it to me! Order your roadster, now.

Then give me about five minutes on your telephone. I'll leave here before you go."

Mark Graddon spent the five minutes giving careful instruction to some of his men over the phone. Those not on duty, he got out of their beds. Like the experienced officer he was, he gave orders that would result in the Worthington Arms being surrounded by a cordon, every exit guarded.

Then Graddon hurried away, to get a taxicab and journey to the scene of what he hoped would be The Mongoose's capture. Five minutes later, Robert Garsell went down in the elevator, carrying the bag. His roadster was waiting for him, in charge of a sleepy garage attendant. Garsell got behind the wheel, and drove off down the street.

CHAPTER VII

EXCITING VICTORY

IT WAS A distance of only about fifteen feet across the little court of the Worthington Arms, from the apartment Garsell had visited to the room from which The Mongoose had watched him. Across that distance, from the window of the room to the open window of the bathroom in the apartment, a heavy rope was stretched. A grappling iron held it securely to the casement of the bathroom window. In the other room, it was fastened safely to a radiator. Eleanor Carleigh had aided her brother in stretching the rope soon after arriving at the apartment house from the hotel where the Bohemian Ball had been held.

In that little room across the court, The Mongoose had the receiving end of his wireless dictograph, a compact piece of machinery arranged so it could be destroyed almost instantly. One of the disks was in the living room of the apartment—and another had been planted some days before in the lobby of the building.

In the little dark room, The Mongoose smoked and waited patiently. Once he got up and moved to a closet, and took from it a canvas bag, such as is used sometimes by hunters for carrying game they have shot. There were several articles in the bag, one being a close-fitting black hood, with a tiny slit for breathing purposes and two more tiny slits for eyes.

With misgivings preying upon him, Robert Garsell drove his roadster through the almost deserted city streets, encountering little traffic except taxicabs, milk wagons and early morning delivery trucks.

It would have suited him, under the circumstances, to simply trade the fifty thousand dollars for immunity, and consider that he had done his share toward completing The Mongoose's plan for revenge. But Mark Graddon was in command of the situation.

Garsell parked his roadster half a block away from the Worthington Arms, got out, and walked briskly to the entrance. Again, he tried to look and act naturally. There were a number of people in the lobby, returning from parties or leaving parties that had been held in the building. Nobody gave Robert Garsell attention as he hurried to the elevator.

Again he ascended to the fourth floor and walked down a flight. In front of No. 345, he hesitated a moment, made certain nobody was observing him, then opened the door and stepped inside, carrying his bag. Quickly he shut the door behind him.

His first glance revealed that the living room was empty, and that nothing seemed to have been changed in it. Garsell walked to the end of the couch, and put the bag containing the money down upon the table.

He felt rather silly. Nobody was there, and nobody talked to him. He did not know what to do next. He thought of the horror in the bedchamber, and shivered. And then he heard the low voice of The Mongoose:

"Remain where you are for a moment, Garsell."

With the cold perspiration of fear standing out on his forehead, Garsell waited, pacing nervously back and forth in front of the couch. He wondered where Graddon was, and what he was doing, whether he had his men posted and the doctor ready. Garsell was particularly concerned about the doctor.

In the little room across the court, The Mongoose slung the canvas bag over his shoulders. He opened the window, swung out, grasped the heavy rope, and traveled hand over hand across the distance to the bathroom of the apartment. He seemed to accomplish this feat easily, though aware that a drop of three floors to the pavement of the court would result in death or serious injury.

Crawling through the window of the bathroom, The Mongoose opened the canvas sack and took therefrom a long black robe, in which he enveloped his body. His hands already were encased in thin black gloves. He slipped the black hood over his head, and his disguise was complete.

Now he stepped noiselessly from the bathroom and into the tiny hall. Through the half-opened door, he could see Garsell pacing nervously around the living room. The Mongoose stepped to the door and stood in it, a menacing figure holding an automatic pistol in a threatening position.

"Garsell!"

Robert Garsell whirled and gasped.

"Careful! Don't make a sound, or this little toy I'm holding is liable to bark and bite. You brought the money?"

"Yes, Here it is."

"Take it out of the bag and put it on the table."

Garsell opened the bag and heaped the bundles of currency where he had been told.

"If the amount isn't correct—" The Mongoose began.

"It's there—fifty thousand. Now, give me the antidote!"

"There's plenty of time."

"But I'm in agony, man!"

The voice of The Mongoose cut like a knife. "And what of the hours and days of agony my father suffered in the prison where you helped send him? I should let the poison do its work."

"You promised—"

"**AND I** always keep my promises," The Mongoose said. "You'll get the antidote in ample time. We'll talk a little, first. Look at the hall door, Garsell. Just above it. See that glass ball about six inches in diameter, filled with a liquid? In the bathroom, I have just thrown a little electric switch, Garsell. And, if that door is opened now, that ball will drop and crash. Smoke and flame will turn this place into an inferno. So, if you have friends in the hall, and expect them to enter and annoy me, better call to them to stay where they are."

"I—I only want the antidote, and to get away," Garsell said.

"Sit down on the end of the couch!"

Garsell obeyed. The Mongoose went forward, carrying his canvas bag. He tossed the bundles of currency into the bag, and retreated to the door of the little hall again.

"Now, Garsell, go to the fireplace," he directed. "Feel behind that vase, and you'll find a powder done up in paper."

"I've got it."

"Bring it back to the couch. Pour yourself some water out of the carafe. Take the powder, Garsell."

"It's the antidote?"

"Take it, and you need have no fear of the liquor you drank."

Garsell opened the paper, tilted it, let the powder pour upon his tongue, and washed it down with a gulp of water.

"There are several ingredients in that powder," The Mongoose said. "Part of it is an ordinary good headache powder—always an antidote for present day liquor. And the other part—sit there on the couch again, Garsell. That's it! May save you a nasty fall."

"What do you mean?"

"The other part, I was going to say, is a drug which makes a man unconscious almost immediately."

"Why, you—you—"

Garsell started to get up, opened his mouth to voice a cry for help. But weakness had descended upon him. He seemed unable to make a sound. His knees sagged, and he sank back upon the couch again.

The Mongoose laughed. "Don't worry, Garsell. No permanent ill effects, I assure you. Inside an hour, you'll be yourself again—and not even a headache. But there'll be a lot of people around here, and you may have some explaining to do. At least, the public will learn you've been indulging in another of your sordid intrigues."

"You promised—the dead woman—" Garsell mouthed.

"Don't worry! I keep my word. You'll never be accused of her murder," The Mongoose said.

Garsell heard his laughter again, only now it was very soft and seemed to come from a far distance. And then Garsell ceased to hear anything for the time being.

The Mongoose darted across the room to the hall door, and listened there. He could hear whispering. He knew that Graddon and his men were scattered around the building. For The Mongoose had one of his wireless dictaphone disks in Mr. Robert Garsell's living room, too, and had heard the conversation between Garsell and Graddon a little before. He had placed that disk himself, in the guise of a telephone inspector.

The Mongoose retreated to the door of the little rear hall again. He reached to the wall just inside the bathroom, and threw a tiny electric switch.

The glass ball above the hall door dropped from the hook upon which it had been fastened. There was a sharp blast. A cloud of pungent smoke lifted, and grew and rolled. From the midst of it came a sheet of flame.

The Mongoose had slipped something into his mouth, and now put goggles on his head, so that they fitted closely over the eye slits in his hood. One whiff of that smoke, and a man would be unconscious for an hour or more. One touch of it to his eyes, and he would experience something considerably worse than tear gas. The Mongoose had chemical knowledge, and he used it.

Those flames were such in appearance only. They were consuming the chemicals in the smoke, and not the woodwork around the door and in the front hall. But The Mongoose knew that the explosion had been heard, that smoke was issuing from beneath the door. And, as he started to retreat, the door was thrown open, and two men staggered into the smoke, to gasp and reel and fall.

The Mongoose heard a chorus of shouts in the corridor, but he did not tarry to hear and see more. Into the bathroom he dashed; closed and locked the door. He tore off and tossed away the black robe. He put the canvas bag containing the money over his shoulders, got through the window, and went swiftly along the rope and through the window of the little room opposite.

He unfastened the rope in the little room, and tossed it out so it would fall down into the court. The other end was still securely fastened to the grappling iron in the bathroom window. There was a measured length of the rope that The Mongoose had not used in crossing the court. When it fell, it ended only a few feet above the pavement. Investigation later would lead to the belief that The Mongoose had gone down the rope from the bathroom window, and dropped to the court floor.

NOW HE tore off his hood, and tossed it down into the court also, and sent his automatic after it. He closed the window. In that apartment across the court, lurid flames were leaping and black smoke was billowing. The place seemed to be burning furiously, though it was only the chemicals in the air that burned.

The Mongoose darted to the telephone.

"Fire!" he shouted into the transmitter, when the switchboard girl answered. "The apartment just across the court's on fire! Better get everybody out!"

Then he darted to his compact machinery by the window, and spoke into the transmitter of the wireless dictograph:

"Graddon men! Third floor, quick! Everybody! Mongoose on the third floor!" That would be heard down in the lobby.

The Mongoose picked up a light overcoat, and put on his hat. He held the canvas bag in the crook of his left arm, and draped the overcoat over it naturally. He hesitated a moment longer, to touch a match to a tiny fuse, which soon would result in the destruction of the compact mechanical and electrical apparatus he was leaving behind.

There was a tumult in the halls now. Men were shouting. From a coat pocket The Mongoose took a small glass tube filled with liquid, a small edition of what the big glass ball had been. He hurled it to the floor. Smoke arose, and flames sprang up. The Mongoose jerked open the door and rushed into the hall.

"Fire!... Fire!" he shouted.

His shouts were only added to others. There was an auxiliary fire alarm box in the hall, and The Mongoose stopped to send in an alarm, though he supposed one had been sounded already. He dropped another of the tiny glass tubes behind him, and smoke and flames shot up.

The hall was filling with terrified tenants, some dressed, some who had been asleep, some evidently guests at late parties and in a condition of befuddlement. The Mongoose sped through them, joined with them in their mad rush to the stairs. He attracted no attention. This was only the third floor, so nobody bothered about trying to get elevators. Down the stairs they rushed, intent only on getting out of the building.

The Mongoose dropped another glass tube, and a chorus of shrieks and cries of alarm came when the smoke and flame arose. Some inhaled, and dropped. The others became terrified. On the second floor, there was a mob fighting to get down the stairs, and those from above joined with them. The Mongoose dropped another tube, and started a fresh panic as somebody crushed it with a heel and caused the tiny explosion.

The spacious lobby of the Worthington Arms was a scene of confusion. A crowd was fighting to get through the doors and into the street. Men were fighting to get inside. In the street, sirens were sounding, and the gongs of fire apparatus already were clanging.

The Mongoose dropped a final tube where he thought it might add to the panic, and made for the door in the midst of a fighting, jostling, throng of terrified men and woman. He almost smiled when he saw Nelson, Graddon's right-hand man, standing to one side and trying to shout orders. Graddon and his few operatives were swept aside. It would have taken two hundred efficient regular policemen to stop that wild crowd and check through it for a possible suspect.

There was a crash as one of the big front windows of the building went out. Another chorus of screams arose. Now firemen were shouting and adding to the din. They came charging into the building.

The Mongoose fled into the street with the others, still clutching the canvas bag beneath his overcoat. He rushed along toward the corner, where an excited crowd was gathering. Windows of other apartment houses had been thrown open, and tenants were leaning out.

"Keep going... keep going!" some policeman was barking at the fleeing guests.

The Mongoose kept along, almost smiling at the command. He went around the corner and down the side street, almost to the end of the next block.

There, a sedan was waiting at the curb, and Miss Eleanor Carleigh was behind the wheel.

The Mongoose got in, and she started the vehicle down the street before he got the door closed. He glanced at her, and grinned.

"Everything all right?" she asked.

"Everything is very much all right, my dear sister!"

He stripped the thin black gloves off his hands, and tossed them through the half-opened window.

"So disappears The Mongoose for the time being," he said.

"Now, Sidney Carleigh will smoke a well-earned cigarette, while his charming sister drives him home. And kindly remember that we have been to the Bohemian Ball, and had quite a nice time!"

ABOUT THE AUTHOR

BEFORE HE BEGAN writing fiction, Johnston McCulley
spent years in newspaper work, and during a large part of this
time was a police specialist. What knowledge he has of the
underworld, the criminal element, the police and their methods,
was gathered from actual experience. It is not surprising then
that, when he writes stories which have to do with criminology
or crime solution, he has the sure touch of an author who knows
what he is writing about.

He was personally instrumental in solving half a dozen
murder mysteries. He has been present at battles between the
police and criminals, has interviewed men in cells, and watched
murderers die on the scaffold and in the hot chair. In those days
he learned to read men and their motives, and studied a thousand different characterizations. He understands the point of
view of both the professional and accidental criminal, and knows
how early environment can make or break men.

Police methods, scientific crime detection, the never-ending
battle of wits between the law and the lawless furnishes this
author with an endless source of study. He likes to trace the
evolution of the "gang" of to-day from the old "tough bunch on
the corner." And he will tell you that, stripped of his "hop" and
away from his associates, when the odds are anything like even,
the gangster is a cowardly rat.

Johnston McCulley is known for fiction along several lines.
But when he writes of crime and criminals, peace officers and

their work, he gets an added enthusiasm into his manu-script. His characters react naturally and normally under different conditions, talk as they do in real life. From the old desk sergeant sitting in his easy chair and yawning in the face of the turmoil around him to the alert, death-risking detective of the homicide squad, this author knows police. And from the common sneak low enough to be even outside the pale of the underworld, to the aristocrats of crime, he knows crooks.

Johnston McCulley

THE ARGOSY LIBRARY ™

SERIES 6 INCLUDES:

* BRAND * CUMMINGS * BRENT *
FARLEY * AUBREY * ROSCOE *
* GIESY & SMITH *
* LAMB * FOOTNER *
* MCCULLEY *

THE BEST FICTION
FROM THE FRANK
A. MUNSEY LINE

www.ingramcontent.com/pod-product-compliance
Lightning Source LLC
Chambersburg PA
CBHW020252030726
47499CB00001B/170